THE MAVERICK

WATERFYRE RISING 7

NADIA HAN

PROSE & CONCEPTS

For those with the "fyre" to create a better tomorrow.

•

•

"Love sometimes wants to do us a great favor: hold us upside down and shake all the nonsense out."
— *Rumi*

•

•

"You sow in tears before you reap joy."
— *Ralph Ransom*

Prose & Concepts LLC

210 Park Avenue, Suite #280

Worcester, MA 01609

www.proseandconcepts.com

This book is a work of fiction. All characters, places, names, and events are a product of the author's imagination. Any resemblance to events, locations, or persons alive or otherwise, is entirely coincidental.

Library of Congress Cataloging-in-Publication Data

Library of Congress Control Number: 2025937676

First edition Ebook ISBN: 978-1-952820-51-9

First edition Paperback ISBN: 978-1-952820-61-8

Special edition Paperback ISBN: 978-1-952820-62-5

Hardcover ISBN: 978-1-952820-63-2

PROLOGUE
ATTIKUS

I SAT with my three classmates on the stage, looking down at the auditorium filled with students and teachers from my high school. My heart was pounding so loudly that I was afraid the audience would hear it. We were all waiting for the principal, Mr. Stephen Perry, to announce the winner of the Best Advertisement Competition, which was open to all high school students.

I was one of three finalists waiting patiently for Principal Perry to get on with his long speech. This year, The Cozy Family Restaurant needed someone to create artwork to help promote their new business. The winning artwork would be used on flyers and displayed on several billboards across the city. The monetary prize urged me to compete. Five hundred dollars in cash from the restaurant and three thousand dollars in scholarship funds from the Best Advertisement Competition, a nonprofit program run by my city's Cultural Committee.

That money would help my family tremendously. My mom worked as a lunch lady at an elementary school, but she also occasionally took on side jobs. My dad was an auto mechanic.

Mom's schedule helped her stay home with me and my younger sister, Amelia, who was in eighth grade. If Amelia were in high school, she would've competed too. She was extremely talented.

I was a senior in high school, so I had to think about life after that. A college education and a part-time job would ease my family's financial burden—mortgage, car payments, and insurance. Everything cost money. I was good at math and helped my parents balance their checkbooks.

"Attikus!" Ashton Lindor leaned into me, then whispered. "Prick. You got lucky."

I narrowed my eyes at the high school bully, who was eighteen, three years older than I was. But we were both in the same grade. Thanks to my outstanding academic record and Mensa IQ test scores, I skipped a few grades.

I didn't reply because saying anything back would give him and his friends, Bobby Cooney and Harry Sullivan, a reason to create more trouble for me. He and his friends were older and bigger than me, and they were known as TTB or The Three Blowhards. They came from wealthy families and didn't do their homework. But somehow, they always got good grades.

"Attikus Mount." Principal Perry looked at me and smiled.

Crap. I'd been daydreaming.

"Me?" I asked.

Laughter filled the room

"Yes, *you.* Is there anyone else named Attikus in this room?" Principal Perry waved me over. "You're the winner! The Cozy Family Restaurant chose *your* artwork for their promotion. Come get your certificate!"

Joy and excitement filled me. I stood from my seat, walked up to him, shook his hand, and took the certificate and the small envelope. I couldn't wait to share the news with my mom. She'd be thrilled.

"The city will deliver the scholarship fund to you next week. The Cozy Family Restaurant will also join for a picture for the newspaper." He whispered in my ear. "That envelope contains the cash prize. The owners figured kids your age could use it for school supplies."

"Thank you so much," I smiled.

When I got to my locker, I peeked into the envelope and saw the five hundred dollars in cash. My heart raced with happiness. I should treat my family to dinner tonight. What would they want?

As I walked home, I felt like my life was changing for the better. I already had a full scholarship to a few colleges based on my grades and test scores. But I wanted to take a year off to work and help my mom. She didn't want me to, though.

Out of nowhere, somebody jumped on my back and started punching me. I fell to the ground and scraped up my elbows. My vision got distorted from the shock and pain. Laughter erupted around me.

Ashton stepped into my view, with Bobby and Harry flanking him.

"Give me his backpack!" Ashton barked.

Bobby tried to yank the backpack off me, but I fought him.

"No!" I threw a punch that landed on his shoulder.

"Asshole!" Bobby, Ashton, and Harry attacked me at once.

I kicked and punched at everyone. Pain erupted in my body.

Ashton stepped on my wrist, and it cracked. Then he stomped on my knee and ankle while Bobby and Harry held me down. Bones cracked, and pain soared. Blood poured from my nose. My entire body hurt like hell. They continued to punch me, even though I barely fought back. My lips and eyes swelled. Noises sounded around me, but I was in too much pain to concentrate.

"Fucker!" Ashton threatened, wincing as he crouched beside me. "If you tell anyone about this, I'll destroy your entire family. I know where you live. I know where your sister goes to school and where your mother and father work." He rose and told his friends, "I got the cash. Let's eat."

Anger, fear, and pain overwhelmed me.

"Hey!" someone shouted. "Help! Stop those boys!"

Ashton and his buddies cursed as they ran off.

"Oh, my God!" Gigi cried, gathering me into her arms. She was the lunch lady at my high school and my mom's friend. "Call the police!" she shouted to someone.

Voices boomed in the background, but I was losing consciousness.

"They took my money," I muttered to Gigi.

"Shhh, baby. You're bleeding a lot. Don't worry. We'll get them."

I vowed to get those assholes back as I lost consciousness.

When I woke up the next day, I could barely move. The nurse entered to check my vitals and said my wrist and right leg were injured. The doctor would be in to talk to me soon. I asked the nurse to turn on the TV. I wanted to know if the police got those assholes.

Channel 5 news made no mention of my attack. They were covering a deadly fire that killed three members of a family. The camera zoomed in on the blue house with a red star on the siding. Angry flames and smoke devoured the porch with a yellow wreath on the front door. When I saw fire eating up the smiling sun on a decorative flag that my dad had recently hung up, my heart shattered, knowing my family was dead. My body trembled with hatred and grief.

"No!" Tears streamed down my face as I knew my life was forever changed.

CHAPTER ONE

VANESSA

I WASN'T in the mood to attend a fancy event, but I forced myself to dress for the invitation-only art auction at The Ritz-Carlton Hotel in Boston. I'd donated my *Hope in Bloom* painting to the charitable event to help raise money for Brigham and Women's Hospital. It was one way to help the community and meet potential art collectors. Serious art buyers would pay an obscene amount of money for original artwork.

Right now, I needed to refill my empty bank account and figure out a way to make Emmanuel stop harassing me. Thinking about my ex infuriated me, so I shoved my thoughts of him aside for now.

I didn't need to stay long at this event. One to two hours would give me enough time to browse and chat with any collectors who might have questions for me. Perhaps they'd want to visit my new art gallery, which was scheduled to open at the end of the week. This was my first art gallery that would showcase all of Nessa Lambert's work. Joy burst in me, but then fear clouded the happiness.

Stop thinking about the jerk.

I wore a long black dress with matching heels. It was a simple dress I'd worn to several events, but with different accessories. I'd have loved to have the freedom to buy a new dress for every occasion, but money was tight, so I had to be creative with this sophisticated black dress. Today, I added a gold belt that matched the gold earrings, transforming my look from last month's art exhibit at the Museum of Fine Arts.

With my embroidered clutch, I stepped into the spacious room, where a unique chandelier hung at its center. Perfect lighting showcased the paintings on the gray walls, metal easels, and felt panels. Men in tuxedos and women in extravagant gowns browsed the area with auction tablets in their hands. I walked up to the desk and gave them my invitation.

"I love *Hope in Bloom*. The colors remind me of Monet, and the gold details make me think of Gustav Klimt," said the woman wearing a blue dress with a name tag that read Jennifer. She checked me in and offered me a tablet.

"Thank you, Jennifer. You're very perceptive. I love those two artists."

She glanced at her computer and gasped. "Someone just placed a bid on your painting for fifty thousand dollars!"

"That's wonderful." I smiled. "Do you know who placed the bid?"

"It says anonymous. That's normal, though. Most donors with a lot of money want to keep their identities private."

More people arrived to get their tablets, and I made my way around the room, admiring the various artworks from artists from all over the country. I spotted *Hope in Bloom* against the wall. A couple stood in front of my painting with two men standing behind them like bodyguards.

Hope in Bloom differed from my current paintings, which depicted a more somber mood. Since this was a charity, I wanted to offer hope with a kaleidoscope of pretty colors, gold aspects, and textures bursting like abstract flowers.

When the couple turned to walk to the next painting, I saw their faces, and my heart leaped.

Was that President Collins and his wife, Madeline? Always posh and stylish, she was a well-known supporter of women's health. I loved her British accent. Everything sounded more elegant when she spoke. I read in the magazine that she was only forty-one years old compared to her husband, who was sixty. Despite the age gap, they made a lovely couple.

The media usually covered news of the President's visit, but I hadn't heard anything about him being at this charity. Had they bid on my painting? I would love to have my art displayed in The White House. Who wouldn't?

I looked at the tablet and saw that all the paintings had a bid, which made me happy. Several more bids came in for *Hope in Bloom*, bringing the total to over one hundred and fifty thousand dollars!

A shiver ran down my spine, and my heart gave a nervous jolt. I sensed someone watching me. I looked around but didn't recognize anyone. Had Emmanuel sent someone to follow me here?

The room had become crowded since I entered, making it hot. Or maybe the rise in temperature reflected my fear that someone would push me into a corner and demand money I didn't have.

I walked to the refreshment area for a lemonade instead of a cocktail.

A man dressed in black with a bushy beard approached. "Excuse me, I'm Jack Connor. Are you the artist of *Hope in Bloom*?"

He was the bodyguard—probably a Secret Service Agent—who had been standing with President Collins and his wife.

"Yes, I'm Nessa Lambert. Do you have a question about the painting?"

"Someone has a question for you. He's in the other room." Jack gestured to a room across the hallway.

"Okay." I followed him to the room where the other Secret Service Agent with the bald head nodded at me.

Jack opened the door and ushered me in. I entered, and he closed the door.

President Collins and Madeline Claude-Collins sat at a round table with a flower centerpiece and a fancy tray of fruits. Madeline popped a handful of blueberries into her mouth. Spotting me, she wiped her hands with a white handkerchief. The couple rose from the table and walked up to me.

"Would you like some fruit? The blueberries are exceptionally sweet." Madeline smiled, revealing perfect white teeth. "They're my favorite."

"No, thank you," I said. "What can I do for you?"

President Collins offered me a handshake. "*Hope in Bloom* is a gorgeous painting."

"Thank you for your kind words, Mr. President." Excitement coursed through me, but I remained calm.

"It's exquisite." Madeline offered me a cheek-to-cheek kiss and asked, "Do you take commissions?" She had curious blue eyes and flawless skin that would make supermodels jealous. Her auburn hair gleamed with incredible highlights, making her appear stylish and sophisticated.

"I do," I said. My plan to cut back on custom orders had just shifted. How could I not make an exception for the First Lady? "What kind of painting do you have in mind?"

I only had one custom order left to fulfill, but that order was accepted a year ago. Plus, I was almost finished.

"A portrait of me in a floral dress. But make it unique." She pursed her lips, thinking. "I don't want a generic portrait.

Something innovative—something unexpected." She turned to her husband. "He's going to pay for it. So the price doesn't matter, right, darling?"

He draped an arm around her shoulders and kissed her cheek. "Don't worry. I'm not using tax dollars to pay you."

Madeline stood a few inches shorter than her husband. She smiled at him while interlacing her fingers with his. "Does that sound like a project you'd want to take on?"

"I love a challenge, and I'll do my best to create a masterpiece for you. I'll send over a form for you to fill out. Please fill out the delivery date, the color scheme you prefer, and anything else you'd like me to know."

"I'm hosting a gala in November, and I'd love to display this. Do you think that's achievable? As for colors, use the color palette from *Hope in Bloom*. It speaks to me."

"Absolutely," I said. "I've paused on taking custom orders, but I'm making this exception for you."

"Really?" she emphasized with warmth in her eyes. "That's so kind of you. I appreciate that. Thank you."

The extra money would help me tremendously. I'd used up my savings and taken out a loan to save my mom and to pay Emmanuel to keep his mouth shut. Mẹ was serving time for a crime she didn't commit, and no one could help us. I had to take matters into my own hands.

We chatted for a bit, and they offered me a deposit of one hundred thousand dollars. An additional hundred thousand dollars would be paid upon delivery of the painting.

I sent the order form to Madeline's assistant's email. They asked me to keep the custom order private, and I confirmed I didn't share information about my clients with anyone.

Madeline had a firm grip when we shook hands. We all exited the room, and I watched as they walked off to greet some friends. Madeline's shoulders weren't balanced. Her left shoulder dipped slightly when she walked. As an artist, I noticed details that others often missed. Despite that, she was still beautiful, especially now that she wanted me to paint for her. Having them display my art would boost my name and business.

I couldn't wait to share the news with *Mẹ* later this week when she called from prison.

As I left the hotel room, I couldn't shake off the feeling that someone was still watching me. Was I being paranoid?

CHAPTER TWO

ATTIKUS

TENSION THROBBED in my neck as I shook off the dark energy from Calvin Wong's exclusive farmhouse and entered The Ritz-Carlton Hotel. Calvin was Arrow's good friend and an honorable triad leader who knew how to get rid of bodies. Before meeting Calvin, I didn't know there was such a thing as an honorable gang leader. He possessed an integrity the leaders of this world lacked.

The triad leader had lent me his warehouse to interrogate Harry Sullivan—the second member of The Three Blowhards. They probably thought I had forgotten about that day and moved on. Nothing could be farther from the truth.

The dark past was like a cinder block tied to my feet. Wherever I stepped, it came along. The events of that day had seeped into my bones—into my blood. That fateful day fueled everything I did.

After an hour of interesting techniques used to interrogate the worst scum of society, I realized Harry didn't know where Ashton was hiding. Fear splashed onto his face when I told him Bobby had been in the same chair only a few months prior.

Both Harry and Bobby had wives and kids. The two swore they didn't know Ashton's whereabouts. Maybe they knew but were afraid of what could happen to their families if they told me the truth.

I could have threatened their families, but I had my limit. Perhaps that was the difference between them and me—I wasn't a monster and didn't kill women and children who had nothing to do with the issue. When they murdered my family, they created a monster—a beast that wielded immorality to deal with other immoral beasts. But my parents' love stabilized my moral compass.

The animals at Calvin's farm would be full and satisfied this evening. My fingers flexed as I gripped my metal cane, remembering Harry's blood on my hands and clothes. I'd changed out of them for this black-tie charity event that could offer me clues on my missing curator.

Joseph had been missing for a month. The more time that passed, the slimmer the chances of finding him. He wasn't a child but my seventy-two-year-old museum curator. A loyal employee who had been with me since the museum opened.

He had written a charity event at Brigham and Women's Hospital in his agenda book and circled it on his wall calendar. Did that signify an event he wanted to attend? Or was it a clue for me to follow? Detective Farmer was working on the case, but I knew he had several others on his plate. The city worked at a snail's pace, so I also had my team working on finding Joseph.

Blowing out a breath, I browsed the room full of exceptional art. I walked slowly with my cane, surveying the area. Joseph often found exceptional art for the Mount Museum at small exhibits. Perhaps that was why he had this event on his calendar. When he stumbled on an incredible piece, he researched the artist—if they were still alive—and would offer to host an exhibit at my museum.

Two men in black suits stood in the corner, staring at someone. They didn't look like they were here to admire the art or place a bid. I followed their gaze to Nessa Lambert. Surprise overcame me, followed by an attraction that rushed through my body. The long, dark hair, olive skin, exceptional figure, and gorgeous face made an extraordinary painting. She was my new tenant. I was scheduled to attend the grand opening of her gallery in a few days.

What was she doing here? More importantly, why were those men eyeing her like vultures? A surge of protectiveness rose in me. Nessa was my tenant—an asset to my new business venture.

I kept my eyes on Nessa as she walked around. The men also kept their gaze on her. I stayed close to them as they moved around the room, pretending to look at the paintings. Nessa exited the room with someone she probably knew. She had a smile on her face, so I wasn't worried.

When the men came to *Hope in Bloom*, they stared at the painting.

"That shit looks pretty," said the man with the spiky hair. "Maybe she'll get money for this."

I approached. "What a lovely painting. I would pay anything for it."

"You would?" the man with the dark hair asked, revealing a missing tooth.

"Absolutely." I gestured around. "I'd pay a lot of money for any of these original artworks."

"Why do people pay shitloads of money for splashes of color? I can do this, right, Pedro?" Spiky Hair asked his friend with the dark hair.

"Go ahead." Pedro smiled. "Let's see if anyone will pay money for it."

"Are you art collectors?" I asked.

"Nah," said Spiky Hair. "We just wanted to see what the event was about."

"This is a silent auction to raise money for the hospital. All the money goes to that cause, not the artist," I said, ensuring they understood Nessa wouldn't benefit financially from this event.

"Oh." Spiky Hair made a face. "That ain't gonna help us then. Yo, we should go."

"Then you can call him and tell him why," Pedro said, looking worried.

Who had sent these men?

"Fine," Spiky Hair said. "The funds are for a hospital. How are we supposed to get them?"

The two men walked out of the room. I followed them, pretending to talk to someone on my phone while I snapped a picture of them and sent it to my team. I didn't know if these men also had something to do with Joseph missing or if they were thugs targeting Nessa because of her artwork. It appeared that whoever sent them knew her or what her art was worth.

I stayed a while longer, studying the art in the room. I didn't recognize any of the artists' names except Nessa Lambert. A couple of paintings surprised me. One was an abstract dick with flowers blooming around the balls. Another was several dicks with flowers strategically covering them. These two paintings had high bids so far. There was all kinds of art for all kinds of people. I searched for the artist Richard C. Muller. He was a gay artist proud of his male genitalia.

Where are you, Joseph?

I looked at my watch and flipped through the tasks I had to

do today. Praying my curator was safe, I headed to my office to prepare for a conference and to ensure the renovation of Nessa Lambert's gallery was all set for her grand opening.

CHAPTER THREE

VANESSA

I GLANCED at myself in the long mirror, nerves wreaking havoc in my stomach. I was wearing the rose-colored dress I'd chosen for my gallery's grand opening. It had a V-neckline, and the skirt gathered to one side, revealing a slit that showed off my legs and black heels. I'd worn these shoes to Boston earlier in the week. With the deposit money from the First Lady, I bought a new dress for this special day. I had purchased nothing new in a long time, so I deserved it.

My art had graced several galleries across the country, but this gallery was all mine. With the support of my loyal collectors, who consistently purchased everything I painted, I gained the courage to open my art gallery.

You're forgetting someone important.

I wasn't. But I didn't want to think about the magnetic man right now. Every time I thought about Attikus Mount, my body took a detour down an unexpected path. I didn't need unpredictability. Stability and practicality were all I wanted.

I had to stay focused today. The media would be present, and so would my art collectors and Attikus. He'd invested a lot of money into the retail strip and especially this gallery, which had been renovated after a fire. He allowed me to lease this prime retail spot down the street from his Mount Museum. Not only that, but I also leased the office space next door, which served as a small studio for touch-ups or to add wire to the frame. I already had a large studio on the ground level of my apartment building, so I didn't want to dirty another place with paint all over the floor.

I was surprised when Attikus offered me free rent for the first three months. He said we could work out the details after the gallery opening as he was busy traveling. What details did he have in mind? What exactly did he want from me?

I had to be cautious with wealthy and powerful men. I had experienced firsthand how they could destroy people's lives.

If it weren't for them, I wouldn't be here living alone. Because of them, I was Nessa Lambert, an artist known for her floral, landscape, and abstract paintings, instead of the botanist Vanessa Lam, who loved studying plants. My mother had been in prison for the last eleven years for something she didn't do because of these people who brandished their wealth and power like weapons.

My phone buzzed, reminding me the gallery opening was in an hour. I wanted to get there early to meet my friends and loyal collectors. My assistant, Willow, would already be there.

Out of habit, I glanced at my email inbox. I had been putting off checking it for the past two days, trying to finalize the details for today's event. My gaze landed on an anonymous email with the subject line: *I know who you are.*

Fear poked me like an icicle spear. I shivered, knowing it was my ex, Emmanuel Valencia. It had been a year of horrendous blackmail. It got worse until I'd gathered enough money to pay him. I'd worked extremely hard to keep my past hidden. I didn't need an ex-boyfriend with ties to major media companies unraveling all my hard work.

Money had paid him off. It had kept him away until two months ago. I'd ignored his demands. What did he want? How had he spent the five hundred thousand dollars so quickly? That money was supposed to go into a fund for my mom and me to start over when the time came. I wanted to buy a house and live comfortably. But this asshole wouldn't leave me alone. He didn't act like this when we were dating. I guessed deceptive people were everywhere, and I was unlucky.

Greed destroys all morality.

Mẹ used to tell me this when I was little. I didn't know the meaning of that statement until I got older.

I didn't want Emmanuel's email to ruin my special day. But curiosity was my weakness. It would hang over me like a dark cloud all day if I didn't know what he wanted. That would be worse. I'd learned to face the monster because once I looked at it, the monster changed. Right now, I didn't want this monster to claw at me on my grand opening day.

I inhaled a breath and opened the email.

Dear Nessa, or should I say, Vanessa?

After careful consideration, I've decided that the amount you've given me isn't enough to bury the truth. You see, I could sell your story to DailyThoughts or Real Rumors, and your career would be over. Not only that, but you'd also be arrested for fraud and . . . murder.

I need more money—three hundred thousand dollars. Don't lie to me. I know you have money. You have a grand opening today. Congratulations, by the way. Your paintings sell for a lot of money.

I have a particular lifestyle that demands expensive things. If you don't respond, I'll reach out to my media contacts and give them all the dirt.

Yours truly,
Emmanuel

The muscles in my stomach tightened, and pain sprouted through my chest and legs. How could I make him leave me alone? Why bother emailing from an anonymous source and then signing off as himself?

I dropped onto my couch, and all my excitement for the gallery opening vanished.

"Don't let him get to you," I reminded myself. "Be strong. Mẹ needs me. People need to pay for what they took from my mom and me."

I had a bigger goal. Emmanuel was a distraction—a thorn in my side. I regretted dating him for two months over a year ago. The two months had turned into a year of hell. He was attentive in the beginning, but when his personality changed, I broke it off. He didn't seem bothered by it.

I didn't know how he knew my real name from the incident eleven years ago. Had he targeted me from the beginning to blackmail me? Or had he discovered my past after we broke up?

It didn't matter. The mess was getting messier, and I had to figure out a way to resolve this issue fast. What would people think when they discovered Nessa Lambert wasn't my real name? It wasn't unusual for people in the creative industry to have multiple aliases. But most of them were upfront about it. I never mentioned that Nessa was my artist's name. What about the murder in the alleyway? Would anyone support a murderer like me?

A wave of anxiety rolled through me, and I inhaled a deep breath to ease the flow.

Life was about choices. *Listen to your heart; it will always show you the way.*

My mom's words rang in my ears, reminding me of the power I had over my life. I shoved the jerk out of my head. I'd deal with him after the event.

My phone buzzed with a text message.

Elena: *We're heading to your gallery. Can't wait to see you all.*

Vivian: *Sorry I can't be there today. Will stop by soon!*

Nessa: *No worries. Stop by anytime.*

Michelle: *We need a painting for our family room when we come back from vacation.*

Audri: *I'll be there. Need another masterpiece for my office.*

Nessa: *You got it.*

Natalie: *Congratulations! We're still in Paris. See you soon.*

Nessa: *Please bring back some of those macaroons you gave me last time.*

Natalie: *Already got a box for everyone. (smile emoji)*

All the girls chimed in with cheers.

Kiera: *I need a lot of art! Will contact you for some commission work soon. Sorry I'm missing our girls' day out. Catch up soon!*

Nessa: *Sounds good.*

. . .

I smiled at these amazing ladies who were my biggest supporters. They'd become friends over their love for my art. I didn't have many friends. Privacy was important to me because it protected my past, my mother, and what I needed to do.

But after getting to know these women, I'd opened up a little more. Being closed off made me miss out on a lot of things.

I checked on my hair, makeup, and dress, making sure I looked presentable instead of angry, sad, and wanting to strangle all powerful men.

CHAPTER FOUR

ATTIKUS

ARRIVING EARLY at Nessa's grand opening, I sat in my Maserati and studied the area around the retail strip. The renovation to the brick-front facade had increased the value and appearance of all the stores. Nessa Lambert's Art Gallery stood out with the gold lettering and large windows.

I glanced at my watch. Twenty minutes before the event officially started. I turned on the spare tablet I kept in my car and reviewed the files of the two suspicious men at The Ritz-Carlton in Boston.

Facial recognition software gave me their identities. Pedro Lopez was the man with the missing tooth, and Martin Brown had the spiky hair. They worked in maintenance for Ultra Health and Fitness, which owned several gyms in New England. Three gyms were in Rhode Island.

Each of them had served time in prison for drug possession and theft. Who had ordered them to target Nessa? My team had hacked into their phones, but they used burners, and so did the other person, which made everything even more suspicious.

Were these men tied to The Trogyn? My friends and I had

been working to eliminate this crime syndicate for a while. This dangerous crime organization had an extensive reach world-wide with powerful elite members who would do anything to keep their identities private. My boys and I had destroyed several of their businesses, so we knew they were after us.

A headache bloomed as I turned off the tablet, setting it aside on the passenger seat. I opened the glove compartment, retrieved the bottle of painkillers, and popped two into my mouth, washing them down with water. The past month had been hectic as hell, with no time to breathe. My body was crying out desperately for me to slow down.

After this event, I'll take a week off.

The calf muscle in my right leg tightened, reminding me I had canceled my physical therapy session for the past few months.

If you don't take care of yourself, who will?

My sister Ellen's words echoed in my head, increasing my headache.

I leaned back in the seat, studying the passing cars and people walking along the street to Nessa's gallery. It still baffled me why I'd leased this retail space to her and offered her three months rent-free.

You know why.

God, if only I could strangle my inner voice.

I owned a painting by Nessa Lambert. It hung in my house instead of my museum. Something about the desecrated water lily called to me. This was before I knew Nessa or her work. The painting I bought didn't have the same signature as her current work. I didn't even know what the painting was called. The art had spoken to me, and I'd bought it at an estate auction.

I'd seen my share of astounding work from artists all over the world, yet I'd never given anyone the space to do as they pleased.

Maybe my spontaneous decision would backfire in a few months, making me lose some money. I'd never done anything spontaneous for business. Research, numbers, facts, and foresight had made me a billionaire. So this was out of the norm for me.

My phone rang, and I debated on picking up the call from my sister.

"Yes, Ellen? What do you need?"

"Is this how you treat your big sister? The sister who toiled over the stove to make you spaghetti and meatballs?" she demanded.

I could picture her standing in the kitchen wearing a bright pink apron, her hands propped on her hips.

"You mean the pre-made meatballs you got from the grocery store?"

"That's not the point. I cooked them with a delicious sauce for my little brother. But it seems he's not interested in eating it."

"Who says I'm not interested?" I retorted. "I'm heading to an event—a gallery opening. I'll stop by to pick up your amazing meal on my way home."

"You have too many events. Mom Gigi wants you to cut back on them and start dating. Her friend, Mary St. Pierre, wants to set you up with her daughter, Daisy St. Pierre, who's a family doctor. I heard she's beautiful."

"I'm not interested." This conversation wasn't helping my headache. I was about to say as much, but I knew Ellen would retort with, *She can prescribe you something. It's a sign from the universe!*

Mom Gigi adopted me after my family was murdered. Ellen was five years older than me and was adopted the year before. Living with two women taught me that patience was the magical key that solved a lot of issues.

"Why not? You're not getting younger. She's worried about you."

"I've got things to do, Ellen," I said as Nessa's face popped into my head. "Why aren't *you* dating?"

"Because I need to take care of my younger brother first. Besides, I'm sick of men right now."

She'd recently come out of an abusive relationship. The fucker had broken her leg and given her a black eye during one of his drunken episodes. When I discovered this, I gave him a stern warning and broke some of *his* bones. I also discovered he was involved in a lot of illegal activities and used that to keep him away from Ellen. He now lived in another country, so I didn't have to see him.

No one hurts my family ever again.

"I'll let you know when I'm ready to introduce a girlfriend to you. Gotta go."

"All right. Don't forget to stop by to pick up the food because Mom Gigi and I can't eat all of this."

I shook my head, knowing she cooked when she was stressed. Ellen worked at a nonprofit company in Boston, helping homeless women and children get back on their feet. I offered her a job at one of my businesses, but she refused.

I guess I dealt with stress by spending money on spontaneous things. Ellen's method was a lot cheaper. Nessa Lambert's Art Gallery was a new adventure for me. It took me away from the stress bombarding my life. Art was my relaxation, and I was investing in my self-care. That was it.

Satisfied with my conclusion, I adjusted my black tuxedo and exited my car. I scanned the several shops on the retail strip. As I walked past Loretta's Café, I turned and glanced inside. A zing zipped through me when I saw Nessa standing in the far corner of the shop. She looked stunning in the red dress, but her facial expression showed agitation toward a man with wavy brown hair. He wore a gray suit with a blue tie. He reached for her hand, but she shoved him away and walked out of the coffee shop.

Nessa didn't see me standing off to the side.

"Asshole," she muttered and walked toward the gallery, which was two doors down.

Her hips swayed back and forth, stirring something in me. The man who had ruined her day left the coffeehouse and bumped into me.

He looked at me, didn't apologize, and walked off, talking into his phone.

"Do it," he said. "She'll pay."

CHAPTER FIVE

VANESSA

FRUSTRATION WHIRLED inside me as I avoided the busy crowd around the gallery. I stepped into my office, closed the door, and dropped onto the couch by the wall. I didn't expect Emmanuel to be waiting for me outside the gallery. Fearing he'd cause trouble, I agreed to talk to him at the nearby coffee shop.

My hands trembled, remembering his threat.

"Pay up, or you'll regret it."

I dug into my clutch bag and retrieved my phone, checking my bank accounts. If I gave him the three hundred thousand dollars—which was everything I had—there would be nothing left to protect my mom's safety in prison or pay for her escape to another country. That amount also included the deposit from the First Lady. Tears filled my eyes, but I willed myself not to cry. I had to be presentable. I didn't want the media to capture me looking like a zombie.

Breathe, Vanessa.

I closed my eyes and dropped into the darkness, a place that had been my sanctuary growing up. In the dark, there was nothing to see. Nothing could bother me here. It was in this emptiness that I could think clearly—start anew.

The darkness was my blank canvas.

Think outside your comfort zone. Reach beyond the confinement of the norm.

Emmanuel knew I'd be selling a lot of art today. He was betting on that. When would this blackmailing stop?

I got up from the couch, walked over to my desk, and turned on my computer. I clicked on the security cameras to see how many people were in the gallery. The crowd had increased since I walked in. I saw my friends and their men.

Then Attikus Mount, the investor of this gallery and the owner of this retail strip—looked right into the camera. My heart quickened. His brown eyes bore into me, and my stomach churned. The anxiety I'd felt with Emmanuel shifted to something else. The tension in my body loosened, allowing me to breathe better.

Maybe all I needed was a distraction from Emmanuel. I needed to get through the grand opening and deal with everything else after.

Shoving Emmanuel aside, I adjusted my long, dark hair and the lotus flower clip on the side. It highlighted the red dress I wore. I looked in the mirror. For a moment, I didn't recognize the person standing before me. My face was still the same, with my olive skin tone from my Vietnamese and Haitian heritage. I wasn't the same girl who had wanted to paint memorable things for fun anymore. Now I painted because I needed the money to rescue my mom.

With that thought in mind, I squared my shoulders and walked out of the gallery. Today was the debut of two new collections: *The Shattered Lotus* and *Bleeding Dreams*. The collections both sounded morbid, but the colors I used gave hope to the hopeless. These paintings were parts of me sent out into the world in secret. No one knew what they truly meant but me.

Inhaling a deep breath, I stepped into the main room and glanced around. People crowded around a table with refreshments and appetizers. Others scattered around the gallery, looking at the curated collection.

My nerves calmed when everything seemed to flow smoothly. Nothing urgent erupted, needing my attention. My paintings were all displayed in their proper places, being appreciated by people who had money to spend.

"Everything okay?" asked Willow Thomas, my assistant. "You look stunning, by the way." She had been my part-time assistant until this gallery. Now she worked full time for me. Willow looked adorable in her short, black dress. A blue butterfly clip gleamed in her curly brown hair, which she wore down.

"Thank you. I'm okay, just tired and nervous. You know?" I embraced her. "Thanks for everything. The refreshment and appetizer table looks fantastic."

"You're so welcome. I love your work, and event planning is my hobby." She smiled. "Everything is running smoothly. You've sold quite a few paintings already. Are you ready for some questions?" She gestured to a group of people standing in front of my *Shattered Lotus* collection.

"Of course," I said and waved to some art collectors I recognized.

Willow led me to a group of people with questions about my lotus painting collection.

"Your paintings have transitioned to something dark, dear," said an old man wearing a black suit with a navy tie. "It's beautiful, though."

"Thank you," I said. "Change is a good thing. It's the only thing that's constant."

"What inspired your paintings?" a woman with a sparkly dress and a lovely French twist hairstyle asked.

"Justice." I smiled, surprised at my quick reply. If I had thought about it, I would have chosen a different word—a word that didn't hint at my problems. But the truth flew out of me like a trapped bird escaping its cage.

"Justice is like karma?" asked a man in a blue-striped suit. "Do you agree?"

A lady in a peach gown replied, "Karma and justice are like intimate lovers. They are better together."

"I love that perspective," said the old man.

I didn't intervene in their art critique of my work. That was the beauty of art or any kind of creative project. A hundred people could look at the same painting, and each would interpret it differently. We saw art through our experiences—our pain, hope, and dreams.

An intense energy suddenly slid down my spine, making me shiver. I looked up; Attikus was staring at me from the corner. He wore a black tuxedo, standing like a masterpiece in my gallery. His swept-back dark hair enhanced his fine-boned face, chiseled jaw, and cheekbones that made supermodels jealous. He stood with his friends, Orion and Remington. His hands were placed on the intricate cane. Attikus responded to something they said, but his eyes remained on me. I didn't know why, but my body hummed from his gaze.

"You look beautiful!" Elena placed a gentle hand on my back, pulling my attention away from Attikus.

She wore a cream-colored dress that accentuated her curves. Her wavy brown hair cascaded down her shoulders, looking elegant as usual.

"You too." I gave her a one-armed hug. "Thank you for coming."

"Have you tried the appetizers? They're delicious!" Elena gestured to the table. "I couldn't stop myself."

"Glad you're enjoying yourself." I laughed as I walked over to admire the appetizers on the pretty plates. I feared if I ate anything, I might puke it all out tonight.

I first met Elena and her friends when they bought my paintings and commissioned me for additional work. Then Elena invited me to do a live painting at her wedding on this exquisite island her husband owned. I'd encountered many wealthy art collectors, but something genuine about these women drew me to them.

They didn't pressure me about my family when that topic came up during a conversation. They respected my privacy, and that was important to me. I had unresolved issues I'd rather not talk about, and trust was a rare commodity these days.

Emmanuel had been my boyfriend, and look at what he'd done to me.

"No!" Elena gasped, staring at a couple standing in front of one of my floating island paintings. "Gotta grab Orion. I don't want that couple stealing my painting." She embraced me. "We'll catch up later. You have a spectacular gallery! I'll tell everyone about it." She rushed over to Orion, grabbed his arm, and led him to the purchasing counter.

Audri walked out of the restroom, looking stunning in her baby blue dress. She saw me, beamed, and walked over to embrace me. "I *love* this gallery. It's quaint and elegant. The location is perfect too."

"Thanks." I beamed. "Attikus knows his real estate." I looked at him and quickly regretted it. *Why is he still staring at me?*

"Is something going on between you and Attikus?" Audri smirked.

"No," I said, surprised by her question. "He invested in this gallery, and I'm grateful for that."

"Oh." Audri studied me. "He didn't invest in the gallery—he invested in *you*." She tapped my arm. "There's no gallery without the artist."

I didn't know what to say. Attikus had mentioned he had a painting by me, but I didn't know which one. Regardless, his investment allowed me to make more money without paying a commission to another gallery.

"I'm sure my little gallery is nothing compared to the other businesses he's invested in."

"I heard he's working on a few projects with the boys. These men are exceptionally amazing." Audri looked at Remington, who asked Attikus a question, forcing him to look away from me. "I'm not saying that because Remi's my boyfriend. The boys are finalizing this fabulous WaterFyre Rising video game. I'm not a game person, but it was fun."

More people surrounded the purchasing desk.

"I need to purchase two paintings I want before someone else takes them." She squeezed my hand. "Talk soon."

Audri walked over to Remington and congratulated Attikus on the gallery. This was also his opening. He'd put in a lot of money renovating this space for me. To be honest, I was so ecstatic when he offered me space with free rent for three months that I thought nothing of it. Was there a separate agenda behind the business deal? Was he this generous with his other tenants?

Attikus made his way toward me, using his metal cane with intricate etchings on it. He walked with a slight limp that didn't deter from how gorgeous and powerful he was. The cane was an accessory that enhanced his persona, adding a touch of mystery to him. How had he gotten injured?

"I think all your paintings will sell out today," Attikus said.

His baritone voice slid over me like a deep-tissue massage, removing the tight knots within me. A magnetic man with a magnetic voice was dangerous to someone like me who was sensitive to things like that. An artist notices details that others often miss, and Attikus Mount was a mysterious man made of fascinating details.

"That means I have to paint more quickly." I smiled. I had several more paintings in storage that would be displayed there.

"Thank you for letting me lease this space and for coming today," I said, trying my best to stay composed. I had shoved Emmanuel out of my mind so I could stay calm, but here I was, trembling distinctly with nerves.

"Your paintings are different from others I've seen. I prefer to invest in things with great potential." Brown eyes stared at me.

I looked into those mysterious eyes, surprised to see they held pain and sorrow. How could I see that? How could I know that? Was I projecting my issues onto him?

Confusion washed over me as I studied the sunburst of topaz and gold within his brown irises.

"I appreciate your support," I said, breaking our gaze to watch a couple holding hands as they looked at one of my *Shattered Lotus* paintings. The woman stepped forward and tripped on the hem of her long dress. Her husband caught her, helping her to her feet.

"How are you doing?" Attikus asked.

"I'm okay," I said. "A bit stressed, but that's understandable. This is my first gallery, so I want to make sure everything goes without a hitch."

"As far as I can tell, everything is working out beautifully."

Willow approached me. "The media would like some photos of you both, if that's okay."

"Of course," Attikus said. "It's a great opportunity to show the community the fabulous new art gallery here in Providence."

After Attikus and I answered questions and had our photos taken, I walked over to the appetizer table and grabbed a bacon-covered avocado, popping it into my mouth. The savory taste settled the erratic nerves inside me.

"Would you like anything to drink?" Attikus asked me.

"Water would be great. Thank you."

He walked over to the drink stand.

"You have a package." Willow handed me a small brown box. "Maybe it's a gift from a collector who couldn't make it today."

I'd received lovely handwritten letters congratulating me in the last few days from loyal fans around the country.

"A gift on opening day?" Attikus returned with my drink and placed it on the tall table. "Let me help you." He reached into his pocket for a pen. Then he twisted the other end of it, revealing a small blade. He cut the tape and handed me the box.

"You have dangerous gadgets." I smiled. "Thank you."

I opened the box, saw the bloody finger, screamed, and dropped it. Fear for my mother overwhelmed me. My body swayed as I met Attikus's concerned eyes.

Then I blacked out.

CHAPTER SIX

ATTIKUS

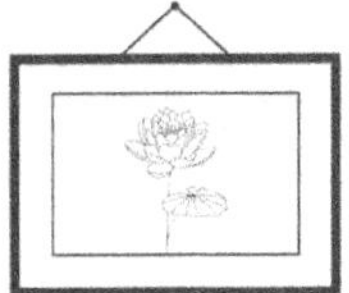

"SHE'S STILL SLEEPING," I said to Detective Gary Farmer, who stood in the hospital waiting room with me.

He had curly red hair, a determined expression, and integrity I'd never seen in any police officer. We had a history, and I trusted him.

Detective Farmer had arrived, wanting to question Nessa about the severed finger. But I didn't want him disrupting her rest. I debated telling him what I'd seen at Loretta's Café but held back.

What if that incident had nothing to do with the severed finger? What if it was a personal issue she didn't want anyone to know? I'd wait to ask her those questions later.

Why? She's not your family. She's not your girlfriend.

I grunted at my inner voice. It wasn't wrong. But I was a businessman who valued my investment. Nessa Lambert was my most recent investment. Her well-being ensured I profited. I didn't spend all that money renovating the retail strip—the gallery—to let some fucker ruin it on its first day of opening.

I briefed Detective Farmer on what I'd seen in Boston and

sent him a picture of the men. Maybe they had something to do with this.

"I'll take a look," he said, glancing at his phone.

"Please keep me posted on your findings."

"Will do." He tucked his small notebook into his chest pocket. "If you can have her stop by my office to give her statement when she wakes, I'd appreciate it."

I nodded and watched him leave the waiting room.

Who had sent the severed finger? I remembered the fear on Nessa's face when she opened that box. The image replayed over and over again. I wanted to hurt whoever was responsible for this. It was her grand opening, and he'd ruined it.

Nessa had expected a congratulatory gift, but her world collapsed figuratively and literally. Fortunately, I was there to catch her.

Dr. Li, the emergency room doctor who was also an acupuncturist, had checked Nessa's pulse and said she was extremely tired. What would she say if she checked mine?

Beyond help. Hopelessly doomed.

I walked back to Nessa's hospital room and sat in the chair beside the bed, watching her. When she passed out, I wanted to reach out to her family, but Willow said she didn't have anyone. That intrigued me. Everyone had some kind of family or a close friend. Who was Nessa Lambert? What was she hiding? Was she more than the artist I'd invested in?

Nessa was friends with Elena, Audri, Vivian, Michelle, Natalie, and Kiera, but I didn't know how close they were. Elena and Audri had offered to accompany Nessa, but I told them I'd do it.

Orion and Remi had stayed behind, apologizing to people for the abrupt closure of the gallery. My friends knew what to do while I went with Nessa in the ambulance. They'd check the cameras at the surrounding businesses to help with the investigation. Though the police were called and Detective Farmer was on the case, the city often took its time. Orion had a team of people who were excellent at retrieving data that others couldn't.

I didn't know why I offered to accompany Nessa. Elena or Audri would have been more suitable. They knew each other better, whereas Nessa and I were only business partners.

Yet, I felt this inexplicable urge to protect her. She reminded me of my sisters, Ellen and Amelia. Ellen had an abusive boyfriend, and Amelia was the thirteen-year-old budding artist whose life was cut too short.

Why did I feel this need to keep Nessa safe? It made little sense. I was no saint, and I certainly didn't have time for this. But here I was, sitting in her hospital room. I'd rescheduled my conference call, which was supposed to happen in an hour, to another day.

"*Me* . . ." Nessa mumbled as tears streamed from the corners of her closed eyes. She shifted and screamed, "No!" Her hands flung out, and her eyes flipped open, glancing around.

"You're safe." I rose from my chair, standing over her.

She looked at me, and confusion splashed over her face. Then remembrance registered in her eyes, and her demeanor changed. She pushed herself up, and I placed a pillow behind her back.

"Thank you. How's the gallery?" she asked, looking embarrassed.

"Everything's taken care of," I said. "No one was angry that we had to close early."

Should I sit on the edge of the bed to talk to her? Or should I stand here looking like a fool? Why should I care what she thought of me?

More importantly, why was I asking these stupid questions? Annoyed at myself, I sat in the chair.

"Why are you here?" She studied me.

Yeah, why are you here, idiot?

"You're the star of the art gallery—a property I own. I need
to make sure my investment is safe."

She stared at me, and I desperately wanted to know what
she was thinking. Something shifted in her brown eyes as
though she were forming ideas for an intricate painting.

Her fingers clutched the bedsheet. "What happened to the
finger?"

Of all the questions she could've asked me, I didn't expect
that. Instead of asking me if the authorities had captured the
person responsible for that horrendous act, she wanted to know
where the severed finger was.

"Do you know who the finger belongs to?" I asked.

Her lips quivered as she squeezed the bedsheet until her
knuckles turned white.

When she didn't reply, I said, "It's a man's finger. The
police will run a fingerprint and DNA."

"The finger belongs to a man?" A spark of hope flashed in
her eyes. "Are you sure?"

I nodded. "Based on the shape of the finger and fingernails,
the CSI said it looks to be a man's finger. But DNA will
confirm the gender." I leaned forward. "Do you know who sent
the finger to you?"

She took a deep breath, closed her eyes for a moment, and
released it slowly. When she reopened them, she looked me in
the eye. Desperation, determination, and anger swam in them.
I'd seen the same emotions in my eyes when I was in the
hospital years ago, recovering from a beating that crippled me.

Nessa clasped her hands together, rested them on her lap,
and looked at me. I sensed her nerves, but also the calm that

came when someone had endured too many storms. She had mastered the skill of forcing herself to remain calm to do what was necessary.

I admired that.

Who are you, Nessa Lambert?

She blew out another breath. "I have a business proposal for you."

The surprise dropped into my lap like an asteroid that didn't belong. No one had shocked me more in one day than her.

My business radars perked up. "Let's hear it."

CHAPTER SEVEN

VANESSA

I BLINKED AT HIS WORDS. I'd expected him to ask me more questions before wanting to hear my proposal. But I supposed a billionaire like Attikus Mount was used to people tossing out proposals. I knew mine would probably be the most unexpected.

You don't know that.

We were the only two people in this room. My body became fully aware of his presence. Energy resonated from his body, slamming into me. Though it was a hospital room, the intimacy was palpable. It thrummed in the air, tingling my skin.

Attikus stared at me, waiting for my reply. I stared back, still trying to process my thoughts. He didn't press me, so I studied his attractive features close up. That was when I realized only one set of lights was turned on in the room. Did he leave the rest of the lights off for me to sleep?

The dim lighting made his brown irises look like spears of molten copper bursting around darkening pupils. His angular face had the perfect bone structure. I imagined the shadows rejoicing as they skipped along the tight creases on his forehead, climbed over the rise of his strong nose, and slid around the curve of high cheekbones to settle on his square jaw. The contrast of dark and light over his lips did something strange to my stomach. When he pursed his lips slightly, the muscles in my inner thighs flexed.

The mystery around him increased by the second. I wanted to discover him as though he was a painting. What was his history? What made him bleed?

What would make him *smile?*

As an artist, I understood the beauty of contrast and composition. This man possessed those aspects perfectly. He was the most gorgeous man I'd ever seen. But I would never tell him that. Men like him already had big egos. If they got any bigger, the world would be unlivable.

Beauty is deception, Vanessa.

Oh, I know. Emmanuel was that horrendous mistake.

But right now, I wanted to see, feel, and wonder about a man without consequences.

"Are you done staring?" he asked, his Adam's apple bobbing.

My eyes darted to it as though it was a splash of paint that completed an artwork perfectly.

"I'm an artist, so I appreciate a great canvas when I see it. You have a well-balanced face."

"Are you buttering me up for your proposal?" he asked with a straight face.

"No."

That was the truth, but I could see why he wouldn't believe me. What normal person would say that to a man she didn't know well? Technically, he was my landlord. We weren't even friends.

I shook my head clear of whatever trance I was under. "I

was studying your face. It's something I do—most artists do that often. I can't help it."

"I'm not asking you to," he said, and the tension in his forehead relaxed. "Your art captures your emotions. Now I know the depth in which you study something."

"You're an art collector, so you understand it too."

He considered me. "Art was an escape for me—"

He blinked as though he hadn't meant to say that. "I mean, art is an escape for people. Just like writing and music. It takes you to another place, another time, so you can forget the pain."

Did he know he spoke like an artist? These were deep words from a man who had endured too much. Only a man who had touched the darkest of the dark would know how to describe it beautifully.

I felt his pain like a serrated knife had scraped over a raw wound. I shivered at the sensation. There was more to Attikus Mount than the man staring at me.

I had no idea why I was sharing so much about myself with him. Maybe it was because he saw my vulnerability. Maybe because he was the only person I saw when I woke up in this hospital room.

Was I doing the right thing with this proposal? Or was I making a horrible mistake? Doubts swarmed me like nasty hornets, but I kept my focus on the idea that seemed more real the more I thought about it.

That horrific dream of seeing men holding down my mother to cut off her finger had tossed me into a panic. When I woke and saw Attikus staring at me with concern, he yanked me away from that panic mode to help me land safely. Even though he didn't know what he had done, I considered that a sign from heaven—he was the path to my escape.

I entertained this idea when I saw the lovely couple in the

art gallery. The man's wife had tripped, and he caught her before she fell. At that moment, I had wondered if I'd ever have anyone to catch me during my fall.

Attikus kept his gaze on me, his eyes searching and probably wondering if I was being serious about my proposal.

I inhaled a breath and said, "Do you want to be my fake husband?"

His eyes widened as he studied me. Silence and something else pulsed in the room. After a moment, he rose from the chair, stepped over to the bed without using his cane, and sat on the edge.

"Why?"

"Because a smart business person like you would want to protect your assets."

An eyebrow arched, and the slow way it moved on his forehead fascinated me.

"Is that so? You believe you're my asset now?"

I pushed down the nerves multiplying in my stomach. Was this a bad idea? I didn't know why, but I had the impression Attikus could be more dangerous than Emmanuel.

"You spent a lot of money on renovating the gallery. I want to help you profit by being successful and continuing my lease for years to come."

He let out a half laugh. "If you want me to help you, I need the truth, Nessa."

Would Attikus be the temporary help I needed to overcome this obstacle? Could my proposal push Emmanuel away once and for all? He probably sent that finger to scare me. Threats about revealing my true identity and ruining my career had been his MO, but cutting off someone's finger? I never thought he was that violent. Plus, he didn't know about my mother being in prison. Did he?

I'd tried ignoring Emmanuel for months, but he'd gotten violent. What if he showed up at my house or the gallery again? A restraining order wouldn't be effective. I'd heard of women getting killed by their significant others even with a restraining order. I needed someone powerful by my side.

I licked my dried lips. "You might not help me if you knew the truth."

He reached out to tuck an errant strand of hair behind my ear. His finger touched my skin, and tingles rippled through me.

"But if I don't know, it's an absolute no. As a businessman, I need to scan the horizon and see things from all angles so I can anticipate what's coming my way. How can I fight a war if I don't know my enemy or my surroundings?" He tipped up my chin. "I don't join a battle to lose. Nobody likes to lose."

Of course, he was right.

"I'm being blackmailed, and I think if I was married to you, he'd leave me alone. The marriage would be fake. We can draft up a proposal. The time frame can be three to six months. After that, we can get it annulled."

"Who's blackmailing you?" The muscle in his jaw ticked.

"My ex-boyfriend, Emmanuel Valencia. We only dated for two months," I said, unsure why I added that tidbit.

"What does he want?" His eyes darkened, reminding me of a lion ready to attack.

"Money." I yanked at the bedsheet. "I've already given him a lot."

"What does he have on you? Or rather, what do you need to protect?"

"My true identity."

That eyebrow arched again. Why did I find it so attractive?

"Does that make me a victim of your false identity?" he asked.

"Nessa Lambert is my artist's name." My stomach clenched. "You invested in the artist. There's no pretense." I swallowed. "My real name is Vanessa Lam, and I killed a man."

CHAPTER EIGHT

ATTIKUS

NOTHING COULD'VE SURPRISED me more than Nessa's proposal and her admission.

Sitting so close to her, I sensed her nerves and saw the determination in her eyes.

"Who?" I asked.

"I'm not ready to talk about it today. My body needs a break from that trauma." She pressed her lips into a tight line. "Emmanuel wants money to keep his mouth shut. But I know he won't stop pestering me after he gets the money."

Understanding, I didn't pressure her. I'd seen what trauma had done to my sister. Time and patience were precious healing remedies.

I got up from the bed, reached for my cane, and walked around the room. The cane was my thinking friend—a comrade who had seen my pain, heard my vow for vengeance, and held a hope I never showed anyone else.

During my darkest days, when I couldn't walk, I leaned on it—literally and figuratively. My injury was the constant reminder I needed to find these fuckers and make them pay.

Let it go, Mom Gigi and Ellen had said. *You'll be happier.*

I'll think about it, was the safe reply I'd given them many times. They didn't need to know my plan had already been in motion the day after my family's funeral. The less they knew about my plan, the safer they'd be.

Right now, I needed the familiar comfort of my cane to make an important decision.

It's a fake, temporary marriage that will end in six months.

Could it be that easy? How would I navigate this scenario? Nessa wouldn't have asked me if she had another way.

I looked at her. "Why me?"

She shrugged. "Because you're the *lucky* one sitting in my hospital room."

I appreciated her sarcasm, remembering she didn't have family or close friends. If a man other than me had been in this room, would she have asked him?

That thought bothered me more than it should, but I didn't know why.

Pushing that irritation aside, I concentrated on her situation. It seemed too familiar to me. When I was at my lowest, a stranger became my savior. Gigi had helped me when I was lying on the sidewalk, bleeding to death. Then she adopted me. She was friends with my mother, but I didn't know her well.

My heart raced as I made a decision that would shock my family and friends. Orion would grill me for this.

"I'll be your fake husband under one condition."

"What?" Her eyes sparked with hope, brightening her face and making her even more beautiful.

"I get to draft the agreement for this fake marriage. After six months, we'll review the terms."

She twisted her lips, considering me. "Can I add some things to the agreement? This is an agreement between two people. I want a say in my marriage."

She made it sound real, but I didn't call her out on it. I wasn't a man who would force a woman to do something she didn't want to. I thought about my sisters. What would I do if someone forced them to sign an agreement that didn't benefit them?

"You can make some suggestions." I stepped up to the bed. "But I'll review them." I didn't know who Vanessa Lam was. Though something in me wanted to help her, I had to be careful. What if she was a decoy? What if she was working for The Trogyn, playing the role of an innocent woman who attacked me when I least expected it?

I had to rule out these questions.

She blew out a stressed breath, probably not liking that I had the upper hand.

"Right now, you need my help. But I'm an entrepreneur, Vanessa. I have to protect my business. We'll discuss the details of the agreement. Feel free to hire a lawyer to review the contract before you sign it."

I knew she wouldn't, but the offer was there.

"Fine," she said. "But I won't commit any crimes."

"But you already did." I tipped her chin up, wanting to look into those defiant brown eyes. "Lying about your real identity to a man who invested in you is a crime." I loved the way her eyes intensified on me. Vanessa had a dark story too, and I wanted to know it. "But it's a crime I can dismiss since you're going to be my wife."

The reality of it sent a shockwave through me. How would I share this news with my mother and sister?

CHAPTER NINE

VANESSA

I LOOKED out the window of Attikus's fancy car, replaying the surreal events of the day. When I woke up this morning, preparing my grand opening, I didn't expect to end the day with an arranged fake marriage.

I turned and looked at Attikus, who was focused on the road. He knew I was staring at him but didn't comment. He was going to be my husband.

As a child, I dreamed of getting married one day and having a family. Many people had this dream. It was sold to them in fairytales and romance novels. I had believed in it until I realized that the world was cruel, and the men who ran it were the reason.

I didn't dare think about such things anymore. My fairytales were scattered all over my artwork. Sometimes, I poured love and hope into them. Other times, I channeled my rage.

Like everything else about Attikus, his profile drew me in. More shadows played out over his features as the evening city lights cascaded over his face.

"See something interesting?" He turned to meet my gaze.

Heat blossomed on my face, and I turned away quickly, praying the evening hour hid my embarrassment.

"Just trying to get to know my future husband," I lied. "If people question me about him, I want to reply without hesitation."

The car stopped at a red light, and I stared at the couple walking in the street holding hands. They seemed happily in love. How long did that phase last until the real person emerged? It was too difficult pretending to be someone else. Eventually, your true self would be revealed.

The car moved, but Attikus didn't turn down the street toward my apartment.

"You missed the turn."

"No, I didn't. I'm picking up dinner at my sister's house. It's time you meet your in-laws."

"Isn't it too soon? Is that necessary?"

He looked at me. "If you want this marriage to be believable."

I just wanted to stay with my small circle of people. I didn't want to meet new people who would ask questions I didn't want to answer.

"Well, I don't have anyone for you to meet on my side."

Curiosity sparked in his eyes, but he didn't comment.

"We met online and chatted for several months. We wanted to keep it quiet, but you fell in love with me and demanded I make a move. I gave in, and here we are."

"Why do I have to be the one to fall in love first?"

"Because they'd never believe it otherwise. Trust me." He turned down a street with lots of trees on the sidewalk. "That would prevent a lot of questions."

"We don't need a wedding reception."

"No, we're doing it at City Hall and then going on vacation to where I have a business meeting. That's our honeymoon."

I stared at him. "How romantic."

"This isn't an actual marriage, remember? I've got things to do. And you can tell me about the man threatening you. I want the entire story. Then we can figure out a way to stop him."

"Wait a minute." My heart raced, and I held up a hand. "You're helping me stop him?"

"Isn't that what you want?"

Do I want that?

I'd wanted to use his social status so Emmanuel would back off. No one would get hurt. I never expected him to help me with whatever he had in mind.

"I was hoping he'd just leave me alone knowing I was married to you," I sighed. "It's not your business to intervene."

"As you pointed out, you *are* my investment. We have a business deal. This marriage is a business contract, isn't it?"

I thought about it for a moment. To my dismay, he was right. My marriage with him had many strings attached to it. I wasn't thinking properly when I offered the proposal.

"Okay," I said. "We'll discuss it later."

Fear and hesitation nibbled at me. How much should I reveal about myself to him? I didn't want him to know everything. What if the truth was too much for him to handle? Would he divorce me?

A thought occurred to me. I looked at him, horrified I hadn't thought about it earlier.

"Are you . . . with anyone?"

"Don't you think it's too late to ask about that now?"

Silence hummed in the air. Not knowing what to say, I chewed on the inside of my mouth.

He broke the silence. "I'm not with anyone. I wouldn't agree to this marriage if it didn't benefit me." He looked at me. "I require a one-of-a-kind painting from you when this marriage is over."

"Then I require something at the end of the deal too," I said. Why should he be the only one to get something?

"What do you want?"

I didn't know what I wanted at the moment. I needed the time to think clearly. He obviously had a list of things he wanted from me. All I wanted was for my mother to get out of prison so we could start over where people didn't know us. But that was something I wanted to do on my own.

"I'll let you know when the time comes."

We arrived at a house outside of Providence. It wasn't a mansion like I had thought, but one of three brick Colonials in the cul-de-sac. He pulled into the driveway, got out, and grabbed his cane from the back seat. I was about to open the door, but he met my gaze, shook his head, and mouthed, "Stay."

A second later, he stood outside my door and opened it for me.

I got out. "You didn't have to open the door for me. I'm capable of doing that."

"This isn't about capabilities, Vanessa," he whispered in my ear, his warm breath sending heat skipping down my spine. "We're playing our role as husband and wife. My family will be looking out the window. If I'm introducing my fiancée to them, we need to play our part." He offered me his hand.

This was all happening too quickly for me. I didn't realize it required so many details. Attikus seemed to be a man who already had the map spread out in front of him. He saw miles ahead and understood what was required to make this fake marriage successful. I, on the other hand only saw a few feet ahead of me.

My limited perspective was due to limited resources, stress, fear, and exhaustion.

I was grateful he had a map to guide us along. If I got lost, perhaps I could borrow that map. But I wouldn't tell him that right now.

I placed my hand into his grip, and energy zipped through us. My body jerked, and I looked at him. He didn't show any response. Perhaps I was the only one who felt anything. I shoved down the strange attraction to him. What else could it be if it wasn't an attraction? The last thing I needed was to complicate matters.

I stared at our joined hands, wondering if I was making a mistake. I felt like someone who lived without direction, making abrupt decisions that I would later regret. This spontaneous marriage would forever change my life. Fear bubbled in me, but I kicked the self-doubt away.

This arranged marriage *had* to be successful for me to save myself and my mother. I had to cut ties with Emmanuel once and for all. If he knew I was married to a powerful billionaire, he wouldn't dare ask me for more money, right? I didn't have any other options.

"Thank you, darling." I squeezed his hand. "How am I doing?"

A smirk slid onto his face before disappearing quickly.

Attikus said nothing as he led me to the front door. A pretty wreath of spring flowers hung on the door.

His finger reached for the doorbell, but then the door opened.

CHAPTER TEN

VANESSA

"WELL, HELLO THERE!" A woman with a friendly smile beamed at me and Attikus. "Come in."

She gripped Attikus's arm, dragging him into the marble foyer.

She smiled at me and reached out her hand. "I'm Ellen, Attikus's sister. You are . . .?" Her voice trailed off as she looked at our joined hands. Then she whipped a look at Attikus. "Have you been hiding your gorgeous girlfriend from Mom and me?"

I studied the siblings and didn't see any resemblance. Attikus had dark hair and brown eyes, whereas Ellen had fiery hair and ocean-blue eyes.

"Ellen, this is Nessa Lambert, my fiancée."

"What?" Her mouth dropped as she looked at me. "Nessa Lambert, the artist?"

I nodded.

"Oh, my God!" She embraced me, then drew back. "I love your work. I have the *Dive into Hope* painting."

I'd sold that abstract painting at an auction years ago.

"Thank you. I'm glad you love it. It was one of my favorites."

Ellen smiled, inhaled a deep breath, pouted, and slapped Attikus on the arm. "What the hell? You have a fiancée and didn't tell me?"

"I'm telling you now." He looked at me. "Would you like anything to drink?"

I wasn't thirsty, but I needed to hold something in my hand. "Water would be great. Thank you."

Ellen lifted a hand. "Let me get her the water. This is *my* house."

"That I paid for," he retorted calmly.

"Because you love your big sister and your mom so much." She narrowed her eyes at him. "Don't make me look like a poor host."

She opened the fridge and took out two bottles of water, gesturing for us to sit at the kitchen table with six chairs. "Let's chat."

"We won't stay long." Attikus pulled out a chair for me to sit on. "I'm here to pick up dinner."

"I'll give you dinner after I introduce myself to my future sister-in-law." Ellen sat down beside me. "So, how did you guys meet?"

Attikus knew this was going to happen. I sipped my water and placed it on the table. "We met on a dating app called Heartstrings."

Attikus flicked me a look, probably wondering how I knew about it. Vivian told me that her sister, Kaylee, had developed the app while attending Whiz Kidz. It was a program by her husband, Arrow Holt. Arrow was one of Attikus's billionaire friends. He had taken over the dating app since it was first developed.

"I can't believe this." Ellen's eyes flashed. "If I had known you were actively looking for someone, I would've backed off. I'll tell Mom Gig to cancel the blind date with Mary's daughter."

Attikus rolled his eyes. "It's only a blind date if I didn't already know Daisy. Now you can stop trying to be the matchmaker."

I couldn't imagine him being with someone named Daisy.

When his mother entered the kitchen with groceries, the mystery around Attikus Mount ballooned. Unlike Ellen, who had red hair and fair skin, Gigi possessed olive skin and blonde hair. Even if she had dyed her hair black or red, I couldn't see any resemblance to Attikus.

She entered, saw us sitting at the kitchen table, lifted a perfect eyebrow, and pinned her gaze on Attikus. "Did I miss something? I didn't know we were expecting guests today."

Attikus got out of his seat, walked over to his mother, and took the bags of groceries from her hand, placing them onto the marble kitchen island. "I want you to meet my fiancée, Nessa Lambert."

The shock on his mother's face was more prominent than Ellen's. She almost looked pissed. Maybe she was but didn't want to show her disappointment in front of me.

Awkwardness set in, and I wanted to leave. Guilt nibbled at me as I tried to imagine doing this to my mother. How would she react? It would devastate her.

Wanting to ease the tension, I rose from my seat, walked over to Gigi, and offered my hand.

"We met online, and I couldn't stay away from his serious and boring self." I shrugged. "I guess the alias 'boring as hell' intrigued me."

"It's nice to meet you." Gigi took my hand in hers. "I'm sorry. I don't know what else to say. It's going to take me some time to adjust."

"Of course. I understand."

Attikus looked at me across the counter, but I couldn't read him. Did he want time alone with his family to inform them of our marriage?

He turned to his sister. "Do you have the spaghetti ready? We have to get going."

"Already?" Gigi asked. "You can't just barge in here, inform your mother you're engaged, and *leave*."

He walked over and embraced her. This was a softer side of Attikus I didn't expect. Not that I knew a lot of billionaires or how they conducted themselves with their families. But I sensed Attikus was close to his family—protective of them.

"I'll be back to chat with you." He kissed his mom on the side of her head. "Nessa experienced a horrific event at her grand opening today. I'm sure she'll need some rest."

"Oh, I heard about that on the news," Ellen said as she opened the refrigerator door and pulled out a container.

"What happened?" Gigi looked at me.

"Someone sent her a severed finger to the grand opening," Attikus replied.

"What?" Concern and disdain flashed over her face. "Who would do something like that? What did the police say?"

"They're looking into it. Maybe it's from a competitor gallery. Or another artist." I shrugged. "People can be cruel."

"Here you go. I gave you an extra container for Nessa." Ellen handed him a bag and looked at me. "Come back so we can get to know each other. Do you need help with wedding planning?"

I looked at Attikus. "We haven't thought about that yet."

I couldn't crush his sister's heart. We'd have to ease her and his mom into our eloping plan. This entire scenario was becoming more complicated.

Gigi and Ellen walked us to the door.

"Go home and rest." Gigi hugged me. "We'll make a trip to your gallery soon. Welcome to the family."

"Thank you. I look forward to getting to know you."

My chest constricted as guilt rose in me. These people seemed so genuine, and I didn't know how they'd react when Attikus and I had to part ways.

Think about that later.

Inside the car, Attikus said, "You should move in with me."

"What?"

He turned to me. "What kind of married couple lives separately?"

I blew out a breath. "I'll move a few things to your place to make it believable. But I'm keeping my apartment so I can return to it after six months."

"I'll pick you up in a few days." He pulled into a parking spot in front of my apartment and glanced around. It was in a quiet neighborhood near downtown Providence. The apartment came with a studio space where I could paint my oversized canvases.

"You still want to go through with this?" I asked.

"Why wouldn't I?"

"Your family seems . . . disturbed by this announcement."

"They've been more disturbed." He looked me in the eye. "I think you're more unsettled about this situation than I am."

"And *that* disturbs me."

The corner of his lips tilted. "I'm used to adapting to abrupt changes. You're an artist. Go with the flow."

Easier said than done, smart ass.

I grabbed my purse, getting ready to leave.

"Nice addition about Heartstrings. Have you tried the app?"

"No," I lied and didn't care if he knew it. "We need to make this relationship believable. Online dating is how people meet these days. Thanks for the ride home."

When I got into my apartment on the fourth floor, I rushed to the window and glanced down. Attikus was still parked on the street.

"What is he doing?"

After ten minutes, he left. I didn't even know why I was watching him. Scrubbing a hand down my face, I dropped onto my couch and released a stressful sigh. I wanted to scream, cry, and curl into a ball that would roll me somewhere away from this reality. I wanted time to stop so I could catch up with life.

Needing comfort, I reached for a throw pillow and placed it in front of me. It became a barrier between me and the new life I'd created for myself.

You're doing the right thing. Mẹ will be out of prison soon.

I desperately needed a hot shower to clear my head so I could research Attikus. I had to know everything I could about my future husband. Then I had to make sure I wrote down all the things I wanted from the marriage. Six months would give me enough time to get rid of Emmanuel.

CHAPTER ELEVEN

ATTIKUS

WHEN I GOT HOME, several text messages from my mother and sister appeared. I'd expected this.

I stared at my mother's texts.

Mom: *What the hell is going on? When did you meet Nessa?*

Mom: *What is her background?*

Mom: *What do you know about her?*

Mom: *She's beautiful and courteous, by the way.*

Mom: *What's her financial situation?*

Mom: *I need to have a chat with my son. SOONER RATHER THAN LATER.*

Her questions were all valid. No mother wanted her son to be attached to a gold digger. I'd met several of them.

Her anger and disappointment pulsed through the screen. I didn't want to call her tonight. She needed more time to let this news settle. I needed time as well.

Something still bothered me.

Most sane people would take more time before making an

important decision. This had been my method—scan the horizon to gauge for any unexpected pitfalls before making the next step. So why did I agree to her proposal so quickly? The abrupt decision perplexed me.

For some damn reason, I knew without a doubt that I had to help her. What the fuck was wrong with me? I couldn't go back on my word now. I had to weather the storm no matter what came my way.

When she spent time with my family, talking to my sister and my mother, I knew there was no turning back. I was a man of my word, and I expected the same of others. This society had become a place where money talked loudest and people's words meant nothing. I knew if I wanted to establish myself amongst these people, I needed wealth. For a while, I assumed wealth and success could fill the void in me. But that never happened because my heart died with my family.

But a tiny spark lit up inside me today. It warmed my chest to see Vanessa catching on to our plan easily. The way she inserted her creative storyline into how we met added to her mystery.

Vanessa Lam was more than an artist. Who was she? Perhaps that was the reason that intrigued me.

I walked over to my mini-bar and poured myself two fingers of whiskey, swirling it in my glass. I brought it over to my desk, sat down, and sipped, letting the liquid roll around my mouth before swallowing. The heat traveled down my throat as I savored the flavor of oak, sherry, and vanilla. The earthy, smoky, and woody aromas calmed me.

The calm allowed me to organize myself easily. With my marriage to Vanessa, I needed to shift some things around to accommodate this schedule change. My mother used to say I worked a lot and needed a hobby—a distraction. Vanessa was that distraction, though I knew my mother had meant something else.

I turned on my computer and opened a folder with several files I'd collected over the years. My mother and sister didn't know vengeance still occupied my mind. I still remembered my childhood home becoming a pile of ashes. Like the decorative flag with the smiling sun that had burned away, the joy and warmth of my family had diminished to nothing in a single day. I remembered walking by that property years later, even though another family had moved into the newly built home, and wondering what life would've been like if my mother, father, and sister hadn't been murdered. They were innocent people. Amelia had been so excited to go on her field trip to the zoo. Their deaths occurred because of me—because high school bullies had taken their hatred out on my family.

How could I let that pain go? Ashton, Bobby, and Harry had been responsible. Even though they'd only been teenagers back then, these boys were ruthless. It was odd how they all disappeared after my family's murders. Their parents said they went to a boarding school overseas.

My research on them showed they'd attended private schools in Paris, but they'd remained out of the limelight for many years until I recently located Bobby and Harry.

I stared at their photos on my computer screen as I did many times a week. I'd found some photos of them as men, but there weren't many. Their families had sold their businesses and moved away from Providence. The Lindors lived in Miami now. The Cooneys settled in Texas, and the Sullivans moved to Los Angeles.

It had been a long time since I had a restful sleep. Whenever I closed my eyes, I saw my burned home and remembered the pain from that traumatic day. The only thing that could give me a restful sleep was the deaths of those who killed my family. A debt must be collected, and I wasn't going to wait for karma to collect. Two down and one to go.

Despite my desire to find these assholes, I didn't want to worry my family. I told them I was expanding my business, which wasn't a lie. The less they knew, the safer they'd be. Besides owning a successful museum, I'd also invested in vacation rentals worldwide and a company that developed mobile apps for children's entertainment and education called Fresh Perspective.

Inspired by Forrest's holistic approach, I created Healthy Horizon. This innovative farm cultivated herbs and vegetables using cutting-edge machines that emitted light and sound frequencies to stimulate optimal growth in the plants. Orion's company created these machines, for which I received a discount. The crystal-infused water was used for irrigation, which assisted in the steady growth of healthy plants. Healthy Horizon was both an indoor and outdoor farm.

My greenhouse didn't need pesticides, growth-induced hormones, or any of the chemicals that large companies used in their recipe for rapid growth. This was the new way of farming. Every family could have a small greenhouse in their yard, allowing them to be self-sufficient. We'd be rolling out the HH-Pods in the next few months for homeowners to start their indoor farming. Returning to the basics of the natural world was something that interested me. I didn't like what the world had become, and I wished for a simpler way to live.

My phone rang, and I picked up the call.

"Hey, how's Nessa?" Orion asked.

"She's at home resting now," I said.

"Did you watch the recordings I sent you yet?"

"Not yet. I just got home."

"Let me catch you up. A man delivered the package," Orion said. "He's a homeless man. Someone gave him a hundred bucks to deliver the package. Before the police took the package, I swiped the fingerprints. My team is working on it now. We'll get the DNA soon too."

I released a sigh. "You work fast."

"You've been off the past few weeks, so I assume you have a lot on your plate. I know what that feels like."

I said nothing for a moment.

"Is there something going on with you and Nessa?" he asked.

"Why do you ask?"

"Elena seems to think something's going on."

Amused, I asked, "What did she say?"

"Nothing, really. It's just how she said it. 'They make a good couple, don't you think?'"

"We're getting married soon."

"*What?*" Orion laughed. "Man, it's too late for that kind of joke."

"It's not a joke. It's only temporary. Six months at most."

"The fuck?"

I briefed my best friend on the situation and told him I'd inform the other boys later.

By the end of our conversation, he said, "You're insane, man. You're being too radical."

"Says the quadrillionaire thief who steals for fun."

"I've cut back on that now. I have Elena to occupy my time."

"So I guess you can say Nessa Lambert will be my distraction for the time being."

"You need a tight prenuptial. *No exceptions.*"

There was no doubt about that, but I said, "It's an arranged fake marriage for six months. It'll be annulled right after. She won't get anything from me." I leaned back in my chair. "She's not in it for the money."

"How do you know?" Shock emanated from his voice. "We both know what women want from men like us. You *need* to protect yourself."

"You sound like my mother."

"Someone needs to pull off your distorted rose-colored glasses. You're not seeing things right, man."

"I don't wear glasses."

"Shut the fuck up. You know what I mean."

I enjoyed riling him up. "Listen, I know these precautions. I just have a weird feeling that I have to help her. I don't know why. So I'm waiting it out. Maybe time will reveal the reason. Know what I mean?"

Orion went quiet for a moment. "I know exactly what you mean. I was drawn to Elena from the beginning, but I didn't know why. I soon realized she was an integral part of my life." He sighed. "Just be careful, okay? For all we know, maybe The Trogyn planted her in your life to start a war with us."

That had occurred to me.

"I'm very careful. Don't worry." I scrubbed a hand down my face.

"How are you doing on Level Seven?" Orion changed the topic.

"It's going. The demo is almost ready. Only a few more changes. How's the marketing going?"

I'd invested in the WaterFyre Rising video game, which was started by Remington Starke. It was a spectacular game consisting of seven major levels, with numerous layers and portals in between. Each boy had designed a fantastical world. The world I created for Level Seven consisted of a magical forest that existed underneath the city of Providence. I'd say my demo was eighty percent finished, but there were a few things I wasn't sure of.

"Don't rush on it. Take your time. The marketing is going

well. We had a friendly reception from players at the recent Games Convention."

When our conversation ended, Orion offered his assistance with whatever I needed. I asked him to keep quiet about my marriage until Vanessa and I announced the news.

Maybe I could show Mom Gigi a snippet of Level Seven so she understood how busy I was. A man like me with a lot of businesses didn't have time to date, so I'd turned to Heartstrings and met Vanessa. I needed my mother to stop asking questions.

Long-term relationships weren't my thing. Still, I was a man and had needs, so casual dating had been working beautifully for me. I didn't have the patience for needy women who only wanted my credit cards or access to the rental halls in my museum to host their galas. Mom Gigi knew this and was probably worried I'd progressed from casual dating to casual marriage.

I could understand her worry. But if I told her the truth, it would make things more complicated. It was already complex with only Vanessa, me, and now Orion knowing the truth. The wider the web, the more unnecessary things it could catch. Things needed to remain simple.

However, I didn't know why I hadn't been in the mood for casual dating recently.

You know why.

I pursed my lips, wondering why there was such a thing as an inner voice. It was annoying as fuck.

Yes, I knew why—since I'd hosted Nessa Lambert's art in my museum. Her style of art spoke to me. Each of her paintings was like a hidden message I couldn't decode, and I considered myself extremely versed in paintings.

Besides the mysterious artwork, she was also beautiful and unreachable. It was as though she had built an invisible wall around herself, keeping people away. I'd never met a woman like that. Most women wanted me to get close to them so I could know their desires. Those women didn't want to be with a physically disabled man. They only saw my wealth and success.

"Have you tried walking without a cane?" Kelly asks, *pointing to the cane leaning on my chair.*

"I have," I say. "But I prefer my cane. Does that bother you?"

"Of course not." She smiles and twirls a golden lock of hair. "I just don't want you to trip when we dance."

My patience snaps. "Who says we're going to dance?"

That kind of conversation had occurred too many times. It was hard to find someone who truly saw me for who I was beyond the cane. I had more to offer than what was in my bank account.

My mind wandered back to Vanessa. She and I were similar. We were islands, detached from the mainland. There were things we didn't want others to know. We were close enough to hop back onto the mainland when necessary, but we preferred being away to protect ourselves. What was she protecting?

She'd been present the day at the museum when Orion revealed his identity to Remington, Royce, Grayson, Forrest, and Arrow. He'd shown them one of my private rooms that held Orion's precious art that he'd stolen from members of the Trogyn. He'd given it to me to do with as I pleased.

How would I reveal Vanessa's identity to my family? They'd find out sooner or later about her real name. There had to be a way for her to work under her artist's name without the public knowing about Vanessa, at least not until she was ready. I had to intercept whatever Emmanuel planned to do.

I needed to find out everything about this fucker.

More importantly, who had Vanessa killed? I needed the entire story.

Slow down.

The muscle on my right leg twitched, and a slight pain shot up my thigh. I knew my body well. Stress showed itself in my injuries. Twitching, aching, numbing, and cramping were all symptoms that told me I had to slow down. I had a habit of trying to do too much. Even my doctor told me to cut back.

Sighing, I stared at my priority list and the names of my enemies. Sometimes, I had to break the societal rules to get things done *appropriately*. Sometimes, punishment for criminals required breaking the law. These fucking laws didn't help me when I needed them. Rather, they protected the people who destroyed my family. The principal of my school, the police officer who claimed I lied about the "good" boys from prestigious families, and the judge who sided with those families. These were "respected" authorities who were supposed to help me.

Where was the justice in that? Those names were on my shit list too, but they weren't a priority yet.

Corruption reigned supreme these days. For that reason, my WaterFyre Rising friends and I created the V.A.T.V.—Vigilantes Against the Villains. I never imagined being part of such a unique group of intelligent men who thought beyond the norm.

Below my family's killers was The Trogyn—a dangerous crime syndicate with ties to powerful people all over the world. They knew my friends had ruined their business and were now retaliating. We had to stop them. It all started when Remington and his friends witnessed a crime by this organization. From that day, the past had followed each of these boys. The Trogyn's crime businesses ranged from sex trafficking and drugs to money laundering, racketeering, and so much more. If I didn't get rid of The Trogyn, they'd come for my businesses too. I'd worked too hard for anyone to take them.

Next on the list was to find Joseph Gallo, my seventy-year-old curator. He'd been gone a month, and nothing on the recordings at the museum showed anything worthwhile. Concern warred in me. I hadn't heard about any dead bodies being reported, so that meant he was still alive. But then again, what if he'd been taken and transported elsewhere? But who would take an old man?

Think positive, Attikus.

I released a sigh as I typed in my next priority: Vanessa Lam.

I sat back, staring at the name. Who was my "wife?" What kind of past had caught up to her? I had to know who was going to live in my house. That thought reminded me I had to move some things around the guest suite, which had its own bathroom, kitchen, and living room. She wouldn't need to leave that suite if she didn't want to.

We would remain professional. Our relationship was a business one. I typed in her name in the discreet search engine owned by Orion's company. A few Vanessa Lams popped into the search. I clicked on an image from Bangor's Daily News, showing a group of students from the University of Maine. A young girl resembling Vanessa stood with her classmates, holding a tray of seedlings. Joy beamed from her face.

The article stated these were botany students volunteering their time at the Horticulture Club. I dug deeper and discovered my future wife was the top student in her class. She was offered a scholarship to attend Harvard for a masters in botany, but she didn't go.

Why? What made her turn to art? There was nothing wrong with being an artist, but it was a tough profession. She could have made a stable living as a botanist or a horticulturist. I could see those interests in her paintings now. She'd incorporated all kinds of plants and flowers in them.

This discovery made her even more attractive to me. Would she consider working for Healthy Horizon? My innovative farms would benefit from her knowledge. This was something to discuss later.

Who taught her how to paint?

CHAPTER TWELVE

VANESSA

I WOKE up the next day full of vigor. Usually, I'd have slept in on a Saturday, but curiosity burned in me. I blamed it on the dream I had about my future fake husband. It wasn't the dream I expected. A fake marriage and a quick wedding had muddled my mind. So my subconscious mind devised a sexy wedding night that could never happen. I shivered as the vivid dream replayed in my head. Attikus had been covered in edible paint, and I was the artist spreading it around his body with my hands, mouth, and tongue.

"Stop thinking about it." I patted my cheeks, horrified at myself for thinking it was real. "It's never going to happen. You're just stressed, and you're releasing it through a dream." There had to be a psychological explanation for this. I'd find it later. "Coffee, my best friend. Where are you?"

Shoving the annoyance aside, I washed up, twisted my dark hair into a messy bun, and applied moisturizer to my face. While the coffee brewed, I dressed in a cotton T-shirt I'd designed a while ago when I had more time on my hands. It showed a little cute sprout with a smiling face, holding a sign that read The Beginning of Everything.

The soft T-shirt had been worn too many times. It had two holes on the side seams. Paint splatter covered the once-white T-shirt. I pulled on cotton pants that also had paint splatter—my outfit to wear when I needed time in my art studio. Today was one of those days. I felt the call to paint—to release untamed emotions.

With my phone and coffee in tow, I slipped on my old sneakers, grabbed my keys, left my one-bedroom apartment, and walked down to the first floor. I walked past three other art studios to reach mine, which was at the end of the hallway. I unlocked my studio, which was the largest studio with three tall windows that allowed sufficient sunlight. Lighting was essential to painting. My studio neighbor, Adam, was a sculptor by night and worked as a plumber by day. Most artists had a day job to pay for their passions. I was one of the fortunate few who could do it full time. But it wasn't always like this.

What's your true passion?

My love for painting had developed over time. It had been an interest, a hobby I was good at. But my passion had always been the world of plants. I sipped my coffee, savored the flavor, and felt the caffeine energize me. Today, the coffee was more of a comforting friend instead of an energizer. The orgasm from last night was something I'd never experienced. It still hummed in me.

After sipping more coffee, I swiveled my chair to face the residential street full of parked cars. A jogger strode by with his dog. An older woman walked with her friend across the street. Life seemed simple for these people. If only mine were like that. I prayed for a day when stress didn't tug at me.

I'd steal a few minutes this morning to research Attikus Mount. What was his personality? What did he like or dislike?

I had to know the man I was going to marry, right? Even if it wasn't a real marriage, I had to know who I was attached to for the next few months.

Had he committed any crimes? What were his ex-girlfriends like? Where did he go to school? I typed in his name, and to my surprise, there wasn't a lot of information about him.

There were pictures of him at his museum and a few at a farm or warehouse full of plants. The farm interested me. After reading the article on Healthy Horizon and checking out their website, I developed a newfound respect for him due to his innovative indoor and outdoor farming practices. Most of the images were from the present day or a few years ago. Nothing dating back to ten years or earlier. Why?

In almost all the pictures, he didn't smile. I tried looking for pictures of him and his family, and nothing showed up. I couldn't find Gigi or Ellen Mount. Maybe they had different last names. Who were these people? Were they frauds? *Shit.* Had I inserted myself into a fraudulent family?

My phone rang, yanking my attention away from the Mount family. My heart raced when The Women's Facility flashed on my screen.

"Hi, *Mẹ!*" Excitement filled my voice.

"Hi, baby. How are you?" Mom didn't sound stressed.

Every time we spoke, we were careful with our words. Phone calls between my mom and her lawyer were the exception to being recorded.

"I'm well. Is everything okay with you?" I'd been so worried something horrific had happened to her.

"I'm okay. I saw on the news about that horrific event at the art gallery. Be careful."

"I will. Don't worry. The authorities are investigating."

"Good. I can't wait to see you. I miss the grilled pork *bánh mì* so much."

Our secret code for the escape was *bánh mì*, which was a popular Vietnamese sub.

"I'll buy you five of them. Rest up. You'll get to enjoy them soon."

"Are you sure? Don't stress about it. We can just go out to eat to celebrate."

"No stress at all, *Mẹ*." My voice cracked. "I miss you too. I'm so sorry."

"Stop," she said firmly. Though my mother didn't get to finish college, she was the smartest and strongest person I knew. I admired her perseverance. "You're worth it. You have a beautiful life ahead of you. Make me proud."

"I will." We caught up for a few more minutes until her twenty minutes were up.

"I'll visit you soon," I said, even though she didn't like me visiting her. She said prison wasn't a place she wanted her daughter to be near.

I sat back, wiped the tears from my eyes, and gathered myself.

When my emotions settled, I took out the commission piece that needed a varnish. I smiled at *Three Roads Diverged in a Dark Wood*. I had taken this commission from the twenty I'd received because of the buyer's concise description on the request form.

Something dark but offers hope. A crossroad that leads somewhere.

The description and the long delivery time made it an attractive option. I had over a year to create it and appreciated the extra time. Edgar Moore added nothing else, so I had free range to create something extraordinary from his description.

Three Roads Diverged in a Dark Wood was inspired by a poem I read in middle school by Robert Frost: *The Road Not Taken*. In his poem, the person had two options to choose from.

In my painting, there were three options. Why? Because aside from the lovely and ugly roads in front of me, there was also one that *I* created on my own. The third road was a reality that came to fruition as a result of it. No one presented it to me—that was the difference.

When I finished the varnish, I placed it inside a makeshift tent I created in the far corner of the studio. The tent kept the dust from falling onto the varnish. I'd send it off this week, and Edgar would pay the balance.

With this payment, I could fulfill the two million dollars to Leo Rossi, who owned the Bread and Butter restaurant in Boston. I met him at a party when one of my clients offered me a ticket to an exclusive club. I thought I'd network for more potential clients, but I overheard the two men discussing how to break someone out of prison. The conversations at that club terrified me. Crimes were negotiated and conducted there. I was one of them when I hired Leo to extract my mom.

I'd driven up to Boston to visit him at his restaurant. Did I fear he'd take my money and not help me? Yes. So I took detailed notes about him and his restaurant in case something happened to me. But Leo was my only hope. He'd sold me a believable plan. Leo claimed he knew people in The Women's Facility who could make the extraction go smoothly. Research on The Women's Facility revealed that three inmates had escaped successfully. The information was swept under the rug. He also claimed he knew someone from the media and the governor's office who would help him keep everything out of the public eye.

Two million dollars was a lot of money, but I'd pay anything for my mother's freedom. I also had to save up so we could move elsewhere to start over. Buy a house and live a simple life.

Feeling accomplished, I grabbed my sketchbook to brainstorm ideas for the First Lady. I held my pencil and drew quick sketches, but none of them called to me. I found a few pictures of Madeline Claude-Collins to inspire me, but I wasn't in the mood. Sometimes, art had its own mind. I couldn't force it. The most extraordinary art was usually created when it came naturally.

Putting the sketchbook down, I filled the water pitcher and watered the plants on the metal rack and windowsill.

If I had become a botanist or a horticulturist, I wouldn't have made enough money to help my mom. The salary couldn't compare to what I could demand for my original art. However, I worked for the American Horticultural Society, documenting data while painting on the side until my art sold well. When Nessa Lambert became popular, Vanessa Lam stepped to the side.

I open the letter and jump with joy! Harvard University has offered me a full scholarship for my masters in their Botany Program. Tears stream down my face as I hold the letter to my chest.

Mẹ is going to be thrilled! This is a huge financial relief for us. She doesn't make a lot of money as the front desk receptionist for a hair salon. She also volunteers at local shelters. It's been hard the past four years because I was in Maine for college and only came home during the summer.

Now she can drive into Boston to visit me. I can even commute from home. I'm not sure yet. My mind races with various scenarios to save more money. I don't want my mom to work so hard anymore. She's been through a lot.

To be honest, I'm surprised she wanted me. I wasn't conceived because my parents loved each other. My mom was raped. She was a sophomore in college when she was kidnapped and forced into prostitution for several years. She didn't know she was pregnant until after she escaped with two other women.

When she came home, her mom and dad and uncle were dead. People said they were in a car accident while searching for her. But she told me it was probably her kidnappers who wanted to stop her family from looking for her. Their deaths were also a warning for her. She had escaped and knew things about their underground work.

My mom is a smart woman, and she also got a scholarship to Harvard University. But she never got to attend. She survived all those years in the prostitution ring by helping the handlers organize their finances.

Now she tries to live a simple life, but I know she's always suspicious of people and overprotective of me. I understand where she's coming from, and I try to be as responsible as possible.

Today is a great day, and I want to deliver the good news to my mom. The Wild Streak is only a few blocks from our apartment. I slip on my sneakers and jean jacket because the weather is still chilly for late March. I'm in Providence for the weekend because Mom called a few days ago about a letter waiting for me.

Tucking the letter into my jacket, I head down the stairs and out onto the sidewalk. Mom still has another hour before her shift ends. She's only working half a day so she can spend time with me while I'm home. The image of the delicious Vietnamese sub on the window makes my stomach growl. I walk into Saigon Bistro to order my mom her favorite teriyaki Vietnamese sub. I also get one for myself. Then I enter the hair salon, waving at my mom and her coworkers, who are all friendly women.

"Almost done, baby," Mẹ says.

"No rush."

Marge, the owner of the hair salon, emerges from the back room and rushes up to me. "Hi, Vanessa. How's everything? I hear you're loving it at UME."

"I am."

"You're making your mom very proud."

I want to share my good news but decide to wait. Mom needs to be the first person to hear it.

When we leave, I lift the bag. "Guess what I got for us to celebrate?"

"Celebrate what?" Mom turns down a shortcut we often take to get home. It's an alleyway that cuts through several brick buildings.

"I got accepted to Harvard on a full scholarship, Mom!" I squeal.

Mom throws her arms around me, and we hug for a moment.

Then, someone shoves us, and our bodies slam against the wall.

"Where's your money?" barks a man with a scar on his lip and a tattoo of a flying pig on his neck. He aims a knife at us. But he's drunk, and he's swaying.

His friend with the mustache rakes a gaze down my body. They reek of alcohol. Fear twists my stomach as Mom wraps a protective arm around me.

She digs in her purse and pulls out cash. "Take it. Please let us go."

The man with the scar takes the money from my mom and shoves it into his pocket.

"Should we let them go, Dillon?"

"After I have fun with the little one, Brody." Dillon grabs me, pushing me to the ground.

Mom reaches for me, but Brody pulls her back. She screams and scratches at him.

I scream too, but Dillon covers my mouth with his dirty hand.

He tries to unbutton my pants, but I fight him with all my might, scratching his eyes. He wails and slaps me. Pain bursts, but I keep hitting him. My mom screams, and the man cries in pain.

I see broken glass near my hand. I reach for a shard and stab Dillon in the face and neck. Blood splatters everywhere. He wails in pain, gripping the glass shard sticking out of his neck.

Terrified at what I'll find and the fury on his face, I kick him away. He drops to the ground as blood pools around him.

"Fuck!" Brody freaks and rushes out of sight.

Mom scrambles over to me as my body trembles.

I can't look away from the dying man on the ground.

Mom tells me, "It's going to be okay, honey. Breathe."

I try to breathe, but my mom leaves my side and walks over to the dead man. She yanks out the shard and stabs him a few more times in his neck. More blood spills out. His body doesn't react to her stabbing because he's already dead from my attack.

With her bloody hands, she smears the blood onto her shirt and khakis.

"Me," I cry. "What are you doing?"

"It was self-defense." She looks at me. Though she appears calm, I know she's pushing the fear aside for me. "I was defending you from this violent man." She drops the bloodied shard on the ground.

Sirens blast in the distance.

We don't know who called the police, but they arrive quickly. Instead of giving us time to explain the situation, they arrest my mom. I tell Officer Caruso that the dead man tried to rape me, and his accomplice ran away.

The officer ignores my statement and says, "Do you know who just died?"

"A criminal," I say, still worried about my mom.

"He's Dillon Claude Harris, the heir to Harris Pharmaceutical."

"I don't care who he is, Officer Caruso. He just tried to rape me. But you arrested my mom."

"Someone has to pay for it," he says, gesturing to the ambulance. "The EMTs will take you to the hospital for a checkup."

As I walk toward the ambulance, I hear the officer talking to someone on the phone.

"Don't worry, sir. She'll pay for her crime."

That's when I realize my mom is going to prison for something she didn't do.

Banging on my door yanked me back to the present moment.

"Be right there."

CHAPTER THIRTEEN

VANESSA

I PLACED my water pitcher down and walked over to peek through the peephole.

"Hi, Adam." I opened the door and smiled at my studio neighbor.

"I saw the light on and knew you were working. Want to go out to lunch?" Adam grinned, running a hand through his mop of messy blond hair.

He'd asked me out twice, but I'd declined. I didn't have the energy to start a relationship. My experience with Emmanuel had forced me to take a break from trusting men.

But you trust Attikus.

He was different. We were in business together, not a personal relationship.

"Sorry, I need to work on a painting." I glanced over my shoulder. "I'm behind on my work."

"Well, you gotta eat to continue, right?" He tucked his hands into his jean pockets.

"I can't."

He smirked. "Why not?"

"Because she has a date with her fiancé." Attikus's voice cut through the space, dismantling whatever Adam had planned.

Adam straightened, looking uncomfortable. "I'm sorry. I didn't know Nessa was engaged."

"Just recently." I smiled.

"Now you know." Attikus used his cane, ushering Adam aside to make room for him. "You can leave now."

Adam stared at the cane, then looked up at Attikus before turning his gaze on me. "Have a good day."

I closed the door as Attikus entered my studio and stared at him. "What are you doing here?"

"Trying to show the world that we're in a relationship by taking my fiancée out to lunch." He glanced around my studio. "And I'd like to know what my fiancée does during the day."

He walked over and stared at several of my paintings I hadn't brought out to the gallery.

"Perhaps next time you should give me a heads up that you're coming."

"I did. I texted you."

With furrowed eyebrows, I walked over to my phone on the desk and glanced at his text.

Attikus: *I'm heading over. Let's go to lunch.*

He'd sent it five minutes ago, probably when he pulled into a parking spot.

I narrowed my eyes. "People usually give me a few hours' notice—if not days—when they want to have lunch with me. But then again, you didn't ask."

"I'm not most people." He lifted a shoulder. "I rearranged my schedule to have lunch with my fiancée. And I assume she would drop everything to accommodate me. Why? Because we are in *love.*"

He emphasized it with an expression that made me want to slap and kiss him.

Kiss him? Where did that ridiculous idea come from?

The dream about him flashed across my mind, and my body betrayed me. The powerful sensations from last night surfaced, making me remember *everything.*

It was only a dream. Get over it.

He ambled over to a dark lotus painting I hadn't finished and crossed his arms, studying it. "Who is this painting for?"

His straight posture demanded attention. For a moment, I forgot he had a cane. I glanced around and saw it leaning against the wall. Did he always need the cane? Had he tried to walk without it?

Why so many questions, Vanessa?

I blinked at my curiosity. It was none of my business. Why was I focusing on his injury? Perhaps it was because he was a gorgeous man despite those flaws. I'd never seen anyone enhanced by a cane the way he was. The cane became a fascinating accessory.

Oh, my gosh. Something was truly off with me. I was an artist, so random things fascinated me, but a cane? That was like admiring a doorknob or a crack on the street when I should admire a tranquil landscape, a lovely sunset, or a bouquet of flowers.

Swerving my attention elsewhere, I studied his light green long-sleeved shirt. He was wearing it with the sleeves rolled up to his forearm over dark jeans, looking as gorgeous as he did in a powerful suit.

I didn't know why, but I liked the light green on him. It made him appear more carefree, less intense. Green was the color of nature, where things grew at their own pace. At this moment, he represented an enigmatic tree standing tall, having an interesting relationship with his environment. I could see him as the CEO of Healthy Horizon.

He flicked me a look that I felt in my core.

Then I remembered his question. "It's not for sale."

"Why not?"

"Because."

His lips lilted. "That's not a good reason."

"It's reason enough."

I expected him to pressure me, but he didn't. "There's a lot of pain immersed in it."

Of all the comments he could have said, I didn't expect that. He had seen through the colors and textures—right into the depth of the painting. My heart raced, and a sliver of fear slid down my back. No one had read my art like that. *No one.*

I stared at him, and he stared back.

A silent conversation occurred between us. The dialogue wasn't conveyed through words, but an energy exchange that I couldn't explain. It was as though we both knew what the other was thinking and feeling, but we respected each other's privacy enough not to push any further.

I felt like a botanist examining the biology and ecology of a unique plant—what made up this interesting man who pulled at me in various ways? He was probably doing the same to me. This was something I had to contemplate later. I'd never wanted anyone trespassing into my private sanctuary. It was too dangerous. I had too many secrets.

Changing the topic, I said, "Five minutes is not enough time to give someone a heads-up."

"As my fiancée, you should always be ready to have lunch with me."

"That's an arrogant statement."

"Is it?" He leveled a stare at me. "I find it to be an accurate statement." He gestured to me. "We're playing a role, and you should practice how to be my fiancée so people won't question our relationship."

Was he taking this marriage too seriously?

"I don't think people will care about that."

He pursed his lips. "Most won't. But the man who's black-mailing you *will*. The entire purpose of this fake marriage is to make him believe you're mine, so he'll leave you alone. Your ex will question our relationship if the media writes articles about how Attikus Mount—the museum owner—and his wife don't appear to be in love." His eyes flashed with amusement. "I'm just trying to cover the bases."

Once again, he was annoyingly right. Why hadn't I thought everything through like him?

He walked over to my counter and grabbed a paintbrush from a container, twirling it between his fingers. Wandering to the table full of plants and seedlings, he examined the string of pearl plants sitting at the top of a bookcase.

"Interesting plant," he said, glancing up at my potted pitcher plant hanging from a rope hooked to the ceiling. "What is it?"

"It's a carnivorous plant. It eats bugs."

I stared at him, wondering what else I could say. We could probably spend all day standing in my studio debating on why sending a text telling someone you're coming over five minutes before arrival was inconsiderate.

But then I realized this was a billionaire who didn't have to follow anyone's rules. People changed their schedules around *him*.

Still, that didn't make me feel any better. I was his fiancée now. Perhaps he should adjust his schedule to accommodate *me*.

"I assumed my considerate fiancée would give me more notice, knowing how busy I am." I turned and grabbed my purse. "Where are we going?" I wanted to get this over with so I could go back to my painting.

"Wherever you want."

I arched my eyebrows. Attikus didn't seem like a man who didn't have a plan. But at this moment, it appeared his visit to my studio was a spontaneous decision.

An idea popped into my head. I might as well make use of being engaged to one of the wealthiest men in the world.

"Let's go to Saigon Bistro. I haven't been there in a while."

My mom and I used to love going there for authentic Vietnamese food.

Attikus just said. "Okay."

As we walked out onto the street, he took my hand. Surprised, I looked over at him.

"We're supposed to be engaged. Smile, people are watching across the street."

I glanced over as two women quickly looked away with cell phones in their hands. A third woman with light brown hair stood off to the side by a parking meter, staring at us. I blinked at the familiar face as unease churned in my stomach.

"How do people even know about us? We only had the discussion yesterday."

"My PR team informed a few friends from the media who told their friends. Things spread like wildfire when you know the right people."

Curious, I paused in my steps and dug out my phone from my purse.

My social media accounts on Real Rumors and Daily-Thoughts had grown to over ten thousand followers overnight! I was tagged in several posts on DailyThoughts and clicked on the one at the top, which indicated it had been shown to the most people.

MirandaNews had an image of my art gallery.

Billionaire Attikus Mount is engaged to artist Nessa Lambert after a whirlwind romance.

But then someone sent his fiancée a severed finger to her gallery opening!

I gaped at the comments.

What could this mean?

Is it her ex?

Does she have enemies?

Is someone giving her the finger?

Did someone dare give Attikus the finger?

I switched to Real Rumors to see the same viral post from MirandaNews.

"Oh. My. God. I can't believe this." I wanted to laugh and cry. "This has grown into some monstrous narrative."

"The media are a manipulative business." He grabbed my phone, turned it off, and dropped it into my purse as though it were his.

"Hey! What are you doing?" I fumed.

"Trying to take your mind off irrelevant things."

My chest heaved. "It has everything to do with me."

Why was he so calm about this?

What else would MirandaNews say next? She had over five million followers—more than my art account. Miranda could ruin me. Would she recognize me? I'd grown up since elementary school.

"You're having lunch with your fiancé. You should focus on me rather than working, right, darling?" Attikus kissed my forehead as Miranda approached.

I inhaled a breath as my body tensed with shock. The past flashed before me. Miranda looked the same as when she bullied me in elementary school. She wore a casual blazer over a pink shirt with jeans.

"Attikus," she said in a tone that told me she knew him. "It's so good to see you. Is this your lovely fiancée?" She looked at me and smiled. "Your art is stunning, by the way. I saw it at Attikus's museum."

"Miranda, this is Nessa." He interlaced his fingers with mine. "Miranda has been a big supporter of the Mount Museum."

What a small world to encounter a childhood bully who had dated my fake husband.

"Do you mind if I take a photo of you for MirandaNews?"

Attikus looked at me. "It's better to see our pics on Miranda's social media page than some other random person's."

Miranda offered me a warm smile. She didn't recognize me.

I looked over to where the two women had taken our pictures earlier, but they'd already left.

Something else was going on behind the scenes, and I hated not knowing the truth. What game was he playing? If we were getting married, I needed to know everything.

When Miranda looked at him, something passed between them. Why the hell was I jealous? What was wrong with me?

This haughty man had taken the reins of my life without my permission. The audacity! I was infuriated with him, stressed about my mom's situation, and now I had to deal with this sudden jealousy squirming inside me like a parasite. My life was becoming a massive mess.

Smiling, I extracted my hand from his grip, slipped my arm around his waist, and posed. Attikus wrapped his arm around my shoulder.

"Smile, Attikus," Miranda said. "Perfect." She snapped a few pictures and showed them to us.

"Send them to my phone, please."

"Got it." She studied me in my paint-splattered shirt and jeans. "How did you meet?"

"We bonded over art and conversation. She's a unique

woman," he replied, even though she had addressed the question to me.

"He wouldn't leave me alone," I smirked and met Miranda's curious eyes. "How did *you* and Attikus meet?"

Her face changed to an awkward expression, and he squeezed my shoulder. "We should get going."

Miranda waved at Attikus. "I'll catch you later." She walked across the street and down the sidewalk.

"Not sure I want to go to lunch now."

"Why?" he asked.

"To avoid meeting another one of your exes."

CHAPTER FOURTEEN

ATTIKUS

WE ENTERED SAIGON BISTRO, a small restaurant with about ten tables. The savory smell snuck up my nose, and my stomach growled. I wasn't hungry minutes ago, but now I wanted to try whatever they offered here.

A long line of people stood to the side.

The server with a pencil pierced through her messy bun greeted us and gestured to a table in the corner. "I'm Lulu, and I'll be back."

Still looking annoyed, Nessa pulled out a chair, sat down, and grabbed the menu. I sat across from her, placed the yellow envelope on the table, and stared at her.

"What's wrong?" I asked, even though I already knew.

She flicked me a look and placed her menu down. "I should be the one asking you that question. You barged into my studio, demanded lunch, and coerced a social media influencer to be outside my studio for photo ops." She leaned into the table. "I thought we had a deal."

"We do."

"It's not a deal if you're doing things without telling me.

You obviously have a plan. I need to know all the details. If I don't, I might do something that would derail this marriage before it even happens." She blew out a breath. "And please warn me the next time you have your ex involved in this. It's weird."

"Why is it weird? She has a wide reach that can help us."

"Maybe it's not strange to you, but it's strange to me." I rolled my eyes. "Especially when she still wants you."

I studied Nessa. Initially, I thought her annoyance stemmed from my unexpected visit to her studio and the disruption it caused to her work. But now I wondered if her moodiness resulted from jealousy.

No, it couldn't be. My attraction to her lived quietly within me. Was she also attracted to me?

This fake marriage had just gotten more complicated. However, I could be wrong about my assumption.

"Miranda doesn't want me," I said.

"Whatever you say," Vanessa replied, dropping her gaze to the menu.

Lulu returned, beamed, and asked, "Do you need a few more minutes?"

"Yes," we both said simultaneously.

Lulu nodded. "Take your time."

"Do you know Miranda?" I asked.

Vanessa lowered her menu. "It's not important."

"It's damn important if it's causing a rift between us."

"I know her, but she doesn't remember me." She huffed out a breath. "And that's all I'm going to say about this topic."

I had to find out, but not today. I didn't know why I felt the need to explain. "We only dated for a few months. Nothing serious. Besides, that was two years ago."

"It's serious enough that she's still attracted to you."

I wasn't going to win this war. "How do you know?"

"I can tell, Attikus." She leaned into the table again.

I did the same and clasped her hands in mine. "How?"

"A woman just knows. I can sense it."

"Really?" I rubbed a thumb over her hand. "What else can you sense?"

"That you have an intricate plan, and you're not sharing it with me."

That wasn't the answer I was hoping for. I wanted her to admit she was jealous. I wanted her to ask more about my relationships.

You value your privacy. Why are you asking for trouble?

"Why don't you ask me why I haven't shared the details with you? Have you considered that I might share them during this lunch date?"

Her expression changed as she weighed my statement. "Why haven't you shared?"

"You had a traumatic experience yesterday. I figure your mind needs a break. If you behave, I might share it after I eat." I flipped open the menu. "Now, what do you recommend?"

"Are you always this annoying?"

"No." I smiled. "Only with you."

She stared at me for a long moment as though something had grown on my face. Vanessa was a fascinating woman, indeed.

My stomach growled, and she asked, "Are you in the mood for noodles, rice, or sandwiches?"

My gaze swung to a man in a suit standing by the window with his sandwich. "How about a little of everything?"

"Have you had Vietnamese food before?"

"A long time ago. Just the fresh spring rolls." I looked around. "But I've had nothing here. It looks like it's been around for a while."

"It has. New owners, though. How about we do this?" She

pointed to a rice dish. "You get the lemongrass beef with rice, and I'll get the lemongrass pork and shrimp with noodles. I'll order beef and cold-cut subs. We'll get plates to share so you can try everything."

"Okay. Sounds good."

After we placed our food and drinks orders, I pushed the yellow envelope over to her. "Review the contract and let me know."

She gasped as she looked at the envelope and tossed me an inquisitive look. "Already? You're efficient." She opened it.

"Things need to get done, and this situation falls under the urgent category."

I was waiting on the results of the DNA testing on the finger. Before the detective took it, I'd taken a blood and skin sample. Orion owned a lab that would garner results quickly. Though I valued Detective Farmer's work, I didn't trust his department. The system had failed me before, so I needed to get results another way.

As she read the contract, I studied the way her eyebrows furrowed and her lips pursed in concentration. She was analyzing every sentence, which demonstrated her thoroughness. She wasn't simply an artist; she was also a businesswoman. I'd met several artists, and some of them didn't have the organizational skills Nessa showed. However, this skill set likely originated from her years of studying botany and horticulture.

Nessa was like a unique painting I couldn't stop admiring. The more I studied her, the more I discovered something new. She was like a portal, with the ability to lure me out of my dark world, helping me remember the joy I once had.

An ache bloomed on my right wrist, and my fingers curled in discomfort. According to the doctor, my wrist had healed from being fractured all those years ago. Perhaps certain things would never disappear.

"Are you done looking?" Vanessa glanced up.

"Is there a problem with me looking at you studying the contract?" I sipped the lychee iced tea with jelly bits she'd recommended. It was light and tasty, and I wouldn't have ordered it if I'd come here by myself.

"Do you have a habit of staring at people?" She considered me while sipping her mango iced tea with the same jelly bits. I loved the way her pink lips wrapped around the straw. My dick twitched, and my mind spiraled out of control.

What the hell was wrong with me?

I had to trek carefully around her if I wanted to maintain my sanity.

"No. Just with you—my future wife." I placed the drink down. "How else will I know everything about you if I don't study you?"

"There's no need for that. I'm not studying you. I think our relationship will be just fine." She gestured to the contract. "Why are there only two pages?"

"Does it need to be more?"

"No." She shrugged. "I just assumed there would be more."

"It's an arranged fake marriage that will end in six months. Nothing ties us together other than a marriage certificate. A document that will mean nothing when this marriage is nullified."

I didn't know why, but that knowledge bothered me.

She pursed her lips. "Is it an arranged marriage, a fake marriage, or a marriage of convenience?"

"Does it matter? It's not a marriage of convenience." I leaned into the table. "It's more convenient for you than for me. I'm just helping you out."

"Because you've spent a lot of money on the gallery," she retorted. "If I fail, you lose money."

That was only a small percentage of why I agreed to help her, but she didn't need to know that.

"I'd say this is both an arranged and fake marriage." She took the document. "We're both arranging things to suit our needs for the six-month duration. I'd like to add a few things that weren't mentioned in the contract."

"This is only a draft. I left room for your input. What do you want to add?"

The server came with our food, and the savory scents made my stomach growl again.

"Enjoy," said Lulu. "Let me know if you need anything."

"Thank you," Nessa replied and looked at me. "You didn't have breakfast? I can hear your stomach."

"No. I went to physical therapy and then to the gym to spar with Orion."

"Like martial arts?"

I nodded. "It's a good workout."

Sparring with Orion had helped release the tension in my body as I continued my search for Ashton.

Nessa scooped some noodles and rice onto my plate. Then she cut the subs in half. "If you like chili peppers, you can add them." She gestured for me to try the food.

I grabbed the sub and bit into it. Flavors burst on my tongue. I wolfed it down in no time.

Nessa smiled and dug into her noodles with a pair of chopsticks. "I'd like to add four more requirements to the contract.

"Okay," I said, devouring my meal.

"One, we can't date anyone else while we're in this fake relationship."

"That should be a given."

"But it's not there. I need it in black and white. Dating

someone else while we're 'married' makes it too complicated. I want to avoid all the drama." Seeing my confusion, she added, "Let's say your girlfriend is visiting you at your house or you're out to dinner with her. Then the two of you bump into me. What if the media or people we know are around? A small thing can turn ugly fast, and I'm not in the mood to deal with a jealous girlfriend."

The woman's mind astounded me. She'd come up with an intricate scenario that would never happen. Did she think I was the type of man who could deal with multiple women at once? I was already having a hard time focusing when she was around. I didn't have space for anyone else.

"Same goes with you—no boyfriends," I said. "But I'll avoid drama by getting rid of him quickly. A marriage demands respect, whether or not it's real on paper. We will depict our marriage as real in every way."

She nodded slightly. "Two. Respect each other's privacy even if I'm living in your house."

"Of course. The guest suite is being prepared for you."

"You noted that in the document. Thank you." She nodded. "Three. No extension to the marriage contract. We annul it on the dot after six months. This will give us the freedom to go or do whatever is necessary."

Did she think I wanted to trap her in this marriage?

"What's the last request?"

"No kissing, no sex, no crossing boundaries—no exceptions."

I chuckled. "How are we supposed to get married if the groom can't kiss the bride?"

She considered my comment. "Okay. Just kissing on the wedding day and during photo shoots. But no sex."

I finished my meal, feeling satisfied. "Why do you think there would be any?"

Her eyes darted away from mine too quickly to focus on the document. Had she been thinking about it as much as I had? Was this clause a line she drew to restrict herself?

Curiosity rose in me, and I couldn't help but ask, "How many times?"

"What?"

"How many times have you thought about it?"

What are you doing?

I shoved my inner voice aside quickly as Nessa's eyes flashed. An adorable pink bloomed on her face.

I already had my answer without her having to reply. Being a gentleman, I saved her from embarrassment. "I can have the revised document for you to sign tomorrow."

"Okay, thanks." She looked relieved that we were no longer discussing that topic.

"Why do you need therapy? I'm only asking because I need to know details about my husband's injuries."

"My right leg." I stretched it out under the table and touched her foot. "Sorry."

"It's okay. Is that why you need the cane?" She gestured to where it leaned against the wall. "How did your leg get injured? Running around trying to seal all the billion-dollar deals?" Amusement flickered in her eyes.

I took a moment to process her question. It wasn't a hard question at all. But she was the first woman to ask me, as if she was genuinely interested in my injury. Like she wanted to know how I'd acquired it without sounding too nosy or awkward. The women I'd dated hadn't asked, or if they had, they'd only inquired because it was a conversation filler. Though they hadn't outright said it, I knew they hadn't liked that I was physically disabled and needed a cane.

Perhaps one day, I'd share it with Vanessa, but not today.

"It's an injury from when I was younger. It didn't heal properly."

"Things like that take time." Her expression softened. "Some things take longer to heal."

"And some things can't be healed."

She cocked her head. "Everything can be healed. It just takes time."

"Are you saying this from experience?"

"Let's just say it's a healthy perspective from an artist whose tummy is full and happy. Ask me that again when I'm hungry. You'll get a different answer."

Before I forgot, I pulled out my phone and showed her an image of the two thugs. "Do you recognize these men?"

She looked at the pic. "No. Who are they?"

I didn't want to reveal that I'd been at the auction searching for my curator and had taken it upon myself to track these men down. She didn't need the extra stress.

"Just thugs on the detective's radar. Maybe they delivered the box to the gallery opening."

Vanessa shook her head. "They don't look familiar to me."

Her phone rang, and she reached for it in her purse. "Unavailable number," she muttered.

She was about to put her phone back when it buzzed again, and her face paled.

I yanked it from her hand.

You have twenty-four hours to deposit the money into my account, or this image will be splashed everywhere.

The blurry image was of a young Vanessa in an alley with blood on her hands. Another woman was with her, along with two men. One man was on the ground.

I immediately blocked Emmanuel's number.

"I don't understand. He wasn't like this before."

"How was he?"

"Not crazy. Not aggressive." She shrugged. "Normal. Friendly."

"Greed changes people. You won't be receiving any more messages from this number." Anger rose in me. "If you receive another threatening text, let me know."

"I blocked him before. He always gets a new phone." She scowled. "This is my phone. You can't just block a number without asking me."

She sounded more annoyed that I had taken over the situation than the act of blocking his number.

"You're not in the right mindset to think logically. You're scared. It shows on your face, so I decided for you." I looked at her. "You're my fiancée now. Nobody threatens you and gets away with it."

CHAPTER FIFTEEN

VANESSA

ATTIKUS PULLED into the parking spot in front of my apartment. "You should pack some of your belongings. I'll pick you up on Friday."

I gawked at him. "That's so soon."

"Does your ex know where you live and work?"

"Yes." I couldn't afford to move and hide. It was hard to find an apartment with a studio space in the same building.

"You shouldn't be here while he's blackmailing you." His nostrils flared. "Desperate people do desperate things. I'm not going to gamble with your safety."

A fresh wave of emotions overcame me. I was trying my best not to show how unsettled I was after seeing Emmanuel's threatening text. But Attikus's concern subdued the nerves. No man had ever displayed genuine concern for me.

We weren't married yet, so he didn't need to take on the protective husband role. His quick reaction proved he wasn't doing this because it was part of a contract. Not that this detail was on it, but it showed a different side of him.

Emmanuel had grown desperate. What if he came to my studio one day when no one was around? Though he'd need a key to enter, that didn't mean he couldn't sneak in with a group of people pretending he lived there.

I was used to taking care of myself and doing things on my own. I didn't know how to react to Attikus handling this situation. He was shouldering some of the weight for me. For the first time, someone had my back.

Sighing, I said, "I'll be ready on Friday."

"Are you okay?" He studied me, probably wondering what had transpired in my head, from being angry at his demand to now surrendering to him.

"Yes." I looked at him, wanting to explain more, but I couldn't. Not right now.

"Okay. If you need anything, call or text me."

He stayed in the car, watching me enter the building safely before taking off.

I wasn't in the mood to finish my painting, so I took the stairs up to my apartment and packed. How many clothes should I bring? One piece of luggage should be fine for now. I could always come back here if I needed more things.

As I shoved toiletries into my makeup bag, my phone buzzed.

Attikus: *I have a studio space you can work in. Bring your art supplies.*

He didn't mention this earlier.

Vanessa: *Art can get messy. Don't want to ruin your house.*

Attikus: *It's not being used.*

I chewed on my bottom lip. Having a studio space at my temporary residence would be helpful.

Vanessa: *Are you sure?*

Attikus: *I wouldn't offer if I weren't.*

Vanessa: *Bring a truck because I have large canvases.*

Attikus: *Got it.*

A small smile slid onto my lips as I stared at my phone. We already sounded like a couple. It baffled me how we had eased into this "relationship" so naturally.

I placed a few pairs of shoes into a duffle bag and realized I didn't need to bring so many. I wasn't going anywhere fancy, so one casual pair of shoes and sneakers would suffice. My phone buzzed again, and my heart leaped, thinking it was Attikus. But it was the girls.

Elena: *What happened?*

I knew they would eventually find out about Attikus and me. I might as well inform them now. But what could I tell them?

I walked over to the couch, dropped onto the cushion, and stared at the messages.

Vivian: *What's going on?*

Audri: *We just saw the post!*

Michelle: *Is it true?*

Natalie: *Why didn't you tell us?*

Kiera: Give us the deets!

Chatting with them would give my mind a rest.

Nessa: *It's complicated.*

Kiera: *Don't give us that and expect us to stop. (eye roll emoji)*

Vivian: *Tell us! I'm dying to know.*

Elena: *Are you attracted to him?*

I smiled at Elena's message. She was trying to help me out.

Nessa: *I am. But he doesn't know that.*

Audri: *So how did he become your fiancé?*

Natalie: *Is there a hidden agenda here?*

Michelle: *Do you need our help with anything?*

Elena: *The more heads, the better we can think.*

Audri: *Girls! We need a girls' evening out!*

Kiera: *Time for SSG!*

Nessa: *What's that?*

Kiera: *It's when we help you get your happily ever after.*

Nessa: *Really?*

Vivian: *Don't doubt us, babe.*

Audri: *You're in trouble now.*

Elena: *Come over on Sunday. The boys are meeting up. We can have our gathering.*

Natalie: *Be prepared to answer questions.*

Michelle: *I'll bring appetizers.*

Natalie: *Got some sexy lingerie for you ladies.*

Audri: *Make Nessa a lingerie package because of her fiancée status.*

Natalie: *Glad to. (heart emoji)*

Nessa: *See you soon.*

Audri: *You make a great couple, just saying.*

Kiera: *See ya. Gotta go now!*

Oh my gosh. This was getting so complicated. I didn't want to lie to them. These were my friends. Was there a halfway point? Could I tell them part of the truth and leave the other part out? Would that be lying? I didn't want to involve more people than I had to.

I could tell them about my attraction and how it was getting stronger every time I was with him. And that this fiancée thing was . . . What?

Shit. Why couldn't my life be simple?

I turned to my rack of plants in simple pottery. Looking at them placed me at ease. Nature had a way of soothing you with its uncomplicated presence.

I prayed I'd come up with a brilliant idea before Sunday.

After I packed, I sat down to check out Emmanuel's social media. Did something happen to him recently to make him erratic and violent? He wasn't like this when I dated him. But then again, maybe this was his true character. His roving eye was why I had to end things. No woman would settle for that. Did Emmanuel take drugs?

I browsed his DailyThoughts feed and saw selfies of him with various girls at wild parties. He looked drunk or on something. The women did too. I scrolled past several pictures of him with a woman with massive red hair. She was all over him. Maybe she was his new girlfriend. I recognized his friend, Nico Messina, whom I met once.

I scrolled to the pictures of him before we met. He posted photos of him hiking and swimming with a different group of friends. I found an old image of him with his sister, Thea. I'd never met her, but he'd mentioned her to me. Why did he stop posting pictures of him and his sister? It was like he had two different lives.

What happened to him?

I didn't know why, but I searched for Thea Valencia. Maybe she could stop him from blackmailing me. Then I wouldn't need to go through with this marriage. This option hadn't occurred to me until now. It would save Attikus and me time and energy.

My heart leaped when I saw Thea on the JobNetwork. She was a manager for Elegant Cosmetics in downtown Providence. I'd been there a few times for makeup products. Excitement and confusion rushed through me. If his sister was in town, why hadn't he posted any current pictures of him with her? What happened to their relationship?

I knew I shouldn't go out right now. Attikus's words rang in my ear, but something nudged me to go. He was being overprotective, which I appreciated and loved. But right now, I had to trust my intuition.

Before more doubts could enter my brain, I grabbed my purse, put on a casual jacket, and slipped on my sneakers. I could pick up some new makeup while I was there. This was my self-care trip to the beauty store.

CHAPTER SIXTEEN

ATTIKUS

INSTEAD OF DRIVING HOME, I pulled into the Mount Museum garage, parked, got out, and walked through the main entrance. The popular Japanese Silk Painting Exhibit had ended yesterday, so the museum wasn't as crowded. This quiet time between events provided the staff with an opportunity to catch up on administrative tasks.

I had a few projects to review and documents to approve. I could get everything done today and clear my slate for the next few days. Arranging for a fake marriage required more work than I had expected.

My lawyer could complete the legal documents once I gave him the terms and conditions. But the other details like the living situation, wedding photos, and how to deliver this information to the media had to come from me. The fewer people who knew about the truth of our marriage, the better. Most of all, how would I share this information with the boys? They weren't like my mother or sister. They'd know something was up.

I had a meeting with them this weekend to review the video

game demo and the status of The Trogyn investigation. Perhaps I could give them some details, but not everything. I could discuss this with Vanessa so our stories matched up.

The simpler we made this marriage, the easier it would be to end it. We only needed professional photos to disperse to the media. My plan for the marriage and honeymoon shifted in my head. Perhaps we could escape to one of my vacation homes and get married there? God knew my body had been desperate for a vacation. I could bring my laptop to get some work done.

That's not a vacation.

Yeah, but it was a fake honeymoon. She would probably do something on her own, so I might as well make the best use of my time.

I had to investigate my wife's history. How had she killed a man? What was the circumstance? Though I didn't know her well enough yet, I knew she wasn't a killer. What had happened to her on that day—that moment?

From my experience, when someone was pushed into a corner, survival mode kicked in, and the person could turn into a monster in an instant. He could kill at that moment. I'd been there, so I understood what it felt like. The day those fuckers swarmed me, I wanted to kill them, but my leg and my wrist were broken. If I'd had the energy, I would have killed them. The second time I felt helpless was when I saw my house burned to cinders on the news. The desire for vengeance clawed through my heart.

Where the fuck was Ashton?

I walked down the arched hallway toward my office.

"Are you okay?"

A voice yanked me out of my reverie, and I turned around to see Agnes, the sixty-five-year-old maintenance manager of the museum. She had sharp brown eyes and wore the museum's gray uniform. Her brown hair was tied back into a short ponytail.

"Hi." I walked over. "Sorry I didn't see you."

She offered a warm smile—one that had gotten me through difficult times. Agnes was another friend of my mom's. They met through a Lunch Lady Club that exchanged clothes, food, and other necessities. Lunch moms made little money, so they shared what they could. Agnes worked at a different school, but I remembered meeting her a few times while grocery shopping with my mom.

When Agnes applied for the museum job, I hired her immediately. Agnes wasn't married and lived by herself. She should have retired, but she claimed to love working at the museum so much that she wasn't ready to leave. She knew the museum's layout by heart.

"Everything okay?" She considered me. "Got a minute? You look like you need some tea and conversation."

"Aren't you heading out?" I gestured to her shoulder bag.

"Yes, but I haven't seen you lately, and I'm worried about you."

"Nothing to worry about." I smiled. "Sure, let's chat."

We walked to the museum café and got tea and cookies. We sat at a table overlooking the new indoor garden. The bamboo, trees, and plants came from Forrest's farms.

I sipped my green tea, which was supplied by Forrest's herbal company. "I know I don't say this often, but thank you for making sure the museum is always looking top-notch."

Her brown eyes beamed as she glanced around. "Thank you for offering me the job. This is a fantastic museum. The best one." She bit into her cookie.

"Mount Museum is small compared to the other museums in the country."

"It's not about size, Attikus. It's about what you offer and what you stand for. I've visited a lot of museums and have met several of their employees." She bit into her cookie, chewed, and swallowed. "The owners aren't as involved as you. You take pride in this museum. It's your passion. It's not just a business that makes money."

"Thanks. That means a lot to me."

"Your parents would've been so proud of you." She placed a hand over mine.

"I'm very lucky to be surrounded by genuine people—you and Joseph." Concern for him surfaced. "I need to follow up with Detective Farmer about his case."

"He's been gone for over a month without a trace." Anxiety stretched her face. "I wasn't working that day. I had a doctor's appointment. I wish I'd been around. Maybe I would've seen something."

"We'll find him. Just let the staff know we won't stop looking for him."

Like Agnes, Joseph lived alone and was a dedicated employee.

"It's bizarre how he just vanished," she said. "He didn't mention going on vacation or anything."

"We checked his apartment. His luggage is still at home. I'll look at the recording again. Maybe I missed something."

"You need to take care of yourself too." Agnes sat back and crossed her arms. "What's this thing about you getting engaged? Why didn't you tell me? I heard from Gigi."

Fuck.

"Sorry." I raked a hand through my hair. "It's been a whirlwind, and I forgot to tell you."

"I can see that. Your mom called me the other day, wondering if I knew anything. She wanted details." She uncrossed her arms and lifted her cup of tea. "When will I get to meet Nessa?"

"Soon."

"I met her during her art exhibit here. She's articulate, friendly, and very attractive." Agnes sipped her tea. "But be careful. Those qualities are often masks for people who want something from you, Attikus. You're a wealthy and powerful man."

I appreciated her protectiveness more than she knew. My mom's friends had become motherly figures, ensuring I didn't take the wrong path.

If only Agnes knew what was between Vanessa and me.

"Do I look like a man who could be swindled?"

"Usually, no." She smirked. "But when an attractive and talented woman is in the mix, things can get blurry. Don't want you going blind."

I finished my tea. "Well, it's a wonderful thing I have you and Mom Gigi to make sure I won't go blind."

"Smart answer." She smiled. "I updated the lock to your safe room."

Agnes and Joseph were the only two people who entered that room. She had access to ensure it stayed clean. He had access to record all my precious treasures and ensure the place was dust-free.

"Thank you."

After a few more minutes, Agnes left. I walked down to the lower level to The Gathering, a safe room that held all my precious belongings and where I conducted my extensive research on Ashton C. Lindor.

I punched in the code, pressed my palm against the screen, and aligned my eye with the scanner to verify my identity. The sensor lights illuminated as I stepped onto the marble floor.

The safe room was made of poured concrete, concrete blocks, high-density steel, ballistic fiberglass, and Kevlar. It had a bulletproof door. The top-notch safe room had all the extra amenities in case of a dangerous storm. I was prepared for an apocalypse. Cameras inside the room linked to a recording I could access anywhere in the world. When I had it built, I needed a place to store my valuable items while I searched for my enemy. Now, there was a separate suite for me to sleep, eat, and bathe in when I didn't want to drive home. I didn't realize it would take me this long to find the fucker.

Who was helping him hide? I wouldn't rest until I found him. This search had consumed me for so long that I didn't know what else to do with my life.

Until Vanessa.

She was the distraction I didn't know I needed.

Walking into the office, I sat down and turned on my computer. I glanced up, and my eyes landed on the illustration that had started everything—the beginning and ending all in one.

I got out of the chair and ambled over, standing in front of The Cozy Family Restaurant ad that had won me a scholarship and cash.

This pen and ink artwork had taken weeks to become a final version. I'd enjoyed every moment of it. It was a magical experience to get lost in the creative process. Right now, working on Level Seven was the only thing that got me close to that magical feeling.

My wrist ached, and the muscles in my leg throbbed.

"Stop." I scolded my body for responding to the memory of the fateful day.

I read somewhere that the body's cells could remember trauma. I believed it. The body produced certain chemicals as a response to fear, anger, and joy. The emotions and pain I'd endured that day were a colossal energy that had infiltrated into my cellular memory.

This was why I couldn't heal from it.

I walked over to my wall of paintings, which ranged in value from a few hundred to millions of dollars. But I didn't measure their worth based on those numbers. They were all gained at various stages of my life.

I ran a finger down the water lily painting from Nessa Lambert. I bought the 11" x 17" painting years ago. It was a raw painting with no varnish, resin, or other protective coatings. The painting had no title either.

I was drawn to the bleeding water lily because I could feel its pain. Exceptional art could reach into you and rearrange your bodily systems, touching you in ways nothing else could. That painting was the first artwork to do that to me.

Vanessa was the first to help me *feel* again. In a way, I felt obligated to help her in return.

Get to work.

I didn't come here to admire art.

I returned to my desk and searched for Emmanuel Valencia. Then I made some calls to assist in the search. Who was Emmanuel? Vanessa mentioned he wasn't like this during their brief relationship. But I knew how people could deceive to achieve a goal. This happened in business all the time.

The fear on her face had dulled her brightness as though a splash of black paint smeared across her vivid red.

After an hour of research, I discovered where he lived, hung out, and worked. I also knew where his younger sister worked. I browsed his social media accounts and noticed his different personalities. There were no images of him and Vanessa.

I also checked Vanessa's social media posts. She only posted about her artwork. I saved a picture of her and me at the gallery opening. I wasn't a social media guy, but I created an account on Real Rumors and DailyThoughts and followed her.

Why? I didn't know.

I returned to Emmanuel's account and continued browsing. My heart leaped when I spotted a familiar face. Dr. Nico Messina was part of The Trogyn. That was my assumption during my investigation into the crime organization. He came from power and wealth and had attended several parties at underground clubs.

I pulled up Dr. Messina's file. His High School GPA shouldn't have allowed him to attend Harvard Medical. His parents probably paid someone for him to attend. He probably paid someone to do all the work for him. Instincts told me to investigate any malpractice lawsuits. There were too many for me to read.

How did he still have a job at Brigham and Women's Hospital? Why hadn't these lawsuits been on the news?

My fingers itched. I compiled a few lawsuits, wrote a summary, sent it to Elena, and copied Orion. Musepaper, Elena's online newspaper, was known for delivering the truth.

My team sent me a file on Emmanuel's school records. At least his GPA proved he qualified to attend Northeastern University. What was the doctor's relationship with Emmanuel?

I printed out a picture of him and Emmanuel and tucked it into my back pocket.

I glanced at the clock. Emmanuel should head home from his office job in an hour. I had questions to ask him.

From the files my team sent me about Emmanuel and his sister, I could tell they were close. But he didn't have any pictures of her on his social media account. Either they had a falling out, or Emmanuel wasn't the monster he appeared to be. A quick visit to Elegant Cosmetics to snap a photo of his sister would make an interesting conversation with him.

As I drove to visit Thea, I stopped at a set of red lights. A black sports car pulled up next to me, and I recognized a face I hadn't seen in a long time. Milton Kalkounis was probably on the phone with someone. He had been part of Ashton's crowd back in high school. Though he wasn't part of the group who beat me that day, he had created a shitty atmosphere for me and others in high school.

A thrill skated down my spine. He would know where to find Ashton. When the lights turned, I took a detour and followed him. Elegant Cosmetics could wait.

CHAPTER SEVENTEEN

VANESSA

I DIDN'T DRIVE my car because it had a good parking spot in the residents-only area. Finding a parking spot close to my apartment was rare, so I avoided using the car unless it was for grocery shopping or big art supplies. I usually had my large canvases delivered because my silver Honda Civic wouldn't fit large canvases.

Across the street, an old couple prepared for the oncoming bus. I rushed over, got on, paid, and sat across from the loving couple. Three other people occupied the back of the bus.

His wife appeared more fragile than him.

"Do you want soup? It's your day, Martha. Tell me where you want to go, and I'll take you."

"It doesn't matter." Martha leaned into him. "I'm just happy to be out of the hospital."

He took her hand. "You're healthy now. So we need to celebrate." Then he kissed her on the head.

Would I ever find someone who loved me like that? I wished my mom could experience this love too. For some strange reason, I imagined Attikus treating me with love and care like this old man. Could he be that caring?

Why? He's only your fake husband.

I didn't know why the thought came into my head. It brought me back to the contract. The no-sex thing was to protect myself from doing something I might regret. That provocative dream of him had set my body ablaze all day. If only he could see my nerves or how wet my panties had been from remembering that dream, he'd probably think twice about having me in his home. The dream was powerful. Even now, my body shivered from remembering his touch.

Having the fine print to state the boundaries would protect both him and me.

When the bus stopped, I got up and smiled at the couple. "You make a lovely couple. I wish you great health and happiness."

Martha and her husband beamed and wished the same for me. I just made their evening better by offering them kindness. Those priceless gestures were rare these days.

I walked into Elegant Cosmetics, which wasn't too busy. Three other customers were in the shop. A sales associate adjusted a sign that promoted a discount on a new makeup product.

I spotted Thea behind the counter, wearing the black uniform with the shop's name on it. She had light brown hair and a pretty face.

I walked up to her and smiled. "Hello. I see you have new makeup."

"Yes, we do." She beamed, looking like her brother. "These are all organic. I'm wearing the foundation and eyeshadow. Do you want to try it?"

"Sure." I slid onto the stool. "I only have a little makeup on."

"You have nice skin." She cleaned my face with gentle aloe wipes and added a toner.

"You look familiar," I said as she tested a foundation.

She paused and studied me. "I don't know you."

I tapped my head. "Yes, I remember you now. Emmanuel showed me pictures of you and him. We dated for a short time."

Fear splashed onto her face, and she whispered, "I don't want any trouble."

Surprised by her response, I said, "I'm not here to hurt you. Emmanuel was good to me when we first started dating, but then he changed. Now, I don't even recognize his character."

Sadness stirred in her eyes. "I know."

"Did something happen to him?"

She bit her lip, ignored my question, and added foundation to my face. "This suits your skin tone perfectly."

"He's been threatening me," I said. "But I don't understand why."

She arched her brow. "What do you mean?"

I gave her a brief account of his blackmail but kept out the part where I'd already paid him some money.

Thea glanced around, making sure no one was nearby. "Some powerful people did something to him. He's not the same person anymore." Tears brimmed in her eyes. "He told me to stay away from him because they'll hurt me."

Was Emmanuel being blackmailed too?

"Who's blackmailing him?"

She looked at me, and I could tell she was weighing how much to trust me.

"I don't want to hurt Emmanuel. Someone is forcing him to hurt me. I want it to stop. What if these people are forcing him to hurt others? Those people might not be as considerate as me. What if they retaliate with violence?"

Understanding flashed in her eyes. "I don't know who they

are. He called me from the hospital one day, and I took him home. But from that day on, he acted differently."

"Did he say why he was in the hospital?"

She shook her head. "He wouldn't tell me. He said it was best I didn't know."

My intuition was right. Something had happened to Emmanuel. What did they have on him? How did these people know about the event in the alleyway?

I looked in the mirror, loving the makeup Thea had used on me. "I love the casual, yet elegant look. What's the eyeshadow color?"

"Lavender pink." She smiled. "It looks great on you. You have naturally long lashes. You don't need extensions."

I loved my lashes, but since I worked in my art studio most of the time, I didn't wear makeup unless I had to go out.

"Thank you. I'll take everything you used on me," I said, slipping a tip into her pocket.

"Oh, no. It's okay. We let the customers try new makeup all the time."

"I know. But you did an exceptional job. And thank you for the chat." I leaned in. "I'll try my best to find these bad men. If you remember anything important, call me, okay?" I wrote my number on a perfume card.

"Thank you." She wrote down her number. "This is mine. When you find them, can you let me know? I'll contact Emmanuel again."

"Let's keep this conversation between us, okay?"

She nodded.

Stepping out of the shop, I inhaled the fresh air. I'd missed the bus, so I walked to the strip mall. I strode by a jewelry shop and clothing boutique before stopping in front of a bakery. A customer walked out, and the sweet scent from the store snuck into my nose. I walked in and bought a brownie and a large chocolate chip cookie. I had a weakness for sweets when I was overwhelmed. They were like remedies to fill a void that couldn't be filled.

I needed something to comfort me.

As I paid and headed out, I noticed a man sitting at a table with the redheaded woman I'd seen on Emmanuel's social media post, but I didn't recognize the man. Nerves stirred in my stomach as I walked to a table behind them and nibbled my brownie. I took out my earbuds from my purse and pretended to watch something on my phone while listening to them.

"You need to make him do it, Becca," said the man.

"I've tried." She sipped her drink. "He's stubborn."

"Give him another shot."

Her jaw tensed. "Enzo, he's already on edge."

The man shrugged. "I don't give a shit."

His phone rang, and he glanced at it. "We have to go." He rose, and the woman did the same.

I slid my brownie into the paper bag and left too.

Outside, he spoke on the phone while walking down the street. I couldn't hear his conversation over the loud traffic.

Someone yanked my arm, and before I knew it, I was flush against the wall of a brick building. My heart raced as I looked into Attikus's intense eyes.

"What are you doing?" I hissed.

His body pressed into mine, and my earlier nerves were now replaced with something entirely different.

"Saving you."

"What do you mean? I was just—"

His lips landed on mine, angry and hungry. I was confused and aroused at the same time. I kissed him back with the same intensity. He tasted so good, better than the brownie. I wanted more.

But he drew back, grabbed my hand, and led me to his car,

which was illegally parked in the no-parking zone. He opened the passenger door, ushering me in. I looked around for the couple, but they had already disappeared.

He dropped his cane onto the back seat before sliding behind the wheel. I looked at him. Oh, he was pissed. What happened? Why was he here?

I wanted to ask those questions, but I needed my heart rate to slow down first. I licked my lips, remembering the kiss. It was even better than the dream. This wasn't good.

He drove in silence, and I stared out the window. Sexual tension throbbed in the car, but neither of us said anything. He waited for a vehicle to leave and slid into a parking spot behind my car.

"I'll walk you up."

"Why?" I asked.

"Because you don't understand the danger around you." He flicked me a look that sent a zing down my spine. "Besides, it's only natural that I get to see where my fiancée lives, right?"

He licked his bottom lip and swallowed as though remembering our kiss from earlier.

"Fine. Just so you know. It's not a fancy mansion like your house."

We got out, walked into the building, and headed up in the elevator. He looked around as though surveying for threats.

"I think we're safe," I said, unlocking the door.

"I love your positive outlook, but you placed yourself in danger today. I didn't like it." He stepped in, closed the door, and locked it. He stared at the lock for a moment. "You need a better lock."

I rolled my eyes, but he didn't see it. "I've lived here for a long time. It's safe. Plus, I'm moving in with you. I'm not wasting money buying a lock for an empty apartment."

Our eyes connected, and he knew I was right.

Dropping the topic, Attikus leaned his cane against the wall near my shoe rack and walked around my apartment. "It's a quaint apartment."

I didn't know why, but embarrassment flushed through me. He was the first wealthy man to enter my one-bedroom apartment. I had an old but comfy couch in the living room with casual furniture. None of these things measured up to his fancy mansion or wherever he lived. Usually, I wouldn't care what anyone thought of me, but I didn't want him to think I wasn't worthy of being his fake wife.

What was wrong with me?

I placed my purse and the bag of pastries on the counter.

"Would you like anything to drink?" I walked over to the refrigerator.

"No, thank you." He ambled over to my rack of plants and picked up my largest terrarium. "This is cool. Looks like a little world."

I gulped down cold water, hoping it would settle the nerves still ringing inside me. Was I the only one affected by that contact? He seemed like he'd already forgotten about it.

"Where did you get this terrarium?" He returned it to its spot.

"I made it." I placed my glass of water on the counter.

As I walked past him, he grabbed my hand and ushered me against the wall. His body was flush with mine. Heat throbbed between us.

"You're very talented. How about I commission you to create a terrarium for my office," he said, looking down at me.

The heat from earlier returned, stronger and more palpable. This relationship was becoming more and more confusing each day. And we weren't even married yet. What kind of chaos would our relationship be when we were actually married?

His cologne snuck up my nose and tantalized my body. My core tightened, and my panties grew damp.

What the hell?

A shiver ran through me, and I tried my best not to show what had just happened. I'd never lost control like this. I blamed it on my nerves from the past few days and not on this magnetic man who could elicit powerful sensations from me.

He brushed his fingers down my cheek. "If I hadn't been there today, that man with the redhead would've suspected you."

"What do you mean?" My cheek heated where his knuckles had brushed.

"Enzo Stevens is part of a dangerous organization. Now that I know he's associated with Emmanuel, this entire situation just got more complicated."

Attikus told me he had work to do and reminded me not to leave my apartment for the rest of the day.

CHAPTER EIGHTEEN

ATTIKUS

IT HAD BEEN a mistake to kiss her. I had assumed if I got the urge out of my system, everything would be fine. She wouldn't fester in my mind, making me crave. But I was wrong. I had underestimated this attraction between us. With every touch, she became the fuel that enticed the fire within me.

I had to get out of her apartment before I did something regretful.

But if I read her reaction correctly, she was struggling with the same issue. Or was that my imagination—my hope?

Maybe she was unsettled because of what I'd told her about The Trogyn. Enzo Stevens was a minor player within the crime organization. His face had appeared in several of my friends' investigations.

I shouldn't have scared her, but she needed to know the surrounding danger. She shouldn't be running around playing detective.

I told her I'd help resolve Emmanuel's threat. Why didn't she believe me?

Today, I'd stepped over that line where I couldn't go back. One taste ignited this desire in me that needed to be tamed.

I pushed all thoughts aside as I parked on a side street, got out, and walked into the lobby of Emmanuel's luxury apartment.

The host with the curly hair smiled at me. "Can I help you?"

"Just waiting for my friend, Emmanuel." I jerked a hand to the gym behind her. I could see him on the treadmill.

"Oh, he's going to be in there for a while."

"I'm Ricky, his cousin, visiting from California. I want to surprise him. Do you mind if I go upstairs and wait in the lounge area?"

His files showed he had a cousin living in Los Angeles, and I'd already looked at the blueprint of this building.

"Sure. I won't say anything." She smiled.

"Thank you."

I took the elevator up to the fifth floor and sat in a comfortable brown chair in the lounge area facing his room. Two people walked past me but were on their phones. While I waited, I had my assistant, Beth, schedule a private shopping at the Happily Ever After Boutique and a photo shoot in Maui. I browsed through the boutique and sent Vanessa a link.

Attikus: *Pick a dress from this shop.*

Vanessa: *I can't afford this. (wide-eye emoji)*

Attikus: *I'm paying.*

Vanessa: *You want to spend this much money on a fake wedding?*

Attikus: *It needs to look real. I splurge on things that matter.*

Vanessa: *In that case, I'll browse.*

I imagined her looking through the website, wondering if she'd choose the one I'd mentally picked out.

Vanessa: *Can I get shoes and accessories?*

Attikus: *Yes. Anything.*

Vanessa: *What's your budget?*

Attikus: *None.*

Vanessa: *Are you crazy?*

Attikus: *You know the answer.*

Vanessa: *I thought you had to work. Why are you looking at wedding dresses?*

Attikus: *I'm good at multitasking.*

Vanessa: *(Eye-roll emoji)*

An idea popped into my head, provoking me.

Attikus: *You're a fabulous kisser.*

The three dots moved and stopped. A few seconds later, they moved again. She was probably struggling for a reply. Would she tell the truth or lie? Or would she offer something between a truth and a lie?

Vanessa: *I'm sure many women would say that about you too.*

Since I was getting married to her for the next six months, I'd make it fun for me.

Attikus: *I'm only interested in what you think.*

A moment of silence.

Vanessa: *You're a dangerous kisser.*

Attikus: *What does that mean?*

Vanessa: *You'll find out later.*

Why was she being cryptic?

Attikus: *Should I leave out the terms for no kissing on the contract?*

Vanessa: *No. Add it.*

Attikus: *But you like kissing me.*

Vanessa: *Exactly. Too dangerous.*

There was the truth.

Vanessa: *I mean. It's not good for us. Will complicate things.*

Too late, darling. You can't take back what I wanted to hear.

Attikus: *Okay. Will add to the contract.*

At that moment, the elevator door opened, and Emmanuel stepped out. Dark hair, about six feet tall, athletic build. He looked at me, and our eyes locked. I rose from my chair, grabbed my cane, and walked over.

He swallowed, knowing exactly who I was. "What are you doing here?"

"Let's have a man-to-man chat. Not here." I jerked my head toward his apartment number 505.

He hesitated a moment.

"Unless you want your neighbors hearing what I have to say. Do you think they want to know you've been blackmailing your ex-girlfriend?"

His jaw tensed as he turned and opened the door. I stepped inside and locked it. He walked down the wooden-floor hallway and leaned against the marble kitchen counter.

Crossing his arms, he asked. "Why are you here?"

"Why are you harassing Nessa Lambert?"

"What did you say?" he asked, placing a hand on his head.

I studied his face, and there was no hint of him being crass or sarcastic.

"Why are you blackmailing Nessa?" I asked.

"I stopped a while ago." Looking uncomfortable, he rounded the counter and opened the refrigerator. "Do you want anything to drink?"

"No, thank you."

The offer surprised me. This courteous gesture didn't match the jerk I'd witnessed in that café.

"Were you at Loretta's Café the day of her art gallery's opening?"

He looked at me with furrowed eyebrows. "I don't remember."

As he stepped closer, downing the glass of water, I noticed marks on his arms. Was he doing drugs? Was that the reason for his erratic behavior?

"Why do you need Nessa's money?"

He blinked and stared at the empty glass as though trying to find an answer that should have been easy. He placed the empty glass down on the counter and scratched the back of his neck. "I'm not sure."

"You're not sure?"

His phone rang, and he reached into the pocket of his athletic pants, pulling it out. He glanced at the screen, grunted, and slid it onto the counter, ignoring it. The buzz signified a new voicemail.

"Is Nessa okay?"

"What do you think?" I glared at him. "She's being black-mailed by her ex. And someone sent a severed finger to her gallery's grand opening."

"I didn't do that." His lips tightened.

"But you know who did?"

I pushed myself off the counter and wandered into his living room. Nothing fancy. A large TV, a video game console with stacks of sports and health magazines. No family pictures displayed on the walls or on the table. It looked like he didn't want people to know about his life.

I pulled out my phone and moved toward him, showing him a picture of his sister from her social media account.

His jaw tensed, and he tossed me an irritated look. "Leave her alone."

"Then leave Nessa alone." I took my phone back. "You're protecting your sister, and I'm protecting my fiancée."

His cell phone rang again, but he ignored it. I glanced at the screen, and my heart jumped at the image. I grabbed the phone, clicked answer, and listened.

"Yo, where are you? Enzo says you're not picking up his calls. Do you have the money? If you're keeping it from me, you're dead, you hear me? Hello?"

I ended the call.

"What are you doing?" Emmanuel plucked his phone from my hand.

"How do you know Milton Kalkounis?"

Emmanuel turned his phone off, shoved it into the charging station, and flicked me an annoyed look.

When he didn't reply, I said, "He's my enemy too. Maybe we can work together."

Emmanuel blew out a sigh, walked over to the couch, dropped down, and scrubbed a hand over his face.

"That's not his name. It's Jean-Claude Dumas."

"Jean-Claude, my ass." I sat across from him. "He went to my high school. I recognize the asshole. It's Milton Kalkounis." The person on the phone didn't sound French. He sounded like the asshole I knew.

Emmanuel furrowed his eyebrows.

Milton's family hung out with the Lindor family, so it was natural for him to follow Ashton around. Why did he change his name? Did that mean Ashton had a new identity too? What kind of crime did Milton commit that required a name change?

"What do you know about him?" I asked.

Emmanuel leaned back on the couch. "He was my trainer when I started the health kick. Gave me a shot he claimed was a vitamin booster in liquid form." He rubbed the bruised spot on his arm. "I became a different person after that. Easily agitated, violent, sporadic memory."

"Was that when you started blackmailing Nessa?"

He nodded. "When he found out her art sold for a lot of money, he told me to blackmail her." He leaned forward. "I don't know how he uncovered information about her past. She never mentioned it to me."

"Why would she? You dated briefly." I should beat the pulp out of him for putting Vanessa through the fear and anxiety. But he was also a victim, and something told me that Milton could be responsible for more crimes. "Did you send her the blackmail threat earlier today?"

"No." His eyes widened. "I've been trying to detox, flush out whatever messed up my body."

"You need to stop using that phone. Milton probably hacked it. Nessa received a threat from your number."

He cursed. "I don't know what to do. I need to get away from them."

"Where did you meet him?"

"At an exclusive club. He's a popular trainer for Ultra Health and Fitness. He has celebrity clients, so when he took me on, I was ecstatic."

I planned on researching Milton when I got a moment. He hadn't been a priority compared to the other members of the high school bully club, but now he'd made himself important.

"He served in the US Army for a few years," Emmanuel said. "That's what he told me."

My mind spun with a plan. "If you're okay with it, my friend is a doctor, and he can examine your blood work. Your trainer gave you something that messed up your body."

I'd give Forrest a call when I left to brief him about Emmanuel's condition. I needed someone I could trust.

Perhaps Forrest could examine him. What kind of injection had Milton given to Emmanuel that altered his character?

The way Milton threatened Emmanuel over the phone didn't sound like any trainer I'd encountered.

Looking nervous, Emmanuel said, "Okay."

"When he calls again, try to act as normal as possible. Make him believe you're still under their control. Play along with their game." I rose from my seat. "If you do this right, you'll survive and keep your sister out of this mess."

Fear splashed onto his face. "Don't get her involved in this.
"

"Then stick to the script. Pretend we never met. They'll kill you both if they suspect you've been compromised. Get a burner phone and call me whenever Jean-Claude contacts you." I gave him a phone number for one of my burner phones. "After the bloodwork, try to stay home as much as possible."

He pinched the bridge of his nose. "Can you let me know when it's safe to contact my sister again?"

"I'll do my best. Is Milton responsible for the severed finger?"

"Yes."

"Do you know whose finger it is?"

"He didn't say. I was just freaked out that he actually did it.
"

"Someone must've told him to do it. Who's his boss? "

"I don't know."

"Have you heard of The Trogyn? Has Milton or Enzo mentioned that name?"

"No, why?"

"It's better that you don't. After I leave, return his call. Make up an excuse for the disruption."

As I drove home, I called the boys and briefed them about

Emmanuel's condition. Forrest agreed to examine Emmanuel and study his bloodwork.

"Do you know of an injection that can alter a person's character or make them lose their memory?" I asked.

"You mentioned he was in the military." Arrow was a Navy SEAL before he retired to create a wine company, which he turned into a billion-dollar enterprise. "They have research centers where they conduct experiments with mind control serums and shit like that. But I wasn't privy to those operations."

"That's legal?" Remi asked.

"It's the government," Orion said. "They make anything legal to suit their agenda."

"Who are the testing subjects?" Royce asked. His blonde hair looked almost white under his office lighting. He was Icelandic and owned travel excursions all around the world.

"Probably their own men and enemies," Grayson said. I could see the sibling resemblance with Audri. "Or random people to test out their serum."

"I see The Trogyn's fingerprints all over this," Remi sighed.

"What kind of fucking trainer threatens the client and injects him with toxic chemicals?" Grayson asked.

"The kind who deserves an injection of his own," Royce commented.

"Once I have Emmanuel's blood work, I'll identify the components," Forrest said.

"Want me to dig into the military research centers and see if Milton Kalkounis or Jean-Claude Dumas was there?" Orion asked.

I nodded. "That would be great. Thank you."

When the call ended, I arrived home and escalated the wedding plan. Initially, I wanted to take Vanessa to Hawaii in a few weeks, but things had become more dangerous. Was Milton taking advantage of a woman who didn't have the means to protect herself from despicable men like him? I needed to solidify this marriage sooner rather than later.

CHAPTER NINETEEN

VANESSA

I WALKED into Saigon Bistro to pick up a platter of fresh shrimp spring rolls and a variety of Vietnamese subs for the gathering at Elena's house. Each of us would bring a dish, even though she told us not to go crazy. I was too tired to cook, so I ordered from my favorite restaurant.

"It's crazy today." Lulu smiled. "Your order will be a few minutes late. Sorry."

"Don't worry about it." I sat in the takeout and pickup area, watching customers come and go. I remembered coming in here when I was little. The shop had expanded, but it was still quaint.

Over the years, I'd seen businesses come and go. That was life; things ended so other things could begin. But Saigon Bistro was like a bamboo stalk that bent with difficulties. Even under new ownership, the food and the service remained the same.

After I got the food and secured it in the passenger seat, I pulled my car into the street. As I glanced in the rearview mirror, Attikus's mother and sister stepped out of Saigon Bistro with brown bags. It seemed like his family enjoyed authentic

Vietnamese food. As their future daughter-in-law and sister-in-law, I should attempt to get to know them. I'd invite them to the next gallery showing.

An idea occurred to me. Perhaps I could host an event at the gallery once a month—Art, Wine, and Conversation. Most art galleries kept things exclusive to art, but I wanted my gallery to be different. My heart swelled when I considered reserving a section of my gallery to sell my terrariums. My first love had always been plants. Science and art were the perfect marriage. A thrill rushed through me as terrarium ideas flooded my mind.

I'd ask the girls for their opinion tonight.

When I arrived, I parked my Honda Civic next to the luxury cars. My money was saved for my mom's freedom and our new beginning. But a girl could dream, right? I'd love to design my car. Something simple, dependable, and functional. Maybe a cross between a Land Rover and a Rivian. A sports car wasn't my thing. I didn't want to be flashy and attract unnecessary attention from thieves. I needed something that could transport my large canvases and floral trees.

An image of Attikus lugging a cherry blossom to some unknown backyard flashed through my vision. Then I saw him hanging up several giant paintings on the wall of an elegant home. I smiled at the ridiculous thought. He wouldn't be with me long enough to do those things as my fake husband.

I carried the box of food and walked by an area with wide windows that showed the men sitting at a table. Attikus turned and met my eyes. Surprise splashed across his handsome face. I smiled at him, walked to the front door, and pressed the doorbell.

The door swung open, and Attikus greeted me. "Hi."

"Hi," I said.

Nerves sprung to life, scattering everywhere. My insides shifted like watercolors dripping slowly over the canvas of my stomach. The kiss at my apartment flashed into my mind, and provocative dreams heated my body.

What the hell? I had to stop this.

"Let me take that." He grabbed the box from my hands. "I didn't know you'd be here today."

"I didn't know you'd be here either," I lied.

My brain wasn't functioning properly. If I told him Elena had mentioned the boy's gathering, he'd ask me why I'd said nothing to him. How could I tell him the girls wanted to know about our relationship, and I was here to give them details? It was easier to lie, and I silently asked God and all the heavenly beings to forgive me.

"Elena invited me to a girls' gathering." That was the truth.

He carried the food into an elegant kitchen and sniffed. "Smells good."

I took out the appetizers. "They're from Saigon Bistro."

"There you are!" Elena approached and offered me a one-arm hug. She wore a soft knit jumper that looked comfy and stylish.

"Where should I put the food?" I gestured to the containers in Attikus's hands.

"I have a table set up in my lounge area."

Attikus looked disappointed.

"Do you have a plate I can borrow? I bought extra food for the guys."

Elena glanced at Attikus and smirked. "Of course. I already gave them portions of what we have." She offered me a plate and tongs.

Attikus surveyed the trays of fresh spring rolls and subs and filled his plate. "Thanks. Enjoy your gathering."

"Enjoy the video game demo." Elena grabbed the tray of subs.

"Video game? Is that what they're doing?" I took the other tray

"Yeah. They're each creating a game for the WaterFyre Rising series."

She led me down a hallway with unique sconces and artwork on the wall. We entered a spacious room with an eggshell-colored interior. Tall windows graced one side of the room with fancy curtains pulled to the side.

"Hey!" Audri beamed and got up from the couch in the lounge area.

My abstract painting was the focal point of that area. Joy sprouted in my chest to see my work in my friend's home.

The other girls strode over, offered me a hug, and glanced at the food.

"I'm not late, am I?"

"Nope," Kiera said. "The boys wanted to meet earlier. So we all came. Can I grab a spring roll and a sub? I'm so hungry."

"You just ate the fried rice I brought." Vivian laughed. Then her eyes sparkled. "Wait a minute."

"Are you pregnant?" Michelle and Natalie surrounded Kiera, examining her.

Her face brightened. "Yes! I've been dying to get everyone together so I could announce it!"

"Congratulations!" I cheered.

We took turns hugging Kiera. Tears filled her eyes. "Thanks! I'm excited but scared."

"Dig in, everyone." Elena gestured to the food. "Get a plate and sit down. We've got stuff to talk about." She winked at me. "And a new mission for our friend here."

I didn't know what they were talking about, but I was ready to eat. I filled my plate with food and sat on a gray patterned couch. Elena dropped beside me.

Not wanting to discuss my relationship with Attikus yet, I

turned to Kiera, who looked beautiful in a long, light-yellow dress. I wore jeans and a peach blouse.

"How far along are you?" I asked, glancing at her tiny stomach.

"Twelve weeks. I'm not due until mid-October." She bit into the sub and sighed. "This is *sooo* good, Nessa. I could probably wolf down two whole subs right now."

We all laughed.

"Elena." Kiera wiggled her eyebrows. "Wanna share your news with us?"

All heads turned to her.

"I'm pregnant too." She beamed and placed a hand over her belly.

"What is going on?" Vivian got up from her seat to give Elena a hug. "Everyone's pregnant!"

"Not everyone." Audri, Michelle, and Natalie lifted their hands in unison.

"I'm so happy for you." I embraced her and gave her an extra spring roll from my plate. "You need it."

"Thanks!" She grinned. "And you'll get to meet not only one but *two* babies!"

My mouth dropped open. I couldn't even imagine two babies growing inside one stomach.

The entire room exploded with cheers and laughter.

"Seems like you've been busy porking." Kiera laughed and almost choked.

"Same to you," Elena retorted.

"He loves this!" Kiera exclaimed and moved her hips, bumping into Natalie, who sat beside her.

I hadn't laughed like this in so long.

Excitement bombarded the space. There wasn't room for anything but laughter, friendship, and food.

"Is everything okay here?" Orion and Attikus stepped into

view at the open double doors. "We heard a commotion from the other side."

"We're fine, babe." Elena smiled.

"Congratulations on your growing family!" We all rose and took turns embracing him.

"We'll find Forrest later for hugs," Audri said. "I can't wait to be an auntie to so many kids!"

Attikus met my eyes, and I knew what had just happened in the other room. He'd told his boys about us. I didn't know how that understanding entered my mind. It was as though he was communicating with me telepathically.

The way he looked at me also said we needed to talk later. This was strange. I'd never been able to communicate with another man in this way. He could probably tell me stories about his life, fears, and wishes all just by looking at me.

Could he tell from my expression that I planned on sharing our fake marriage news with the girls? The answer burst in me when I was laughing with them. These girls were the closest friends I'd ever had. Friendships didn't exist for me because my life was too complicated to explain it to them. But right now, I felt at home—safe enough to share my vulnerabilities.

I offered Attikus a warm smile, and he gave me the same. The men left, and we returned to the lounge.

A thrill coursed through me as I was about to share myself with these girls. I was part of their inner circle, and that meant a lot to me.

I'd shouldered enough burdens without having anyone to talk to. When the isolation and loneliness became too much, I poured the pain into the paintings. But I didn't feel isolated or lonely.

After a few minutes of eating, I learned Elena was having fraternal twins, a boy and a girl. She'd have her hands full. Kiera was having a boy.

The conversations about future baby showers drifted. Then the room went quiet. I glanced up from my plate of food, and all eyes were on me.

"So, tell us." Michelle piled her brown curly hair into a messy bun and looked at Natalie. "You got it?"

"Absolutely." Natalie rushed over to a table and grabbed an ivory shopping bag for me. She'd lightened her blonde hair, making her look like a chic movie star. "This is for you. The other girls already got their gifts."

"Thank you." I took the bag and pressed it to my chest, feeling grateful.

"Look at it, silly." Michelle smiled.

I opened the bag full of clothes I could never afford. Natalie had a flagship shop downtown that showcased the latest fashions. I'd browsed it a few times when I needed inspiration. Her fabric had unique textures and colors.

"These are beautiful, thank you!"

"They're the new Spring Collection. Wear them around and promote them for me."

"Check out the special box!" Kiera waved an air-fried chicken wing that Michelle had brought.

I pulled out the ivory box with foiled designs, removed the lid, and gasped. "Oh, my gosh!" I flicked her a look as heat flushed my face.

Vivian got off the ottoman and kneeled on the rug in front of me. She'd braided her black hair, making me wish I'd done something different to mine. Then she plucked a cream lingerie set and held it up for all to see. "What a lovely set for the newly engaged couple."

I stared at the lacy bra and teeny-tiny panties.

"That won't cover anything," I said as I picked up a soft baby-doll set that made my loins tighten. I'd never owned anything this provocative and had never imagined myself in them.

"They're not meant to cover," Natalie said. "They're meant to entice and provoke."

"Drive him crazy with them," Audri said as she adjusted the pink hair claw in her dark hair.

Kiera blew out a heavy sigh and leaned back on the couch. Pregnancy had made her brown hair look so full and vibrant. "So tell us what's going on with you and Attikus."

"I can't believe you're engaged." Michelle looked at my hand. "Where's the ring?"

Oh. Right.

I hadn't even thought about it. We'd never spoken about it. My mind had been on the contract, fine print, and trying to get Emmanuel away from me, so the ring wasn't even in my thoughts.

"No ring yet."

"What?" the girls all said at once.

Kiera leaped up from the couch. "I need to ask him why he didn't get you a ring! It's a token of love."

"Don't go!" I got up and grabbed her hand.

"You need to sit and calm down." Michelle ushered Kiera back down. "You're hyper. I don't think that's good for the baby."

Audri laughed. "Keep the dessert away from her."

"Get her some calming tea," Vivian suggested.

"I don't think that's gonna help." Elena laughed.

"Why are *you* so calm?" Kiera blew out a breath.

"Maybe my body is in shock that two babies are growing inside me," Elena replied.

Natalie turned to me. "So why did you stop Kiera?"

Where should I start?

"It's complicated," I said.

They all made a disappointed sound.

"It's *always* complicated," Audri said. "Who proposed?"

"I guess I did."

"What do you mean, you guess?" Elena inquired.

"I have something to confess." I looked at them. "But please keep this between us, okay?"

"Babe, you're part of this strange family now." Kiera leaned forward, looking calmer. "We protect our own."

They all nodded and waited patiently.

Inhaling a breath, I told them about the fake marriage that would end in six months.

When I was done, they gaped at me.

"So you're Vanessa Lam and not Nessa Lambert?" Elena gawked at me.

"She's both." Vivian held up a finger. "One is her artist's name."

"Sorry I didn't tell you guys earlier. I haven't gone by Vanessa in a long time."

I didn't tell them about my mom's situation. That would take all night, and I didn't want to complicate things even more.

"We'll address you as Nessa in public until everything is resolved," said Audri. "In private, you're Vanessa."

"Attikus will crush Emmanuel like a cockroach." Elena squeezed my hand. "Some men are just shitty."

"I can see how you'd miss the ring aspect of the engagement," Michelle said.

"Are you sure everything is fake?" Kiera arched a perfect eyebrow. "I've seen him look at you. It doesn't look fake to me."

"So you're arranging a fake marriage to protect yourself," Vivian said to herself. "And he agreed to it because if something happened to you—his tenant—he'd lose money?"

"Yeah," I said, wondering why her reason for his agreement

didn't sound plausible. It made sense to me. "He's a business-man, so he wants to protect his assets."

"Honey," Kiera held up a hand, "Attikus doesn't *need* any more money. None of those guys over there playing their video games need more money. Together, they probably own the world." She pointed at the open doors. "He didn't agree to this outrageous proposal for *money*."

"Oh," was all that came out of my mouth.

Elena looked at me, offering me a warm smile as though she'd always known about the attraction.

"There's more to his agreement." Natalie placed all the clothes and lingerie back into the bag for me.

"You know what that means." Audri rubbed her palms together with a spark in her eyes. "Our Vanessa needs an SSG mission."

"Mission?" I remembered them mentioning it.

They explained SSG stood for Super Spy Girls, sort of like a Bond girl mission. Each of them had a mission to see if their significant other had true feelings for them during their courtship. I laughed at the interesting mission names: License to Kiss, From Iceland with Love, The Man with the Golden Angle, Opals are Forever, A Kiss is Not Enough, and The Thief Who Loved Me.

"What should her mission be?" Vivian looked around the room.

The sexy dream of Attikus flashed into my mind, giving me an idea. "How about For Your Heart Only to follow the theme of *For Your Eyes Only*?"

"That's perfect!" Audri clapped.

"I love it!" Vivian beamed.

"So, are you planning on seducing his heart with paint?" Elena smirked. "Or painting hearts all over his body?"

"You'll know it's the real thing if he strips and becomes your nude model." Kiera laughed.

Wild suggestions erupted, filling the room with laughter. I prayed Attikus and the other boys would stay in their room and ignore us.

Little did these girls know I had dreamed of Attikus naked in my studio. We'd done more than me painting on the canvas. But I wouldn't share that private moment, even if it was only a dream.

"One more question." Kiera held up her finger.

"Yes?" I smiled at how pregnancy gave Kiera even more energy than before.

"Are you attracted to him?" she asked.

How could I not be? Even as I sat there, my body sensed his nearness. The attraction had always been there from a distance. When I first met him at the art exhibit in his museum, my body reacted to him. But I hadn't even considered more at that time.

Everything had escalated recently as I spent more time with him.

"Yes," I admitted.

Amusement gleamed on their faces, like sisters who were happy for their siblings.

"So it's not really a fake relationship," said Michelle.

"But it's not a real one either," I replied.

"Use your mission to find out if he considers this marriage temporary," Audri said. "See if he has any genuine feelings for you. It won't hurt to find out."

"We've all been there." Natalie cracked a juice bottle. "We need to know the truth instead of assuming. Assumption is the worst."

"Communication is everything," Michelle said.

An enormous weight slid off my chest after sharing the fake marriage with them. They were like the sisters I'd never had.

To have this kind of support system after doing things all on my own for so long gave me a moment to breathe.

A novel idea for my gallery popped into my head. "What do you think of having a gathering once a month for art, food, and conversation at my gallery? I was thinking I could offer an art class or how to make a terrarium while we chill and chat?"

"I love that idea." Elena's eyes sparkled. "Call it Chill and Chat. I can promote that segment on Musepaper."

"People would love that," Audri said, and the others agreed.

We lounged around, eating and chatting about random things. The girls told me how they'd met their significant others, and I was astounded to learn that each of them had undergone an insurmountable loss before the gain. I knew then that it was the right decision to share my issue. We all had weaknesses, and none of them judged me.

Tears brimmed in my eyes, and my heart swelled with happiness. I blinked back tears, wondering what Attikus was doing now. What kind of video games was he creating?

"The boys meet up often to play video games?" I asked.

They all exchanged glances, and Audri gestured to the doors.

Michelle was closest, so she got up to shut them.

When Michelle returned, Audri said, "They're not just playing video games. They're strategizing how to destroy The Trogyn."

I gaped and listened as they briefed me on the dangerous crime organization that had been trying to hurt their men. I remembered Attikus warning me about them. If he already had his plate full, why did he agree to help me? Guilt stirred in me.

"The boys are worried about us," Elena said.

"They want to protect us." Audri looked at each of us.

"Because they love us," Vivian added.

"But we love them too," Natalie said.

"So we're secretly strategizing." Kiera smirked.

"We need to protect our men too," Michelle said, looking at me. "We can't just sit around and let The Trogyn hurt them."

Elena wrapped an arm around me. "You can help us strategize."

The love these women had for their men and each other inspired me. This was more than friendship. This was a family, and now I was a part of it.

I'd come here tonight thinking we'd be discussing my fake marriage, but the gathering had turned into a bond of friendship I'd never experienced.

We decided the first Chill and Chat would be for us girls to discuss how we could help the boys without them suspecting anything.

CHAPTER TWENTY

ATTIKUS

I SAT at the table with a wide view of Orion's yard. The magnolia tree was blooming. My yard had the Yoshina Cherry and Magnolia trees. More flowers surrounded his yard and home since Orion got married. More importantly, it was now full of dandelions, Elena's favorite flower.

My head kept turning toward the other room, where laughter echoed.

"Sounds like they're having fun," Orion said, offering me a glass of wine.

Remington, Grayson, Royce, Arrow, and Forrest were all playing the demo for my Level Seven. An element was missing from my fantastical world, and I needed more time for the solution to come to me.

"Are you nervous?" I sipped the wine and let the warmth coat my throat. "Having two babies won't be easy."

"Scared shitless." Orion smiled. "But Elena doesn't know that. I don't want her worrying about me."

"It's natural to be scared. This is a major life change. You'll have mini versions of you and her running around the house."

I recalled playing with my sister when we were younger. Five years younger than me, Amelia had looked up to me, wanting me to teach her how to draw and claiming I was better at it than her.

"Elena is the one having to deal with most changes. She has two humans growing inside her. That's a miracle to me." I could hear the joy in Orion's voice. "I didn't have any siblings growing up, so I'm happy my kids will have each other." He turned to the lounge area with the wide TV screen. "I bet Forrest feels the same way. But he's a doctor, so he can check up on Kiera more than I can with Elena."

"I thought you had a nurse coming here to examine Elena?"

He waved a hand. "I did, but Elena claims it was obsessive and unnecessary."

"You're also having a life-changing event with this marriage thing." Orion tossed me a look. "I have to ask—is the contract tight?"

My best friend was being protective of me, and I appreciated his thoughtfulness. "Yeah. Don't worry."

Orion nodded and finished his wine. "I can see why you're helping her."

"Why?" I arched an eyebrow.

"Because she's an artist like you and your sister."

The truth of it hit me hard. I knew that was the reason, but I'd let it linger on the side. Facing it would acknowledge that I was no longer an artist. That my passion had died a long time ago. Those assholes took that passion away from me.

Of all the boys, Orion knew me best. Vanessa was like my sister and me—victims of a greedy and callous society. I didn't want her passion destroyed the way mine was. I didn't want her to lose her life and the opportunity to share her creativity with the world. Amelia would have been an astounding artist if she were still alive. She was more of a painter, and I was more of an illustrator. Based on the art I'd observed, Vanessa had both skills.

I lifted my hand and wiggled my fingers. "I have drawn nothing since that day."

"You should try again," Orion said.

I lifted a shoulder. "Maybe."

"Level Seven is the *bomb*. I can't wait to see the last game." Grayson walked over, sat down, and grabbed an egg roll. He wore a yellow stylist shirt that Natalie probably designed for him. I'd hired his architectural firm to renovate my museum and other properties a while ago, and we'd become good friends. He filled his plate with wings and the dumplings Audri had brought over.

"Not anytime soon," I said.

All the boys came to the table, expressing their thoughts on Level Seven.

Remington pulled out a chair next to me. "Do you need me to look into Dr. Nico Messina?"

I told them about seeing him in Emmanuel's social media feed.

"That would be great," I said. "Enzo Stevens, Nico Messina, and Milton Kalkounis are all part of something big. I can feel it."

"Enzo and Nico were just names on our list of Trogyn members, but now we'll move them to the priority section." Royce shoved a French fry into his mouth. He'd recently returned from vacation with Michelle and now looked like a tan Thor.

Each of the boys had taken a different angle into The Trogyn. This crime syndicate was a colossal monster with ties to extremely powerful people with hidden identities. We had to be careful how we attacked them now. They knew about us, and I knew they were planning to hurt our families and businesses.

Remington had destroyed a profitable sex-trafficking warehouse. Grayson destroyed an underground tunnel used to transport drugs and shit. Royce had eliminated key members of their organization. Forrest had closed down another sex-trafficking ring. Arrow had brought down several elite members, including a Supreme Court judge and a European prince. Orion had eliminated their money laundering business and life insurance scams involving multiple banks worldwide.

"Milton Kalkounis changed his name to Jean-Claude Dumas," I said.

"The fuck? Why?" Arrow asked.

"Not sure. But I'm gonna find out."

More laughter erupted, and the boys shook their heads while smiling.

"It sounds more fun over there," said Grayson.

"You can join them." Arrow slung an arm around Grayson.

"If they let you," Remi said, his expression turning contemplative.

He didn't need to say anything. I knew what he was thinking. We had to eliminate The Trogyn to protect the joy in that room.

CHAPTER TWENTY-ONE

VANESSA

THE NEXT DAY, Attikus shoved the last suitcase into the trunk of his Maserati SUV, closed it, and looked at me. "Is that all?"

Most men would ask me why I had three suitcases if I were only staying at his place temporarily with the option of going home to retrieve more items when necessary, but he didn't.

"What's wrong with you?" I asked.

"What are you talking about?" He walked me to the passenger side door and opened it for me.

"I just gave you three large suitcases and two duffle bags. Aren't you going to ask me why I need so many when I could just drive back to my apartment to get what I need?"

His lips twisted into a sardonic smile that did something strange to my stomach. "You haven't seen my mother or my sister travel yet. I'm used to it. This is nothing."

"I should drive my car there."

"Why?"

"Because I might need a car to go places?"

"You can use one of mine. It's best to keep your car parked here."

Now it was my turn to ask, "Why?"

He leaned in. "Because I want to give the impression you're still living here. People will cause trouble when they think the apartment is empty."

I knew he was right. Still, I didn't want to depend on him for everything.

He probably saw my frustration. "I have a lot of cars and use only a few. I don't mind my wife using any of them."

I wasn't going to win this argument, so I slid into the passenger seat. "Why do you need so many cars if you don't use them?"

"Why do people buy art?" He reached for the belt buckle. His cologne slithered into my nose, making me want to grab him for a longer sniff. "They just like it. It's a collectible item."

I supposed he was right again, or I was too exhausted to debate with him.

We remained quiet on the drive to his house. I appreciated a moment to catch up on things. I'd been through a whirlwind of changes. It was probably drastic for him too. He went from an eligible bachelor to engaged in only weeks. Now I was moving into his house.

I stole a glance at him. His eyes were trained on the road, but his features appeared more relaxed than days ago. The more I studied him, the more I wanted to touch him, explore him.

So I stopped and looked out the window. He started to whistle. Surprised, I turned to look at him again.

"Are you okay?" I asked.

He met my eyes with amusement and curiosity. "Why do you keep asking me that?"

"You're acting strange."

"Me?" His eyes gleamed. "I should say that about you."

"Me? I'm not acting strange."

A small smile crept onto his lips. "Says the person who keeps staring at me and asking weird questions." He stopped at the red lights and turned to me. "I know why you're nervous."

"I'm not nervous," I said as a new series of nerves skated down my spine from the way he studied me. How could he know I was nervous when I was trying hard to shove that emotion aside?

"You cross your legs and tap your foot a lot when you're nervous."

Shit. It was that obvious? They were annoying traits, but I didn't realize others noticed them.

I was relieved when the lights turned green and his attention swerved back to the road. I didn't like that he could see right through me. How could I not be nervous about moving in with him? My attraction to him had increased tenfold. I feared I'd do something to ruin this arranged fake marriage.

"Are you okay?" He repeated my question, but there was no sarcasm in it like I'd expected.

"Why are you so calm? You have a stranger coming to live with you. Aren't you nervous?"

"You're not a stranger, Vanessa. You're my fiancée. Before that, we were acquaintances. I was a business investor who admired your talent." He turned down a street with extravagant homes. "And your beauty."

I froze at that comment. Was he flirting with me?

I narrowed my eyes at him. "Are you trying to make things difficult while I'm living at your house?"

"No. Just playing the role of a man who's extremely attracted to his gorgeous fiancée. You should try playing that role too."

Oh. He was only acting.

"It'll make the next few months fly by," he continued. "I know you can't wait for the contract to end so you can resume your life." He turned down another road where a beautiful home sat by itself, surrounded by flowering trees. A set of deciduous trees created a peaceful backdrop. It must be mesmerizing in the fall when the leaves turned to various shades of orange and gold.

I had expected a mansion surrounded by luxury fencing and a security gate to keep curious people out. But this modern home wasn't intimidating. It had lovely curb appeal. The entrance, marked by a wide front door and flanked by Japanese maple and dogwood trees, made the location warm and welcoming. The doors just needed a floral wreath for the final touch. But that was subjective. If I had a home like this, I'd have a wreath for each season.

"I want to get back to my life too." His words cut into me, yanking me back to reality.

Unease bloomed in my body. "Don't worry, I'll make it as painless as possible."

"That's not what I meant." He pulled into the driveway and parked in front of a garage with four cars beside it.

What was wrong with me? I had to rein in my emotions so we could both survive this marriage.

"I'm sorry. I'm just anxious. You're doing me a huge favor, and I should be grateful and not take things too seriously."

He reached over and brushed a knuckle down my cheek, surprising me. "You want to resume your peaceful life. There's nothing wrong with that. I've lived alone for a while, so this is the first time I've had someone here."

"No one has stayed over?"

"No." He got out of the car.

I stood next to him as he opened the trunk. "Not even your mom or sister?"

"They only visit." He dragged out my luggage. "They prefer their house like I prefer mine."

I didn't know what to think about being the first person to stay at his house. He must've been feeling uncomfortable too. But he was better at keeping calm than I was. This was going to be interesting.

"Are you sure you're going to survive sharing your house with me?" I grabbed the third piece of luggage and followed him into the house, which had marble flooring.

Out of habit, I stopped at the mat and kicked off my sneakers.

"You don't have to do that," he said.

"I prefer it. It keeps the house cleaner. My mom used to make me sweep the floor whenever I forgot and trekked in dirt from outside. You should try it. It's good feng shui."

"You know feng shui?"

"Only a little. But it's common sense. If you bring nasty things into the house, most likely those nasty things will breed negative energy." I glanced around his home and saw some plants, but not enough. "Having plants in the house would help transform that heavy energy into something better."

"I see my fiancée already knows how to improve my living situation." He left the luggage, walked back to the doormat, and kicked off his shoes, placing them next to mine.

The act surprised me. I didn't think he would adopt my preferred way of entering the home this quickly.

"This is your house. You don't need to change it for me."

"I'm not." He walked to me and grabbed the handle of the suitcase, pulling all of them down an eggshell-colored hallway. "I'm an open-minded person. I can adapt to a new environment with ease, especially when it makes sense. Who doesn't want more positive energy in their home?"

I didn't know if I could adapt to things the way he could.

He came to a door, opened it, and walked in. "This is your suite. There's a compact bathroom, a living room, and a small kitchen here."

I gaped at the lush living room and modern kitchen with appliances that still gleamed. "Has anyone lived here?"

"No."

"Why do you have a suite when you never have guests over?"

"It came with the house, and I didn't need to change it." He shrugged. "I had a feeling it would be useful one day, and I was right." He stepped closer and tipped my chin up. "Are you ready to play the role of my beloved fiancée?"

"I'm not an actress," I murmured, struggling to think clearly. "But it seems like you're good at it."

"Sometimes, we have to wear a mask to survive," he breathed into my ear, the warmth of his breath making me shiver. When he drew back, his brown eyes had darkened to a lustful chocolate.

"I'm afraid I might forget who I am if I wear a mask."

"Or you might find a part of yourself that was dormant."

Was there a hidden message woven within his statement? Probably. But my brain cells were all frozen. How many masks had he worn to survive? What did he discover about himself?

"Try it for a few weeks and see. You have nothing to lose. It could be fun."

I was in a fake marriage. When I stepped out in public, I had to play my role correctly, or the news media would start rumors. Then again, I saw how they could start trouble regardless of what people did. Attikus was doing me a favor. The least I could do was make this situation easy for both of us.

What harm would it do to pretend to be his fiancée? *It could be fun.*

My inner voice wanted to retort with sarcasm, but I shut it

down before it could form. A part of me wanted to see how far we could go—or rather, how far I could go with this fake relationship.

"So you want me to call you by a pet name and flirt with you?"

His eyes sparkled. "That would make this situation interesting. Wouldn't you agree, Lily Pad?"

"Lily Pad?" I asked, my heart racing for no reason.

"Do you remember the dark purple water lily painting?"

I sucked in a breath. "That was my first oil painting. I sold it to an old couple at a farmer's market." I'd loved that painting, but I needed money to pay bills, and the couple had offered me a thousand dollars. That was a lot for a new artist like me. "How do you know about it?"

"I own it now."

I didn't know what to say. "How? I sold it years ago."

"I bought it at an estate sale."

"For how much?" A strand of my hair fell over my face.

"I got it as a bargain." His finger skimmed my jaw. "But it's the most precious painting in my collection."

"You're lying." I snorted and pushed him away from me. "You own art that can sell for millions of dollars, and you're telling me *The Lost Lily Pad* is worth more?"

"I don't measure worth with numbers, Vanessa." He pulled me back and wrapped both arms around my waist. "That's what it's called? There was no title on the painting. And the only initials were VL."

"Then how did you know that's me?"

"Educated guess and trusting my gut. Based on all the new paintings you've done. Every artist has a certain style."

I couldn't believe this. Of all the people in the world, he had my first painting. That had been a difficult time for me, and I'd channeled that into the art.

"Why is it called *The Lost Lily Pad?*"

I didn't want to share that with him yet. "I'll tell you one day when you're ready to share a dark secret with me, okay? We're newly engaged. It's gonna take time for us to get to know each other, Whistler." This role-playing thing wasn't so bad. It was helping me escape his questioning.

"Is that my pet name?"

"It is." I ran my fingers along his powerful jaw. "The whistling caught me off-guard earlier, but I like it."

"Oh, yeah? Why?"

"Because you seem carefree when you whistle."

He blinked at my comment, and I couldn't tell if it surprised him in a good or bad way. His phone rang, interrupting the flow between us.

"You can get settled. Make yourself at home. I'll get the rest of the bags."

"I'll do it. Take the call."

He nodded and walked out of the suite, leaving me in this luxury suite that I could never afford.

My phone rang, and I reached into my purse to see that it was my mom. I closed the door to the suite and walked toward the tall windows that looked out to a private yard. A greenhouse was attached to the side of the house, but it was empty.

"Hi, *Mẹ.* Is everything okay?" I asked, trying to calm the nerves stirring in me.

I didn't know why, but I always got this way whenever I received a call from her. She was in prison—an unsafe place where things could turn bad quickly. I wouldn't be able to stop worrying until she was home with me.

"I'm safe, sweetie. Is everything okay with *you?*" she asked. "Have you had the *bánh mì* lately?"

The code for her escape reminded me how serious things were. Minutes ago, I was flirting with my fake husband, and all the anxiety bombarding me had faded away. But this was reality.

"Yes. We should be all set. I'm going to call the *bánh mì* shop to double check on my order after our chat." When I last called Leo for an update, he told me his team would rescue my mom during the street cleanup.

Two months from now, my mother would join other female prisoners to pick up trash in the city. Leo and his men would extract my mom and put her on a flight to Mexico with a new identity that I'd paid for.

"Have you carved out time for yourself? Dating anyone?"

It had been a while since we'd discussed my personal relationships. She knew nothing about Emmanuel. What would she think if she knew I was engaged to a billionaire and we were getting married soon? My mom didn't have any social media accounts that could reveal my engagement. She mostly watched the local news.

"No time for personal relationships."

"How many times have I told you to slow down and live? I'm okay. It's not so bad here. I've met some wonderful friends who were also wrongly accused. We have each other."

Whenever I sent money to my mom, I sent extra so she could help her friends, Sheila Brown and Josephine Smith. Their families couldn't help them like I helped my mom.

"Can you do something for me?" *Mẹ* asked.

"What is it?"

"Start dating."

"Why?"

"Because I want my daughter to be happy. I don't want to see anxiety in you when you visit. A mother can sense things about her daughter, and I know you're carrying a heavy burden." She choked up. "I know what you've been through to get me the *bánh mì*. But my only wish is for you to live a happy life."

I couldn't respond right away because tears were sliding down my face. She shouldn't worry about me. She was the best mother I could ever ask for. I'd give her a sliver of happiness so she could sleep better tonight.

"Well, I was going to wait until I visit you to share this. But since you're so worried about me, I'll tell you now."

"Tell me!" Excitement filled her voice. I could imagine her pretty smile.

"There's this man I like."

"Who is he?"

"My landlord." I laughed, wondering what Attikus was doing now. Technically, he was my landlord and my fake husband.

"Does he have a stable job? Is he handsome?"

"He's well off, and he's very hot." These were all truths that would remove any concerns regarding my private life.

"Those are excellent qualities. But be careful. Men like that aren't always trustworthy."

"I'm careful, which is why I'm not making any moves. I didn't want to tell you until I was sure."

"I have the most intelligent daughter. Whoever he is, he better be on his toes."

We chatted for a few more minutes until she had to go.

A knock sounded on my door.

"Come in."

Attikus brought my duffle bags and placed them on the floor. "I've got to head out. You can give yourself a tour or wait until I get back. What do you want for dinner? I'll pick something up."

"It doesn't matter. Anything is fine."

"Anything?"

"I'm not picky."

"Okay. How about I get some Vietnamese food from Saigon Bistro again?"

"You really like it there?"

"The food is amazing. Can you text me what we got last time? That way, I'll know what to order when I call it in?"

"Okay."

When he left, I called Leo to triple-check that my mom's escape was solid.

CHAPTER TWENTY-TWO

ATTIKUS

I WALKED into Detective Farmer's office. "Thanks for calling me about the news."

"You're welcome. Please have a seat." He gestured to the leather chair in front of his mahogany desk.

I closed the door, leaned my cane against the chair, and sat down. He'd lost some weight since I last saw him. Or maybe the blue-striped shirt made him look slimmer.

"Is the department working you to death?" I asked.

"Oh, you know how it is working for the city. Overworked and underpaid."

"Public service is a hard job, and it's rare to have someone dedicated like you. I've met a lot of city workers. Not all of them have the same integrity as you, detective." I leaned into the table. "So what do you have for me?"

He slid me a folder. "This case has become interesting."

I arched an eyebrow and opened the folder. A muscle on my cheek twitched as the past flashed across my vision. How in hell did my high school principal's finger end up in a box sent to Vanessa?

"Are you sure it's him?" I read the report.

Detective Farmer nodded. "We tested the DNA twice. Both times, it showed Stephen C. Perry."

I'd looked into all the names of those who had sided with Ashton and his family back then. Stephen C. Perry had taken money from the Lindor family many times. He hadn't cooperated with the investigation regarding Ashton, Bobby, and Harry bullying me and others. He had been a minor character until now.

"Do you know where he is?" I asked, remembering he had a wife and a daughter.

"Yeah, he's in the morgue with his wife and daughter."

"What? How?" I furrowed my brow.

"A friend came to visit and found the family dead in the living room this morning. We're still investigating."

"How did they die?"

"It appears like a murder-suicide. Stephen killed his wife and daughter, then turned the gun on himself."

"With the hand that had the missing finger?" I asked sarcastically.

"How do you know?" Detective Farmer looked at me suspiciously.

Fuck. "I was being sarcastic. If that's true, the actual killer is stupid, careless, or wants to send a message."

"What kind of message?"

I pursed my lips. "Maybe Stephen is involved with something bigger. Maybe his death is a warning for those wanting to look further."

Detective Farmer considered me. He knew about my past because he was the only police officer who had listened to me back then. Detective Farmer had just graduated from the police academy and had sat with me while I waited to talk to the other two detectives assigned to my family's murder case. Detectives

Mike Matthews and Benjamin Jones weren't helpful because I didn't have money for a top-notch lawyer. My family's murder case file was ruled as a fire accident caused by an electrical error and signed off by the fire investigator, Anthony Young.

But I'd looked into these men, and they were also on the Lindor's payroll. Just last year, they were all found dead. Detective Matthews died when he fell off a cliff during a hiking trip, and Detective Jones died from a heart attack even though he had a clean bill of health, according to his family. Anthony got into an accident during a whitewater raft trip with his friends.

It seemed like the Lindor family was removing anyone with links to them. Why now?

I met Detective Farmer's eyes. "Maybe you should step back with this investigation. It seems like everyone linked to my family's murder case is dying."

"I can't step back now. If I stop now, there will be questions. Everyone knows I'm like a bulldog with these cases—I won't let go until I get answers. Also, the system let you down back then." His jaw tightened. "But I won't. I take my job seriously."

"If they came to you with a blank check to buy your loyalty, what would you do?" I asked, knowing too many men had taken that offer in the past.

The country was ruled by men who were easily bought. For all I knew, our government had been compromised by foreign enemies for some time now.

"I'd write 'fuck off' on it and return it to them." He smiled. "Do you still have the check I returned to you?"

A smirk slid onto my lips, remembering when I'd given him a blank check to test him. "No, I fed it to the shredder."

He laughed. "I'll keep you posted on what I find out."

"Thanks."

Stephen C. Perry would go on my investigation board at

home. How powerful was the Lindor family? I'd looked into their finances, and they had a substantial amount of money, but not millions. There had to be other accounts. Who was funding them? They had to be doing something illegal if they were killing people off like this. What did Stephen do for them? Or did he have information they wanted to bury?

Questions crowded my head.

"Nothing on Joseph?" I asked about my curator.

He shook his head. "That's another mystery baffling me. Let's hope we'll get news on him soon."

Could Joseph's disappearance be related to the Lindor family? Was it possible that they were trying to sabotage me?

I rose from the chair and grabbed my cane. "Thank you for the update. Please keep me posted on everything."

"Will do," he said.

I walked toward his door.

"Attikus," he called.

I turned around and met a pair of serious blue eyes. "Yeah?"

"Be careful, okay?"

"You too. Call if you need anything."

"How's your leg?" he asked.

"Better every day." I tapped my cane on the floor.

Detective Farmer was the official the public needed. He was a rare find, and I'd make sure he remained safe not only for my sake, but for those who needed a voice—those who needed justice.

He didn't know I had my own investigation on the side. It would complicate things if he knew, and I didn't want him to lose his job for me.

Inside my car, I checked Vanessa's text message for the food. Then I called it in and headed to Saigon Bistro.

You seem carefree when you whistle.

Her voice echoed in my head. I hadn't noticed that I'd whistled again until she pointed it out. I used to whistle whenever I sketched. It was a calm trance when I was at ease. The whistling used to annoy my sister. Vanessa had put me in a comfortable state of mind that allowed dormant aspects of myself to emerge. No one and nothing had been able to do that.

What else could she lure out of me?

There was no doubt that she was as attracted to me as I was to her. I desperately wanted to know how long my Lily Pad could refrain from kissing me. I knew she wanted me to add that clause to the contract to protect herself. But I saw through her and had my own agenda.

She should have reviewed the contract more carefully when I gave her a copy so we could both sign it in front of each other. All she had cared about were the demands she requested and not the fine print that was added, which benefited both parties who were attracted to each other.

I got dinner and drove home, loving the idea that I was going home to her.

CHAPTER TWENTY-THREE

VANESSA

I ACQUAINTED myself with every room in Attikus's house, including the art studio. However, I struggled to enter his bedroom. I stood at the open door, staring into a room with gray walls and a massive bed. The door had been left open, so I could see plenty without having to enter. I didn't want to invade his privacy, yet curiosity anchored me to the doorway. One step over, and I'd be inside. But that one step would be like stepping over the demarcation line, wouldn't it?

You're his fiancée. You should know what his room looks like.

But I was his *fake* fiancée. That didn't give me permission to be nosy, right?

Not nosy. *You're researching a mysterious man who agreed to be your husband for six months. To ensure your safety, you need to analyze him like a plant under a microscope.*

I slapped a hand on my forehead. I'd never sounded as ridiculous as I did at this moment.

What was wrong with me? This was his home, and I should respect it. When he said to make myself at home and take a tour, I was certain he was referring to the kitchen, living room, bathroom, and dining room. I was certain he did *not* mean his bedroom or the office across the hall.

I'd walked past his bedroom to see that his door was open. If he didn't want anyone to look inside, he should've closed it.

Would I want him to enter my bedroom when I wasn't home? Probably not. But this was his home, so he could enter any room he wanted, including my suite.

I valued my privacy, and I hoped he would do the same for me. Turning around, I walked back past the three empty bedrooms and down the wide staircase to the first floor, where my suite was.

Why did wealthy people need such big houses if only one person lived in them? The bigger the house, the more maintenance and cleaning required. Then again, Attikus probably had a service that came weekly.

I walked back to the living room, admiring the homey decor. He'd likely hired an expensive interior designer to achieve this comfortable living space with its masculine flair. Earth tones, paired with wood and metal furniture, illustrated a pleasant elegance. Despite that, the home would improve with more greenery. He had only three plants in the entire house, and one of them was plastic. For an owner of vegetable farms, he had little flowers or plants around. I made a mental note to check out the greenhouse later.

I envisioned a design plan for him as I walked through the house. Maybe I'd add some colorful accent pillows to the brown couch and loveseat. I planned on making this place prettier while I was here. After the six months, he could remove everything or keep it.

I sat on the wide couch and propped my feet on the matching ottoman. My mom's predicament surfaced, but my conversation with Leo settled my nerves. My heart pounded as the truth sank in. I'd hired men to break the law—men who didn't hesitate to cross lines I'd never even approached before. And now? I was no different. An accomplice. A lawbreaker. Maybe even worse. But then again . . . who really bore the weight of guilt here? Who was the true villain in this story? Those who placed my mom in prison for something she didn't do? Or me trying to save her so she could live a comfortable life?

The prosecutor had an enormous pile of evidence against my mom—witnesses who said they had seen her stab him. They claimed to have recordings from their cell phones to support their statement. The police officer hadn't listened to what I had to say and probably tampered with the evidence. The judge had appeared to sympathize with the dead man's family and ignored the fact that he had attacked us first.

Money had so much power; it ruled everything. It could destroy the lives of innocent people in a flash. My mom and I were victims of that. I needed wealth to combat wealth.

Was it wrong of me to step outside of the law to protect those I loved? Sometimes, things weren't black or white. Shades of gray existed for this reason. As an artist, I loved every shade of every color that wasn't defined as the typical red, blue, green, yellow, and so on. I appreciated things could be sea-foam sky blue, mystical green, petal pink, or angry red.

The palette of life consisted of various hues that couldn't be defined. That inexplicable aspect was its beauty and wisdom.

I heard Attikus's car in the garage and jumped to my feet. My heart thudded erratically, and I cursed myself for my ridiculous reaction.

Stop it. Behave like a normal person.

I walked over to the kitchen and stared at the door connecting to the garage. When he opened the door, a swoosh of energy overcame me, washing off the worry that had clung to me minutes ago.

His face brightened, and a question sparked in his eyes. He was probably wondering why I was standing in his kitchen like a fool. I wanted to know the answer to that too.

"Hello, Lily Pad." He smirked, kicking off his shoes on the mat. I'd never heard of Lily Pad as someone's nickname. But somehow, he made it unique and interesting. Or maybe I was under his spell. That was the only rational explanation for my strange behavior.

Attikus was indeed excellent at adapting. Before today, he'd walked around his home with his shoes on, spreading dirt and germs on his pristine floor. I didn't know too many men who paid attention to details like him.

"Hello, Whistler," I said, wondering if he liked me calling him that.

A small smile formed on his lips as he placed the food on the marble island. The scent of the delicious dinner filled the space.

"Did you give yourself a tour of the house?" He looked at me.

"You have a lovely home. I saw everything on the first floor, but I didn't look at the second floor."

"Why not?"

"Do you want people going into your office or bedroom when you're not around? Especially people you don't know well?"

He took out two pretty plates from the cabinet and placed them on the round kitchen table. The dining room had a long rectangular table made of petrified wood. It was a gorgeous art piece that shouldn't be eaten on.

"You're not a stranger, remember?" He removed the food containers from the bag.

I helped him bring the six containers to the table. "What if you have things you don't want others to find out?"

"Like what?" He pulled out a chair at the table and gestured for me to sit.

I sat down. "Like personal things that might embarrass you."

He folded himself into the chair across from me. "I'm a boring man, Vanessa."

I didn't know why, but my inner thighs quivered at the way he said my name. His baritone seemed to sing to it.

"Now that's a lie."

An eyebrow lifted. "Do you find me as interesting as I find you?"

Was he playing the role of fiancé?

"You're a fascinating mystery," I said, also playing my role. The pretense hid the nerves and heat blooming in my body.

"Then I give you permission to uncover the clues. Nothing in this home embarrasses me."

Everyone had secrets. Why was he being so open with me? Or did he have another place that held his dark secrets?

He rose from his seat. "Do you want anything to drink? Wine, juice, water?"

"Water is fine, thank you."

He walked to the fridge, pulled out two bottles of water, and brought them back to the table.

I stood and walked to a drawer. "Do you have spoons for the food?"

"Left drawer near the second sink."

I took out the spoons and brought them back to the table. One of the food containers held four Vietnamese subs. I thought about asking why he'd bought so much food for two people but remembered how he'd wolfed down everything at the restaurant.

When he sat down, I scooped the rice with the teriyaki beef onto his plate. "You love this dish."

"I do." He beamed like a little kid. "Here, let me." He piled up my plate, surprising me.

"You're very thoughtful," I said.

"I had a mother who taught me well. And an adopted mother and sister who made sure I didn't forget my manners." He eyed me. "But I'm only thoughtful of those I consider family."

I opened my mouth to say that I wasn't his actual family, then closed it again. I didn't want to ruin the mood.

"This couple recommended the crêpes with chicken and shrimp." He gestured to it with his chopsticks. "Do you like that dish?"

"Yes, it's good."

"Do you know how to make any of these foods?" he asked.

"Of course."

This casual conversation about food was so normal that I didn't know what to think.

"Wanna make some for me?" Amusement gleamed in his eyes.

"That depends."

"On what?"

"On how well my fiancé behaves." *On how well you help me solve my issues.* I had to tell him about my mom's problem eventually. What if I was caught and sent to prison? That would be the worst-case scenario. Still, I had to let him know what he was in for.

He chuckled, and we ate in silence. His gaze flicked to mine often, and I didn't look away.

So far, we were having fun role-playing.

CHAPTER TWENTY-FOUR

VANESSA

AFTER ATTIKUS FINISHED his plate of food, he sipped water from his bottle while watching me eat.

I lifted my eyes and met the heat of his gaze. "Are you done?"

"I'm done eating, but not done admiring my fiancée's lovely features."

I grabbed a sub from the box and placed it on his plate. "Here. Occupy yourself while I finish my dinner."

Laughter sparked in his eyes. "My home is more entertaining with you here."

I imagined him eating at this table all by himself, and sadness stirred in me. "Do you invite your mom and sister over for dinner often?"

"They've been here, but it's not the same thing." He flicked me an inquisitive look. "I can't sit and stare at them like I stare at you."

"You mean you can, but you *won't*."

"My mother and sister don't interest me the way you do."

He bit into the sub, chewed, and swallowed. "They don't make me wonder about things."

I finished my dinner and gulped down water to cool the heat coursing through me.

What did he wonder about me? Would that question lead to more sexual tension? I didn't want the thermometer in the kitchen to burst because of us.

He was enjoying this fiancé role a bit too much. I supposed I shouldn't disappoint my future husband.

"Do you want to know what I'm wondering?"

"Yes." He wiped his mouth with the napkin and drank some water. "What are you thinking?"

"Why are you exceptionally attentive to me tonight?" I glanced at his empty plate and the crumbs from the sub. How did he stay so fit if this was how he ate?

"I had an interesting day." A muscle twitched in his jaw. "You're the perfect distraction for me."

"What happened today?"

His eyes darkened as he rose from his chair and walked over to me. "I got to experience the bad and the good today." He offered me his hand.

I took it and stood. Whatever happened today must've been awful. If he wanted to tell me, he would have already, so I didn't pressure him. Based on my experience, you had to push the ugly aside sometimes so you could breathe.

So I gave him the space he needed and became his perfect distraction simply by being his fiancée.

"Let me give you a tour upstairs. I don't want you getting lost when I'm not home." He held my hand, leading me up the stairs.

"I fear I might spot a woman's underwear hiding in your bedroom," I teased.

He squeezed my hand. "You must have hidden yours in there while I was out."

He tossed me a lustful look that had my core tightening. Was that an act too?

When he stepped inside, I glanced around at the spacious room with the king-size bed, which looked welcoming with its taupe and gray sheets. I turned to a spacious extension with tall windows and comfy couches.

"This must be where you hide your sex toys."

"You're so smart." He lifted my hand and kissed it. "How do you know everything?"

My skin heated where his lips touched. The SSG mission sparked in my head. I'd almost forgotten about it. I could use this opportunity to confirm his intentions. Was this all fake, or did he have genuine feelings for me?

What if I discovered they weren't real? My chest tightened. I'd think about that later. He considered me a distraction from whatever had bothered him today. But he was also my distraction.

We were using each other to fill a void.

The fancy curtains dressed the tall windows beautifully. Framed kids' drawings hung on one wall. I released my hand from his grip and walked over. Some drawings had burned edges. I smiled at the happy sun with the adorable clouds. One drawing of a family of stick people was incomplete because the other portion had been burned away. I loved looking at children's drawings. They conveyed a sense of wonder, magic, and hope that adults often forgot. The residual of fire had tainted the joy in these drawings. What happened to them?

I turned to see Attikus leaning against a side table, watching me. "Whose drawings are these? They're precious."

He walked up to the family drawing and ran his fingers along the gold frames. "My younger sister. Amelia was a great artist. She drew our family when she was only four. When she was in middle school, she could illustrate anime better than me. I wish I had some of those illustrations. She wanted to be an artist when she grew up."

The tone of his voice changed, and his fingers curled. I sensed his pain, so I took his hand in mine.

"I can see her talent."

I wanted to ask what happened to his family, but he pulled me to him. "You have an incredible talent, Lily Pad."

"What's that?"

"For making me feel better."

I sensed his erection against my belly and lost my breath. Things were moving too fast. Right now, he seemed vulnerable. I didn't want him to make a mistake he'd regret later.

My eyes darted to the family picture frame sitting on the side table behind him. "Is that you?" I broke free from him, stepped over to the table, and picked up the picture frame. "You were a cute boy. What a beautiful family photo." When I looked closer, I saw it also had smoke stains. "You and your sister are a beautiful blend of your parents."

"Thank you."

The photo also showed the spark of a young Attikus. His eyes revealed a powerful glimpse into his soul—hope and motivation that could inspire the world.

I looked up at him.

"What?" he asked.

"You still have that spark." I patted his cheek.

"How can you be sure?"

"It's like looking at art. Sometimes, you just feel it."

He considered my comment for a moment. Then he slipped his hand behind my neck, massaging it gently. He bent and pressed his lips gently to mine.

When he drew back, I said, "You're breaking a rule in the contract."

His lips pursed. "Some rules can be bent temporarily."

"Says who?"

"Says the two people who are in heat right now."

"I'm not in heat."

"Okay." He smirked, seeing through my lie. "Then it's just me." His Adam's apple bobbed. "Please forgive me, Lily Pad."

The sexual tension in the room increased several notches.

"I'm going to unpack and call it a night."

Attikus nodded. "Okay. I need to get some work done. If you need anything, you can call, text, or walk upstairs."

I nodded. "Let me help you put the food away."

As we walked out of his bedroom, he said, "You're welcome to leave your underwear in my drawers if you need more room."

Was that an invitation? He knew he was unsettling me and didn't back down one bit. Did he want me to jump him or something? Because if I had to stand next to him for another minute, I would.

Rolling my eyes, I stalked past him, rushing down the stairs.

He caught up to me. "As for the sex toys, I don't have any. But we could start a collection if you want."

Heat blossomed on my face and traveled down my neck. I glared at him. "Sounds like you want it more than me."

He stood with his hands tucked into his pants, smirking as he rocked back on his heels.

"Where's your cane? Is it safe to walk around without it?"

"Are you worried about me?"

"I'm worried about *me*. If you fall and knock yourself out, I'm not strong enough to drag you to safety." I looked around and spotted it leaning against the kitchen wall. "Here." I offered it to him. It was heavier than I had imagined.

"Thank you." He took it but leaned it against the kitchen island. "The doctor told me it's okay not to use it at home. During my physical therapy sessions, I don't need a cane." He walked back and forth in the kitchen like a lion owning his domain. "See?"

He walked without a limp. I wondered if his pain was sporadic, but I didn't want to ask any more questions. I was supposed to get away from him.

As soon as I finished putting the food away, I said good night, rushed into my bedroom, and locked the door.

When I sat on my bed, I blew out a heavy breath, trying to calm my erratic heartbeat.

We weren't even married, and he'd already broken one rule on the contract.

But you're not mad about it.

I wasn't, which made this entire situation dangerous. I didn't want to get hurt, and Attikus was a man who had the potential to do just that. I could tell because my body had never reacted this way to anyone.

A hot shower would help me clear away his energy so I could unpack and get a restful sleep.

CHAPTER TWENTY-FIVE

ATTIKUS

I SAT INSIDE MY OFFICE, staring at my computer and wondering what Vanessa was doing. Was she asleep or unpacking?

Today had revealed a lot of profound things. So many emotions packed into one day didn't serve me well.

My meeting with Detective Farmer had placed me in a sour mood. The research into Ashton Lindor had become complicated. How was he linked to my high school principal?

Despite the stress tugging at me, when I got home and found Vanessa waiting for me in my kitchen, it did something to me. Her presence changed the energy in my home and transformed everything around me.

It was as though she brought a fresh perspective that illuminated my portrait in a new light.

Picking up a pencil, I twirled it around my finger and grinned, remembering what I'd overheard when I went to her suite after I took Detective Farmer's call. I wanted to inform her I'd be out, but then I heard her mention me to someone.

Anyone would pause and listen if they heard themselves

mentioned in a conversation, right? It was a natural reaction. Though she had closed the door, I could hear her perfectly. I hadn't meant to eavesdrop, but I couldn't help it when she admitted her attraction to me.

After I heard that, I walked away with a smile and a plan forming in my head. What would it take for her to admit she wanted me?

I loved the way she blushed, trying to hide her attraction.

You have a contract with her. Respect it.

But I wanted her to break a rule. When that happened, I'd propose something else to her.

A strange sensation overcame my body. It was something I hadn't felt in years—not since that day when hope became a tiny ember in the ashes.

Tingles rushed down my fingers as I held the pencil. The desire to sketch coursed through me. My right hand shook from this profound revelation. This was the new beginning I hadn't thought was possible.

I took out a new sketchbook and pressed the pencil to the paper. Magic occurred, and I immersed myself in that bubble. Two hours later, I stared at Vanessa's beautiful face.

She had inspired me to sketch again.

CHAPTER TWENTY-SIX

VANESSA

I WOKE up at five the next morning without an alarm. I was a morning person, but based on my fatigue yesterday, I should have slept until six or seven in the morning. Feeling motivated to complete my For Your Heart Only mission, I walked into the bathroom—which was bigger than my entire apartment—to wash up. I brushed my hair, but it wasn't doing what I wanted, so I sprayed on some leave-in conditioner and added curlers. This usually tamed the frizz.

Usually, I wouldn't care what I looked like, but I wanted Attikus to see the best version of me today. A first impression was important, especially to my fake fiancé, who owned a museum filled with extraordinary art. He knew what it took to impress.

I glanced at my planner. Unlike most people these days who used online planners, I preferred my physical planner. I liked the tangible touch. An artist knew the difference between using a Photoshop paintbrush versus a real one. The organic touch of the real thing connected me to nature—back to the basics. There was nothing wrong with digital art. I'd created amazing art with it many times, and it helped with my social media graphics. But I preferred to walk in the woods rather than on a treadmill.

I flipped through my planner, crossing off the things I had completed, and reviewed what needed to be worked on. I'd finished *Three Roads Diverged in a Dark Wood* and sent it off. That custom piece had earned me two hundred thousand dollars. I still had the painting to do for the First Lady. I didn't like any of the rough sketches I'd drawn of her. Why wasn't I inspired? This wasn't good. I had to deliver a unique portrait of her. Maybe some time off to clear my head would help me start fresh.

It was only five forty-five when I opened my bedroom door and peered out as though I didn't belong in the house. Attikus was probably still asleep. I walked down the hallway to the room he'd turned into an art studio for me. I only brought what I needed to work and some blank canvases. The studio was spacious, with a lot of natural lighting. One side was all glass, allowing me to look out at a blooming garden.

I walked over to the sliding door and opened it, allowing the fresh air to enter. I remembered I'd brought some flip-flops with me. Rushing back to my room, I dug out a pair of green flip-flops and wore them out into the garden. I had no idea why I'd brought them with me. Apparently, my subconscious mind knew I'd need them.

Sometimes, I loved walking barefoot on the grass, but I didn't want dirt in my new art studio. But as soon as I stepped onto the stone path, I realized there wasn't dirt anywhere. It was stone, mulch, and grass. The private yard was fenced off with a locked gate. This was my private oasis, where I could paint or do whatever I wanted. I twirled as if I wore a dress, but I was still in my cotton T-shirt and knit pants.

Mid-May weather meant the sun rose early. I glanced up at

the warm pink sky and smiled. It was going to be a wonderful day. I walked around admiring the daffodils and tulips.

"Thank you for your beautiful colors." I blew kisses at them, imagining them giggling at me.

Skipping along the stone path to the gate, I unlocked it and walked into a larger yard. Someone had tended to the grass and plants by adding brown mulch to the area. I spotted the greenhouse I'd seen yesterday. It had solar-like panels on the roof. I approached and saw a metal box attached to the side of the wall. Opening it, I saw a keyboard. Closing the box, I surveyed the textured glass wall that wrapped around the space. Something about the design and textured glass made it appear more advanced.

I yanked the door, and it opened. Stepping inside, I browsed the tables, racks, and displays. There were no seedlings. Just empty trays with a variety of seeds and gardening tools spread out on a table. What was he planting? Why hadn't he started?

I walked out of the greenhouse and explored. Attikus had an abundance of flowering trees and shrubbery. The fresh air invigorated me. With joy radiating in my heart, I skipped around the yard in my flip-flops as though the space was mine.

No one was here but me, so I could sing if I wanted to. It had been a long time since I felt this carefree. I didn't know how long this would last, so I had to take advantage of this rare moment. A rabbit raced out from behind a budding Azalea bush and darted across the lawn. It paused and looked at me.

"Hey, there," I said, stepping forward.

The bunny hopped into a bush by the kitchen sliding door.

When I looked up, my heart galloped at the gorgeous man wearing only cotton pants. Attikus's bare shoulders and chest showcased a spectacular form with taut muscles. Saliva pooled in my mouth. Who knew he had such an incredible abdomen? I could use it as my painting palette. I wanted to run my hands over those fantastic ridges.

My throat grew dry, staring at him. My dream about him resurfaced. Then I saw my reflection in the sliding glass panel and gasped. My curlers dangled from my hair—one clinging haphazardly to one side—and my thin T-shirt revealed my breasts and pebbled nipples. I could die from embarrassment.

Why was he up at this hour?

Attikus opened the sliding door. "Would you like some coffee?"

CHAPTER TWENTY-SEVEN

ATTIKUS

"NO, THANKS." Vanessa rushed past me and out of the kitchen.

Smiling, I stared after her, noticing she hadn't taken off her flip-flops. If I were a decent man, I'd leave her alone, but I was an aroused man who needed one more look at his striking fiancée.

"You forgot the flip-flops, Lily Pad."

"Ugh." She cursed, removed the flip-flops, turned around, and walked back to me. My eyes darted to her chest, loving their shape and wondering what they'd feel like—taste like.

She took my empty hand and placed the flip-flops in it. "Here. Since you wanted to see *them*."

She knew me so well.

"They're perfect," I said, placing the flip-flops on the mat. "Who wouldn't? They're the best thing I've ever woken up to."

She rolled her eyes and turned to head out of the kitchen. "Wait."

She huffed out a breath and whirled to face me. "What?"

"Do you have any pressing projects?"

"Why?"

"I need to take you somewhere important this weekend."

"Where?"

"You answer me first."

"Why?" she asked, looking annoyed.

Despite that, she turned me on.

Her eyes darted to the bulge in my pants.

"If you answer my question quickly, you can leave the kitchen."

"I have nothing pressing."

"Great." I placed my coffee cup on the counter and looked at her. "Start packing. We're flying out this evening."

"To where?"

"Hawaii."

"What? Why?"

"We're getting married."

Speechless, she blinked at me.

"When we come back, you'll be Mrs. Mount."

CHAPTER TWENTY-EIGHT

VANESSA

I'D NEVER FLOWN first class, never mind on a private plane. Apparently, Natalie's husband, Grayson, owned this plane, which he allowed his friends to use. It baffled me how the wealthy folks lived.

I wiggled in the comfortable seat as I flipped through a wedding gown magazine that Attikus had given me. The man thought of everything. He'd already given me a website to look through, but this magazine offered dresses from several boutiques on Maui.

"Do you want anything to drink?" Attikus asked, sitting across from me, looking through a folder.

"No."

"Are you still mad?" He placed the folder down.

"You could've given me a heads up about what you were planning. This is *our* wedding. I want a say in it too."

I was used to doing everything, so it was a relief to have him take over this wedding planning. After we sealed the deal, perhaps I could share more information with him. I didn't want him to back out once I revealed I was breaking my mom out of prison and his wife could be imprisoned. That could be too much for any husband to accept.

"I was trying to help you. You're dealing with a lot. Do you want me to ask the pilot to turn around, and we can reorganize the wedding?"

"No." I rolled my eyes. He knew I wouldn't waste time like that. "What else do you have planned? I want to see the agenda."

He smirked and pulled out a paper from the folder he was looking at. I glanced at the organized document. We had an appointment with Happily Ever After Boutique after we landed.

A justice of the peace would fly in tomorrow to meet us for the ceremony in the afternoon. Then a photographer would take photos of us. He had a dinner reservation at some restaurant on the island. Nothing was scheduled for Sunday or Monday, and we'd fly back on Monday evening.

Astounded, I looked up and met his eyes.

"I left two days open for my wife to do as she pleased."

"Where did you find the time to organize all of this?" I asked.

"I have several assistants who help me run my businesses. I told them what I needed, and they got it done. Like I said, you were stressed."

"You're doing so much for me that you're neglecting your greenhouse."

He shrugged. "I'll work on it soon. There's no rush. The HH-Pods will be available for everyone to purchase by the end of the year."

I remembered reading about it on the Healthy Horizon website. "What are you planting?"

"Anything I can eat." He eyed me. "Feel free to help whenever you want."

"I might take you up on that offer."

"I don't want my fiancée to look anxious in her photos," he said. "Push all your worries away for the next few days."

The image of the severed finger popped into my head. "Do you know who the finger belongs to yet?"

"Yes."

"Who?" I leaned into the table that separated us. "Why didn't you tell me?"

"Because of this." He pressed a finger to the space between my furrowed eyebrows. "You're stressed again. I only found out yesterday."

I recalled him mentioning he'd had a bad day yesterday. "So you kept the news to yourself to protect me from anxiety?"

"What's wrong with that? Isn't that what a caring fiancé should do?"

I wanted to retort that this was a fake relationship and he didn't need to go overboard. But my heart softened toward him. No one had ever been this thoughtful or protective of me.

"Nothing's wrong. You make me look like I'm failing in the fiancée category."

His eyes darkened with mischief. "You can always make it up to me later. I'll take a rain check."

How could he still joke like this?

I didn't reply to that comment. "Whose finger was it?"

"You don't need to know."

"I certainly do." I gaped at him. "It was sent to my grand opening. That was a message. We're in this together, aren't we? You agreed to help me, but I'm not going to sit here and do nothing if someone is threatening you or me."

Something shifted in his eyes. "What would you do if someone threatened your fiancé?"

"I'm an artist, Attikus. I have extremely creative ways to hurt my enemies."

"You've piqued my interest, Lily Pad." A sly smile tilted onto his lips. "How?"

"If I tell you, I might incriminate myself."

"It's okay. I won't tell a soul." He pressed a finger to his lips.

"Let's just say that a pencil, pen, or paintbrush can be a useful weapon." I pursed my lips. "I'll attack when they least expect it." Pretending to hold an invisible paintbrush in my hand, I stabbed it into the air. "Unpredictability is an advantage."

"You sound like a war general who's been strategizing an attack plan."

He had no idea how many sleepless nights I'd experienced trying to find a way out of this mess. I'd envisioned several ways to retaliate against those who had hurt my mom and me. It was my therapy to live out the fantasy in my mind.

"When you're surrounded by dangerous people, you have no choice but to come up with several attack plans . . . and several escape plans."

His expression shifted, and I could tell he wanted to ask me a question. But he said, "I should be extra careful around you."

"You should," I said. "I have to protect my assets."

He smiled, knowing I'd repeated his words.

"So whose finger was it? I'll keep asking you until you tell me."

"My high school principal."

"What?" My eyes widened. "What does he have to do with me or the gallery?"

"That's what I'm trying to figure out. Maybe the package was meant for me."

No name was on the package, but I'd assumed it was for me. Even so, something seemed off.

"Let's not talk about this anymore, okay?" He leaned back, looking casual and handsome. "We're heading to our wedding, so let's put the stress aside so we can relax. We both need a vacation."

I couldn't remember the last time I'd been on vacation. My mom's freedom and the blackmail had loomed over me for so long that I had become used to the stress.

"Okay," I said.

"Have you been to Hawaii?"

"No."

"Do you have any idea what you want to do for those unscheduled days?"

"Not yet. Let's play it by ear and see what happens. Sometimes, it's best to let things be."

Though I could see something swirling in his eyes, he said nothing.

Attikus was a scheming man who fascinated and terrified me. What if I wasn't careful enough and fell into one of his traps?

"What are you scheming about?"

"What makes you ask that?" He tapped his fingers on the manila folder.

"I can see it in your eyes."

"I had a plan, and it had nothing to do with you." He reached across the table and grabbed my hand. "But now it has *everything* to do with you." His gaze intensified as he kissed my hand and each of my fingers.

I couldn't take my eyes from his lips nibbling my skin. I sucked in a breath, trying to control the moan that wanted to come out. "What do you mean?"

"Would you believe me if I said you're the reason I have to reorganize my life?" He opened my palm and dropped a kiss on it. "You have beautiful hands and elegant fingers."

I lost all train of thought. All I could think about was him standing shirtless in the kitchen with the knit pants hanging low on his hips.

"You have a beautiful face and an exceptional body," I said before I could stop myself.

Realizing my mistake, I tried to yank my hand from his grip, but he wouldn't let it go. A wide smile stretched his face, transforming it. He was gorgeous when he smiled like that.

"You're welcome to explore it anytime you want." His eyes sparked. "I think we should do a lot of exploring in the next few days. What happens in Maui stays in Maui."

I couldn't believe what he was proposing. I wasn't thinking correctly and feared I'd say something I'd regret.

So the safest reply I came up with was, "We can explore snorkeling."

This time, he released my hand. I busied myself in the magazine and looked at the same page for the rest of the flight.

Attikus turned on his laptop and began working as if the provocative conversation and crazy proposal hadn't occurred. He was pushing my buttons, but why?

I scolded myself for even considering the proposal. This was our vacation—my escape from reality. Could I have a moment of fun without repercussions? Was that what he meant? Was I reading too much into his offer? Was this vacation exempt from the contract? Did I want it to be?

Stop it with the madness, Vanessa.

Then the pilot announced we'd be landing in twenty minutes.

CHAPTER TWENTY-NINE

ATTIKUS

VANESSA and I had eloped to get married. It was better this way. My mom and sister wouldn't like it, but they'd forgive me when I gave them the news after the fact.

I sat inside Happily Ever After Boutique, waiting for Vanessa to try on her dress. We'd arranged a private appointment, so no one else was there.

While I sipped the champagne offered by the manager, I thought back to our conversation. I wasn't lying to Vanessa when I told her I'd rearranged my life because of her. I didn't fully understand why I had done it. All I knew was that I *had* to protect her. In doing so, I had to shift a few things on my priority list so that Vanessa was at the top. Somehow, she had become more important than Ashton. Nothing had swayed my vendetta until her.

The attraction between us had grown exponentially. I couldn't wait for her to admit she wanted me.

After having her in my home, I couldn't imagine anyone else there. This morning had been a lovely surprise I didn't know I needed. I woke up early like I usually did. While making coffee, my security system informed me someone was in the yard. The motion detector had picked up squirrels, rabbits, and groundhogs before, but when I went to check on the computer, I saw my fiancée skipping in the yard and talking to the flowers. She had those curlers in her hair that looked ridiculous yet insanely sexy. I never thought hair curlers would turn me on, but since Vanessa, I found myself attracted to odd things. Her thin T-shirt had given me an unforgettable view of her gorgeous rack. I stood frozen as she danced and skipped in the yard outside the kitchen, my dick hard.

I wanted to strip her so I could touch and taste those breasts. This unpredictable woman had brought me more joy than I could ever have imagined.

The door to the changing room opened, and Vanessa walked out, knocking the breath out of me. I swore my heart stopped beating for a moment as I absorbed her beauty in the elegant gown that hugged her body and flared out at the bottom.

Smiling, she twirled. "What do you think?"

This was the dress she'd picked from the website and the dress I'd had in mind.

"It's perfect." I got up from the chair, grabbed my cane, and walked over to her. "You're perfect. Stunning."

"The dress is gorgeous on you," said Chloe, the manager. "It's from our new collection."

"You think so?" she asked, then leaned in and whispered, "The price is too much for you-know-what."

"I don't care about that. If you love this dress, get it."

She chewed on her bottom lip and glanced at herself in the mirror. "Let's try on the other two dresses." She turned to me. "I'll decide after."

The other two dresses didn't suit her the way the first dress did. Her eyes didn't light up, but she liked the more affordable price tag, saying she didn't want me to waste money on a fake wedding. I'd pay anything to see her wear that perfect dress and promise herself to me.

"Get the first dress," I told her. "I like it better on you."

"I have to agree," Chloe said. "Other women have tried it on, but it doesn't look as good on them. I'm not saying it to make a sale. It's the truth."

Vanessa offered her a warm smile. "The other two are nice as well." She looked at the dresses hanging on the rack.

"I know you prefer the same dress I do." I inhaled a breath. "If you choose another, I'll buy all three."

Her mouth dropped open, and Chloe looked to the floor, hiding her smile.

"That's wasteful and makes no sense at all." Vanessa pouted.

"What's wasteful and makes no sense is *not* buying the dress you love for *your* wedding, Lily Pad." I offered Chloe my credit card. "Ring it up."

Chloe looked at Vanessa. "Would you like to look at the shoes, veils, or jewelry?"

Vanessa glared at me for a moment. When she knew I wouldn't budge, she sighed. "Okay. Let's rack up his credit card so he can stop being so bossy."

Chloe whispered, "Most women want their men to shower them lavishly. You don't?"

"I'm not most women. I'm an artist. I'm used to being poor."

After paying for the dress, shoes, veil, and jewelry, we left the boutique to explore the surrounding retail area.

"Should we take everything with us now?" Vanessa asked outside on the street.

"No, someone will take care of it. A hair and makeup team is arriving tomorrow morning. They'll bring the dress."

She stared at me and shook her head. "You've planned everything, huh?"

"I'm a master at it."

"You're the maverick, an unconventional man who likes to do radical things like buy expensive wedding gowns for a fake wedding."

She knew me more than she realized.

"I've always been an outsider," I said. "The norm is too boring. Just enjoy this vacation with me. Don't worry about anything."

The weather in Maui couldn't have been better. Vanessa had worn khaki capris with a floral shirt. I wore jeans and an aqua polo shirt.

I bought a pink lei made of orchids and plumeria for her, and she bought me a jasmine lei.

"Stop paying for me."

"I don't mind."

"But I mind. Just because you have all the money in the world doesn't mean you should spend it carelessly."

"It's not careless when I'm spending it on my stunning fiancée. She deserves to be spoiled."

"I can't argue with you."

I wrapped an arm around her shoulders. "That's why you shouldn't. You should obey my every demand."

She laughed and elbowed me in the ribs. "Dream on, Whistler."

We walked to a beach with tables and umbrellas. Several vendors sold food on the side. A band played in a nearby restaurant.

"I haven't had that in a while." Vanessa gestured to the vendor selling coconut drinks.

We found a table with an umbrella.

"You sit." She pointed to the chair took my cane, and

leaned it against the table. "Let me treat you to a coconut drink, okay?"

"Okay. Since I'm *obeying* you, does that mean I get a reward later?"

"Yeah, a *straw* to drink from the coconut." She smirked.

No woman had made me smile more than her.

As I sat and watched her walk up to the vendor to place her order, peace filled my heart. I hadn't felt that in a long time. I inhaled the ocean breeze and took in the pretty blue sky.

As she walked back, a man wearing a red backpack rushed up to her and shoved her to the ground. Anger shot through me as I clasped my cane, rushing over to her. No one else was near to help her.

"Get off me!" She scratched him.

I whacked him on the head with my cane and yanked him off her.

The man looked at me with glazed eyes. "Must kill!" He whipped out a pocketknife and swung it at me.

I dodged him and tripped over the coconut Vanessa had dropped. He leaped onto me, but I punched him. His nose cracked, and blood poured out of it, but he showed no pain.

Vanessa picked up my cane and whacked his back. "Help us!"

Her scream for help appeared to enrage him even more. I shoved my knee into his balls. That should have been a painful blow, but he rolled off me and lunged at Vanessa.

I gripped his leg, making him fall.

Three men approached and helped me subdue the madman. They held him down by the legs, arms, and shoulders while I examined Vanessa.

"Are you okay?" I asked her.

Though her hands trembled, she said, "I'm fine."

The police arrived and apprehended the man.

"The fucker is high," said the man with the purple shorts who had helped us.

Two EMTs examined and released us.

"You have a cut on your ankle!" Vanessa exclaimed in concern. She crouched on the ground to examine the minor cut I didn't even feel.

She huffed, looking toward the ambulance where the madman was restrained. We could still hear him shouting nonsense.

I'd gotten his identity from the EMT and had already passed it along to my team. Who was he? Why did he attack Vanessa? Was this a random event?

"Come on." She offered her hand for support. "Lean on me. I'll drive back to the house."

I slung an arm around her as she assisted me back to the car. Though my cut didn't affect my walk, I took advantage of the opportunity to let my fiancée take care of me.

"Does it hurt?" she asked when I settled into the car.

"Not really."

Vanessa rolled her eyes. "You don't have to pretend to be all macho if it hurts." She pulled the Land Rover into the street and headed to our private oasis, which wasn't far from the shopping area. "Everyone gets hurt, and it's okay to say so. You won't embarrass yourself."

I supposed it would be inconsiderate of me not to comply with my concerned fiancée. It wasn't my fault she wanted to hear me moan in pain, even though I wasn't experiencing any.

"I can massage your ankle with the hot and cold ointment. Where's the closest drugstore?" she asked.

"The medicine cabinet at home is fully stocked. There should be some in there."

Vanessa pulled into the driveway, got out, and rounded the hood to open the door for me, offering her hand to assist me.

I'd never received this kind of attention from any woman I'd dated. I could get used to it. Once inside, she helped me into the living room. I pretended my leg gave out and fell onto the couch, dragging her with me.

"Oh, my gosh! Are you all right?" She pushed herself up, sitting on my lap.

"I'm fine." I held her in place when she wanted to get off. "Don't move. I need a moment to breathe."

"Does it hurt if I move?"

No. "A little."

She flicked me an inquisitive look. "Are you misbehaving?"

"I wanted to know what my fiancée would feel like sitting on my lap. This was the perfect opportunity."

Vanessa narrowed her eyes. "You got hurt because of me. So I'm going to be nice to you and sit here for a bit. Then I'm going to head back out to the car to retrieve your cane." She shifted and straddled me. "Is this better, Whistler?"

"A lot better." I gripped her hips with my hands. My cock grew, and she gasped, looking at me. "You do this to me all the time."

Her eyes darkened. "All the time?"

"Every time I think of you."

"Really?" She moved her hips back and forth, driving me crazy.

"Don't stop." My hands lowered her buttocks. "I've forgotten all about the pain."

"Will you be okay for the wedding ceremony?" She gyrated her hips.

I gathered every ounce of control so I didn't burst. "Nothing will stop me from marrying you tomorrow." I jerked my chin to the beach beyond the sliding door. "It's going to be out there."

She placed a hand on my cheek. "Thanks for planning this."

I remembered her trembling hands earlier. "Are you really okay after the attack?"

She got off my lap and sat next to me, her hand still in my grip. "I'm okay now. The attack brought back an awful memory."

"Want to tell me about it?"

She looked at me. "Maybe after the wedding. We're on vacation, so I don't want my past to ruin it."

I wanted to break the man's bones for making her suffer. What had happened to her? Did this have anything to do with the man she claimed to have murdered? That was a story I needed to know sooner rather than later.

"When you're ready, I want to know everything."

She smiled warmly. "Let me get your cane and the ointment."

CHAPTER THIRTY

VANESSA

EVEN THOUGH THIS was a fake wedding, nerves still wreaked havoc in my stomach. I should be calm since this wasn't a real ceremony. No one would be in attendance except me, Attikus, and the justice of the peace.

The gorgeous Kealoha sisters, who owned Maui's Beauty Salon, came early this morning with the dress and everything I'd bought at the Happily Ever After Boutique.

In my bedroom, Alanna, the older sister wearing a long yellow dress, worked on my hair. She added big waves, piled up my hair, and secured the veil.

She stepped back, studying her work. "Beautiful."

When the younger sister, Nalani, finished my makeup, I didn't recognize myself. I'd never had a professional do my hair or makeup for any special events. I usually did my own for art exhibits. I felt like a celebrity.

After the sisters helped me get into my wedding gown and put on my jewelry, I dug out cash from my purse to tip them.

Smiling, Alanna shook her head. "Mr. Mount has already paid us with an exceptional tip."

"You're such a stunning bride. Thank you for letting us be part of your special day." Nalani beamed.

"Thank you for making me feel and look like a princess."

"It's easy when the bride is beautiful and not a Bridezilla." Nalani made a face. "We've dealt with all kinds of brides. You're the calmest."

If only they could see the wild party inside my stomach. If only they knew this wasn't an actual ceremony.

"Let's check on the groom before we head out." Alanna headed for the bedroom where Attikus was getting dressed. I hadn't seen him since last night.

We didn't follow the tradition of not seeing each other prior to the event. Times had changed, and this fake ceremony didn't warrant any cherished tradition.

Was he nervous?

I gasped, realizing we didn't prepare or review any vows.

As the Kealoha sisters said goodbye, they reminded me that their photographer friend, Hoku, would arrive soon.

I waited to hear the door click closed and walked out of the bedroom in my new heels, wondering where my groom was. I walked as quietly as I could to the bedroom at the other end of the house. This marvelous home had four bedrooms with oceanfront views. Being a gentleman, Attikus had given me the primary bedroom to sleep in last night. We'd spent some time in the living room with me massaging his ankle. I'd learned the technique from an online video when I twisted my ankle during college.

Attikus seemed to enjoy the massage. Something strange had occurred yesterday. Maybe it had started when he'd spotted me in his backyard. Was it only yesterday? Gosh, it seemed like a while ago. It didn't matter when, where, what, or how. What mattered was that something had shifted between us.

Last night, we'd talked about random things as though we'd been dating for years. Perhaps being away from home allowed me—us—to detach physically and mentally. That was why people went on vacation.

I didn't mind massaging the ointment into his ankle since he'd been injured because of me. The cut was minor, but it could've been a lot worse. What if that crazy man had broken his ankle again? Attikus had mentioned that his ankle and knee were healing from a wound he'd acquired in his youth. I couldn't live with the guilt if he had broken them again.

The experience had been traumatic, but I'd enjoyed Attikus taking advantage of his injury by pulling me onto his lap and had played along with my mischievous fiancé.

Two could play that game.

Like a fool, I stood in front of his bedroom door, giggling to myself.

"You won't find me in the door, Lily Pad."

I jumped at the deep voice behind me. Heat blossomed on my face as I turned to see Attikus leaning against the wall in the lounge area, staring at me. How long had he been standing there? He looked sexy and sophisticated in his black tux. His eyes raked over me, moving slowly over my body. His magnetism was something I'd never experienced. I couldn't break his gaze or step away—not that I wanted to.

Attikus pushed himself off the wall and walked over to me. My heart skipped at how gorgeous he was. Tall, handsome, powerful, mysterious, and cunning. The list went on and on.

He took my hand in his and kissed it. "You're absolutely breathtaking."

I swallowed, finding my breath again. "You're dashing, Whistler."

"Ready to tie the knot with me?" His eyes beamed.

"Where's your cane?"

"I don't need it for the ceremony."

"Did you ask the justice of the peace to prepare a generic vow?"

"Everything is all set. Just relax."

Simplicity was the word of the day. We stood in the backyard with the beach behind us. Pots of exotic flowers surrounded the lounge area. Apparently, he'd instructed people to decorate the backyard early this morning.

Hoku arrived and took photos of the wedding décor, setting, and of us checking out the area. Attikus offered me a gorgeous bouquet of lilies and orchids. I had forgotten about the bouquet. How could I have overlooked such an important thing?

"Thank you for remembering," I said, gazing at the flowers. I placed the bouquet down, grabbed the boutonniere, and secured it to his lapel.

"Like I said, just enjoy the day."

The justice of the peace stepped outside and offered us a friendly smile.

"It's you," I said. "You work for the Mount Museum."

"I do." The justice of the peace smiled. "I'm Agnes Sullivan, and I'll be conducting your ceremony. It's a fun side job. So when Attikus asked me for a last-minute favor, I couldn't resist it."

"Thank you for accommodating us," I said.

"He's a good man, and I'd do anything for him." Agnes offered Attikus a hug. "You look dashing."

"Thanks for being here." He smiled.

Hoku positioned himself for photos of us exchanging vows. Velvety butterflies fluttered inside me. Was this what all brides experienced? The nerves, the excitement . . . and the fear that this blissful moment wouldn't last.

"All right, let's get started." Agnes nodded at me. "Repeat

after me."

"I, Vanessa Lam, can create the most extraordinary painting," I said. "But when *you* entered my life, you became the paintbrush I couldn't live without."

I looked at him, speechless at the power and beauty of the short vow. Agnes hadn't written this. From the look in his eyes, I knew he had. Why? Where had he found the time to write this vow? Had he written it for someone else and used it for this fake wedding?

He looked at me as though he understood the questions floating in my head. He smiled and squeezed my hand.

"I, Attikus Mount, cannot resist a soul-searching masterpiece. So when I saw you, I recognized my soul. That was the day my life started. I cannot wait to see the masterpiece we'll create together."

My heart burst with love and emotions I couldn't comprehend. Why was I so emotional when this wasn't real? But it seemed too real to me. When he looked at me and spoke those loving words, I couldn't help but accept them.

Agnes said, "Do you, Attikus, agree to color Vanessa's life with the rainbow from now until the end of days?

"I do," he said.

Agnes turned to me and asked the same.

"I do," I replied.

I didn't know what Attikus was feeling, but my heart was bursting with emotion. Why had he written such a beautiful vow for something that wasn't real? This marriage wasn't supposed to be this serious. We would separate in six months. Did he always put this much effort into everything he did?

"Do you, Vanessa, agree to be Attikus's forever masterpiece?" Agnes asked.

"I do." I laughed.

Attikus reached into his jacket and pulled out a set of rings.

I'd forgotten about the rings too! *Ugh.* A spark gleamed in his eyes, understanding my reaction. Goodness, I wasn't good at this wedding stuff. The girls had asked me about the ring before, and I still hadn't remembered to inquire.

He slipped the ring on my finger, and I did the same to him. I lifted the ring for a closer examination. I'd never seen anything like it. It was twisted, petrified wood molded into a ring.

"You may kiss the bride."

Attikus pulled me to him, and we kissed. His lips were soft on mine at first, nibbling, tasting. Then he deepened the kiss, and I lost my balance. His arms tightened around me as the kiss lingered. When he drew back, desire darkened his eyes.

"Okay, lovebirds. Enjoy your day. I'll be enjoying my time here on the beach for the next week. See you back in Providence."

It sounded like Hoku snapped a gazillion pictures of us in the backyard before we kicked off our shoes and strode out to the beach. Two hours later, Hoku left, and we relaxed in the lounge chairs. Though I didn't have to mingle like actual brides and grooms who had real wedding banquets, I was exhausted from everything—hair, makeup, getting dressed, the vows, and the surge of emotions. The nerves had added a layer of unnecessary stress.

He looked at me. "Want to go out or stay in for dinner?"

I didn't know why, but a thought popped into my head—an outrageous idea.

"Stay in."

"You're missing a diamond ring," he said. "I haven't had time to get you one yet."

He'd already spent so much on me and this wedding.

Shaking my head, I smiled. "No need for that, Attikus. This

petrified wood is perfect. I don't need anything else. Where did you get the set?"

"I know an artist who specializes in petrified wood. I asked him to create them for me from a sketch."

I looked at him. "You sketched them? You can draw?"

He interlaced his fingers with mine. "Lily Pad, there are a lot of things you don't know about me."

"I guess so. Have you always drawn? What kinds of things do you draw?" This man fascinated me more and more. I knew he loved art because of the museum, but I didn't know he could also create it.

He considered me for a moment. "It's not a cheerful story, so I don't want to ruin our wedding. How about I share it with you later?"

I wanted to ask when later would be, but I didn't want to pressure him. He hadn't pressured me on topics I didn't want to discuss.

As though he knew what I was thinking, he said, "I'll tell you my story if you tell me what the madman triggered in you, okay?"

An uncomfortable feeling overcame me. I knew I had to tell him sooner or later. When I looked into his eyes, I didn't see judgment, just honesty.

"Okay."

"Want to go snorkeling and exploring the island? Then we can order dinner to eat out here and watch the sunset."

"Sounds wonderful."

CHAPTER THIRTY-ONE

ATTIKUS

I'D VISITED Maui many times before and loved the magic of the island. But this visit was different because of Vanessa. She'd made the trip unforgettable. I saw more of the island than I had on all the other occasions combined.

During our snorkeling adventure, more fish came out to greet us. I'd only seen a few during my previous experiences when I'd gone alone. Not only that, but a friendly dolphin swam close to us. It was so magical. I didn't know what to say. Unlike me, who watched in awe, Vanessa clicked her tongue as though speaking to the animal. It clicked back. Joy radiated from Vanessa as she conversed with the dolphin. A boat in the distance roared, startling the dolphin. It disappeared into the water.

We swam back to the shore, returned the snorkeling equipment we'd rented, changed into our casual clothes, and headed to pick up dinner.

"You were good with the dolphin. Have you swum with them before?"

"No." She smiled. "I was surprised too. We were blessed that it came to us. It was an auspicious sign."

"You spoke to it."

She laughed. "I've watched videos of people swimming with dolphins, and that's what they do to communicate. Dolphins are intelligent creatures." She shrugged, looking ahead. "I couldn't afford vacations, never mind pay to swim with dolphins. So I fantasized about whatever I wanted to experience by watching videos of the actual event or through my imagination."

"Is there anything you want to do while we're here?"

A sign promoting the botanical garden appeared in the distance.

Her face brightened. "Are you in the mood to visit a garden? It might be boring to—"

"Let's go," I said, making the turn to the garden. "So far, it's been an adventure with you. If a bear comes out to greet us, don't start talking to it, okay?"

Laughter erupted in the car. "There aren't bears or wolves here."

The garden wasn't crowded because it was only open for another two hours. We walked down the path, taking in the various exotic plants.

"Why didn't you pursue a botany career?"

Vanessa stopped and looked at me. The joy in her eyes vanished.

"I had to research my wife," I said, pulling her close. "You searched me, didn't you?" I massaged her shoulder blades. "I want to know everything about you."

"My life isn't that beautiful, Attikus."

"I don't define beauty like other people. Besides, we all have ugly things in our past." I brushed a knuckle down her cheek. "Wait until you hear about my past."

A small smile crept onto her lips as we continued down a path full of unique ferns. "I still love plants." We stopped by a bed of flowers, ferns, and tiny mushrooms growing on a log covered in moss. "I became an artist because of circumstances."

"You have a talent for it."

"You don't realize what you have until you step out of your comfort zone." She watched an orange monarch butterfly land on a fern. "Plants have taught me so much about life. On my lowest days, I look at a flower, and it gives me hope. I admire its ability to just be."

I stared at her while she examined the plants. She became more beautiful as she described what I had always taken for granted. I didn't look at the flowers or trees the way she did. After my family was murdered, vengeance was my hope. It gave me the strength to find those responsible and make them pay. Vengeance had consumed me. But at this moment, it stayed off to the side. There was no room for that darkness here.

"Maybe that's why people say a walk in nature is the best medicine. You're teaching me a different way of looking at plants."

She snorted. "Me? Teach a billionaire like you?"

"Billionaires don't know everything, especially things that money can't buy."

Vanessa inhaled a deep breath and released it slowly. "Nature has a certain unapologetic quality. It simply *is*." She walked over to a eucalyptus tree with its rainbow bark and glanced up. "Trees are majestic in their steadiness, maturity, and wisdom." She walked over to an area full of plumeria flowers. "Flowers grow with no self-doubt or reluctance. They're rooted to a pragmatic way of living—of common sense."

"Many people lack that these days."

Nodding, she grabbed a twig and poked it into the soil. "It's in the dirt where we find ourselves and our purpose. At least, that's where I found myself."

Those words exposed something raw and sad about Vanessa. What had happened to her? "Are you defining dirt as the soil plants need to live, or are you looking at it as something you're ashamed of? Like the dirt you want to keep outside your home?"

She met my eyes. "Why are you so smart?"

"Because I'm talking to an intelligent woman who's making me think."

"Let's just say dirt has many meanings. I've learned to accept and appreciate its wisdom."

I placed my hands on her shoulders, spinning her around.

"What are you doing?" she asked.

"Trying to make sure you're the same Vanessa who came here with me. She seems to have transformed into a new person."

"You're being silly." She rolled her eyes. "Nothing's changed. You just haven't really looked at me until now."

Oh, I've been looking, Lily Pad.

She pressed a finger to my forehead. "You were too busy planning." Something gleamed in her eyes. "Let's go home and have dinner and enjoy the sunset before it's too late."

"What do you want to eat?"

"You decide. I'll be happy with whatever."

She took my hand, swaying it back and forth as we headed back to the parking lot. "Are you in the mood for another adventure?"

"What kind?"

"It's dangerous, and we can both get hurt," she said. "It will require your absolute trust in me."

I stared at her. "What do you have in mind?"

"I'll only tell you if you promise me one thing."

What was going on?

"I'll promise my wife anything." Mischief glittered in her eyes, and I wanted to kiss her so badly. "Tell me."

A serious expression splashed onto her face. "You can't tell anyone about it. What happens in Maui stays in Maui, okay?"

"Are you planning on murdering someone?"

She laughed. "No."

"Then we won't have a problem. When are we heading to this so-called dangerous adventure?"

"Tomorrow at four in the morning."

I widened my eyes in horror. "If that's the case, then we need to hurry and eat so we can go to bed."

"That's right," she said.

I didn't know what my wife had planned, but I loved seeing the happiness on her face. I wished she could be like this all the time.

As we got to the car, my phone buzzed. I looked at it and frowned.

"What's wrong?"

"Nothing important."

"Don't lie to your wife. We're in this together. I need you to trust me if you want me to trust you."

"I do trust you, but I don't want to ruin our wedding day with upsetting news."

"Didn't you learn anything from our walk in the garden? Life is full of unapologetic events. You can't stop it in the same way you can't stop a tree from growing. Look at the issue for what it is, and we go from there."

I wished I'd met her years ago.

"It's news about the man who attacked us on the beach."

She gasped. "Who is he?"

"A former CIA agent named Ryan Evans."

"What?" She gaped at me.

"He's not a simple, unapologetic weed now, is he?" I teased, trying to hold on to the joy and amusement.

She smirked. "Shut up."

When we got into the car, I said, "I need to do some research on him. And I'm not going to talk about him for the rest of the night. So don't ask. I just want to have dinner with my wife."

Her lips formed into a pout. "Okay, Mr. Mount."

CHAPTER THIRTY-TWO

VANESSA

THIS VACATION WAS EXACTLY what I needed. I'd gotten closer to Attikus and found myself wanting more than what was good for me. The contract stated that there was to be no touching or kissing. These were *my* requirements. But the attraction between us was like wildfire, burning out of control. At least for me, it was.

I wanted to kiss him, touch him, and know what it felt like to have his body on mine. Was I just horny since I hadn't been with anyone for a while? Or was it being in paradise that made me believe anything was possible? That I could live out my fantasy and not deal with the consequences?

Attikus was busy setting up the food outside while I stared at the silky dress Natalie had given me as part of the For Your Heart Only mission. She also got me a set of bridal lingerie I didn't think I'd ever wear. I held up the ivory sheer lace bra, wondering how the cups would ever cover my breasts. I didn't have large breasts, but they weren't tiny either. The thong was just a floral patch. My core tightened as I imagined this evening with Attikus.

I couldn't believe he'd agreed to wake up at dawn for an adventure with me. He didn't know the dangerous adventure was for tonight, not tomorrow. *Surprise.* I held onto my courage and put on the bra and thong before I chickened out. I was breaching the contract and hoped he wouldn't say anything about it.

I glanced in the mirror, loving the new version of myself. The sexy lingerie enhanced my curves and made my breasts look bigger than they were. I slipped on the silky short dress with narrow straps and bows on the shoulders. The heels I'd worn during the wedding ceremony also worked with this dress. I added gold dangling earrings, sprayed perfume, straightened my spine, and prepared to seduce my fake husband.

This was my escape. When I returned to Providence, reality would come knocking. Our fake marriage would be announced, and the dark world would resume. I deserved a moment of fun with a man who also seemed to want me.

When I walked out to the backyard, Attikus stood at the table with his back to me. He'd changed into a sage T-shirt and athletic shorts. Strings of light glowed all around us. My heart warmed, knowing he'd prepared the serene ambiance. I'd discovered so much about him in the past few days. I feared I could travel down a dangerous path that would shatter my heart. But I couldn't help it. Did that make me stubborn or stupid?

I shoved that negative thought aside and focused on the present moment. Things could change tomorrow, and I'd deal with them then.

In the distance, the horizon glowed a warm pink as it said goodnight to the world. Nerves thrummed in my body. A sliver of mischief and happiness slid down my spine, making me release a sigh. Attikus turned, and our eyes locked. My heart quickened as his gaze slid up and down my body.

Smiling, he walked over. "You look lovely. I'm underdressed compared to you."

I looked down at his right leg. "How is your knee and ankle?"

"Fine."

"Where's your cane? Are you supposed to be walking around without it?"

"I don't need it when you're around. So don't go anywhere."

"Are you trying to be cute?"

"Do I need to try?" he asked without a hint of sarcasm.

Shaking my head, I smiled. "You're the most arrogantly handsome man I've ever met."

"You look spectacular." He tugged at a strap on my dress, and his touch sent goose bumps blossoming across my skin.

"It's my wedding night, so I figured I'd wear another dress. Like you said, it's our vacation. I'm making the best of it."

A wicked smile crept onto his lips. "Why do I feel you have a surprise for me?"

"Maybe I do."

"Tell me now." He clasped my hand. "Or I won't feed you."

"What kind of husband starves his wife?"

"The kind who's hungry for something that's not the Polynesian food on the table. The kind who's been desperate for a wedding night with his hot wife. You have no idea what kinds of things I've been dying to do to my wife, but feared she might not want them."

My heart raced. "What are you thinking?"

He shook his head. "You can't play this game with me, Lily Pad." He tipped my chin up, looking into my eyes. "You tell me, and I'll tell you."

His confession about wanting a wedding night surprised and elated me. "What happens in Maui stays in Maui?"

He lifted his hand to his mouth, locked it, and tossed the invisible key behind him. "No one will ever know."

I grinned and slid my hand around his neck. "Then give me what a wife deserves on her wedding night."

Without hesitation, he crushed his lips to mine, kissing me with desperation. My body jolted awake, molding into his arms. I moaned as he devoured my mouth, sliding his tongue inside to greet mine. Sensations bloomed in me, and I felt like a flower experiencing its first spring. This kiss was everything. This man was everything.

Urgency grew in me, and I gripped at his shirt. "Off."

He laughed into my mouth. "So demanding. I love a woman who knows what she wants."

He stripped off his shirt, revealing the firm abdomen I'd seen days ago when he'd spied on me. I ran my hands over them, learning the taut grooves, before traveling up to his strong shoulders. He watched me explore him as his gaze intensified on me. My fingers traced the powerful line of his shoulder—strong, sturdy, and stable. All qualities that drew me to him—he made me feel safe.

My gaze darted back to his abdomen as his breathing deepened.

"Done exploring?"

"No."

Attikus smiled. "It's my turn, now." He twirled me around. "I like you in dresses. It makes it easier for me to explore." He slipped his hand under the hem, gripped my ass, and gave it a squeeze. "You're wearing a thong. *Fuck*."

I bit my bottom lip. "Exactly my thoughts."

"Wicked woman," he growled.

Whatever patience Attikus had vanished as he lifted the

dress off me. The warm breeze brushed my skin, and my nipples pebbled. His shorts tented, and desire strained his face. "You should always wear sexy lingerie like this." He cupped my breasts, kneading, and watched me respond to his touch. I arched toward his hands, offering him all of me. He yanked down the cup of my bra, exposing my nipple.

Our eyes connected, and a deep yearning erupted between us. My reaction to him was carnal, primal—nature's unapologetic way of creation and reproduction. Creative energy was at its utmost. I wondered what kind of art we'd create tonight.

When his mouth closed over my nipple and sucked on it, liquid heat leaked out of me.

"Oh, my god," I moaned. "Don't stop."

My legs wobbled, and I fell onto him. His touch was like a paintbrush that brought me to life. His arms tightened around my waist as I leaned back, letting him feast on me. Fire bloomed where he tugged on my nipple, sending me into a world full of magic and possibilities.

"I need to see all of you now," he breathed. "I'm giving you an unforgettable wedding night, Lily Pad." He tossed me over his shoulders like a caveman.

"What are you doing?" I laughed in shock as he carted me off like cargo.

"Fucking my wife in our bed," he said. The dominance in his voice rippled down my body.

He stalked into his bedroom and dropped me onto the massive bed with exceptionally soft sheets. We'd been sleeping in separate bedrooms, but the rules of the game were blurred tonight.

With predatory eyes, he stared at me. He swallowed, and his Adam's apple bobbed. The sexual tension in the room throbbed. I flipped to the side and propped up on my arm, resting the side of my face on my hand.

"Strip, Whistler." I crooked a finger at him. "I need to see my husband."

He smirked and dropped his shorts and boxers, exposing his glorious cock. I gasped at the magnificent sight and crawled over to examine him. Veins corded his length, and I wrapped my fingers around him like a prize. He pulsed in my grip, hot and desperate. As I stroked him, his face transformed, struggling with restraint. I felt powerful, having this control over him.

"Like what you see?" he crooned, eyeing my hand on him.

"Very much." I pressed my thumb to the tip of his crown.

He groaned, and his thighs quaked. God, I loved seeing him teeter on the edge of his self-control. His cock twitched and increased in size. What would it feel like inside me?

He growled as I bent to kiss his tip. "You're going to make me come before I get to do everything I want with you." He clasped a hand over my wrist, lifting it away from his cock.

"I need you in my hand," I begged.

"Later," he said, his voice hoarse with desire. "I have things I want to do to you."

Goose bumps scattered down my spine.

He nudged me down on the bed. Keeping his eyes on me, he pressed a palm to my sex, massaging me. I moaned and opened my thighs wider, moving in rhythm with him. The friction increased, and the wicked smirk on his face promised a night I'd remember. I gasped as he shoved aside the floral patch covering my sex and plunged a long finger inside me.

"Attikus!" I screamed as his thick digit pummeled me.

"You're so fucking wet." Fire blazed in his darkened eyes.

I wanted to say something, but my brain cells had scattered elsewhere. When he pulled out his finger and licked it, I almost lost it.

"I've been wondering how you taste. Now, I'm addicted." He kissed me and plunged two fingers deep into my sex.

The sound of my arousal and his fingers pumping me echoed in the room. The kiss grew animalistic as our tongues, teeth, and lips clashed.

I broke for breath and bit his shoulder. "You're a wild beast."

He pushed my knees up, draped them over his shoulders, and stared at my center. "So beautiful." He swiped his tongue over me once and groaned. "God, you taste so fucking good." He licked me again and again, opening my folds and plunging in with his tongue.

I gripped the sheets to anchor me as he buried his face between my thighs, devouring me. My fingers tugged at his hair. Part of me wanted him to slow down, but the other part needed him to increase his feasting. I licked my dry lips as my head thrashed from side to side, trying to find something to stabilize myself. I was on the edge, with nothing to secure the fall.

His mouth and tongue worked their magic, and my thighs trembled as a massive orgasm rolled through me. I shuddered hard and clung to his head. "Attikus!"

"That's right, baby. Come for me." He sucked on my bud, and I arched into him.

My ears rang, and my eyes fluttered closed. I heard the crinkle of a wrapper, but I was too enraptured in bliss to pay much attention.

Attikus lifted my ass. "Look at me, Vanessa."

I opened my eyes and saw his condom-covered cock positioned at my entrance. Anticipation overcame and invigorated me.

He held my gaze as he slid into me. A primal moan escaped him as he plunged deeper and deeper. My muscles tightened at the sight of his massive size. He thrust in and out, and my body welcomed each thrust. We stared at each other as we exchanged energy and power, giving each other what we needed. His hardness needed my softness, and I needed his steadiness.

His face was strained with passion as he bent to kiss me. "Is this what you had planned, Lily Pad? Seducing me like this?"

"Yes."

He growled and pumped into me harder.

CHAPTER THIRTY-THREE

ATTIKUS

VANESSA WAS the catalyst that changed everything for me. This vacation was supposed to solidify our fake marriage. We weren't supposed to be fucking at all. The kissing during the ceremony was a one-off, as specified in the contract. I was supposed to keep my distance from her, even though I knew that was impossible.

You added a beneficial line with the fine print.

Still, I'd tried to honor the contract as she knew it but failed miserably. My gorgeous wife hadn't made it any easier when she wanted to have an unforgettable wedding night. The way she looked in her ivory lingerie and how she responded to my touch proved this wouldn't be over after Maui. But I wasn't about to tell her that.

I figured we needed time to deal with this powerful attraction before it burst out of control. But now I'd tasted her, and my dick was inside her, I couldn't stop wanting her. Her sweet and tangy taste still lingered in my mouth. I breathed in her unique scent, and my entire body heated a few more degrees. Being connected to her like this made me recall a longing I'd forgotten. A passion that an unfortunate event had snuffed years ago. Now that lingering ember had caught fire, there was no going back.

Grunting, I pummeled her sex, loving the sound of skin slapping against skin. Each thrust was a burst of flame kindling the ember.

Her muscles squeezed my cock. "You're so thick. I love it."

"So good, baby." I crooned, staring at her in awe. She was mesmerizing and all mine.

She reached up and dragged me down to her swollen lips for a kiss. How could I resist her?

"I love the way you fill me."

My heart quivered. "Glad I could satisfy my wife tonight."

She gyrated her hips, taking me deeper. My orgasm rose to the surface, waiting for me.

"Fuck me," she begged. "Give me everything."

I slammed into her, giving her what she needed. My orgasm shot through me, knocking the air out of my lungs.

"Vanessa!" I cried as pleasure ripped me apart. Energy ricocheted through me as I lowered my body to hers. "Fuck." I moaned as the momentum continued.

I remained still, trying to fill my lungs with air.

Finally, the orgasm ebbed, and I rolled off her. "That was cataclysmic, Lily Pad."

"Indeed, it was." She smiled warmly.

I gathered her into my arms, kissing her slowly, tenderly. She caressed my face as our tongues explored each other. A tenderness I'd never experienced stirred between us, and my heart ached. I didn't want to know what it was trying to tell me.

I drew back and looked at her. "Let me get a towel to clean you."

She smiled and propped up on an elbow, watching me get

off the bed and rush into the bathroom. After cleaning myself, I returned with a fresh towel.

"I'll do it," she said with a hint of blush on her cheeks.

After all the things we'd just done, she was embarrassed at me cleaning her?

"It would be an honor to clean my cum from my wife. I've seen and tasted all your secrets, and I want more."

"Is this something you do often?" she asked.

"I've never been married until now," I said, not answering her direct question.

CHAPTER THIRTY-FOUR

VANESSA

I SNUGGLED INTO ATTIKUS, my heart beating erratically. A sense of dread overcame me. I thought giving in to my desires for this one night would satisfy my craving for his touch. But I'd made things worse.

Don't think about it now. Just enjoy the moment.

I could see my issues snowballing into an avalanche. It was just waiting for the moment to hit me hard. I'd have to face reality when I returned to Providence. What happened in Maui stayed in Maui.

My body tensed as tears brimmed my eyes.

Shit. What was wrong with me? Why was I being so sensitive?

Attikus shifted, looked at me, and smirked. "What's wrong, my sexy wife?"

"I'm not your real wife."

"As I recall, you sounded like a satisfied wife not long ago. Want me to remind you?" He tickled me, and I giggled. "There." He touched my lips with his fingers. "I love your smile and your laugh." His expression turned serious. "Want to tell me what's wrong?"

Oh. Gosh. I wasn't in the mood to talk about my emotional state. So I replied, "Nothing important."

He arched an eyebrow. "You're not a good liar. Tell me."

Before I could share my emotional mess, I had to sort out *why* I was feeling this way. Most of all, what did I want from Attikus? This fake marriage would end when the time came, but right now, as I lay in bed with him, I didn't want it to end. I was the one who asked for the concrete terms and conditions. But now I wished I hadn't.

Was he taking advantage of this situation like I was? This vacation was an escape for both of us. My heart shouldn't hurt. What was wrong with me?

You want him to want *you regardless of the contract.*

The stark truth of it terrified and confused me even more. Why couldn't things be simple?

"If you don't tell me. I'll keep asking." He brushed a tear away. "Did I hurt you earlier?"

"No. Not at all. You were magnificent."

Concern warred in his eyes. He wouldn't drop this topic unless I gave him a satisfying answer. This was something I had to tell him anyway.

"You asked me what triggered me that day on the beach when we were attacked." I sat up. "Ready for a story?"

"I've got all night." He straightened and took my hand in his.

As I prepared to share the horrific event in the alleyway, I shared another story that had been etched in my memory.

I stand outside Jacksonville Elementary School, waiting for Mẹ to pick me up from the after-school program. My fifth-grade science teacher, Mrs. Bumpus, is teaching us how to garden for healthy eating. There's a garden bed outside her classroom. Students can sign up to grow a vegetable.

I smile down at the cucumber plant in my hand.

Two other classmates, Miranda Sargent and Mary Forcier, stand near me. But we don't talk. I'm not friends with those mean girls.

Miranda holds her tomato plant and says, "Some kids need to know how to dress."

"Yeah." Mary glances at me and laughs. "Did your mom buy your clothes at the Goodwill store?"

I look down at my ripped jeans, plain T-shirt, and dirty old sneakers. They wore designer jeans, cool knit tops, and sneakers I could never afford. My simple clothes aren't purchased at the fancy stores in the mall. My mom works very hard to pay the rent and utilities. We don't have extra money for fancy stuff.

"Some kids need an attitude adjustment," I say. "I don't shop at snobby stores."

They roll their eyes. I don't know how the rumor started, but they know I don't have a father. They often make silly jokes about it. Just because I don't have a father doesn't mean I'm a bad kid.

I see Miranda's dad flirting with the fourth-grade teacher, Ms. Palacios, all the time. But he's married. I don't say anything because it's not my business. Miranda and Mary are mean girls who bully others. I'm not afraid of them, but I don't want detention. I don't want to make Mẹ sad.

"I bet your father saw how ugly you were at birth and left you and your mom." Miranda laughs.

Anger rises in me. "I know your father is cheating on your mom because he can't stand you."

She pouts and narrows her eyes at me. "You're such a brat."

"So are you, but worse." I return her narrow-eyed glare.

Mary glowers at me. "Everyone knows your father left you and your mom."

It's strange what these girls assume. What if my dad died, and I don't want to talk about it? But they don't have an ounce of kindness in them, so they think the worst of others.

"And everyone knows you're both stupid and cheat on your tests." I paste a smile on my face.

I've been teased about not having a father since the first grade. Kids are mean, and I hate this school. I don't have any friends here. My mom says we're moving to Rhode Island soon. I can't wait to get away from here.

Miranda stalks toward me and knocks my cucumber plant container from my hands. I do the same to hers.

She huffs. "I'm telling my mom."

"Go ahead. I'll tell mine too. Then I'll tell the principal you've been paying Kevin to do your homework." I flare my nostrils. "Try me."

Mary helps Miranda pick up her tomato plant as Miranda's mom pulls up to the curb. "Ready girls?"

"Yup!" Miranda beams.

I know Miranda won't say anything about the plant because I know her secret. Mary is just a follower and does whatever her friend tells her.

When they leave, I stand at the school entrance feeling sad and mad. I turn when I hear voices behind me. More kids come out to wait for their parents.

Mẹ reminds me to always be wary of my surroundings. She was kidnapped and forced to do bad things. Then she was raped and got pregnant with me. Sometimes, I wonder who my dad was. But I get angry when I think about him. I don't want to know him. He's a bad man.

At ten years old, I shouldn't know about these things or how babies are made, but I do. We already have sex ed in health class.

Mom says the world is cruel, and I have to be watchful. The kidnappers planned on killing my mom and the other women who were with her. But she escaped to Florida and gave birth to me. Mom loves me despite how I was conceived. She tells me I'm a miracle baby. She had polyps, and the doctor told her she couldn't have any children. But after she had me, the polyps disappeared. So she loves me because I gave her hope.

I'm protective of my mom. She must have been terrified to raise me all by herself. I hate my dad and the people who kidnapped my mom.

I see my mom's car approaching, and I walk to the curb.

"Hi, baby," she greets me.

I see anxiety in her eyes. "Is everything okay?"

She looks at me. "Remember that plan I told you about: papaya salad?

Oh, no. Nerves tighten my stomach. Papaya salad *is the code phrase for an emergency escape.

Danger is here, and we have to follow the plan she's explained many times. Mẹ drives me to a parking lot with an old warehouse and parks next to a pickup truck. The large wooden treasure chest is in the back bed. I hop on and crawl into it.

"Be quiet, okay?" Mẹ presses her fingers to her lips and covers me with folded sheets. "We'll be safe soon. I'll be in the front seat."

"Where are we going?" I ask.

"You've always wanted to go on a road trip." She smiles. "We're driving to Rhode Island."

I feel like Mẹ is hiding something from me, but there's no time to ask. Why do we have to run? Who's after us? What if that person knows we're in Rhode Island?

"I'll explain when we get there, okay?" Mom puts on a red wig and a Miami Dolphins baseball cap. Why is she in disguise?

My mom is so smart. She was a sophomore in college, studying chemistry at the University of California, Berkeley, when she was kidnapped.

I nod as I lie quietly in a treasure chest filled with clothes. Mẹ closes the lid. I look through the tiny holes on the side of the wooden chest, but I see nothing. The humid Florida air sneaks in, allowing me to breathe more easily. Then I hear women's voices, but I don't recognize them.

"We're ready." Mẹ is talking to some women, but I can't see them.

The door slams shut, and the truck roars to life. A loud boom rends the air, followed by another. The force of it rattles the chest. A few minutes later, police sirens blast to life and fly past the truck.

I don't know what exploded, but I have a feeling it has something to do with my mom.

Sighing, I looked at Attikus. "You've had a traumatic childhood." He pulled me closer. "So that's how you know Miranda."

"I was surprised when she showed up to take pictures of us for MirandaNews," I said. "She doesn't remember me. The past is in the past. She seems to have grown up since elementary school."

I still couldn't believe my elementary school bully was his ex.

He nodded. "What exploded?"

"My mom's car with two bodies in it. She made it look like we were dead." She knew someone who worked at the morgue and paid for the bodies.

"Why?" His voice carried a protective edge that made me shiver.

"I guess when my mom escaped, she blew up a large section of the warehouse where they were producing drugs. It was a tremendous loss for them. They pursued her afterward."

"What's your father's name?" Attikus asked.

"My mom told me his name is Charles Laurent, a Haitian citizen. I don't know much about him."

There wasn't a lot of information about him on the internet, so I stopped my research. I didn't want to waste my time on a man who had hurt my mom.

Nodding slowly, he kissed the side of my head.

I inhaled his comforting scent and confessed, "It was hard feeling worthy while growing up."

"The world isn't worthy of you," he said. "The way you see things and interpret them in your art tells me you have wisdom few people can understand." He shifted and looked me in the eye. "You're teaching me how to live and see life. Never think that you're unworthy. If anyone says that to you, I'll kill them."

I stared at him, appreciating his protectiveness. But I wouldn't want him to kill anyone for me. I didn't want another person I cared about in prison.

"Kids are petty. I knew I shouldn't let their words bother me, but what they said made me question my existence, you know?" I leaned into him, letting his musky scent cloak me. His skin warmed against mine, and I felt like I could tell him anything. I could share all my fears with him because everything would be okay. "That's why I'm drawn to the water lily and the lotus flower."

"How so?" He rubbed circles on my hand, soothing me.

"Because they grow from the mud—something people find disgusting." I sighed. "From the filth, something beautiful emerges."

"See how much depth is in that statement?" He tapped my chin gently. "You're worthy of everything you dream of,

Vanessa. How you're made has nothing to do with your self-worth."

His conviction in me tightened my chest.

"Do you know the difference between a water lily and a lotus?" I asked.

"They look the same to me."

"At a glance, they are. But the lotus grows taller than the lily pad, whereas the water lily sits on the lily pad."

He thought about it. "You're right. I've never paid close attention to it." He interlaced his fingers with mine. "You're the lotus—reaching above expectations."

"*The Lost Lily Pad* painting was me conveying how lost I was. I was that lily pad surrounded by the dark and without a flower."

"It's a powerful painting. I sensed the despair but also the hope in it."

"You did?"

"I *felt* it. The flower was budding," he said, giving me his interpretation. "Working its way through the muck. Just because you can't see it doesn't mean nothing's happening."

I didn't know why, but tears overflowed from my eyes. Attikus understood me more than I realized.

"I'm not crying because I'm sad," I said to relieve the worry in his eyes. "You've read all the messages woven into the painting so well."

He reached for a tissue on the side table and offered it to me. "So what happened after you escaped Florida?"

"We settled in Providence. Mom changed my name to Vanessa Lam."

"What was it before?"

"Van Kha Lam is my Vietnamese name. To be safe, I went by Vanessa, and Mom went by Hannah because it was similar to Hanh in Vietnamese. Miranda only knows about Van, not Vanessa or Nessa."

"People who have multiple aliases seem to have multiple personalities." He smirked.

"It's for safety reasons." I pinched his cheek playfully. "Sometimes, survival of the fittest requires adapting."

"You're with me now." He kissed me gently. "I won't let anyone hurt you. You can be Vanessa in private and Nessa in public; it's your artist's name. I'll make sure of that."

I thought about Emmanuel and his blackmail. If he wasn't behind it, would the people he worked with give me trouble?

"The story I told you is a prologue of what triggered me at the beach." I straightened, resting against the headboard.

Attikus did the same and took my hand in his while I described the event in the alleyway. I told him about the man who tried to rape me, how I stabbed him with the shard of glass, and how my mom was sent to prison because she protected me.

"What?" Attikus curled his fingers in a fist.

I placed my hand over his fist. "*Mẹ* is doing well in prison. I'm not ashamed of having a mother in prison. She's innocent."

"You defended yourself." He seethed. "Your mom shouldn't be in there."

"I'm trying to get her out."

"Who's your lawyer? Fire the fucker. I'll have my lawyer take over your case. Your mom can sue the officials and the state for not doing their job properly. She'll get the justice she deserves."

"I'm telling you this so you understand me better. I don't want it to burden you."

He gripped my chin, tipping my face up to meet hardened eyes. "It's not a burden to help my wife."

CHAPTER THIRTY-FIVE

ATTIKUS

VANESSA OPENED her mouth to reply, but I kissed her. She sighed, and her lips opened for me. I could kiss her all night. I didn't want to hear her say this was a fake marriage or that I'd done enough for her already.

My life had been difficult, but after hearing her story, I admired her resilience and determination.

"You're not a burden," I spoke against her soft lips. "You're the hope I've been waiting for—the spark of light that showed me new possibilities."

She showed me the way to my salvation. That profound revelation hit me hard, and I needed time alone to ponder on that later.

She sucked in a breath, gripped my face, and kissed me hard.

I didn't know what my relationship with Vanessa would be after six months. But in my eyes, that timeline was irrelevant. That contract we signed was now insignificant. I didn't need signatures to define what she meant to me. What we did tonight and what we shared was an invisible promise we made to each other. She trusted me enough to pour out her dark past. Those who had hurt her would pay.

She broke the kiss and smiled. "Now I want to know your story." She lifted my right leg and patted my knee.

My cock hardened as she massaged my knee. "Someone's jealous."

She chuckled. "I'll give him attention after you share your story. If I touch him now, we won't be talking much."

God, she's so perfect.

"Then come here. If you keep massaging me, I won't be able to think properly."

She snuggled into me, and I loved how soft her nude body felt against me. Her hair smelled like fresh flowers, and her skin held an intoxicating hint of perfume.

"It all started with an artwork that won a contest," I began.

Sharing the story brought back all the emotions I'd locked up. As with Vanessa, there were people who looked the other way when my family needed justice.

Even though the doctor tells me to stay in bed for a few more weeks, I sneak out of Gigi's house to visit my old home. Only one side of the house still stands. The next windstorm will knock it down. The ground is black from the soot.

I enter, looking for anything I can salvage. This was my home. I need something to remind me of my family. Tears and anger roil through me.

I find a folder of my sister's artwork. I hold it close, wondering if she was scared. Were my mom and dad sleeping during the fire?

I tremble, trying to imagine what they experienced. I know it's not good for me, but I can't help it.

Ashton, Bobby, and Harry will pay for this. They murdered my family and got away with it. My leg hurts, and I sit on a kitchen chair that's still intact. I lower my crutches and breathe in the surrounding air. It's tainted with smoke, death, and vengeance. I know breathing it in isn't healthy, but being here gives me the strength to move forward. I see cars pass by in the street, but the people in them don't look. Even if they did, they probably wouldn't care.

I don't know why those boys hate me so much. Is it the cash? Is it because Ashton can't fathom losing to anyone? If they can kill so easily now, what will become of them?

"Rest in peace, Mom, Dad, and Amelia," I say as tears stream down my face.

Vengeance courses through me as I sit in my former home. My life is now dedicated to making those boys pay.

"There you are!" Gigi appears. "How did you get here? I was so worried."

Gigi maneuvers around the debris and reaches me. She's my mom's friend and has already submitted paperwork to adopt me. A week ago, she helped me scatter my mom's, dad's, and sister's ashes in the ocean.

"Sorry to worry you. I took a taxi here." I push myself up with my crutches. "I wanted one last look at my house before it's torn down to be rebuilt."

She pats me on the shoulder. "I would've driven you."

"I know, and thank you. But I wanted to be alone with them, you know?"

She nods. "The school sent you all your belongings, including the artwork that earned you the prize. The restaurant heard about your story and made another donation in cash. It's at home."

"Oh, my god, Attikus." Tears filled Vanessa's eyes. "I'm so angry at those boys! Why are people so evil?"

Vanessa sat up, touching my knee and ankle with delicate care. She held my ankle in her hand, examining it like a plant specimen, turning it this way and that way. Then she bent and gave it a gentle kiss. My knee got a kiss too. She gripped my right hand and kissed my wrist. My body thrummed with heat as though her kiss was the medicine it had needed all these years.

I couldn't take my eyes away from her kind gesture. No one had shown me this much love.

"You're not embarrassed to be with someone like me? Most people don't want to be with a physically disabled man."

She shot me a disapproving look. "We all have flaws, Attikus. Some of us have unseen flaws. Some of us have physical flaws." She rubbed my wrist. "My mom told me about this mythical character named Chiron. He was a centaur, half-human and half-beast. He was an outcast. Even his father didn't want him. So he had a wound of unworthiness. But he used that wound of being different to move forward. He took classes from the other gods and goddesses, mastering the arts of medicine, science, astrology, astronomy, mathematics, and the arts. He surpassed all his teachers and proved that his weakness didn't hinder him. Instead, he transformed the wound into a gift for the world."

"I've never heard of Chiron, but I'll definitely read up on him. I was an outcast, and so were you."

"An outcast is the maverick who lives out-of-bounds. Because of this, he thinks and acts from an innovative perspective." She poked me in the chest. "You are the way you are *because* of your flaws."

I could sit here listening to her for hours. Everything she said made sense. Would we have connected and fallen for each other if we had met earlier?

My heart quickened at the admission. I was falling for her. How could I not? How could any man not want her? But could we have a long-lasting relationship? My life had been consumed with vengeance. Nothing was going to stop me from locating Ashton and making him pay.

And yet, my chest hurt thinking of not being able to have Vanessa. What if she got hurt in the crossfire? I'd spent years planning what I wanted to do to Ashton. I couldn't change my curated plan for a woman.

Stop thinking negative thoughts. Enjoy the moment. She deserves that.

She drew circles on my stomach like it was her canvas. "I think people who don't fall into the 'normal' category carve their own path. Take Beethoven, for example; he was deaf, but that didn't stop him from creating so many masterpieces. That's so inspiring, isn't it?"

"Can I hire you to be my therapist? My wrist, knee, and ankle already feel a hundred percent better from listening to you."

"I'm so angry at those boys for hurting you. Your entire life changed in an instant." She held up a clenched fist. "Do you know where they are?"

Amused, I asked, "Will you hurt them for me?"

"I would. The world is a better place without people like them."

"You'd be a great addition to the V.A.T.V. team."

"What's that?"

"Vigilantes Against the Villains," I said. "We believe in eradicating the scum of society by any means."

"Are you referring to bending or ignoring the laws?" Her eyes gleamed as though she understood exactly what I was referring to.

"Laws are made by people who don't follow them. I view laws as guidelines that I can either follow or break if necessary. So yeah, the boys and I are busy with V.A.T.V. and video games."

"I heard about WaterFyre Rising. Can you show me yours when you're ready?"

"You play video games?"

"No." She smirked. "I just want to peek into your complicated brain. You own a museum, art galleries, innovative farms, properties all over the world, children's educational apps, and now you're creating a video game." She tapped my forehead. "I admire your mental capacity."

"I see you've done a lot of research on me."

"You've transformed your pain into a gift for all to appreciate, Attikus. Your museum is a collection of beautiful things that symbolize something to somebody. Your innovative farms help people eat healthy, and your educational apps offer kids creative ways to learn. I don't think you realize how much you're contributing to society."

Money was power, and I'd used it to benefit those in need. My family had been the victims of a cruel world. I wanted to add some goodness to it for them.

"Thank you for your wisdom." I wrapped my arms around her. "I'm a lucky man to have a wife like you."

"Don't you forget it," she teased. "You're an artist like me."

"More like an illustrator. My sister was more creative. You would've gotten along well."

"Can I see the drawing that earned you the prize?"

"It's old."

"I don't care."

I reached for my phone, which was charging on the nightstand.

"You have it on your phone?"

"It's a reminder of what changed my life—the beginning and ending." I opened the phone, swiped to my photo folder, and showed her.

"No way." Her mouth dropped as she held my phone in

one hand, and the other hand went to her chest. "I can't believe this."

"What?"

She pointed to the photo on my phone and zoomed in on it. "I remember this!" Excitement filled her eyes. "My mom and I helped her friends at The Cozy Family Restaurant choose this artwork. I can't believe that was you!"

I couldn't believe it either. "You picked my artwork out of all the submissions?"

She nodded. "My mom worked part time at The Cozy Family Restaurant. She was friends with the owner, Cindy, who couldn't decide on the best ad for her restaurant. So Cindy asked my mom and me to help them pick. Yours stood out because I liked the illustration of the happy family in the restaurant setting." She held the phone to her chest and wiggled her eyebrows. "I guess I chose you back then, Whistler. We were meant to meet."

I was still baffled at how I was indirectly linked to her back then. Would we have become friends if I had met the restaurant owner? Would Vanessa have been there?

She swiped to some new pics. "Who are these people?"

I glanced at the image, and my mood soured. "My enemies."

"Is this the doctor who cared for you?"

"No. Dr. Messina was a resident shadowing Dr. Noah Marks, who cared for me. But my doctor died suspiciously a day before I was released."

She pursed her lips as she looked at the doctor. "You think he has something to do with it?"

"I suspect, yes, but I don't have any proof. Right now, he's on my shit list like so many others."

"Aside from running your multiple businesses, you're also investigating an old crime. When do you sleep?"

I grabbed my phone, placed it back on its charging station, and yanked her to me. "When my wife fulfills her promise to me. I don't want to talk about my enemies on my wedding night."

"What did I promise?" Amusement sparked in her eyes.

I took her hand and placed it over my hard dick. "To give something your attention."

"Like this?" She stroked me slowly, making my breathing heavy.

"Yes," I moaned in pleasure.

When her mouth came over me, my eyes rolled back, and I let my talented wife have her way with me.

CHAPTER THIRTY-SIX

VANESSA

THE NEXT DAY, we woke at nine in the morning, which was late for both of us. We showered together in the massive bathroom and had another memorable escapade. We couldn't get enough of each other. After the long shower, I chose a coral T-shirt with khaki shorts for Attikus. I wore a coral top with white flowers and a flowing white skirt.

Attikus took a phone call in his office and told me to start the breakfast order he'd placed after our steamy shower.

Sitting at the kitchen table, I smiled as I ate a bowl of papaya and mangoes. Last night was unforgettable. Maui now held a special place in my heart. My body was sore from several rounds of wild sex, but I'd never been more alive. My body zinged with energy. Attikus was the best lover I'd ever had—a sex warrior who knew how to please me. He knew how to touch me everywhere.

"Why are you smiling?" Attikus stepped out of the office, eyeing me.

My core tightened, remembering what had happened last night.

I finished my papaya and mango and placed the fork down. "Just thinking."

"About what?"

"About how good you are in bed."

"You've just made my day, Lily Pad." He bent to kiss me. "Let's do it again tonight."

We should probably take advantage of our last full day together. Tomorrow, we'd be heading back to Providence—back to reality. This vacation had been a dream. But like all wonderful dreams, it would soon end.

"Okay." I bit my bottom lip, wondering what other skills he had. "I want to walk along the shore today. You want to come with me? We can bring a sketchbook."

I couldn't believe I'd shared so much with him last night. But he'd also shared a lot with me. My husband was an artist, but one incident had destroyed his passion and motivation. I would probably have lost interest too. I wanted to erase the pain and grief he'd endured.

Who were these people who had hurt him? They didn't deserve to live.

"Okay, but I'd rather watch you sketch." He folded himself into the chair next to me. "We can go after I have my croissant." He took two croissants from the container, placing one on my plate and one on his.

"I just finished the bowl of sweet papaya and mangoes. It's delicious. Try it."

Attikus took a fork, poked a cube of papaya, and popped it into his mouth. "It is sweet." He poked another cube and fed it to me.

I broke off a piece of my croissant and fed him. We enjoyed breakfast in silence, like a couple who had been together for a while. The bright sun, the sound of the waves, and the salty breeze created a peaceful mood. I could live like this—a carefree life with no deadlines, no worries, and no expectations. But this blissful state was temporary.

He smiled as he finished his cup of coffee. I wanted to see that smile on him forever. His story had touched me deeply. Most people in his situation would have succumbed to life's cruelty and chosen a dark path, but he'd succeeded in building a thriving business. He inspired me with his persistence and determination.

We were similar in some ways.

Though he seemed stable, I knew that kind of darkness lingered in a person like a dormant illness. It lingered in me. There were days when I hated the world.

I wanted to create something for Attikus. According to our contract, I owed him an artwork. However, this would be something that came from my heart, not because of a contract. A few ideas popped into my head, and one of them made me blush.

We strode hand-in-hand as we walked along the shore. We had the private beach to ourselves.

"How's your leg?" I asked.

He hadn't used his cane since the attack. What if he was hiding the discomfort?

"It's fine. I'd rather hold your hand than a cane." His eyes gleamed. "The other hand can carry your sketchbook."

"Why do you have sketchbooks in your vacation home when you don't sketch?"

"I married an artist, so I need to stock up on art supplies in every home from now on."

"You think of everything, don't you?" I swung his hand.

"Part of being successful is planning ahead."

"And for survival. If you want to defeat your enemies, you need to be several steps ahead of them."

"Want to be my war strategist?" He smirked.

"No." I laughed. "It's common sense."

"Oh, right. The pragmatic way of living like plants."

"Hey, nature is intelligent, okay? If we paid more attention to plants, we wouldn't have so many problems."

"I'm only teasing you." He kissed the top of my head. "I agree with everything you've said about nature. I'm trying to weave that wisdom into my life."

We found a shady spot under a few palm trees that bent low to the ground. Attikus spread out the beach blanket, sat next to me, and watched me sketch the seashell near my foot.

I glanced at him. "Can I ask you something?"

"Anything."

"How long did it take for your leg to heal? Did you need constant surgery? How often do you go to physical therapy?"

He looked at me for a moment. "Why do you want to know?"

"Just curious about my husband."

"It took a long time to heal and many surgeries. I go to physical therapy once in a while or when I feel like it."

"When you feel like it?" Appalled, I gawked at him. "You should go as directed if you want to get better."

"I *am* better."

"Not if you still need a cane to walk."

His expression changed, and he stared out at the ocean. "Does the cane embarrass you, Vanessa?" His tone turned icy.

"What?" I blinked. "No."

"Are you sure my handicap doesn't bother you?"

Confusion hit me for a moment, then revelation surfaced. *Oh, my god.*

"That's not what I meant." I placed a gentle hand on his shoulder. "I'm not embarrassed by anything, Attikus. I just don't want you to depend on something if you don't need to be. You should be strong and free." I sighed. "I imagine the cane would remind you of a painful past. If I were you, I'd want to be free of that reminder. That's all."

"Sorry, I overreacted." He scrubbed a hand over his face. "You want to accompany me to my physical therapy? It's at Forrest's Clinic. He has an amazing team."

"If you'd like."

His phone rang in his back pocket, but he let it go to voicemail. The silly man was glued to my pencil drawing of his foot.

But the phone rang again.

"I think you should take the call."

He reached for his phone, looked at the screen, and answered. "Yeah?" He listened while keeping his eyes on me. "It's okay. What's up?" His expression darkened, and I paused my sketching. "Send what you have. I'll look soon. Keep me posted. Thank you."

"What's wrong?" I asked once as he ended the call.

"Emmanuel is dead. He was in a car accident."

CHAPTER THIRTY-SEVEN

ATTIKUS

WHEN WE ARRIVED IN PROVIDENCE, Vanessa excused herself to unpack. I knew Emmanuel's death had affected her. Though he'd been her ex, he was also a victim in this fiasco.

Forrest had sent me the toxicology report on Emmanuel's bloodwork. He had high levels of toxins. He hadn't seen that combination before, but he recognized some of the dangerous chemical agents that damaged brain cells.

"I'll be in my office." I kissed her forehead. "If you need me, just come in."

"His sister will be devastated. Do you think she's also in danger?"

"I'll have someone watch over her."

"You'd do that?"

I tipped her chin up. "I'd do anything to remove the despair on your face."

"Thank you." She embraced me. "Do you need me to help you unpack?"

"You'd do that?" I repeated her words and earned a smile.

Nodding, she pinched my cheek. "I'd do anything to remove the despair on your face."

I watched her enter her bedroom, and my chest tightened a little more. I wanted her to move into *my* bedroom. But now wasn't the moment to bring that topic up.

I walked into my office, shut the door, and moved to the bulletin board with pictures and notes of my family's murderers. A second board had been created for Vanessa's blackmailer. More individuals needed to be added after what she'd told me.

I wrote a note and slapped it on the board.

Emmanuel had given me a list of gyms affiliated with Ultra Health and Fitness, where Milton worked. My friends had uncovered that Milton Kalkounis—the man who hung out with the bullies—was part of The Trogyn. Vanessa's father was too. When she'd told me his name, I sent it to Orion to search through the database. Charles Laurent had died a few years ago in an explosion in Mexico.

Yesterday, Emmanuel was supposed to be on a flight out of the country to a remote village in Brazil where Forrest had an herbal farm. Emmanuel was going to work there until things settled in Providence. I should hate this guy for dating and terrifying Vanessa, but I'd obtained a new identity card for him to start over.

I opened the file containing recordings of Emmanuel's apartment over the past few weeks. He'd left the building twice. The first time was to a convenience store a block from his home. He'd been in disguise and returned home safely. The second time was yesterday. He'd been in disguise again and gotten into a ConvientRide. Two recordings from a few blocks away showed the ride had run a red light and was hit by a truck, flipping the vehicle several times. People rushed to pull him and the driver out. According to the police report, the driver was drunk, but my instincts told me it was no accident. The driver was still at the hospital. I needed to ask the fucker a few questions before someone else got to him.

I reached for my phone and called Detective Farmer. "Do you have anyone watching Sam Thornton, the ConvenientRide driver from yesterday's car accident?"

"No. Should I?"

I briefed him on the situation.

"Understood. Someone will check on him."

"I need to ask him some questions. Do you want to meet me there?"

"Be there soon."

My gut told me Emmanuel's death wasn't as simple as it looked. Was his death a warning to anyone who went against The Trogyn?

I walked into Vanessa's room. "I've got to head out for a bit. Do you need anything while I'm out?"

She shook her head. "Is everything okay?"

"Yes." I stepped up to her. "Just meeting the detective to go over Emmanuel's death."

She sighed. "Is he also investigating the man who attacked us in Maui?"

I had to follow up on that later. Shit was erupting all around us.

I wrapped my arms around her. "No. It's not his jurisdiction. But I'll get to the bottom of that incident. As soon as I get more information, I'll let you know."

She looked up at me. "Promise?"

"Yes."

"Okay. I'll unpack for you." She smirked. "Do you have anything in the luggage you don't want me to see?"

"You have access to everything in my luggage, bedroom, or any room in this house. If you find something interesting, let me know."

"I've got the key to everything?" She waved an invisible key in the air.

"Everything."

As I left the house, the meaning of "everything" rang in my ears. I meant what I'd said—she had access to everything that belonged to me. No other woman had that. But Vanessa had burrowed into a deep spot in my heart, and I'd do anything to protect her.

CHAPTER THIRTY-EIGHT

VANESSA

I REMOVED Attikus's clothes from his luggage and inhaled his musky scent, which comforted me. Emmanuel's death had unsettled me. My shoulders tightened with anxiety. I wasn't breathing properly. Though he'd blackmailed me and made my life hell for a while, he was also a victim.

Would the people who'd killed him come after me? What did they want from me?

Stop stressing yourself out.

I concentrated on putting Attikus's clothes and toiletries away. Then I walked into the office, wanting to see where this complex man worked. We weren't pretending to be a couple anymore. At least, I wasn't. One, I didn't have the energy to pretend. Two, I was falling for him. That emotion, on top of everything in Maui and Emmanuel's death, sent me into an emotional whirlwind. I tried my best to squash the confusion and fear, but it didn't help.

I'd made a mess of things by falling in love with him. I'd broken every single rule in the contract.

No kissing. No sex. No crossing boundaries.

We'd done all of those things more than once. And we couldn't stop.

I had to raise the issue with him. He'd agreed to look into my mom's case. Could his lawyer win? How long would that take? Should I still go through with the extraction process to get my mom out of prison? I hadn't told Attikus about that part yet. But I'd already paid those men. I doubted they'd give me a refund.

Vacation was over, and now chaos was showering down on us.

Sitting in his chair, I blew out a heavy breath. I ran my fingers along his sturdy desk, trying to envision him sitting here thinking, reviewing files on his computer, or making a business deal.

Standing, I browsed his office. I turned to a nook with a lounge chair by a window, offering a view of the yard. I sucked in a breath at the painting on the wall. My heart raced as I stepped closer. I thought President Collins and the First Lady had bought *Hope in Blossom* at the auction. Attikus was the anonymous buyer all this time. Why hadn't he said anything to me?

I moved to the long conference table. Two boards on stands were positioned close to the wall. I approached the first board and examined the pictures of the three high school boys. Two of them had a large red X marked over them. Bobby C. Cooney and Harry C. Sullivan. These were the boys who'd attacked Attikus. The picture of Ashton Lindor stood out to me. His calculating brown eyes, ruffled blond hair, and knowing smirk gave off negative vibes that sent chills down my spine.

I studied the pictures of bloody clothes and blood on the sidewalk. My heart cracked when I saw a picture of a broken Attikus in the hospital bed. His face was bruised and unrecognizable. Tears filled my eyes and slid down my face. I hated these boys.

Where was Ashton now? He needed to be punished for his crime.

My eyes slid over to the burned house. Only part of the house still stood. My heart shattered, and I dropped into the chair at the table. I could only imagine the pain and grief Attikus had endured. I wanted to help him capture these people.

I glanced at the notes posted on the board and the boxes filled with files on the floor and table. Attikus was consumed with this case. I would be too, if my family had been murdered like his. I admired his persistence.

Walking over to the second board, I gasped when I saw it was about me. Notes and pictures of Emmanuel, his sister, Enzo, the missing finger, and some fitness centers took up parts of the board.

I stared at the Post-it note that read, *Get Vanessa's mom out of prison.*

He must've written this down in his office before he left.

I didn't know what to say. I'd mentioned it to him yesterday, and now it was a priority on the board. He was doing so much for me already, and I felt guilty that I couldn't offer much in return. He'd only asked for a painting from me, but at this rate, I'd be painting him a hundred.

I remembered how he had assumed I was bothered by his cane. Maybe he'd dated the wrong women who'd made him insecure about his injury. But those things didn't bother me. In my eyes, his cane represented a powerful symbol that showed he was a survivor—that he built himself up from nothing.

The need to take care of him overwhelmed me. I wanted to erase his pain and insecurities. Though he portrayed himself as a powerful billionaire who could achieve anything, I saw his vulnerabilities. I knew things about him that no one else did, and vice versa.

Two ideas popped into my head. One was the greenhouse, and the second was food.

Food always made me feel better. I knew he enjoyed the Vietnamese food at the Saigon Bistro. That could be our dinner tonight.

But first, I went to the greenhouse, found a new pair of garden gloves, put them on, and got to work. I opened the bags of soil on the ground and filled up the trays and pots. Two hours later, the greenhouse had containers of vegetables and herbs that would sprout soon. Attikus had an irrigation and solar light system with unique-looking light bulbs that were already set up. Four panels with speakers hung on each corner of the greenhouse. Reading the pamphlet on the table, I activated all the functions in a low setting.

Satisfied that we'd have vegetables and herbs to eat in a few months, I removed the gloves, washed my hands in the small sink, and returned to the house.

Then I called Saigon Bistro to place my order. Minutes later, I drove to pick it up. As I walked out of the restaurant, Attikus's mom and sister arrived. Gigi had trimmed her bob cut, making her look chic. Ellen wore her red hair in a ponytail.

"Hi," I said, wondering if I should address her as *Mom*.

I didn't know if Attikus had told them about our wedding yet.

"Hi, Nessa! How are you?" Ellen offered me a hug.

"Wonderful," I told Ellen.

"Hi." Gigi smiled, but I sensed a slight hesitation. Maybe she'd heard about the wedding and resented us? Awkwardness stirred between us.

"Now that you're back from Maui," Gigi said, "we'd like to visit you at your gallery."

She knows.

"Sure, I would love to have my mother and sister-in-law visit. I'm sorry that we eloped. We should have alerted you. It was a last-minute decision."

Gigi huffed, holding up a hand. "It's not your fault. It's Attikus's. He's been making outrageous decisions and won't listen to anyone." She eyed me. "Except his wife."

Did she think I forced Attikus to elope?

"Mom, Nessa has nothing to do with it. He does things no one understands. I'm sure he's confusing her too." Ellen smiled at me.

"He is," I admitted.

"Honey, you need to grip tight on the reins so you don't injure yourself." Ellen gestured with her hands.

I nodded. "I'll try."

"Look on the bright side." Ellen leaned into Gigi. "Attikus hasn't taken a vacation in forever. When we invited him to Honolulu a few months ago, he declined. He also declined Paris, Costa Rica, and Singapore. He didn't want to cancel his meetings to go with us. Our Nessa inspired him to take some time off. That's a victory, isn't it?"

Gigi sighed. "I suppose."

"Stop by the gallery this week, and I'll be there."

Nodding, they both offered warm smiles.

I walked out of the restaurant and made a mental note to have Attikus talk to his mom. I turned back to see if Gigi was still angry and saw Agnes talking to them. Wasn't she supposed to be vacationing in Maui? I thought Attikus had bought her a week's vacation. Maybe she took a rain check and came back. Was she the one who told Gigi and Ellen about the wedding?

Anxiety gripped my stomach. Agnes had married Attikus Mount to Vanessa Lam, not Nessa Lambert. If Gigi and Ellen knew this, they would assume I was a fraud. I had to speak to Attikus.

When I got home, I placed the food on the kitchen island and set the plates and chopsticks on the table. I didn't know when Attikus would be back.

I went to my studio, hoping to work on the painting for the First Lady. The large-scale gallery-wrapped canvas measured seventy-two inches wide and one hundred and twenty inches high. It sat on two containers of primer, leaning against the wall for security. My easel wouldn't fit. I had a three-step ladder for when I needed to paint the top portion. Madeline wanted a statement piece, and I would deliver it for her.

I threw on a baggy T-shirt with paint splatter on it, stood in front of the canvas, closed my eyes, and dropped into myself. I calmed my breathing and cleared my head, making my mind a blank canvas. Distractions would affect the flow of my creation. When I was ready, I opened my eyes, poured paint onto my palette, and began the magical journey.

My mind stopped thinking, and my emotions took over. Beautiful colors filled the background. I stepped back to see what I'd accomplished so far. Satisfied with the blend of colors, I stepped on my stool to paint the top portion.

An image of me painting Attikus's naked body popped into my head, and I knew what I wanted to gift him.

Would he pose for me to paint him?

CHAPTER THIRTY-NINE

ATTIKUS

WITH MY CANE, I headed to the nurse's desk and smiled at the older woman with the name Kerry embroidered on her nurse's scrubs.

She offered me a friendly smile. "How can I help you?"

"Hi, Kerry, I heard about Sam's accident. He's my cousin. May I visit him, please? I flew up from Florida as soon as I heard the news. Is he doing okay?"

"The doctor examined him this morning and said he should recover. It's always good to see family. You can head down this hallway." She pointed. "Sam's in room twenty-six."

"Thank you. Has anyone visited him yet?"

"Not that I'm aware of."

I walked down the hallway and found the door left ajar. I stepped inside to see a police officer with a beard standing by the bed. Was he one of Detective Farmer's men?

Clearing my throat, I hit my cane gently against the open door. "Hi, Sam."

The officer whirled around, looking startled. "What are you doing here?"

"Visiting my cousin. The nurse told me to come in. Are you the officer sent to watch over Sam? The nurse told me an officer was supposed to stop by today." I glanced over at the bed, and Sam appeared to be muttering something. "Sam, are you okay?"

"Yeah, they sent me. Sam seems fine. Have a good day." The officer exited the room.

I knew he wasn't a real officer based on his sneakers. As I watched him walk down the hallway, I called Detective Farmer to notify him about the fake officer.

I returned to check on Sam, but he was foaming at the mouth. I pressed the emergency button on the wall, and a doctor and a nurse rushed in.

As I paced in the waiting room, Detective Farmer appeared.

I rushed up to him. "How's Sam?"

He shook his head. "He died of a poisonous injection."

I cursed. "Did you get the fucker?"

"He's in the back of my cruiser."

"Can I have a word with him?"

"I'll be busy interviewing the nurses and doctors here." He dropped his keys on the nurse's desk. "I'll be looking for them in an hour."

I picked up his keys and headed outside to his cruiser. Another police car was in the parking lot, but no officers were in sight. They were probably in the hospital. I approached the cruiser, opened the back door, and slid in next to the fake officer. He met my eyes but didn't seem to recognize me.

"You just murdered Sam Thornton. If you don't tell me who sent you and why, I'll make sure you end up like him." I offered a slow smile. "But your death won't be that quick. Animals will feast on you limb by limb."

The man looked confused for a moment. "What did I do?"

"You injected Sam Thornton with poison."

Fear splashed onto his face. "I . . . I did that?" His eyebrows furrowed. "Why can't I remember?"

I studied his trembling hands. Something wasn't right with him. A brazen criminal usually remembered their crime unless they were lying through their teeth. But he didn't look like he was lying. If he were an actor, he'd be the next Academy Award winner.

"What's your name?"

"Paul Exinor."

"Where do you work, Paul? Do you know Sam?"

"Sam and I work for the CIA. In their research labs."

What did the CIA have to do with any of this? Then it occurred to me that the man who'd attacked Vanessa and me in Maui was also a CIA agent.

"Do you know Ryan Evans?"

"Yes. We worked together for a while. He volunteered for a well-paying project."

"What kind of project?"

"I don't remember." He looked at me as though begging for help. "Something's wrong with me. I can't remember what I did this morning."

"What kinds of research were you working on for the CIA? Where's the location?"

"They're working on innovative medicine, serums, and mind-control programs. There's a base in Texas and . . ." He shook his head. "I can't remember . . ."

Then a seizure overcame him.

Shit. I rushed out of the cruiser and into the hospital to alert a nurse.

CHAPTER FORTY

ATTIKUS

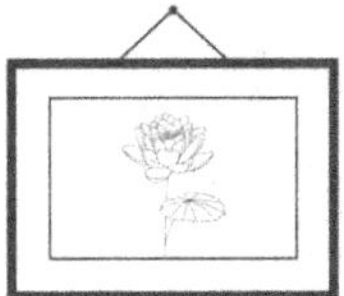

THOUGHTS CRAMMED my brain as I entered my home, wanting to see Vanessa. So much was happening around us, and I needed a moment to sit still and look at everything carefully.

Why were CIA agents killing people? Who had ordered this? It seemed like Paul had lost his mind and memory, but he was still alive.

I paid for a private hospital room and hired two security guards to watch over Paul, ensuring he was protected. No one was allowed in except an approved doctor or nurse. Detective Farmer didn't object to my actions, which meant he understood my needs and the direction this investigation was taking.

I needed Paul to remember who had ordered him to kill Sam Thornton, the CIA agent who had killed Emmanuel. Whoever was behind this was killing off potential witnesses to their crimes. Before Detective Farmer left, he mentioned that the two thugs, Martin Brown and Pedro Lopez, also died in a car accident the day before Emmanuel. He showed me pictures of the other two deceased people who were in the same car—Enzo and Becca.

At a glance, things seemed chaotic. The mastermind behind this shitshow was trying to create confusion, trying to distract me from seeing the truth. This meant I was getting close. If I zoomed out and ignored all the flying debris, two powerful entities rose to the surface: The Trogyn and the CIA.

How were they connected? What did they want to hide?

I texted my friends, asking them for a conference call tonight. Arriving home, I walked around my house. I needed to see Vanessa. I inhaled the delicious aroma, knowing she'd ordered dinner from Saigon Bistro. That made me feel better. Before her, my place had been quiet, empty, and cold. But now, warmth stirred in my home and my heart.

I'd never felt so anchored. Even though I had all the wealth in the world, I'd never felt fulfilled. Vengeance had propelled me forward, disregarding everything else. My house had been a place to sleep. Now it was a home.

My home with Vanessa.

I heard a noise in the studio and headed there. I stood at the open door, watching her adjust the stool. She stepped on it and stretched out her hand to paint a lovely peach color on the massive canvas, which was bigger than she was. The beautiful colors reminded me of *Hope in Bloom*, a painting I'd bought in Boston.

Though she wore a baggy T-shirt, seeing her painting in my house was as hot as hell.

"Who's the painting for?" I asked as I stepped into the studio.

She whirled around and beamed at me. Placing her brush and paint palette on the side table, she wiped her hands on her shirt and rushed over to me.

"Hi! I'd give you a hug, but I've got paint all over me."

I wrapped my arms around her, inhaling her scent. "I don't care. I've got plenty of shirts and jeans."

"Are you hungry? I got us dinner."

"I saw. Thank you. I want to see what you're painting first." I took her hand and walked over to the canvas. "The colors remind me of a painting I have."

"Why didn't you tell me you bought *Hope in Bloom*?"

I smirked. "I didn't want you to think I was a creepy art collector who was stalking you."

"You were at the Brigham and Women's art auction? I didn't see you."

"I saw you."

At that time, we had already signed an agreement for her gallery.

"Why didn't you say hello?"

"I was about to, but you left early. I hadn't intended to be at the auction, but a clue sent me there."

"A clue?" She furrowed her brow. "What do you mean?"

"Do you remember Joseph Gallo? He's my curator, a long-time employee of mine. He went missing two months ago. I found a handwritten note on his desk about the auction, so I went to check it out." I left out the part where I encountered two men planning to extort her. Even though they were now dead, she didn't need the extra anxiety.

"And you still haven't found anything on him?"

I shook my head.

"I remember Joseph. He was friendly and thorough."

"Agnes and Joseph were with me when the museum first opened. I have to find him, dead or alive. He and Agnes are family to me."

"I know." She touched my face. "Speaking of Agnes, I saw her at Saigon Bistro. I thought she was still on vacation in Maui."

"She came back to help at the museum since Joseph is still missing. There's a lot of administrative work that needs to be completed."

"That's a dedicated employee you have." Vanessa elbowed me. "I also saw your mom and sister at the restaurant. Seems like that place is where I keep bumping into people."

"Was she mean to you?"

"Not mean, more like irritated. I don't blame her, though." Vanessa looked at me. "She's your mom. You need to soothe her anger. Did you tell her about us eloping?"

"Yes. She didn't like it."

"Does she know my real name?"

"Yes."

Relief settled on her face. "Well, you need to figure out a way to make her happy again. She thinks I lured her son to the dark side."

"No, she doesn't." I chuckled. "You lured me back to the light."

Vanessa gave me the side eye. "Trust me, she does. She believes I've corrupted you beyond saving."

I laughed. "I was corrupt when she took me in."

"Seriously, I don't want her to think ill of us whenever she sees us. What does she like? How can I warm her up?"

"Just be you. She likes plants, though," I said, loving the idea that Vanessa wanted to win over my family. "Ellen is more understanding."

"A mother would take something like this to heart, whereas a sister is more forgiving. Let me get a plant so you can give it to her. Say you're sorry."

"I'll comply with my wife's demands if she fulfills her obligations."

"What obligations?"

"You don't remember, love?" I placed a hand on her shoulders. "If you breach your contract, I get to ask you for anything."

She sobered, and her mouth twisted. "I'm sorry I broke—"

I pressed a finger to her lips. "Don't be sorry. I *wanted* you to breach the contract."

"What?" She gaped at me.

I smirked. "What can I say? I'm a greedy man. I wanted to see where this relationship could go without the contract. Don't tell me you haven't been thinking about it."

"What are you saying?"

"Let's date. Forget the contract. People will assume we're married, and that's fine. But I don't want you to think I'm pretending to want you. There was no pretense in Maui, and there's no pretense here."

She smiled, but then fear squashed it. "Is that going to complicate things even more?"

"Lily Pad, it's going to make things easier for me. A contract makes this relationship too fake, you know? I want us to be real. I wanted it from the beginning."

She narrowed her eyes at me. "What do you mean?"

"I had a fine print added to the contract. You were so focused on your requirements that you didn't read it."

"You're so sneaky! What did it say?"

"That the contract is voided from the moment you kiss me." I grinned. "That happened during the ceremony."

Vanessa stared at me for a while as a small smile slid onto her lips. "What am I going to do with you?"

"Kiss me." I pursed my lips. "Do all the things you want to me. But seriously, you don't have to give me an answer right now about us dating. Think about it."

She chewed on her bottom lip. "So you want to be my official boyfriend instead of my fake husband?"

"I don't want anything fake with you." I smiled. "We'll let

our friends know the fake marriage has dissolved and we're dating. Emmanuel is dead, but the people behind his death are extremely dangerous. For now, we'll let the world believe you're still married to me until the chaos settles, okay?"

I feared The Trogyn or the CIA would hurt Vanessa regardless of whether she was married to me or not. The game had become more perilous. I knew my enemies would target her first to get to me, so the closer she stayed to me, the safer I could keep her.

Her eyes sparkled. "What do you want for the contract breach?"

"For you to paint me in the nude."

She grinned. "How did you know I'd thought of that?"

Oh, she had no idea what I was referring to.

I ran a finger down her cheek. "I want you to paint me while *you're* naked."

Her eyes widened, and her mouth dropped open.

Before she could say anything, I kissed her.

"You've got a weird kink, Whistler."

"It all started because of you, Lily Pad." I returned my attention to the painting. "Who's the customer for this one?"

"Promise not to tell anyone?" she asked with pride in her eyes.

"I promise."

"The First Lady, Madeline Claude-Collins."

"Wow. That's fantastic. They tried to steal *Hope in Bloom* from me, but I outbid them by one million dollars. That painting is mine. Just like *you're* mine."

When she threw her arms around me and squeezed, I knew her answer was yes.

She grinned when my stomach growled. "Let's go eat."

"How's Sam? Were you able to question him?"

"He's dead."

"Oh, my god. What happened?"

I briefed her on the situation as we ate. "I don't want you to worry about anything, okay? I need to talk to the boys, so it's going to be a long night."

She nodded. "I'll work on my painting."

"Can you give me more details about your mom's case? I'll have a team review it."

She looked at me for a moment, debating over something.

I frowned. "You don't trust me?"

"No. It's not that." Her lips twisted. "I did something bad. You might not like it."

"That's impossible." I placed down my chopsticks. "What is it?"

"I hired some people to help my mom escape from prison."

"Who?"

She told me about the plan, Leo Rossi, and his restaurant in Boston. I'd add him to my to-do list.

I couldn't believe my woman had the courage to hire criminals to extract her mother.

"Don't go through with it. Give me their names."

"I paid them a lot of money."

"Lily Pad, this extraction spells trouble. There are cameras everywhere that can spot these men. If they're caught, they'll point the finger at you. Your mom will get additional time for escaping, and you'll also be convicted." Based on what Vanessa had told me, these men hadn't given her a detailed, minute-by-minute plan. But she wouldn't have known to ask for that. "Not to mention, if something goes wrong, she could die."

Dread overcame her face. "She shouldn't be in there. She's been waiting for her freedom for years."

"Let me handle this. I need you to trust me, okay?"

She looked at me with so much trust and nodded. "Would you listen to me if I said no?"

"Not if I know you'll be in danger."

"Your mom is wrong."

"About what?"

"That your wife is calling the shots."

The definitions of a girlfriend and a wife were blurring into one another. I didn't mind at all. Right now, they were the same.

"She's not wrong." I smiled. "My wife can do whatever she wants as long as she's not in danger." I tapped her nose. "I've been dwelling in this dark world for a long time. The plan has holes. I care about you, and I don't want anything to happen to you or your mother."

"Okay."

CHAPTER FORTY-ONE

ATTIKUS

DINNER WITH VANESSA was the best thing that happened today. It seemed like everything that occurred outside of this house was chaos, and everything inside calmed my soul.

After dinner, she returned to her studio while I entered my office and logged into the conference call with the boys. Forrest, Arrow, and Royce couldn't make it as they were traveling.

"You okay?" Remington asked. "Your group text sounded urgent."

"I think the CIA is involved with The Trogyn," I said.

"What makes you say that?" Orion asked. "I've got contacts there. I can look into it deeper."

I told them about Ryan Evans (the Maui attacker), Sam Thornton (the driver who crashed the car that killed Emmanuel), and Paul Exinor (the man sent to kill Sam). All were CIA agents.

"That's interesting," Grayson said. "We need to protect Paul, or they'll kill him too."

"He's currently in a private room at the hospital," I told them.

"Why don't we move him to Forrest's clinic?" Orion suggested. "It's safer there."

"Yeah, let's do that," I agreed.

"I'm sending him a text now," Remi said.

I looked at my friends, all of whom wanted to destroy this crime organization. In the beginning, I kept my plan for vengeance separate from eliminating The Trogyn. But now, it seemed like the two were intertwined.

"We need to revise our plan for The Trogyn," I said.

"What happened?" Remi asked.

The only person who knew about my vendetta was Orion. So I shared my past with Remington and Grayson.

"Fuck, man," Grayson said. "You should've told us sooner."

"I didn't want to deter the focus from the group. Besides, it's my personal matter."

"We're all in this together," Remi said. "And you're right—your past is linked to the current issues."

"The severed finger belonged to my high school principal," I said. "His family is all dead."

"Ashton Lindor is the only person still missing." Orion scratched his chin.

"He could hide under a new alias." Grayson sipped his bottle of water.

"I looked at that angle too, but have found nothing." I told them about the now-deceased Enzo and Becca, including their association with Milton Kalkounis. "He was my high school classmate and the trainer threatening Emmanuel, who was Vanessa's ex."

"Sounds like they're cleaning house." Orion leaned back in his chair. "The CIA has been compromised more than we thought. We already got rid of three Trogyn members."

"There's probably a lot more we don't know about." Grayson stretched his neck from side to side.

"Is that why you agreed to marry her?" Remi asked but held up a hand. "You don't have to answer. I already know. Women can make us do irrational things. Just look at Grayson. He bought a plane."

"I don't see you complaining when you need to use it," Grayson retorted.

Remi smiled. "I'm not complaining. Just saying we do illogical things for love."

"He's right," Orion agreed. "I discovered a new constellation and named it after her."

"And you also started a media company for her," I said.

We all laughed at our ridiculous behavior. I briefed them on why Vanessa needed my help, the video of her killing a man while defending herself, and the release of her real name, which was tied to the video.

"Do you have the video?" Orion asked.

"Not yet. Still looking," I said. "She hasn't received any new threats."

"We got you," Grayson said.

"I'll have my team research Milton and his associates." Orion massaged the back of his neck.

"Thanks. One more thing," I said. "I need your help to extract Vanessa's mom from prison."

"Christ," Remi said. "What do you have in mind?"

While I described my plan to them, the door to my office slowly opened. I glanced at the time at the bottom of my computer screen. It was already midnight.

Vanessa peeked in, and I wiggled my fingers, signifying for her to enter. She entered, and I lost my breath. She wore a short, silky robe and untied the fabric belt as she approached my desk. I lost my train of thought, and the boys' voices faded into the background.

"That sounds good to me," I said as Vanessa slipped off the

robe, revealing a lingerie set with open cups. *Fuck*. I could feast on her breasts without having to remove anything.

I pretended to yawn on the screen. "Can we resume this another day?"

"We'll update the other guys and schedule another meeting," Remi said. "Attikus?"

"Yeah?"

"You're not alone in this, okay?" Remi looked at me for confirmation. "Whether it's Ashton, The Trogyn, or the CIA, just let us know what you need."

The other boys reiterated the same.

"Thanks, guys," I said, appreciating their friendship more than they knew. But right now, my brain wasn't functioning properly. My dick wanted my wife.

I ended the call and spun the chair to face my wife—I loved referring to her that way—who straddled me. My dick hardened, wanting to be inside her.

"This is a pleasant surprise." I cupped her breast—so soft and supple.

"Your meeting took too long," she murmured. "I didn't want to wait anymore."

"Is there something you need?" I played with her nipples, yanking each one.

"You looked stressed earlier, so I thought I'd be a thoughtful secretary and help you release the tension." She straddled me and looped her arms around my neck, massaging it.

"Don't stop," I begged. "It feels really good."

"How does this feel?" She gyrated her hips, arousing the hell out of me.

I growled as I removed a hand from her breast to palm her. Then I tugged the sheer panties aside and slid two fingers inside her. Wetness coated them.

Her pink tongue swept across her lips, and I watched its every move.

"You're the sexiest secretary I've ever had."

"And you are the hottest boss I've ever had." Her hand caressed the back of my neck.

"I'll be expecting this kind of assistance whenever I work from home." I bent and claimed a nipple while my fingers continued to pump into her.

She arched toward me. "Yes, sir."

I growled and sucked her nipple harder.

Our eyes connected, and the sexual tension snapped. We were all over each other with our hands, mouths, teeth, and tongues. In seconds, she was on my conference table with her legs spread wide for me. I buried my face between her legs, inhaling her addictive scent and loving every crevice.

She cried out, filling my office with her blissful sounds of pleasure.

I couldn't get enough of her. I wanted to thrust my dick into her, take her in my office. But tonight, I wanted her in my bed. This was a dream I'd thought about constantly.

Scooping her into my arms, I carried her out of my office, down the hallway, up the stairs, and into my bedroom. I placed my sexy wife on the bed and looked down at her. She was so hot.

"I'm having you in my bed tonight. We're sharing a room from now on."

"Is that going in our new contract?" She smirked.

"If you want." I stripped off my clothes and hovered over her, taking in every detail of her beautiful face. "I love that smart mouth of yours."

With so much affection in her eyes, she cupped the side of my face. "Attikus?"

"Yes, Lily Pad."

"Kiss me."

Our mouths crashed into each other like a wild storm that wouldn't end. She gave, and I took. I offered, and she responded with the same hunger. This woman was my perfect match.

When we broke for breath, she looked at me with amusement in her eyes. "Whistler?"

"Yes, Lily Pad.

"I want you to fuck me hard tonight."

"Baby, that's all I've been thinking about all night."

That night, we broke the bedroom chair and cracked the headboard.

CHAPTER FORTY-TWO

VANESSA

FOR THE NEXT FEW DAYS, Attikus worked at the museum and spent time in his home office. He took breaks and visited me a few times in my studio. We fell into a natural routine like a real married couple. Today, he was busy at the museum preparing for an upcoming business trip.

I was close to finishing the painting for the First Lady. All I needed was her face. She mentioned on the order form that the portrait didn't need to look exactly like her. She wanted a unique version of her that was stylistic, which meant I could paint any woman as long as I added aspects of her. I had the figure and even a regal gown painted, but the face needed more time.

When I held my paintbrush, I couldn't make myself start. The artist's block had kicked in, and I needed to take a break. I looked at the time on my phone—one hour before Gigi and Ellen visited the store.

I washed my brushes and left them in a container to dry. Then I went into our bedroom to change out of my painting clothes and put on a floral dress. *Our bedroom.* I'd been sleeping with him in his bedroom. The man was a sex god, but he was also attentive and tender with me afterward.

I hadn't given him an answer about being his official girl-friend. We were a couple—whether it was as boyfriend and girlfriend or as husband and wife. On paper, we were married, but behind the scenes, we were dating. Everything blended together, and regardless of how I defined it, I was *with* him. Girlfriend and wife became the same thing. To an outsider, that might seem confusing. Perhaps one day, I'd want a real marriage. But for now, I was content.

Attikus was helping me carry an enormous burden, making my life easier. He'd discovered that Leo Rossi—the man I had hired to rescue my mom from prison—and his associates were part of The Trogyn. The girls and I had discussed them at our last gathering. It seemed everyone was working for this crime organization. How far was their reach?

Emmanuel was dead, and the trainer who had blackmailed him was missing. Attikus had located the video used to threaten me and said the quality was poor. Regardless, they couldn't prove it was me. The video showed I was defending myself from a violent man—a man who belonged to a wealthy family.

So now I didn't have to worry about people knowing I was both Nessa Lambert and Vanessa Lam. Attikus's legal team was prepared to defend me at all costs. He was doing so much for me, but I feared that something bad was about to happen. I didn't want him to get hurt because of me.

Before I headed to the gallery, I stopped by the greenhouse to check on my plants. My heart burst with happiness at seeing the little sprouts in the trays and pots. The hanging pipes sprayed a gentle mist onto the plants. I could tell hidden pipes were built into the tables where the trays sat because I could hear the water traveling.

This life growing in his garden was like my feelings for

Attikus—each day, it grew more and more. I was in love with this man. My heart raced every time I saw him. In the morning. At night. I didn't realize love could be so powerful. It truly was transformative. I could see it in the colors I chose for my paintings. I could see the change in me—more hopeful about life.

But I was afraid to tell him all this when his emotional state was unstable. He was under extreme pressure. He had a vendetta to focus on, an employee who was still missing, and a crime organization to destroy. And he was helping my mom and me. That was a lot for one person to take on.

Sighing, I exited the greenhouse, walked into the house, slipped on my purse, and grabbed the box with the two terrariums I'd made for Gigi and Ellen. I slid into one of Attikus's Land Rovers and headed out.

When I arrived, several patrons were in the gallery. I had a comprehensive collection of paintings in the back room for when inventory ran low. I'd have to produce more art soon.

As I entered my office and set the terrariums down, a thought occurred to me. What if I sold these here? I'd never been to a gallery that sold items other than paintings. I could organize a section in the front display to showcase novelty plants and pottery.

"Hey, Nessa!" Willow knocked on the door. "There's a customer who has a question about the abstract painting."

"I'll be right out. Thank you."

I approached the older woman and answered several questions about my journey as an artist. She purchased the abstract painting *A Drip of Time* for her new vacation home in the Cape. As the woman paid and signed the documents to pick up the painting at a later time, Gigi and Ellen entered.

"Hi, Nessa!" Ellen gave me a hug and a gorgeous bouquet of flowers. "For you, from us."

Gigi hugged me and glanced around. "Your gallery is gorgeous. Thank you for having us."

They seemed exceptionally friendly compared to last week. Perhaps Attikus had spoken to them.

"I have something for you too. Have a seat." I led them to a table where I usually discussed customized artwork with my customers. "Be right back."

I brought out the terrariums and placed them on the table.

Gigi looked at them and gasped. "Those are gorgeous. Where did you get them?"

"This one is for you." I gave Gigi a terrarium in a glass container shaped like an abstract canoe. "I made it."

"You made it?" Ellen asked.

"I studied botany when I was in college. I love plants, and these give me a reason to work with them again. I hope you like this one."

Ellen's terrarium was inside a round glass bowl with an opening on the side.

"I'll be back in a moment." I walked back into my office, grabbed my laptop, and brought it back to the table. "Would you like to see the wedding pictures? We just got them."

Ellen nodded eagerly. "I'm dying to see them."

I placed the laptop in front of them. "Take your time. I have to help Willow with something."

"Don't worry about us. Do what you need to do," Gigi said. "Thank you for the terrariums. You didn't have to do that."

"I know, but I wanted to. Thank you for the flowers. I need to go get a vase for them."

After speaking to another customer who wanted to meet me, I got a vase, added water, and placed the beautiful flowers inside. The white daylilies and lilac irises looked stunning.

I placed the vase on the desk and sat down at the table next to Gigi.

"The pictures are mesmerizing," Gigi said with tears in her eyes. "He looks so happy. I've never seen him like this." She reached for my hand. "You brought him back to life, Nessa. I'm sorry if I was angry or cold with you."

"No worries." I smiled. "You're his mom, so you have every right to worry. You and I didn't know each other well then, but that's going to change." I placed my other hand on top of hers. "Know that I won't hurt him. I love him."

My heart thundered at the admission. The power of the words filled the space with immense joy.

Gigi cried and embraced me. "If his mom were still alive, she would be so happy." She drew back and looked at me. "Susan and I were good friends."

"You guys make a gorgeous couple." Ellen dabbed her eyes. "My li'l bro is all grown up."

I didn't know what had changed from last week, but I welcomed it. I was sitting with my mother and sister-in-law, having a wonderful conversation. This day had turned out better than I could have imagined.

While Gigi examined the terrarium from different angles, I said, "You know my real name isn't Nessa, correct?"

"That's your artist's name." She lifted a shoulder. "Kind of like an author's pen name. How would you like us to address you?"

"Nessa is best for now. Thank you."

"This terrarium is stunning and so unique," Ellen said. "Have you thought of making them to sell?"

"Great minds think alike." I beamed. "I thought that just now in my office." With hope thrumming inside me, I stood and gestured to an area by the wide window. "I could set up a display there for people to see when they walk by. The gallery could offer unique plants and other art besides paintings. What do you think?"

"That's a splendid idea," Gigi said. "I know many people who love terrariums and plants. I'll send them this way. Just let me know when you're ready."

"Not everyone can afford expensive original art, but they can buy plants in unique containers," Ellen said.

"Or smaller works from various artists," I added.

"Exactly." Gigi smiled. "People love unique things. You can sell these terrariums for a higher price than other places because you're the artist."

"I agree." Ellen held hers up. "I love this so much. It's like a little world."

"Thank you." I clasped my hands together. "I'm excited about this new addition." I'd reach out to Shauna Casey, the artist who made the glass containers, for a quote for more orders.

"Thank you for having us," Gigi said. "I know Attikus will travel for business soon. When he returns, come over for dinner."

"I would love that."

They stayed until they had to leave to meet up with some friends.

"If you need anything, call Ellen or me, okay?" Gigi looked at me as though she knew something about me that I didn't. Despite that, the warmth in her eyes made my day. "We're family now."

"Same goes for you and Ellen. If you need anything, call or text."

When they left, I got a call from *Mẹ*. I didn't tell her about the change regarding her escape. Attikus was still working on it, and I didn't want to worry her.

"How's everything going?" she asked in a tone that made me smile.

"I'm dating him."

"I'm so happy to hear that," she said. "He's a lucky man to be with my daughter. I can't wait to meet him."

"I think you'll like him."

"I know I will," she said with so much conviction.

"How do you know?"

"Because I trust my daughter's judgment." She sighed. "And I trust God to guide us along the way."

My mom wasn't a social media person, so she probably didn't know about my fake marriage. She would have asked if she'd heard. I didn't want to make her worry by giving her unnecessary information.

We caught up on life. She told me about her friends, Sheila and Josephine, who were taking online classes. Mom wanted to get her chemistry degree just because. Sheila and Josephine were doing well in their business and accounting courses.

Before we hung up, I told her not to worry about anything and that everything was going well.

But I was worried about Attikus. How was he going to get her out successfully? If he got caught, his career would be over. I couldn't live with that.

CHAPTER FORTY-THREE

ATTIKUS

AFTER MY MEETING at the museum, I followed up on a clue my team had uncovered. Someone had tried to sell Joseph's watch at a pawnshop.

Though the watch wasn't a Rolex, it was a customized watch. I had a European watchmaker create it with Joseph's name engraved on the back. The interesting thing about the watch was that the dial for the date was changed to something that intrigued me.

The man who'd found it said he'd spotted it near the Canal Walk, an area filled with retail businesses and office space along a section of the Providence River entering the city. I'd been that way several times.

Had Joseph wandered there? Had something happened to him, and he dropped the watch? The dial and the number were set to 020700. Had someone tried to change the number? Had the watch malfunctioned? Or was this a clue to something?

I strode along the Canal Walk.

Where are you, Joseph? Are you okay?

The recordings my team had uncovered around this area

had shown nothing suspicious. I didn't see Joseph or anyone who looked like him.

This was a busy section of the city, and those numbers could mean anything. They could be license plate numbers or a code into a building. I could go crazy trying to decipher this. The numbers could also mean nothing.

After wandering around for another hour, I headed home to work on my video game. The International Game Convention was coming up and ran from late July through to September. This would be the perfect opportunity for my friends and me to showcase the finished WaterFyre Rising. This was our debut to the world.

Two days ago, an idea came to me on how to improve Level Seven. That inspiration was what I'd been waiting for. The main framework and characters were all set. I just needed to fill in the details—the easy and fun stuff. The game was so close to being finished.

I also included the names of those who had hurt my friends and me in the game. They became villains that players wanted to kill. I wanted my game to declare the truth of how corrupt this world was. But I also wanted to show hope.

Vanessa's face popped into my mind. She was the hope that contrasted the dark world I'd lived in for too long. Working on the game would take my mind off Joseph. I didn't want to think that he was dead.

When I got home, Vanessa had just showered and looked happy.

"Guess who came to visit me at the gallery today?"

"Who?" I pulled her to me and inhaled her comforting floral scent. It immediately soothed my tension.

She wrapped her arms around my waist and peered up at me. "Your mom and sister."

Vanessa had spent a lot of time creating the perfect gift for

Mom Gigi and Ellen. One gift—which symbolized us as a couple—was enough. My mom and sister didn't need another plant from me to earn their forgiveness.

Even though Vanessa had been screwed over by many people, she still held onto hope and kindness. I wasn't like her, but she proved that the world still had good people.

"Oh, yeah? Did they like the terrariums?" I held a strand of her soft hair in my hand. "Also, where's my terrarium?"

"They loved them. Yours is in your office. I wanna start selling them at the gallery." Her eyes beamed with excitement. "These would be terrariums inside unique containers."

"I think that's a fantastic idea. I haven't seen any galleries that sell terrariums. You'll start a new trend."

"Thanks! This gives me a reason to work with plants again. Also, you should check out the greenhouse. We can start eating the vegetables in a few months!"

I'd received an alert on my phone that my greenhouse had been activated, but I hadn't gone out there to see what she'd done.

"Thanks for starting it."

"You're welcome. I figured you were busy. It was fun."

"I want to see my terrarium." We walked into the office, and I saw a unique glass jar with a cover on top. A set of steps made of tiny twigs led up to a small gazebo. Small sticks and moss lined the path. Adorable trees and flowers were perfectly placed around the jar to create a peaceful scenery—a safe and magical world inside a jar. That was how she made me feel. When I was here with Vanessa, I felt like I was entering a safe space where nothing could bother me.

"It's beautiful. I love it." I gripped her face and kissed her.

"These would sell wonderfully at the gallery. You should price them high. They're unique art."

"That's what your mom said."

Needing the comfort, I pulled her in for another hug.

"Are you okay?"

I didn't want to talk about finding Joseph's watch and worry her. My job was to protect *her*.

"Yeah. I want to work on my video game today. Wanna see what I have so far?"

"Yes, please." She reached for a chair, dragging it over next to my desk.

But I said, "Sit on my lap."

"How are you going to work like that?"

"It's perfectly fine." I patted my thigh. "I want your ass to kiss my thighs.

Shaking her head, she slid onto my thighs, and all was well with the world again.

I clicked on my computer and opened the folder with all the video games from my friends.

"I like how you named it level one, two, three, and so on."

"Yes, that signifies the elevation of power."

"What power? Is there an element that links all the games?"

"It's WaterFyre—a powerful energy that builds over time. The players gather this potent energy every time they move on to the next level."

"That's an interesting way to link them all together."

"Remington started this with Grayson, Royce, Forrest, and Arrow when they were teens. Orion and I joined later."

I played a trailer for all the levels that we'd be showing at the International Game Convention.

"It's amazing," she said, browsing the levels. "I'm not a

gamer, but this makes me want to play. There's magic, suspense, and mystery. I like the hidden treasure boxes where you reference names and things in Providence and The Trogyn."

I looked at her profile: beautiful and strong—a warrior who would help me defeat the villains.

"My friends and I have sprinkled evidence of all of The Trogyn's crimes into the game. We've changed the names a bit, but the criminals who are part of that organization will know who we're talking about."

"That's brilliant." She shifted to look at me, and her ass made my cock hard.

"Grayson did it first, and the other guys went back to their demos and inserted the details."

"The video game isn't just a game." She searched my face, and pride soared in me. I was fortunate to be with an intelligent woman who saw the plan.

"No, it isn't."

"Top secret billionaire stuff?" she asked.

"Exactly." I kissed the side of her head.

She knew not to ask any more questions, and I loved her more for that. I wanted her to be safe, and part of that protection was keeping certain things secret.

I showed Vanessa Level Seven, where a warrior goddess was a painter, and her weapon was a paintbrush. She could paint portals to escape dire situations. Her brush could also heal injuries, depending on the energy source.

"Wow," she said. "Each color on the palette is a source of power." She zoomed in on the warrior artist's face. "That looks like me!"

"It *is* you."

She whipped her head at me. "What? You made me a character in your game?"

"How can I not add the woman I love into a game that's very important to me?"

She opened her mouth to say something but stopped. Emotion gleamed in her eyes.

Shifting, she straddled my hips to face me. "What did you say?" she asked nervously.

Taking her hands in mine, I lifted them to my chest. I hadn't meant to say those words to her today. But after encountering so many deaths recently and not being able to locate Joseph, I realized that life was unpredictable.

What if something happened to us tomorrow? I wanted her to know how I felt now.

"I love you," I said. "It all started with one painting that set me free."

Her eyes teared up. "How do you know it's love?"

"How does the sun know when to rise or set?" I skimmed her cheek with my fingers. "It just knows."

She said nothing as tears slid down her cheeks.

I grabbed a tissue from my desk and dabbed her eyes. "How does a plant know how to grow?"

She smiled but didn't say anything, probably waiting to see what I would say.

"It just does. Like you said, nature is intelligent." I brushed my lips against hers. "It follows the natural rhythm of what it's made of." I swallowed, trying to calm my heart as raw emotions flowed out of me. I didn't realize how thoroughly I'd prevented myself from expressing my feelings all these years. Vengeance had been my driving force, but it was also my crutch. "You've brought my heart back to life. It was dead before you appeared."

She placed a hand on either side of my face and looked into my eyes. "I love you too." She kissed me, lingered, and then drew back. "Your heart was never dead. It just took a nap." She hugged me. "We all have moments when we need rest." I felt her heartbeat against me as she rubbed circles on my back and muttered, "I'm going to protect you too."

"What?"

She kissed my cheek. "Whenever you need to rest or take a nap, we'll do it together, okay?"

I nodded. "Want to help me add details to Level Seven?"

"I thought you'd never ask." She grinned. "By the way, I think Nessa Lily Pad needs a magic lily pad that could take her places like the flying carpet in Aladdin."

"I can show you the world . . ." I sang an awful rendition of the song.

"Oh, my god." She laughed and shifted her body to face the computer.

"I'll leave the magic lily pad for you to design." I massaged her shoulders.

"Yeah?" Excitement filled her eyes. "And I think the warrior, Whistler Ren, needs a powerful cane that's a magic pen and a spear all in one."

I laughed, agreeing with her design. "The boys and I should hire you to help design the game. You're good at this."

She leaned back and looked up at me. "It's because I'm hanging out with the best of the best. It's like osmosis, you know."

"I sense a cheesy plant line coming."

Her eyes sparked with mischief. "Do you know you have flowers on your face?"

"Where?" I patted my cheeks.

"You have tulips." She grinned, pressing her finger to my lips. "I want to plant a kiss on them, but I'm too nervous. What plant am I?"

"A sweaty palm."

Her face brightened. "You realize we're having a very cheesy conversation, right?"

"Yup, and I'm loving it."

My stomach growled, having missed lunch. It was past dinnertime now.

"Let's have dinner first, and we can resume later." She hopped off my lap and grabbed my hand.

"No, we can't.

"Why not?" she asked.

"Because I haven't *botany*."

"Oh, my god." She rolled her eyes but laughed. "That's stupid."

"It made you laugh. I'm catching on, aren't I?"

"We have plenty of leftovers." She dragged me into the kitchen. "After we eat, I'm going to make Whistler Ren the coolest protagonist in existence. Your friends will be jealous of this character."

Pride and love radiated from me. I was in love with an intelligent, creative woman with a big heart and a strange sense of humor. "I can't wait to see the revision."

CHAPTER FORTY-FOUR

VANESSA

ATTIKUS LEFT this morning for a business meeting in California. Then he was flying to New York for another meeting at the end of the week. He'd been gone for an hour, and I already missed him.

The more I got to know this brilliant man, the more I fell in love with him. Level Seven was ninety-five percent complete, and I was thrilled to help him with the details. He could now cross that off his priority list.

Despite that, I still sensed his stress. I knew he was trying to protect me by not sharing all his concerns. I overheard his conversation with Orion the other day. Something about apprehending a Trogyn member, but then Attikus walked into his office and closed the door. I couldn't sit around and let him do all the work.

Before he left, he told me not to worry about my mom's freedom. Attikus discovered that the prosecutor and judge were linked to The Trogyn. His lawyer was currently preparing documents to submit to the court for a new trial.

Hope sparked in me. Perhaps I didn't need to extract my mother from prison at all. Maybe she'd be released soon.

Creativity had burst in me the last few days, and I couldn't stop painting or outlining the ideas for a terrarium corner. I finished three paintings and even varnished them.

I didn't have to go to the gallery until later today, so I walked into Attikus's office and looked at the research boards he'd created. He didn't know I'd been using these boards for my research. I couldn't sit around while my man put himself in danger trying to help me.

I stepped over to the board that displayed my issues, looking at Emmanuel's pictures and all the people he had been associated with. Becca was the redheaded woman I'd seen with Enzo at the bakery that day. Both were deceased Trogyn members. Milton Kalkounis was Emmanuel's trainer—another Trogyn member. Not deceased. A Post-it note stated that he was also Jean-Claude Dumas.

"Huh?" I said to no one. The trainer had two identities? Why?

My heart raced as I recognized the man who was there the day I was attacked in the alleyway—Brody Harris. The man with the scar on his lip and the flying pig tattoo on his neck. Attikus had probably identified him from the blurry video.

Brody was the cousin of Dillon Harris, the man I'd killed. They were part of Harris Pharmaceuticals, which owned several drug and health insurance companies.

As I surveyed the board, studying more pictures, my eyes landed on the trainer, Milton Kalkounis. He was also on Attikus's board. I saw he was friends with the group who had bullied Attikus. Milton was the link between our cases.

I wanted to ask Attikus so many questions, but if I did, he'd know I was looking into it.

I looked at the picture of the severed finger of his high school principal. Perhaps it had been sent to Attikus that day and not me. Whoever had done it knew he would attend the gallery opening.

My phone rang, and it was Willow.

"How's it going?" I asked.

"I know you're not due in yet, but three art collectors are here. They'd like to speak to you. Shall I ask them to come back later?"

"No. I'll be there in thirty minutes. Getting ready now."

Business at the gallery had increased more than I expected. With my terrarium collection coming soon, I should hire a second or even a third associate. I had to review my finances to see what I could afford. But right now, things looked positive.

When I arrived, five people browsed the gallery. I walked to the back room and brought out three new abstract paintings I'd finished two days ago. I had an urge to show them today.

Two of the new pieces sold while I spoke to the art collectors. After attending to those customers, a man approached me. I stopped breathing, and my heart thundered in fear. Gathering all my strength, I remained calm and pretended not to recognize him.

"Hello. How can I help you?" I forced a smile as I greeted Brody Harris.

Was God trying to tell me something earlier today when I recognized his face on the research board? He looked older and had gained more muscle since the alleyway incident. The scar on the lip and the flying pig tattoo on his neck were still visible.

"How much is that painting right there?" He pointed to the third abstract painting I'd just brought in.

I didn't want to sell it to him. I didn't want him to have anything that belonged to me. So I threw out a price that was way more than what the art was worth.

"Five hundred thousand dollars."

His mouth dropped open. "But I heard the other two customers buy something similar for a fraction of the price."

"Well, this painting has a deeper meaning. And there's more texture to it. The colors are similar to Van Gogh's *The Starry Night*."

"What is that painting called?"

"The Starry Truth," I said, realizing the irony of it.

This man who put my mom in prison was now trying to buy my art. Did he recognize me? Probably not. I didn't look like that college student anymore.

He stared at the painting for a moment. "I'll take it."

I blinked. What should I do now? I didn't want to sell the artwork to him, but I couldn't decline his offer either. What if he created trouble by saying I was prejudiced against him for whatever reason? That would create bad press for my gallery. Plus, he was associated with bad people. They could create more trouble for me.

An idea popped into my head. The shock of seeing him had hindered my ability to think clearly.

"Wonderful. Fill out this form for me." I offered him a tablet with the document to collect his information. "I'll package the painting for you and provide the Certificate of Authenticity."

He nodded and busied himself with the tablet.

Instead of taking the painting to the counter and packaging it, I took it into the office. My heart rate soared as I pulled out the drawer that held the innovative device Vivian had given me. A company specializing in high-tech gadgets had made it.

No one could see the tiny metal device, which was the size of a pinhead. My nerves skyrocketed as I inserted it into a spot on the painting. I used a metallic paint marker to cover up the device, making it look like one of the stars in the painting.

I put the painting into a customized box, then slipped it

into a gift bag. When I walked out, I grabbed the Certificate of Authenticity and placed it in the bag.

After he signed the documents, I asked, "Would you like to pay an installment or the full amount?"

"I can pay it in full today."

"Wire transfer or credit card?"

He gave me his Black American Express credit card with the name Harris Pharmaceuticals LLC on it. When the amount was authorized, he signed it. I didn't ask if he worked for the company or anything.

As he left, his phone rang, and he picked up the call. "Yo. I'll be at the banquet tonight. I'm all set with my gift."

Who was he giving the painting to?

For the next hour, nobody entered the gallery. The rush was over, which gave me time to calm my nerves. I let Willow take an early lunch while I replayed the event. I had to tell Attikus when he returned. If I shared this with him now, he'd probably cancel his meetings and rush back. I didn't want him to do that.

With my heart pounding, I logged into the website that tracked the device.

A blinking red dot moved slowly on the map, signifying that Brody was a couple of blocks from here.

I couldn't believe I had done that. But intuition told me he could offer more clues for Attikus and me.

I set Brody aside to review my financial situation. With the income I received today, I could afford to hire two more associates if I continued selling paintings at this rate. I wrote up the job description and the requirements for the sales positions, then posted them on several job sites.

My business was growing fast, and I couldn't be happier. I checked my email and saw a reply from the glass artist, asking me to stop by her studio for a chat. My terrarium idea was coming to fruition quicker than I'd anticipated. I should visit local garden shops to see if they could offer me what I needed. Another idea bloomed in my mind. I could use the greenhouse to plant mini trees, shrubs, mushrooms, and whatever I wanted to include in my terrariums. But I'd also be supporting the local communities.

Despite everything going so well regarding my business, a lingering dread prevented me from fully celebrating. Sighing, I wished everything would be resolved soon. I missed the care-free lifestyle we had in Maui. I was tired, and I knew Attikus was too.

The front doorbell chimed, and I looked up. My day took another nosedive as I spied Miranda. She stalked in with a stern face as though she owned the place. I wasn't in the mood to speak to her. It seemed my past was taking turns today, and she was a part I didn't want to remember.

I couldn't believe Attikus had dated her. Then again, her family was wealthy, and she probably ran in his circle. Perhaps I should give her a chance. Her post about Attikus and me had benefited us. She seemed professional and had grown up a lot. Maybe she'd experienced something that had changed her attitude.

Miranda stepped up to the desk and smirked. Her demeaning expression from years ago was on full display again. This was the Miranda I remembered.

"Where's Attikus?" she demanded in a rude tone.

"Working," I said. "Is there something I can help you with?"

"Well, he's not at the museum. Where is he?"

Agitation pumped off her body. What had happened to her?

She glanced around the gallery, muttering something to

herself before whipping her gaze back at me. "I need him to pay child support."

What?

I gaped at her. "Attikus doesn't have any children." Not that he'd told me. And his mother and sister would've mentioned it.

Miranda stepped closer to the counter. Her pupils were dilated, but her irises were dull. When she turned, I saw a rash on the side of her neck.

"He has a boy with me. I never told him, but now I need him to pay up."

"Where's the kid?" I asked.

Something was wrong with Miranda. She reached into her purse, pulled out her phone, and showed me a picture of a five-year-old child. "This is Brandon. He's Attikus's son."

He had Attikus's dark hair, but I didn't believe her. What was she trying to do after all these years? Was she trying to make me angry? If so, this was an outrageous way to do it.

"Do you have proof that the kid is his?"

"A paternity test result was sent to Attikus's email. I need him to reply. If he doesn't, my lawyer will reach out to him."

Attikus didn't need an extra problem on his plate.

I stared at her, trying my best to stay calm. "Why are you doing this now?"

"Because Brandon needs to know who his father is. Attikus needs to take care of his son and the mother of his child."

"So you want money because you're incompetent?"

"Don't talk to me like that, bitch."

I was familiar with this Miranda. "Are you on drugs?"

"No," she said too quickly.

"Attikus isn't here. He's away on business. I don't know when he'll return." I picked up my phone. "Do you mind if I take a snapshot of your son?"

"Sure. Isn't he handsome? Just like his father. I already sent Attikus a copy. He hasn't replied to my texts."

She held up the phone, and I took a picture of him. I didn't want to give her my phone number. She also showed me a video of her son playing at the park. He was going down the slide as she commented on the phone.

When Miranda stalked out of the gallery, I collapsed on the chair, unsure of what to think. Had Attikus fathered a child and not known it? That could be a possibility. He would've told me if he had a son, right?

CHAPTER FORTY-FIVE

ATTIKUS

AS SOON AS my meetings concluded in California, I headed to New York City to meet with Remi and Orion. We had scheduled a meeting with a group of popular gamers with a wide following to discuss their help in promoting WaterFyre Rising.

When everything was set, I left Remi and Orion to complete the negotiations so I could attend another meeting.

I was dead tired by the time I returned to my hotel room after dinner. Vanessa had sent me a text saying she missed me earlier, but I hadn't had time to reply to her. I had back-to-back conferences because I'd squeezed a week's worth of meetings into a few days so I could return to my love. Just two more days, and I would be home.

I'd never experienced a stronger desire to be home. My other half was waiting for me. What was Vanessa doing now? Was she missing me the way I was missing her?

After a quick shower, I called her, "What's my Lily Pad doing?"

"In bed, thinking about you."

I smiled as my cock hardened in my boxers. This woman could affect me from miles away.

"How was your day?" I asked.

She told me she sold three paintings and was in the process of hiring two associates. But she feared her income could drop. Selling art didn't offer a stable income. Some days, she didn't sell any art.

"Continue with the hiring process," I told her. "I'll help with whatever you need."

"I can't do that, Attikus. This is my business. And you're the landlord."

That comment hurt. "I'm more than a landlord, Vanessa. I'm your boyfriend who loves you, but I'm also your husband. So I can help. Besides, I want to invest in you. If you need more associates to run the gallery, hire them. I want you to succeed, and I'll ensure you have the capital to do so."

"Why do you care so much?"

Her voice held an edge that told me something had happened.

"Because I love you." It was a simple and true statement. I heard her sigh on the other line. "What happened today? I can hear the tension in your voice?"

"Miranda stopped by, looking for you."

"I received two missed calls from Miranda and some text messages. Haven't checked them yet. Agnes also left me a voicemail about Miranda looking for me. What did she want?"

"She said you fathered a son with her. He's now five years old, and she wants you to pay child support."

"*What?*" I sat up in bed. "That's absurd. I didn't father any child."

"How can you be sure?"

I raked a hand through my hair, trying to wrap my head around why Miranda was suddenly accusing me of this.

"Our relationship was short," I said. "I can count how many times I slept with her on one hand. And I used protection *every single time.*"

"Condoms aren't a hundred percent guaranteed."

I didn't like the doubts I heard in Vanessa's comments.

"Do you trust me?" I didn't care what the rest of the world thought of me, but I needed Vanessa to trust me.

"Yes," she said. "I trust you, which is why I'm talking to you."

Relief settled in me. "I don't know what's going on. She obviously wants money, but why? Her family has money. *She* has money."

"She was behaving strangely today compared to when you introduced me to her. She seemed extremely agitated. Her pupils were dilated, and she was muttering to herself."

What happened to Miranda?

"Today, she acted like the spoiled brat from elementary school. There's one more thing. She showed me a picture of your son. "

"That's impossible."

"Sending an image right now to your phone. Miranda said she sent you a copy already."

My phone buzzed, and I glanced at the image.

"It's fake. An amateur could do this on Photoshop or any AI software."

"I didn't think about that."

"Your judgment was clouded because you were angry and hurt."

"She also showed me a video of the boy at the park playing by himself."

"Don't think about it too much. The video is also fake. AI software can easily create these things. It can take pictures or videos of people and blend them. Technology is highly advanced these days, and that's one of the dangers we have to face."

"I'm afraid she'll hurt your image."

"Don't worry. I'm heading home tomorrow, and I'll reach out to her."

"How was your day?" Vanessa asked, sounding calmer.

"Chaotic, but efficient. Missing you like crazy."

I could picture her smiling on the other end of the phone.

"You know what I want right now?" My voice grew hoarse as I imagined her in bed with me.

"A cheesy plant joke?"

I laughed. "That wasn't on my mind, but I'll take whatever you want to give me." My dick needed attention, and I gripped it, wishing it was her hand stroking me.

"I know what you're doing right now."

"Do you now?"

"You're doing what I'm doing. But I wish it were you . . ."

She was fucking hot and perfect.

"I didn't realize I had such a wicked wife."

"That's because I'm learning from my wicked husband."

Twenty minutes later, my seductive Lily Pad had me rushing into the bathroom to clean myself.

I fell asleep with her voice in my head.

CHAPTER FORTY-SIX

VANESSA

AS I DROVE to work the next day, I stopped by the grocery store to pick up some water bottles and healthy snacks for the refrigerator in the gallery's kitchen.

I bought some fruit, water, juice, and trail mix for Willow and me. I ate her last pack a few days ago.

As I loaded my car, I heard a scream.

"Leave me alone! Help me!"

I stiffened, remembering the traumatic event I'd experienced all those years ago. I rushed to help and saw two men harassing Miranda.

"Help!" I shouted as I reached for my phone and dialed 911.

This was too familiar. My heart hammered, but I wasn't a young, helpless girl anymore. The men spotted me and pushed Miranda to the ground. She was bleeding profusely from her stomach.

The man with the ponytail held a bloody knife and glared at me. "Get her!"

The infuriated men rushed toward me, looking like they wanted to kill me. A group of people exited the grocery store and hurried toward me.

"Help me!" I waved them over. "They stabbed her!"

The two criminals saw the people and tried to run away, but three men rushed after them. A battle erupted as three bulky men shoved the criminals to the ground.

I overheard one of my rescuers calling for assistance. He must've been an off-duty officer.

My body trembled as I pressed a hand to Miranda's wound, trying to stop the bleeding. "Help is on the way," I told her.

Tears streamed from her eyes as she looked at me. Her pupils weren't dilated.

"It wasn't me yesterday." She winced. "They did something to me . . . Can you get my phone?" She looked over at her purse lying on the floor with the contents scattered everywhere.

I reached for her purse and found her phone.

"They want me to blackmail him with a video . . . They're evil . . . Here's the code to my phone." She drew the code on my arm. Another wave of pain overcame her, and her breath hitched. "He didn't have a son with me . . ."

She cried out in pain as blood gushed from her wound. Streams of red slipped through the seams of my fingers and oozed onto her clothes. Fear tightened my chest. It didn't look good for Miranda. I looked around me. Where was the ambulance? Why was it taking so long?

"Be careful . . . These people are dangerous . . . They want him to stop searching. . ." Her eyelids fluttered.

"Searching for what?"

"Ashton . . . I don't remember . . ." She moaned as she looked at me. "You look like someone I knew from elementary school."

This wasn't the time to bring that up.

"Save your energy," I urged.

Miranda shook her head and tapped her forearm. "They injected me with something. It's making me weak . . . I'm bleeding too much . . . I won't make it." She gripped my arm. "If you know of a girl named Van Lam, tell her I'm sorry for being such a bitch to her . . . I made her life hell back then . . ."

"I'll let her know." Tears dripped from my eyes. "She forgives you. Stop talking. Save your energy."

"You have to be careful, Nessa . . . They'll hurt you . . . Be smarter than them . . ." Her face paled from the excessive blood loss.

My hands were covered in her blood. "Who are these people?"

"I don't know . . . My trainer . . . he—" Her body shook with a seizure.

Medics finally arrived and took over. I stood off to the side, watching them try to save her. Foam spilled from her mouth. When her eyes rolled back and her hands went limp, I knew she was gone.

Shock filled me. Why was this happening? People I knew were dying. Emmanuel, and now Miranda. I feared for Attikus and our friends.

The police officers tried to handcuff the men, but they fought back. One of them reached for an officer's gun, but the other officer shot him dead.

"They're on drugs or something!" said the officer as they handcuffed the man with the ponytail.

Were these guys linked to the man who had attacked Attikus and me in Maui and to the driver who killed Emmanuel?

I tucked Miranda's phone into my purse before the crime

scene officials arrived. After answering some questions from the police officer, the EMT cleaned my hands.

What was on Miranda's phone? Why were these people protecting Ashton? Was Attikus getting too close to his enemy?

CHAPTER FORTY-SEVEN

ATTIKUS

I WAS ABOUT to head into another meeting when I received a text from Vanessa.

Vanessa: *Are you in a meeting right now?*

Though it was a text message, I sensed the dread in it. I walked into an empty room in the hotel lobby, shut the door, and called her.

"Is everything okay?"

"Are you busy? I don't want to interrupt you if you are." She sounded stuffy, like she'd been crying.

"I'm not busy. What's wrong, baby?"

"Miranda's dead," she choked. "She was bleeding so much."

Shock came over me. "What happened?"

As Vanessa described the situation, my hand formed an angry fist.

Those fuckers could've hurt Vanessa. What had they injected into Miranda?

This entire situation was getting out of hand.

"Are you home or in your gallery?" I asked.

"I'm home."

"Okay, stay there. I'll be home in a few hours."

"You don't have to," she said. "I'll be okay."

She didn't sound okay. Besides, I wanted to be with her. After what she'd been through, she needed me there.

I was getting close to Ashton. He knew I'd been searching for him all these years. Where the fuck was he? What kind of coward forced a woman to carry out a threat for him?

If he could do that to Miranda, I feared Vanessa would be next. This was the first clue that Ashton C. Lindor was still committing crimes behind the scenes.

"I miss you, so I want to be home."

"Did you finish all your meetings?" she asked.

"I got what I needed."

"Okay. I'll see you soon." She released a sigh filled with distress. "Attikus?"

"Yeah?"

"Be careful."

"Lily Pad, I'm the living devil," I said, appreciating her concern for me. But I'd been waiting for the asshole to show himself. "They should be afraid of me. But for you, I'll be careful."

Rage coursed through me as I wondered how Miranda had become involved in this mess. Had they blackmailed her like Emmanuel?

I called my lawyer, who was also attending today's meeting, and had him handle the final negotiations for the art books and affordable art programs I was rolling out to the public schools. The discussions with the distributor were ongoing, and today's meeting was to finalize the details.

Then I booked the earliest flight home and headed to the airport.

CHAPTER FORTY-EIGHT

VANESSA

I LAY on Attikus's bed, inhaling his masculine scent. It comforted me like a protective blanket.

Today's event drained me of energy and hope. The dark clouds hovered over me, and I couldn't shake them off. Where was justice when you needed it? Where was karma?

I knew deep down that justice and karma would always collect what was due. But sometimes, they took too long. How many more lives would be ruined before I saw any justice?

I could still see Miranda's face in my head—her pain, worry, sorrow, and regret. Her blood had seeped into the pavement of the parking lot. A dark memory was now embedded in that area. This was the second time I'd seen someone die before my eyes. The first time was Dillon, who tried to rape me. But Miranda didn't deserve to die. She had grown up, and she had asked for my forgiveness.

I forgave her, and I hoped she understood that.

However, her death wasn't the only thing that bothered me. I stared at her phone on the side table. A Post-it note with

Miranda's code sat next to it. I was an emotional mess, so I feared if I didn't write it down, I might forget it.

I saw the video on her phone earlier. It shook me to the core. I shivered, remembering the violent video of three boys beating one. How could I not be affected after watching something that vile and malicious? These boys weren't people; they were savages. I wanted to hurt them the way they had Attikus.

My chest hurt seeing what those monsters had done to him. When he'd told me his story, I had an image in my head of the event. But seeing the real thing shattered me. I'd already watched it three times, and each time, my heart broke some more.

I'd cried for a long time before I had gathered myself and called Attikus. I wanted to reach over the phone and hug him— keep him safe. Those boys had put him through hell. It wasn't just the beating but also the murder of his entire family.

Tears filled my eyes again, and I reached for the tissue box. Ashton had stepped on Attikus's hand and broken his knee and ankle. The other two boys were stupid followers. Who recorded this video? Could it be Milton Kalkounis? Miranda said her trainer had done something to her.

I blew my nose and knew my eyes would be puffy tomorrow. But I didn't care. I'd already told Willow I needed tomorrow off. Hopefully, she wouldn't be bombarded with customers.

Feeling drained, I snuggled into Attikus's pillow and stretched out an arm to touch the empty spot where he would be if he were in bed with me. Exhaustion tugged at me, but I forced myself to stay awake for Attikus. I wanted to see him. It was only seven in the evening, but my body was desperate for rest.

I closed my eyes for a moment . . .

CHAPTER FORTY-NINE

ATTIKUS

WHEN I ENTERED THE HOUSE, silence greeted me.

I called out to Vanessa, but no one answered. I walked into my bedroom and found her sleeping in my bed. That image spread warmth in my chest. She was the reason colors existed in this world. She looked so beautiful and peaceful. Then she shifted, and her peaceful expression transformed into a frown as tears streamed down her face.

Why was my baby crying in her sleep?

"No!" She punched the air and kicked at the blanket. "Leave him alone!"

"Vanessa." I gripped her wrist, fearing she might hurt herself.

"I'm going to kill all of you!" she cried as tears flooded her face with her eyes still closed. "Attikus!"

What kind of nightmare was she having?

"Vanessa, I'm here." I held her hands down on the bed.

Then she sobbed and curled into a ball. I gathered her into my arms and held her as her anxious breathing subsided. What would have happened if I hadn't returned home?

I pressed a kiss to her head. Then her body stiffened, and her eyes opened. She whipped her head toward me, and our eyes met.

She sat up and smiled as though she hadn't just experienced a nightmare. "When did you get home?

"Just now."

She cupped my face in her hands and kissed me. Then she hopped onto me and embraced me. We held onto each other for a long moment.

"Are you okay?" I asked.

"Yes, now that you're home."

"Let me see that pretty face of yours."

She straightened up. "It's not very pretty right now."

I brushed away the wetness that still lingered under her eyes. "Why were you crying?"

"It's been an awful day," she said as her expression changed. "I realized I'm capable of violence. There are new people on my shit list." She held up a fist.

I stifled a smile. Was this the reason for her dream?

"Who are they?"

She touched my face and named the three people who had changed my life. She probably saw the question in my eyes because she gestured to the phone on the table. "That's Miranda's phone. She gave it to me."

I grabbed it and used the code on the Post-it note to enter.

A video was already on the screen. I didn't have to play it to know what it was. I recognized the clothing they wore that day.

Vanessa gripped my hand, and her worried expression told me this was the reason for her traumatic dream.

"I'll be fine. I know what that video is all about. It will only push me harder to find Ashton."

Vanessa rolled over and snuggled next to me. She gripped my arm as though she feared I might break from the video.

I hit play and watched the entire attack. Vanessa rubbed her hand up and down my arm during the five-minute video. Something unexpected happened. The video didn't affect me like I thought it would. Instead of enraging me, it healed me to see it from this perspective. It was as though I had detached from the experience and was now looking at it from a different angle. My heart thundered as I looked at Vanessa's hand as she soothed me.

Love had removed the pain from my past. It had allowed me to move on. I hadn't realized it until now. The energetic knots that had twisted me up all these years had loosened. However, moving on didn't mean I'd forgotten what had happened. It didn't mean my desire for vengeance had disappeared. It just meant I could navigate without the dark shackles hindering me.

I knew love was a powerful emotion, but I didn't know its capability until now. No wonder people were transformed by this potent emotion.

I placed the phone down on the table and took Vanessa's hand, kissing it. "You were crying for me?"

She nodded as her eyes filled up again. "I punched those boys in my dream. Kicked one in the nuts. Ashton screamed like a girl. It felt good."

I smiled but didn't tell her I'd witnessed it. I wanted to keep that secret to myself.

"Thank you for kicking their asses for me."

"Anytime." She grinned. "Are you hungry? Did you have dinner yet?"

"I'm not hungry. I spoke to Detective Farmer on my way home, and he told me the man who hurt Miranda died in prison from a heart attack." His accomplice died on the scene when he grabbed an officer's gun.

"So many deaths," she murmured.

"That just means the enemy is scared of what we might find out."

CHAPTER FIFTY

VANESSA

"WHERE ARE YOU TAKING ME?" I asked from the passenger seat.

I woke up this morning to a surprise. Not only did Attikus already have breakfast ready, but he also had a whole day planned for me.

"We're going on a date. I canceled all my meetings today and tomorrow to spend time with you."

Though I loved the idea of spending time with him, I knew he had a lot on his plate. There were urgent matters that needed to be dealt with. He was working with Detective Farmer regarding Miranda and Emmanuel's murders.

"Are you sure? I know you have a lot to do."

He reached for my hand and squeezed it.

"Nothing matters more than you. We both need a break from all this chaos. Consider the next two days like an energetic cleansing so we can recharge."

"Okay." I smiled at him. "I closed the gallery for the next two days too. Initially, I was going to have Willow work, but she deserved time off as well."

What was the point of working to death when I couldn't enjoy anything?

"So where are we going?"

"To the Mount Museum, hiking for some fresh air. Then we'll head home to watch a movie. Lovers things. Unless you have a better idea."

"Today, you get to organize our date. But tomorrow is my day to plan."

"Sounds good."

I'd been to the Mount Museum a few times, but it was mostly for business. An exhibit one time, and other times, I went to support fellow artists. I hadn't browsed as a visitor, though.

After browsing the first floor, Attikus took my hand and led me to the second floor. A few visitors wandered around. A group of college students sat in front of an Impressionist painting and sketched in their books.

As I walked through the rooms filled with art and sculpture, I felt like they were whispering secrets of the world to me.

"Do you sense they're talking to you when you walk through these rooms by yourself?"

"Yes," Attikus said. "I also sense the messages from the creator."

He walked up to an abstract painting with bold colors and powerful brushstrokes. With both hands on the cane, he studied the painting. "This a ten-million-dollar painting that captures the chaos of the artist's mind. Kenzi Kyoto was a brilliant physicist but also an artist. He had dementia at a later age. But during that time, he created some of his best work."

"His mind traveled beyond its confined boundaries," I said. "Society's expectations and family values can condition us to a certain way of thinking. He was freed from his mental grasp."

Attikus walked back to me and touched my face. "He could

capture moments of liberation. There's a genius to that. It's powerful and priceless."

"That's why this piece is ten million dollars."

"Sometimes the price doesn't match its true value. A seasoned art collector would understand that."

"Do you own it?"

"Yes." He glanced around. "There is art here borrowed from other museums, but I own this one."

We ambled by a hallway that was closed off.

"What's in there?"

"That room belongs to Orion. He leased the space to store some of his collection."

I nodded and followed Attikus's lead to the stairwell.

"You don't want to take the elevator?"

"The stairs are fine."

Although he was still using his cane, his walk had changed since I first met him. When we got to the first floor, I gestured to his right leg. "Is your leg getting better? I don't see you limp anymore."

"Magic happens when you're in love." His eyes gleamed. "You've healed me. I'm all better because of you."

"All better?" I walked around him, examining him like a doctor.

"You'll understand in a moment. Follow me."

We walked past the Employees Only sign and passed several offices.

"This is my office." He gestured to a spacious room with his name on the metal plate.

As we continued, Agnes walked out of her office, saw us, and smiled. She wore navy overalls and carried a toolkit in her hand.

"Something broke?" Attikus asked.

"One of the wires from a painting broke, so I fixed it."
Agnes turned to me. "Hi, Nessa. How are you?"

"Excellent. Thank you. You're so handy."

"If you ever need maintenance help, you call me." She
walked up to me and whispered. "Or if you ever want to renew
your vows. I'm always available."

I smiled. "Noted."

We continued down the hallway until we came to a door
with a metal plate that read Maintenance. Attikus opened it
and strode in.

"Are you going to repair something?" I asked.

He smirked. "No, Lily Pad. I'm showing you a special
room."

I laughed. "With an electrical box and boiler?"

"But highly advanced."

The door opened to another hallway. We made our way
along it and entered another door that led us down several
flights of stairs.

"Is this some kind of bunker?"

"A safe room. It's called The Gathering."

He pressed his palm to a screen, pressed a code, and shifted
his position to where something scanned his face. A noise
sounded, and the door clicked open.

"That's some security you have there," I said.

"Before we leave, I'll set you up so the screen recognizes you
too." He stepped in, leaned his cane against the wall, and looked
at me. "If you're ever in danger and need to use this room, you'll
have access to it." He described the concrete walls, made of
high-density steel, and how the door was both bulletproof and
fireproof. It sounded like he was preparing for the apocalypse.

I nodded. "Who else has access to this?"

"Agnes and Joseph."

I didn't know what to say. He was trusting me with this room, which obviously held his most prized possessions.

Attikus walked around the room, which had cream-colored walls and warm lighting. On the walls were more framed drawings that resembled the ones displayed at home.

I turned to admire more art, and my heart swelled. "You're Edgar Moore?" I walked up to the *Three Roads Diverged in a Dark Wood* painting I had shipped off to the buyer in Boston.

"Yeah." He smiled. "I placed that custom order a while ago under an alias. I wanted to see what you could come up with based on my brief description. And you delivered a masterpiece. It's one of my favorites. That's why it's here."

"So *The Lost Lily Pad* isn't a favorite anymore?" I teased.

"I can't store everything in here. I needed reminders of you in my home too. So I chose that piece because it was the first painting I got from you."

"I didn't realize I had a stalker."

He bent down for a kiss. "I guess I was attracted to you back then. Curious about the gorgeous artist who could reach into my soul." He turned his attention back to the painting. "You're the third road—the option that wasn't visible to me. But I discovered it as I discovered you—what love can do to a person. You led me to my healing."

"Attikus." I wrapped my arms around him, appreciating his declaration.

"Come look at these." He opened the door to a room full of my paintings.

I walked up to them, running my fingers down each frame. I'd sold these to people over the years. Some had been custom orders.

"How did you find these?"

"You can achieve a lot with money. Joseph had been helping me locate your work for a while."

I was speechless. "Why do you have this room, Whistler?"

"It was an urge that grew into something complex," he said. "I guess I built it as a way of protecting myself. It made me feel safe knowing I had a place to go to when the world fell apart. I had been planning my vengeance toward Ashton, Bobby, and Harry for a long time." He looked around. "This room gave me a place to rest my mind and soul so I could recuperate."

I spotted an office to the side and also a room with a bed. "You sleep here?"

"Sometimes when I work late." He walked up to me. "But I don't anymore since you moved into my house."

He had a massive board filled with pictures and notes about his enemies. The research board looked like a second version of what he had at home.

I touched his cheek. "Despite how this room can protect you, it feels lonely."

He took my hand. "It is. But I didn't know someone like you existed for me. I don't come here that often anymore."

"You don't need to." I turned to the cane leaning against the wall. "Is your leg healed?"

"It healed years ago." He led me to a lounge area and ushered me to a comfortable chair.

"What do you mean?"

"I had several surgeries on my leg after the event, and I depended on the cane for a while. But the will to survive—the drive for vengeance—helped me get stronger." He opened a refrigerator that blended in with the wall. "Water, juice, or wine?"

"Water, please."

He pulled out a cabinet door that was also integrated into the wall and retrieved two glasses. Then he poured water into each, offering me a glass.

"I continued physical therapy to get stronger until I didn't need the cane anymore. Though I didn't need it, I kept it for two reasons. One, it reminded me of my survival. I befriended it. Two, I wanted my enemies to believe that I was still injured. People get sloppy when they think you're weak."

"So you were pretending to limp all this time?"

"It wasn't pretending. I limped for a long time. That habit was ingrained in me. I had to remind myself to stop, but it was especially hard on days when I was preoccupied with other things. You know how some habits are more difficult to let go?" He gulped down the water and placed the glass on the table.

"Yes," I said. "If people could stop their bad habits easily, they wouldn't have a lot of problems. But then *you* entered my life, and that annoying habit disappeared. It was so easy. I didn't even realize it until recently." He walked up to me and kissed me. "You healed me in so many ways. Your art and your presence."

"I'm happy to help you. So the cane is merely an accessory to manipulate your enemies?"

He nodded. "Yes."

"I like that idea. Do your friends know you don't need the cane?"

"They do now."

I smirked at my cunning billionaire boyfriend, who was also my husband. Our relationship was strange, but somehow, it worked for us. To the public eye, we were a married couple. But in reality, we were in the beginning stages of dating.

"I guess we're manipulating our enemies too. You're not my real husband. We're lovers. Just dating."

"I think we're perfect partners in crime."

"Okay, Whistler." I laughed. "Where's the next crime?"

"A hike in the woods."

"Where three roads diverge?"

He grinned. "Exactly."

CHAPTER FIFTY-ONE

ATTIKUS

I WOKE at eight in the morning—the latest I'd ever slept in—and found the spot next to me empty. Where was she? I wanted her soft body next to me.

Rain splattered against the window, making me want to stay in bed. Last night was adventurous in every way. In the woods and in bed.

I enjoyed every minute spent with Vanessa. It was the best date I'd ever had. We didn't discuss any topics that brought sadness or stress. I could live with this peaceful lifestyle.

I got out of bed and walked into the bathroom to wash up, wondering what she had in store for me. When I entered the kitchen, Vanessa was wearing an apron and stirring something on the stove. It smelled delicious.

"What are you making, Lily Pad?" I came up behind her and kissed her neck. She smelled delicious too.

"Chicken porridge." She turned and kissed me. "Perfect for a day like this. Have you had chicken porridge before?"

"Nope."

"Well, I made a big pot. I hope you like it. If not, I'll have to give some to your friends." She gestured to the kitchen table. "I also made other things in case you don't like the porridge."

"What time did you wake up to make these?" I walked over to the table and glanced at the assortment of breakfast I'd never had at home before.

"Five sharp. But I bought these the other day and put them in the freezer. A lot of it was just steaming and frying. I didn't make them from scratch. Don't have time for that."

"I'll eat whatever you make, love. Thank you."

I smiled at the pretty plates of fried and steamed dumplings, a display of egg custard buns, and tarot cakes.

"But what's that?" I pointed to the white triangle pastries with a creamy sauce.

"A Vietnamese pastry I love to eat for breakfast, but most people have it as dessert. It's a banana pastry with coconut sauce."

"This is a five-star breakfast display. I feel like a king today."

Her eyes sparkled. "You can get these at any restaurant."

"But I love that you made them for me to eat at home."

She scooped some porridge into two bowls—one for me and one for her. Then she added scallions and cilantro, sprinkling in some black pepper before placing the bowls on a tray. She brought the tray over to the table and placed my bowl in front of me.

"Have a seat and eat whatever you like." She gave me a soup spoon and a pair of chopsticks.

I bent down to sniff the steam from the porridge. "It smells so good. You've worked hard today. Are you tired?"

"No. I feel energized." She smiled. "There's nothing on my mind but taking care of you. No stress about work or anything."

I scooped some up with my spoon and ate. "The chicken porridge is amazing."

She smiled. "Thank you. It was my mother's recipe. You should have some dumplings too."

"This is going to be lunch and dinner."

"That's what I was thinking because we're not going out today. It's pouring rain."

"What do you have planned for me, Lily Pad? Today is our second date."

"There are romantic movies we can watch." Mischief gleamed in her eyes. "Or, if you prefer, we have laundry we could do."

I placed two steamed dumplings onto my plate and ate them. "I've never heard of doing laundry as part of a fun date."

"We're creative people. We can make anything fun." She grinned. "We can make *boring* fun."

"I'll pass. But I'll watch a movie with you. I haven't watched a movie in a long time."

I didn't need to do anything today to be happy. Waking up to Vanessa making me breakfast was enough. We could sit around chatting or even doing laundry. I couldn't believe I thought that. But yeah, even doing laundry with her would be fun.

After I finished my bowl of porridge, I looked at her. "I think you should make this for me at least once a week or whenever it rains."

"My mom made it for me whenever I was sick. It comforts the stomach."

"I can see that. It's like a version of chicken soup."

We sat in silence, eating and exchanging glances. She wore a cotton T-shirt and shorts but looked hotter than any lingerie model.

"Oh, I forgot to get you some green tea. Hold on one second." She got up, went over to the kitchen counter, and brought over two cups of tea. "Green tea helps with digestion."

After I drank the tea, she said, "Are you in the mood for a movie or a documentary?"

"Whatever you want."

An hour later, we snuggled on the couch watching *Serendipity*, one of her favorite movies.

"Do you believe in fate?" she asked.

"I do."

"Me too. Certain things can't be explained. Like how I chose your art as the winning piece all those years ago. And how you bought my first painting but didn't know me until later."

"The universe is the perfect orchestrator."

She pinched my cheeks. "God is the most extraordinary artist." She got up from the couch. "I'm craving a snack. Do you want anything?"

"No, thanks." I was going to ask why she wanted a snack when the table was filled with so much food.

Had she made something else for me?

CHAPTER FIFTY-TWO

VANESSA

I LEFT the living room but didn't go into the kitchen. Instead, I walked into my studio and prepared for the surprise. Attikus had wanted me to paint him in the nude. I'd make his dream come true today.

I stripped out of my clothes and slipped on a silk robe that stopped at my knees, tying the fabric belt at the front. The neckline was open enough for Attikus to see parts of my breasts.

I placed a fresh canvas on my easel, preparing to paint my hot boyfriend. Things could get messy, so I covered the wooden floor with a thick canvas fabric. I selected a soft instrumental song on my phone. Then I picked up a metal container holding my paintbrushes and dropped them onto the floor, creating a loud noise.

"Ouch!" I cried.

I smiled as I heard footsteps rushing to my studio and stepped to the side.

"Vanessa? Are you all right? What happened?" Attikus rushed in and glanced around.

"Hi, Whistler. I've been waiting for my model so I can paint him."

"Is that what you've been up to?" He grinned. "I wondered what kind of snack you were getting because it was taking so long."

I walked up to him and placed my hand on his chest, sliding down to palm his cock. "This kind of snack." I fluttered my eyes at him. "I'm in the mood to paint your nude body on this new canvas. The art would be for our bedroom only. Unless you want to show it off at your museum."

"It's going into our bedroom."

"But it could draw millions of visitors to your museum."

"My body is only for one set of eyes." He walked over to me, untied the belt, and slipped the robe off me.

He scanned my body, and heat bloomed inside me. He cupped my breasts before his hands roamed all over my body.

I moaned when he cupped my sex. "Not yet, Whistler. I need to paint you first."

"You're so naughty today, Lily Pad."

"Did you think we were just gonna watch movies all day?"

In seconds, he was naked in front of me, his clothes tossed to the side. "I've never been a nude model for an artist. What am I supposed to do?"

I stared at his magnificent form, strong and muscular. His cock twitched as though wanting my attention.

Later.

"Sit on that chaise." I pointed. "Drape one arm over the back and relax one leg. Find a comfortable position so you won't get stiff."

"I'm already stiff." He looked down at his prominent cock.

I was trying my best not to touch him because if I did, this painting session wouldn't happen. We'd be doing something else entirely.

He glanced at the chaise. "So this is where it went. I noticed a missing chair in the other room."

I smiled. "Yeah. I dragged it in from the other room. I hope you don't mind."

"I don't mind at all. My furniture is your furniture."

Standing a few feet from him, I took a pencil and sketched an outline of his form onto the canvas. It would help me stay focused when I added paint.

I could feel his eyes burning my skin. My nipples hardened even though he wasn't touching me. When I met his eyes, lust smoldered in them. I had never painted naked in my life, but I would do it again and again for this man who had done so much for me.

He gripped his cock and stroked it. "Will this ruin the painting?" he asked in a hoarse voice.

"Are you trying to distract me?"

"You have no idea how much I want to fuck you right now," he admitted.

I placed my pencil down and poured some paint onto the palette. Taking the paintbrush from the brush container, I blended some colors.

"What do you want to do to me while I paint?" I asked.

He growled. "I want to squeeze your breasts, lick them all over." He moaned as his stroking increased. "I want to suck those gorgeous nipples." He licked his lips. "I want you on all fours so I can spank that perfect ass."

Tingles and heat coursed through me as I listened to his seductive words. He looked like a beast ready to pounce on me. I paused the paintbrush, which caused paint to drip down the canvas, creating its own abstraction. I couldn't concentrate. If I continued painting, the artwork might not be what I had intended. My brain was mush.

"I want to feast on your ass and slide my dick inside you."

My paintbrush slipped from my fingers and dropped to the floor. Thank goodness I had it covered because paint splashed everywhere.

Attikus looked so gorgeous leaning on the chaise with his muscular arm stroking himself.

Hot liquid leaked out of me as I walked to the table with a tray of fresh paint. I brought it over to him, kneeled, and placed the tray on the floor. "These are new edible paints. Wanna try them?"

He pointed to his throbbing cock. "Paint him first. He's desperate."

"Love is a painting that lathers you with its colors and textures. Let me show you." I squirted out some red paint on my hands and spread it on his dick. "He's on fire." I stroked him, covering him with strawberry-flavored paint. Then I bent and licked him. Up and down, up and down.

"Fuck," he crooned, placing a hand on my head while watching me. "You're so hot."

I took him into my mouth, sucking him. Red paint was all over my hands and mouth. Our eyes locked, and he dragged me up to kiss him.

"We'll have to clean your chaise later." I sucked on his lips.

"I don't care about the chaise. We can buy a hundred of them for these kinds of painting sessions."

I pursed my lips. "Whatever you want, Whistler."

"I'm going to paint you too." He poured blue paint into his hands and lathered my breasts.

I took yellow and green paint and spread it all over his chest. In seconds, we were on the floor, touching, licking, sucking, and feasting on each other.

He was on top of me, kissing me as we rolled around the canvas fabric that covered the floor. Paint smeared here and there, creating abstract art. Moans and cries of pleasure filled my studio.

Then he spread my legs open and positioned himself between them. "I wanna fuck you without a condom."

"I'm on the pill."

A wolfish smile slid onto his face as he plunged into me, growling all the way. "Feels so good."

"I've fulfilled my duty as stated in the contract, sir." I flicked him a challenging smirk.

He gave my ass a playful slap. "The new contract states you must satisfy your boss like this every day."

"Okay, sexy boss."

He slammed into me again and again. Sensations escalated, sending waves of heat all over me. He took me in all kinds of positions, wild and hot. When I flew over the edge, he continued to pump inside me. I watched his face as he poured himself into me.

"I love you so much," he breathed.

"I love you too," I replied and kissed him.

We collapsed onto the floor and took a moment to breathe. Our bodies were lathered in edible paint, an innovative, delicious, and more costly alternative to acrylic or oil paints. This could be our painting sessions from now on. A glance at the canvas fabric showed the most beautiful abstract painting.

"Round two?" Attikus asked.

We continued our messy painting session all night long. I couldn't wait to see the artwork we created in the morning.

CHAPTER FIFTY-THREE

ATTIKUS

TWO DAYS OFF with Vanessa had cleared my head to return to work. I told Vanessa I had a business trip and would be back in two days.

Reality flooded me with information. Detective Farmer didn't obtain any new information about the two men who had attacked Miranda. One of them had died at the scene and the other of a heart attack in prison.

Paul Exinor had been in and out of consciousness at Forrest's clinic, so we weren't sure how helpful he could be. But we held on to hope. Who had sent him to kill Sam Thornton?

The boys and I had a quick meeting to review our plans. Though I had taken time off to be with Vanessa, I'd ensured things were set in motion. When the boys confirmed our plan was ready, I headed to Chicago to meet Milton Kalkounis.

He was lying low at an Ultra Health and Fitness location in Chicago. Milton took the bait when he heard about a potential client who needed to look buff for a new role in an upcoming movie. He loved it when I told him I'd pay anything for his help.

I sat in the tenth-floor lounge of a hotel I owned. It wasn't as busy as the ground-level lounge. If Milton Kalkounis didn't give me what I needed, I had no qualms about pushing him over the railing to his death.

My men occupied ten tables scattered around the lounge area. I had no doubt the fucker had recorded the beating years ago. Though he didn't beat me that day, he was part of the crime by recording it. He had to know where Ashton was hiding.

I held a tumbler of whiskey as I waited, scanning the area for Milton Kalkounis. A man like him would probably bring backup. I wouldn't address him by Jean-Claude Dumas.

Seconds later, Milton Kalkounis walked into the lounge, wearing a crisp dark shirt and slacks. He had dyed his short blond hair black. No one was with him, but that didn't mean his men weren't on the ground level waiting for him.

I glanced at the two men at a nearby table, who understood what needed to be done. They stood and headed downstairs to ensure Milton's men didn't come up here.

Milton turned to the host. "I'm here to see Jonathan Wellbridge."

"Mr. Wellbridge is sitting in the far right corner by the railing."

I tapped my phone, turned it on, and looked outside, where the large windows were open to allow fresh air to enter. My back would face Milton when he arrived.

"Jonathan Wellbridge? I'm Jean-Claude Dumas," he said in his fake French accent.

I rolled my eyes and turned to greet him.

He recognized me immediately and tried to bolt, but my men rose from their seats.

"Don't move," I ordered, "or things will get ugly."

He glanced at the men surrounding him.

"Empty your pockets and place everything on the table. If you don't, I'll toss you over the railing, and you'll discover how hard Chicago sidewalks are." I looked at him. "I'm not as patient as I used to be."

He placed his phone and wallet on the table. One of my men approached, patted him down, and moved Milton's phone and wallet to another table.

When he was cleared, I gestured to the chair across from me. "Sit."

"What do you want?" He sat in the chair.

"What do I want?" I finished my whiskey and placed the tumbler down. "That's a loaded question. But since you asked, here goes—I want Ashton to pay for what he did to my family and me. I want him to *die* like Bobby and Harry." I smiled. "But his death will be worse."

A question sparked in his eyes. "You killed them?"

"It took me a long time to locate them." I leaned into the table. "I want everyone involved in my family's murder and my beating to pay. Blood for blood. Even the person who took the video."

Color drained from his face. "How do you know?"

"I know a lot of things, Milton. In war, you need patience to win. And I had years to figure things out."

He shook his head. "It's not what you think."

"What should I think?" I eyed him. "If you're trying to tell me it wasn't Ashton, Bobby, and Harry who broke my leg and left me crippled, don't bother. I know what happened that day."

"That's not what I meant." He scratched the back of his head, looking nervous. "What happened to you was awful, but they didn't burn down your house."

This was something I hadn't expected. "Who did?"

His lips trembled. "They're going to kill me."

"Who?" I demanded. "If you don't tell me, what do you think will happen to you? Do you think I'll have more mercy than they will? Who murdered my family and burned down my house?"

"The Trogyn."

Shock washed over me, but I didn't want him to see it. "Why did they murder my family?"

"I don't know. But the Lindor and Harris families work for them. Your mom knows something about them."

My mother? She was a lunch lady at an elementary school. She wasn't a threat to anybody. Had I gotten everything wrong? It didn't make any sense.

"Where is Ashton? Who's hiding him?"

"I don't know." Fear sparked in his eyes. "You can toss me over the railing if you want, but I don't know. Whenever he needs something, he calls me from a burner phone. But something is different about him."

"Like what?"

"He sounds different."

Maybe Ashton had assumed a new identity and was playing out the new role. He was in the drama club in high school, so acting wasn't hard for him.

"So he calls you, but you never call him?"

Milton shook his head. "He calls when he needs something. Then he wires money into my bank account."

"You killed Emmanuel, and you killed Miranda. Why?"

"I didn't kill them!" he exclaimed, losing the French accent altogether.

"Let me rephrase that. Why and how did you get those CIA agents to do the killings for you?" I pinned him with my eyes. "Be careful how you answer that question. I only want the truth. Every time you lie to me, you'll lose a finger."

He blinked and considered me. "You're not the same Attikus. "

"A man adapts when dealing with monsters." I gave him a cold stare. "How can I be the same when my life was turned upside down?"

"I had nothing to do with that."

"When you run in the same evil circle, you're part of it." I leaned back in the chair. "That's how the game goes. Now, answer my question."

Big Mike, one of my security men, approached, standing to the side, ready for my order. He was part of an elite team that conducted underground business for me. My friends and I couldn't fight The Trogyn in ethical ways.

Milton swallowed. "Those agents are part of a military research program called HADES."

"What does the program do?"

"Drug and behavioral experimental shit." Fear filled his eyes.

"You mean mind control?"

This was a conspiracy theory that had been all over the internet for a while. But I had never considered it to be true.

Milton scrubbed the hand down his face. "That's what I heard."

"You're lying." I flicked him a disbelieving look. "What have you witnessed?"

He shifted in the seat and blew out a breath. "The drugs they used are powerful shit. It shuts off your mind. Then they play these recordings with voices and sound waves to train your mind. You become a different person—angry and violent." He paused. "And you don't remember anything once the serum wears off."

This was why Paul Exinor couldn't remember killing his

coworker, Sam Thornton. Maybe Paul's mission was to kill Emmanuel if Sam failed.

"What happens if you inject too much of the serum?"

"The person dies. Serum99 is extremely potent."

Which probably meant it was the ninety-ninth version of evil.

"Where is the research based?" I asked.

"I wasn't privy to that information. If I ask them, they'll suspect me. So I don't ask questions that will pose a threat."

"Why did you force Emmanuel to blackmail Nessa Lambert, who's now my *wife*?"

Milton wiped his palms on his thighs. "She wasn't the original target. I needed money to pay a debt and knew she was a successful artist who sold expensive art. She was convenient because she was his ex."

He'd terrorized her because it was convenient? My fingers itched to pound his face.

"What do you mean she wasn't the target?"

"My order was to target people around *you*. In the beginning, Nessa wasn't part of the picture. She was a tenant leasing your property until you announced your engagement." A bead of sweat slid down the side of his face. "Now she's on their radar."

Fuck. Vanessa's proposal for the marriage had backfired in the most unexpected way. She had wanted me to save her from the blackmail, but I'd made her Ashton's primary target.

"You sent the principal's finger to the gallery opening?"

"Ashton told me to. He knew you'd be there because you love art shit. But he told me not to leave a name on the box to throw you off. Ashton knew you'd been unsuccessfully searching for him. I guess the finger was his way of saying FU."

"Why did he have to kill the principal's entire family?"

"Stephen Perry didn't want to work for Ashton anymore. The Lindor and Perry family know each other well."

"Was Ashton part of the Trogyn when we were in high school?"

Milton nodded. "His entire family was."

That explained why he believed he was untouchable and could do whatever he wanted without getting into trouble. If I destroyed the Lindor family, that would be a tremendous blow to the crime organization.

"Do you know any members of The Trogyn besides Ashton?"

"No."

Milton was a small fish in The Trogyn. He was replaceable. I wasn't surprised he knew little details. The Trogyn only offered important information to elite members.

"Do you know who's running HADES?"

"Dr. Nico Messina. He's creepy. Kind of out there, you know?"

"The doctor who works at Brigham and Women's Hospital and teaches at Harvard Medical?"

"I think so."

Dr. Nico Messina was in residency when I was in the hospital. Had Nico killed Dr. Noah Marks, who'd cared for me?

My phone buzzed. I picked it up and glanced at the screen before placing it face down again. My men had confirmed that the three men waiting for Milton had been apprehended and were locked in a room waiting for me.

Milton glanced around nervously, probably wondering where his men were.

"You can stop looking for them. No one's coming up here."

His eyes widened. "What do you want from me?"

Initially, I'd wanted him dead. But a new idea percolated in my mind. I could delay his death a little longer.

"If you want to live, you need to help me." I steepled my fingers. "Why did you change your name and pretend to be French?"

"Have you heard of the Claude family?"

"No clue. Who are they?"

"An extremely wealthy family in France with ties everywhere. They come from old money. They're connected to other wealthy families all over the world."

Perhaps Orion would know them. The Reimann family was also a powerful banking family with old money.

"Ashton got me a gig to work for The Trogyn. But for them to trust me, I had to show my allegiance by becoming part of their 'family.' They gave me a new name and told me to act like I was Jean-Claude Dumas. They're very proud of their heritage."

"And you sold yourself for money," I said. "Why aren't you just Jean-Claude?"

"Because there are too many of them."

"What else do you know that can save your life today?"

He linked his trembling hands on the table and looked at me. Then he poured out everything he knew, hoping I would have mercy on him.

Shock, confusion, and rage collided inside me. But I had to confirm everything before acting on it. For all I knew, Milton was playing both sides.

My men brought him to a soundproof room down the hall. I turned off the recording on my phone and remained seated for a few minutes. The events of that fateful day played in my head like an awful movie. I saw the faces of my father, mother, and sister. What I was about to do was for them and for me. It wouldn't bring them back, but it would give them a sliver of justice.

I rose from my seat and headed toward the room. Milton sat in a metal chair at a table with a tray covered by a cloth.

I approached him. "Which hand recorded the beating?"

His lips trembled. "We had a deal! I'm supposed to help you!"

"The deal is still on—you won't die." I slipped on latex gloves. "You lied to me earlier, so you need to pay." I jerked my chin toward his hands. "Which one?"

I sensed the fear pumping off him. I remembered my younger self experiencing the same fear while Milton had recorded three heinous boys beating me. I could have died that day. People like them didn't deserve mercy. They were bullies then, but now they were abhorrent monsters.

Milton's right hand trembled as he lifted it slightly. Big Mike gripped his wrist and slammed it down on the table. I grabbed a large knife and chopped off all his fingers except the middle one. His screams filled the room, and he passed out. My men treated his hand, stopped the bleeding, and inserted a tiny device under the fingernail of his middle finger. They wrapped it in gauze and waited for Milton to regain consciousness.

Milton Kalkounis had a message to deliver to Ashton for me.

ATTIKUS

THE NEXT DAY, I sat in the hotel lobby in New York City, sipping my coffee. My meeting wouldn't start for another thirty minutes. I looked at the map of Providence on my phone and smiled.

"So that's where you are," I said to myself.

Along with a tiny device underneath Milton's fingernail, I'd also embedded a tracker in the soles of his feet.

Using Orion's software, I hacked into the Blue Chic Suites, a small bed-and-breakfast, and checked their occupants. When I saw "Picasso" for suite number thirty-five, I knew it was Ashton. He always liked Picasso in high school. I downloaded the blueprint of the suite and looked for his room. It was a corner suite with a private yard.

Scheduling the device to be active in ten minutes, I entered the conference room for my meeting. Ten minutes later, my phone buzzed, and satisfaction rolled through me.

When the meeting was finished, I checked the breaking news. Sure enough, an explosion had occurred at the Blue Chic Suites, with one casualty reported.

I didn't know if Ashton was injured in the explosion. Even if he was, his people had probably kept it out of the news. But he now understood that nothing was going to stop me from making him pay.

I imagined Milton's middle finger ripping off his hand and whacking Ashton in the face. *Fuck you.* But that was just my wild imagination.

CHAPTER FIFTY-FIVE

VANESSA

A MAN WEARING JEANS, a white shirt, a casual jacket, and a red cap came into the gallery asking if I had a bleeding-heart painting. He'd been here before asking for the same thing, and when I told him I didn't have any, he inquired about a custom piece. I'd declined his offer and had expected him to find another artist.

"Sorry, I don't have any paintings that depict bleeding hearts."

"Why not?" he asked. "You have lotuses, waterlilies, roses, calla lilies, and other flowers. Why no bleeding hearts?"

"I don't know," I said. "That flower has never crossed my mind."

"It's a beautiful flower. You should paint it."

"Maybe I will. Is the painting for you or the special lady in your life?"

His eyes gleamed. "The special lady."

"She must be very lucky to have a thoughtful partner like you."

The man seemed happy with my comment. He was the last

customer before I had to close early for my gathering with the girls.

After a moment, he walked up to me. "I'd like to get *A Petal for Your Thoughts* rose painting. The one with the thorns."

"Excellent choice," I said.

"This one's for me." He handed me his credit card, and I glanced at his name. Dan Wilson.

"We all need to gift ourselves sometimes, right, Dan?" I swiped his card for five thousand dollars. *A Petal for Your Thoughts* was a stunning artwork that was more affordable than other masterpieces in my gallery. I tried to offer various price ranges for my customers, but I gave each painting its worth.

While I retrieved the Certificate of Authenticity from the drawer, Willow wrapped up his painting. He exited the gallery with a smile.

I closed the gallery early and gave Willow the rest of the day off. She was thrilled to hang out with her new boyfriend, Andy. They'd been dating for a month, and Andy seemed to be the perfect guy for her.

Each of the girls brought snacks for the gathering. Vivian brought some wine. I had juice and water in the fridge for my pregnant friends.

Kiera sat down and rubbed her belly. "I can't believe you eloped, got married, and had your honeymoon all in three days." Her tummy had grown bigger since the last time I'd seen her.

"It was efficient for sure." Vivian smiled. "No delays. No distractions. Glad you did it."

Audri scooped some fruit into the bowl. "Maybe Remi and I could do this."

"You surprised us all," Michelle said. "We knew it wasn't real, but you guys did things fast."

"Did you try to make babies in Maui?" Natalie asked.

Everyone burst out laughing, and my face burned as I remembered what we'd done.

"Her pink face says it all." Kiera pointed at me.

"How is he in bed?" Vivian asked.

"Fabulous. Unforgettable. Incomparable." I grinned. "Amazingly thick."

Audri choked on her wine, laughing. "I guess he's a keeper."

"We like them thick, don't we, girls?" Elena rubbed her belly.

"We sure do." Natalie grabbed a cucumber slice and dipped it in the ranch dish.

"Eloping could be the new trend. Do you mind if I write an article about it?" Elena asked. "I think the readers of Musepaper will find this new trend innovative for working women and men."

"People want to save money these days," said Vanessa. "Weddings are expensive. If you can squeeze everything into three days, why not?"

"Was it your idea?" Kiera asked.

"No. He planned it all. I was completely surprised but also glad I didn't have to do anything."

"How's your SSG mission going?" Elena asked.

I looked around the table at these women who had become my friends—my family. "I have something to tell you guys."

When I was done, they gawked at me.

"For Your Heart Only mission is complete!" Vivian clinked glasses with us.

"I can't believe you both exchanged those precious words already." Elena smiled warmly. "I mean, I can. The attraction between the two of you is off the charts. I feel uncomfortable standing near you."

"Stop it. It's not that strong."

"It's strong, honey," Kiera said. "And that's coming from a preggo woman who has unstable hormones."

I opened my mouth to comment about unstable hormones creating irrational thoughts, but I didn't want to start a war of words with a pregnant woman. So I asked, "Do you think we're moving too fast?"

Audri held up a grape between her fingers. "That's a hard question. Each relationship is unique. You just started dating, but he's known you for a while. Plus, he's been obsessed with your art for years." She popped the grape into her mouth and chewed. "I think you're moving at a pace that's perfect for both of you."

"Audri's right." Vivian sipped her wine. "We're all different. Some people experience love at first sight, and that works for them."

"I can tell he loves you," Elena said.

"Based on how he's prioritized you, he's in deep." Kiera wiggled her eyebrows.

We all shook our heads.

"What?" She reached for a crab rangoon and bit into it. "Since I'm carrying two babies, my hormones have been all over the place. I've been horny as hell."

Laughing, Vivian placed more appetizers on Kiera's plate. "I'll tell Arrow to let Forrest know his wife *needs* him."

"I have something else I need to tell you," I said. "But before I share anything, I want to let you know I sincerely appreciate your friendship. Thank you for accepting me into your circle. I've never had a lot of friends because I didn't want to answer questions about my past. But you've proven that I can trust you."

"Did you burn someone's house down? Did you kill someone?" Michelle asked. "You can trust us with anything because we trust you."

"I've never burned down any house. But . . ."

Audri leaned into the table. "You killed somebody?"

I nodded and described the incident that had led to my mom serving a life sentence in prison.

"That's self-defense," Natalie said.

"I'd kill him too," the other girls said in unison.

I cried at their empathy for my situation. "Attikus is helping me get my mom out of prison."

"That's wonderful. Your mom is gonna be okay." Vivian reached across the table for my hand.

Audri placed both hands on the table. "Since we're on this topic of danger, let's discuss ways we can help the boys."

Elena looked at me. "We can research individuals associated with The Trogyn."

"The boys are already doing that, but there are a lot of angles to look at. Maybe we'll see something they haven't."

"We could start with Harris Pharmaceuticals," I suggested. "They're connected to The Trogyn somehow."

"I swear there's a scam with health insurance and the pharmaceutical companies," Kiera said in frustration. "They wanted my mom to pay an obscene amount of money for something that wasn't even necessary. The doctor made false claims so he could get kickbacks."

"Ugh. I can't stand people like that," Natalie said. "They're taking advantage of the vulnerable."

"I'm sure the boys have plenty of info on The Trogyn." Michelle grabbed a green baby carrot and dipped it in the sour cream. "We can focus on Harris Pharmaceuticals."

"The boys are doing everything they can to protect us. But we're not useless. We're not going to sit around and do nothing." Kiera smirked. "We're smartasses. We can think of ways to help."

Natalie's face brightened as she looked at me. "Do you have a piece of paper and a pen I can borrow? I've got an idea."

I walked over to the sales desk, grabbed paper and a pen, and returned to the table. "What are you thinking?"

"I've been thinking of creating a new label inspired by us girls." Natalie wrote. "Smart A.S.S.—the initials are for Achieve, Strive, and Succeed. We can have a collection of clothing and accessories to promote independent women." She glanced around at all of us. "We all get to design it together. It'll be our girl's thing. What do you think?"

"We can use the proceeds to fund a women's organization to help people," Audri added.

I nodded. "Love that idea."

"Don't mess with the Smart A.S.S. Enterprise." Kiera laughed.

"Let's do it!" Vivian cheered.

"Sometimes, we have to go outside of the law to get things done properly," I said. "The Smart A.S.S. is like the boy's V.A.T.V.—Vigilantes Against the Villains."

"We should make a themed T-shirt for each," Michelle said. "Have two labels and see which one does better."

"A menswear and a womenswear label." Elena nibbled on a cookie.

"I'll have my legal team start the paperwork to have those labels copyrighted and registered next week." Natalie beamed. "We'll all be owners of the labels."

I didn't expect to become part of new clothing labels tonight, but I loved that we'd come up with something to help people in the long run.

After that idea was settled, we returned to discussing Harris Pharmaceuticals.

"The boys can know about the new labels but not about us trying to help them," Audri said.

"Yeah," Vivian agreed. "They'll get overprotective."

"You know the little tracker you gave me recently?" I looked at Vivian. "I used it already."

The girls gasped, knowing what I was referring to. Vivian had given each of us a device.

"Details, please," Elena said.

"Brody Harris, the man who was in the alley that day. He bought a painting from me."

"Does he have anything to do with Harris Pharmaceuticals?" Elena asked.

"He's one of the heirs."

CHAPTER FIFTY-SIX

VANESSA

MY MEETING with Shauna Casey at her studio turned into an interesting conversation when she showed me her new glass bowl collections. I'd given her a brief description of what I envisioned for my terrariums. She had delivered my vision and more. The glass containers ranged from round, oblong, rectangle, square, and triangle to abstract shapes that would give my terrarium a unique look. She even had lanterns and various jars that had my creative juices going wild.

I appreciated a proactive artist who understood my needs. So the casual meeting that was supposed to be a meet-and-greet turned into me signing a business contract. I placed a large order with her. As soon as that meeting was over, I called the local plant shop to order succulents, moss, crystals, and other items needed for my terrariums.

Excitement zipped through me, making me remember the passion I had when I was younger—when things weren't so dark. My love for plants and nature had returned. Actually, it had never disappeared; it just stepped to the side temporarily.

But Attikus had inspired me to reclaim that passion and do something with it.

As I drove back to my office and parked, my stomach growled. I glanced at the time on the dash and shook my head. It was already three in the afternoon and I hadn't eaten lunch. I rushed into Loretta's Café and got in line. The lunch crowd that usually packed this space had already died down. Still, there were about eight people in line ahead of me.

I glanced at the assortment of pastries and smiled. Maybe I could take some home for Attikus.

I placed my order of a coffee, a turkey sandwich, and an assortment of cookies and brownies. While I waited, I turned, and my heart skipped. Dr. Messina—the man in the photo on Attikus's vengeance board—sat in the corner talking to two college students. They were wearing T-shirts from Brown University and the University of Rhode Island.

My plan to rush back to my office vanished. I couldn't let this opportunity slip by. When I got my food, I grabbed a table nearby with a good view of them and began eating while keeping my ears trained on their conversation. It was noisy in the café, but I was close enough to hear them.

I opened the notepad on my phone and took notes: the date, location, subjects, their description, and so on. Data was crucial, especially for analysis.

"You think we're perfect candidates, Dr. Messina?" asked the boy with the Brown University cap.

"I saw your thesis, and I think it's brilliant. We need intelligent kids like you to join our team, Joshua."

"Do we need to get our parents' permission for this?" Joshua asked.

"You shouldn't have to." Dr. Messina sipped his drink. "It's like a work-study because you're getting paid."

"Awesome!" cheered the girl with blonde hair. "How much money are we talking about?"

"Depends on how well you perform, Ana."

"I'll need time for my homework," Ana said.

"You do this at your own pace. We meet three times a week after six in the evening. The first meetup is tonight. It's more of a meet and greet. Refreshments will be served." He glanced at his fancy watch. "If you know any trusted friends who might be interested, bring them with you. You get a bonus if they sign up with the program."

"Really?" Ana asked.

"Of course. Word of mouth is the best advertisement. But I only want those with serious interest."

They chatted for a few more minutes until Dr. Nico Messina got a phone call and had to leave. But before he left, he told them to meet him at the Modern Research Group at the Canal Walk. This was my opportunity to find out more about this doctor. Any information would help Attikus.

An insane thought popped into my mind as I headed back to my office at the gallery. I spotted Willow showing a couple the triptych of an abstract painting. The gold leaf on each of the three panels glistened under the spotlights. Without interrupting her, I entered my office to get some administrative work done.

When I finished answering emails and paid some bills, I rushed to the mall to grab a Rhode Island School of Design T-shirt and a cap. Then I returned to my office and worked on the layout of where I'd place my terrarium and other plants for sale in the gallery.

My phone buzzed with a text, and my heart leaped.

Attikus: *Busy working?*

Vanessa: *Always. Missing me or something?*

Attikus: *Yup. (smile emoji)*

He'd only been gone for a day, and I missed him so much. He wouldn't return from his meeting in New York until tomorrow.

Vanessa: *Are you done with your meeting?*

Attikus: *For now. Another one starts in an hour.*

Vanessa: *What are you doing?*

Attikus: *In my hotel room, thinking about my wife.*

My inner thighs quivered, and all thoughts of work vanished.

Attikus: *What are* you *doing?*

Vanessa: *In my office, thinking about my husband.*

Attikus: *Are you brainstorming a painting of me?*

He didn't know I'd already finished a painting of him, including the abstract painting we'd done while rolling around on the floor. I'd cut out a section from the canvas fabric and turned it into a gallery-wrapped canvas.

Vanessa*: Are you offering to be my model again?*

Attikus*: A husband is there to support his wife with everything she needs.*

Vanessa: *Your wife needs another painting session with you.*

Attikus: *Why don't you tell me what you'd do to me, Mrs. Mount.*

I grinned at the name.

Vanessa: *Mr. Mount, I'd strip you and make you stand at the center of my studio.*

Attikus: *I'd want you naked too.*

Vanessa: *I'll think about that.*

Attikus: *Non-negotiable.*

Vanessa: *I'm the artist—my call.*

Attikus: *I'm the model you NEED.*

Vanessa: I'll get a new model then.

Attikus: If you want him to DIE.

Vanessa: (eye-roll emoji)

Attikus: I don't share my wife's attention.

Vanessa: Moving on, Mr. Mount—we're in the studio now. Your stalk won't behave.

Attikus: Not my fault. My wife is so hot.

I snorted at this entertaining text.

Vanessa: I walk over and grip you.

Attikus: The artist's grip—my dream come true.

I laughed.

Vanessa: Your face lights up as I move my hand up and down.

Attikus: My hands are all over your breasts.

I sucked in a breath as liquid oozed out of me.

Vanessa: The model must be punished for misbehaving.

Attikus: What will you do?

Vanessa: What do you want me to do?

Attikus: Paint me with your tongue.

I grabbed a glass of water to cool my heated body.

Vanessa: How does it feel?

Attikus: The most incredible brushstroke . . .

Vanessa: Never had this kind of lunch date before.

Attikus: Me too. This needs to be repeated.

Attikus: Gotta go clean up before my meeting.

I gaped at the message. Did I make him come?

Vanessa: You okay?

Attikus: Thanks for the quickie. Can't wait to be home.

Oh, my gosh. I didn't know how to respond because my body was also reeling with arousal.

I should have mentioned Dr. Messina to him, but I'd forgotten during our fun texting. I feared if I told him what I was about to do, he'd cancel his meeting and rush back to stop me.

I had a couple of hours before I had to head to Canal Walk to look for the Modern Research Group, so I began a new painting, pouring joy into it. Thinking of Attikus, I painted an abstract landscape. I was lost in creation when my phone buzzed with the reminder to meet those college students.

I changed into the RISD T-shirt and jeans, tied my hair back, and pulled on a college logo cap. Then I grabbed an old backpack I used for my paint supplies when I took trips to the park or into the woods. It had paint splattered all over it, making me look like a poor art student in need of a part-time job.

I took some cash from my wallet and a fake driver's license with the name Nikki Lau and shoved them into an old, tattered wallet. I had paid a lot of money for the ID years ago when I needed a fake identity while searching for ways to get my mom out of prison. After using it only once and almost getting caught, I realized it wasn't the safest approach.

So why are you using it now?

Intuition and the Chill and Chat with the girls gave me the courage. I supposed this was my way of being a Smart A.S.S. This was a rare opportunity to see what Dr. Messina could offer. I shoved the wallet into the inside pocket of my backpack, pulled on my paint-splattered sneakers, and glanced at myself in the mirror. Poor art student, indeed. I slid my phone into the back pocket of my jeans.

Leaving everything in my office, I went to the front desk and told Willow I was heading out and would return before closing time. I took the bus to the Canal Walk, near Brown University. When I got off, I walked toward the ten-floor brick building with the colorful flags at the front entrance, which faced the Providence River. The Canal Walk was a wonderful route for walkers or joggers. I'd come here often to paint when I was home visiting during the summer. It was a lively area, booming with business and college students from around the world.

I glanced at the metal nameplates to see that Modern Research Group was on the first floor. My phone showed I was still twenty minutes early. I found a bench nearby, sat down, and waited, hoping I'd encounter Joshua and Ana before they entered.

A boat sailed by and caught my attention. I hadn't seen boats along the Canal Walk except during special events like the WaterFire arts performance that occurred on the weekends. As the boat moved past my sight, I saw the city logo. Maybe these were maintenance people ensuring the water was clear of trash.

A few minutes later, I saw Joshua, Ana, and two other students walking toward the building.

I approached. "Hi! Are you here for the part-time gig?"

Ana looked at me. "Yeah. You?"

"I heard about it, and I'm interested in making some extra money. Art supplies are expensive!" I smiled at Joshua, the redheaded girl, and the athletic boy with brown hair. "Is it too late for me to sign up?"

"How did you hear about it?" Joshua looked at me.

"My friend said she had a meeting with Dr. Messina at Loretta's Café the other day. She's traveling so she couldn't participate. I forgot about it until hours ago." I frowned. "Don't tell me I'm too late to sign up."

Nodding, Joshua flicked a look at Ana. "You can add her to your list. I don't mind."

"Thanks!" Ana beamed as she looked at me. "You can be my referral." She took out her list and added my name.

"Thank you so much!" I said as I entered the building with them.

"Welcome to the team. I'm Stacy." The redhead smiled. "And this is my friend, Eric."

"I'm Nikki. So happy to meet all of you. Let's hope for a fun job that pays well!"

CHAPTER FIFTY-SEVEN

ATTIKUS

I'D NEVER EXPERIENCED an orgasm from texting until today. Never knew it could happen, but my wife had revealed an extraordinary hobby I planned on repeating often. I missed her so damn much.

It's only been a day, idiot.

As I walked into the conference, my phone buzzed. Hoping it was Vanessa, I glanced at the screen.

Though it wasn't Vanessa, I smiled at the excellent news. My team notified me that Vanessa's mom would be rescued sooner rather than later. I'd been watching The Women's Facility closely. This was more than a prison for women. Leo Rossi had been using the prison's basement to create illegal drugs for The Trogyn. He had paid off the warden and the chief of security. He wasn't lying to Vanessa when he said he had contacts in the facility.

The facility had scheduled a street cleanup later today, and my team and the boys were all set for the rescue.

Vanessa would be reunited with her mom soon.

CHAPTER FIFTY-EIGHT

VANESSA

AFTER SIGNING IN, we entered a room decorated with fancy chairs, couches, tables filled with appetizers, a juice bar, and a dessert display with a frozen yogurt stand. A DJ played music at the far end of the room. This party vibe would entice any college student.

At a glance, the crowd consisted of college students and young professionals. A pretty hostess wearing an elegant black dress approached our group with a tray of fancy glasses. Her name tag read Tiffany.

"Would you like some apple or pineapple juice?"

"That's juice?" I asked, studying the fancy glass.

"Yes." She smiled. "It tastes better in a fancy glass. We also have water over there." She pointed to the beverage table.

"No cocktails?" asked Stacy.

"Sorry, no," Tiffany said.

"How did you guys hear about this?" I asked my group.

"My thesis on Hollywood, mind control, and the CIA got Dr. Messina's attention," Joshua said.

"He's a nerd." Ana elbowed me.

"He sure is." Stacy sipped her apple juice.

"I heard from my buddy." Eric gave Joshua a light punch in the arm.

Embarrassed, Joshua scratched his head.

Intrigued, I said, "That's an interesting topic. I wouldn't have grouped Hollywood, mind control, and the CIA together like that. Where did you get that idea from?"

Joshua looked into his glass of orange juice for a moment as though considering something.

"The entire class knows why, Josh," Ana said. "You even thanked your uncle in your thesis."

Joshua sighed. "My uncle was in the CIA, but then he died. He mentioned a few things to me that got me researching."

"He's gonna make a fantastic CIA agent." Stacy beamed.

"I don't want to be an agent," Joshua said.

"You're going to be an incredible psychiatrist." Ana patted his shoulder.

His thesis fascinated me. Perhaps Attikus could talk to Joshua about the CIA agents. So many of them had tried to kill me. I took it as a sign that Dr. Nico Messina was interested in Joshua's papers.

Maybe I shouldn't be here. Nerves multiplied in my stomach, but I wanted to stay for the entire event. Though I held a water bottle, I didn't drink anything. I excused myself to use the restroom and told my group I'd join them in the room for the seminar.

I chose the last stall in the restroom. As I flushed, I dumped some of the water from my bottle to show I'd drunk something. I didn't know if I was being paranoid, but something told me to be extra careful.

As I exited the bathroom stall, Tiffany exited the one next to mine.

She smiled at me. "Are you excited about the seminar?"

"I am. How long have you been with Modern Research Group?"

"Over a year."

"Do they pay well?"

"Yup! As long as you do as they say, you'll be fine." She smiled and washed her hands.

"Are they demanding?"

"Oh, no. I meant to say, as long as you do your job, you'll get rewarded." She dug into her purse and pulled out a BMW key. "I paid for this car with my bonus. I graduated from college a year ago as a pharmacist, and I'm now debt-free."

Tiffany was someone who knew medicine and its dosage.

"Wow. That's amazing." I stared at her key, pretending to be mesmerized. "Are you working as a pharmacist and this part-time job?"

"For now." She flicked her long blonde hair behind her shoulder. "Besides, they trust me now, so I can do administrative work on weekends."

"I hope to pay off my bills soon," I said. "Thanks for the chat."

"You can do it!" She smiled. "Just keep the vision of money in your mind."

We entered the seminar room at the same time. She closed the door, and I heard a click. I turned to see if she had locked the door, but the lights dimmed.

"Nikki! Over here." Ana waved at the table on the right.

"Thanks for saving me a seat." I sat down.

A wide screen that took up half of the wall showed a video of Dr. Nico Messina addressing the group. He walked us through his lab, showing us the various parts of the programs.

The room suddenly grew extremely quiet, and someone snored. It was Stacy. I turned to look at the other tables, and they were all asleep too.

Ana yawned. "I don't know why I'm so sleepy."

Shit. Something was in the drinks or the appetizers. Josh and Eric were already out.

"I'm sleepy too." I rested my head on my arm and closed my eyes, pretending to sleep. Staying still, I breathed in and out slowly for about five minutes.

Then I heard footsteps approaching, and someone said, "They're out. Let's get moving. The boat should be there now."

"I'll grab all their belongings," Tiffany said.

The light flicked on, but I kept my eyes closed. A noise sounded from a nearby table. I cracked my eyes open. They were putting the people on rolling cots and covering them with a tarp.

Oh, my god. Fear escalated.

When Tiffany turned, I closed my eyes immediately.

"Where are we taking this group?" someone asked.

"To the warehouse down by the canal," Tiffany said. "The boat should be ready."

"The new research center is open now?" asked a man.

"Yeah. Suite 207. Dr. Messina has a new serum he wants to experiment with. He wants us to give it to Joshua first."

Fear squirmed inside me.

"Why him?" asked the man.

"Something about him being a threat to our program."

I heard more people enter the room. Terror rose in me, but I tried to focus on my breathing. *Stay calm.*

How could I escape them? I couldn't just get up and leave. They'd kill me on the spot. My mom's face flashed across my mind. Then came Attikus. My heart sank as I thought about my loved ones. The fear increased, so I stopped thinking about them and focused on surviving.

Where was this new research center? I had to play this by ear.

Someone came and yanked my arms, shoving me into a cart. A tarp fell over me. I felt another warm body next to me. Fear tightened my stomach and shoulders, but I concentrated on playing dead.

Breathing slowly, I tried not to panic as I was pushed away on the cart.

CHAPTER FIFTY-NINE

ATTIKUS

EXCITEMENT RUSHED through me as I drove home a day earlier than expected. I'd signed a deal with Creative Minds. They had accepted my terms, and now I was part owner of a company that would distribute books and art supplies to schools all over the world.

Even though my creativity was hindered during my youth, I knew what creativity could do for a child—for this world. Innovative ideas were an unstoppable force, possessing the power to bring about massive change. Schools often lacked funds for the arts because society had concentrated on certain methods of teaching. Education shouldn't be a cookie-cutter template. Academics were necessary. But to me, creativity was more important. Creativity expanded thoughts and ideas, opening a person up to limitless possibilities. Combine that with knowledge, and you had a well-rounded person contributing to society effectively.

Vanessa's art had helped me see life differently—that there was beauty in pain and darkness. I now looked at life from that perspective—that wisdom and beauty were woven into everything.

I stopped at a set of red lights, glancing at a mural on the wall. The week before the attack in high school, I'd agreed to help my art teacher, Mrs. Borri, paint a mural on an apartment building that needed an update. It was part of my community service project, but I never got to do it. So much of me crumbled that day.

A car horn blasted behind me, and I realized the lights had turned green. I waved an apologetic hand and drove off.

I glanced at my phone in the charging dock. Where was Vanessa? As soon as I got off the plane, I sent her a text. Usually, she replied right away. But it had been twenty minutes.

Did she want me to pick up dinner? I called her number from my car, but it went to voicemail. Something twisted in my stomach.

I sped home and noticed her car wasn't in the garage or driveway. She'd been working at the gallery today. Maybe she was still there chatting with customers. I drove over to the gallery, and relief settled in me when I saw Vanessa's Land Rover. I'd convinced her to sell her Honda Civic because it was a waste of car insurance. She could use any of my cars.

I parked, got out, and strode to the gallery, but the doors were locked. The lights were still on. I glanced at the business hours, which showed the gallery was closed. I knocked on the glass door.

Willow walked up, saw me, smiled, and opened the door. "Hey, Attikus."

"Hi, Willow. Is Vanessa here?"

"Her purse is still in her office, but I don't know where she is." Willow frowned. "I tried calling her, but it went to voicemail. She was here earlier in the day, but then she left wearing a T-shirt, jeans, and a cap. She said she'd be back before closing . . ."

I headed to Vanessa's office, and Willow followed me.

"I thought she might have gone home and forgot to tell me, but I saw her car was still parked outside, so I waited a while."

Her purse was still on the counter behind her desk.

"I assumed she was meeting up with some friends. But why would she leave her purse?"

"Did she wear these dress shoes today?" I gestured to the pair on the floor.

"Yes. She wore those black flats." Willow placed a hand on her stomach. "Did something happen to her?" Tears welled in her eyes.

"I'll find her, don't worry," I said, trying to comfort her and myself.

I called Detective Farmer to make the report official. It didn't take him long to stop by, as he was already on his way home.

After he reviewed her office and interviewed Willow, he waited for his team to arrive. She'd been missing for a few hours, so it wasn't an official missing person's case yet. But he and I knew something was off.

"I'll do what I can," he told me. "I'll head back to the office and check out the city cameras."

"Thank you."

When Detective Farmer and his men left, I walked Willow to her car. "Go home. We'll find her."

"Please let me know when you hear something."

"I will."

As soon as she drove off, I rushed to The Gathering. I accessed the cameras on her street and hacked into those at the nearby shops. It would take Detective Farmer longer to get the footage. He had to go through city protocols that I didn't.

Fear twisted my gut as I searched the most recent video, starting with the one in front of the gallery. She'd worn a RISD T-shirt with a backpack and took the bus.

I called Orion. "Hey. Can you do me a favor?"

"What's up?"

"Hack into Vanessa's phone. She's missing."

"On it. I'll let you know ASAP."

"Thanks." Orion had access to more intricate software that could locate Vanessa sooner.

After I hung up, I sat back to gather myself. My mind was going a thousand miles an hour, and I knew I wouldn't be able to see this situation objectively. I was too emotionally involved because I loved Vanessa. Had Ashton gotten to her? Or was it The Trogyn? If something happened to her . . .

Don't think like that.

I cursed and blew out a heavy sigh. This wasn't the time for negative thoughts. I continued reviewing the recordings from the stores. My heart leaped when I saw Dr. Nico Messina leaving Loretta's Café. Minutes later, Vanessa also exited the café. His presence meant danger was near. I hacked into the camera inside the café and saw Vanessa sitting near the doctor and two college students. Was this why she had dressed in a RISD T-shirt? What was she up to?

More importantly, why hadn't she mentioned this to me?

An hour later, I was watching videos of areas where college students hung out, particularly where her bus had stopped—the Canal Walk. Joseph's watch was also found in that area. Could this be connected?

The cameras around the walk were suspiciously inactive. Why weren't they working? These were city cameras. Perhaps someone had hacked into them. The area was home to various businesses and college offices. There had to be a private camera I could access.

"Where are you, Lily Pad?" I said to myself.

My phone buzzed with Orion's text message. I clicked on the link to a map with a red dot.

She was still near the Canal Walk.

I called Orion. "I'm releasing my drone to that area."

"Okay. The boys and I will do the same," he said. "The more drones, the more areas we can cover."

CHAPTER SIXTY

VANESSA

MY HEART POUNDED SO loud in my ears that I feared someone would hear it. Under the tarp, I glanced at the warm body next to me. It was a man in an athletic shirt. What kind of mix was in that so-called juice? It could've been in the water and appetizers too. Thankfully, I didn't drink anything.

The boat motor roared, and my body shifted from side to side. I wanted to reach for my phone, which was in my back pocket, covered by the T-shirt, but I feared a slight movement would catch someone's eye. I didn't know who stood watch.

So I gathered my patience and waited.

"Pull under that warehouse canopy," said Tiffany.

When the boat stopped, another boat cut its engine behind us. I swallowed the terror building inside me as someone lifted the cart and pushed it along. Based on the smooth movement, I knew there was probably a plank or level pavement for the wheels to roll without interruption.

I thought I heard sirens, but that could've been my wishful thinking. Did anyone know I'd been kidnapped? Attikus had to know something was wrong when I didn't return his texts or calls. Willow was probably worried too. She'd have noticed my car and belongings were still at the gallery. Even if she'd reported me missing, how would they know where I was?

I tensed as fear resurfaced. I didn't know if I had phone reception. My phone battery was probably dead by now.

"Move the cart with that blond kid into the room. He'll be the next testing subject tomorrow. Dump the others in the storage room," Tiffany ordered. "Get the rest of the bodies, and we can go home."

"When do we have to show up tomorrow to help with the serum?" a man asked.

"Six in the morning. Dr. Messina only has a few hours before his flight takes off," Tiffany said.

My fingers curled, wanting to stab Tiffany with something. My hatred toward her, Dr. Messina, and all these people working for the Modern Research Group intensified. As anger rose, my fear faded. How could Tiffany dismiss people's lives like this? Then I remembered the gleam in her eyes when she showed me the keys to her fancy car. Money turned people into monsters.

We were lab rats for whatever they were trying to do. What was their agenda?

The door opened, and I sensed someone moving the man next to me. I heard a thump and forced myself to go limp as someone lifted my arms and dropped me onto a mattress. Something hit my right rib cage, and pain bloomed, but I bit my lip to suppress my moan.

When I heard the door click closed, I opened my eyes slowly to a dark room. The light from the window on the door cast a glow for me to see. When I didn't spot any cameras, I looked at my rib cage and saw a man's foot resting there.

I shifted away from him. My heart lurched when I saw

about twenty bodies scattered on various mattresses. I reached for my phone—only one bar of reception.

I had several texts from Attikus and a voicemail. My phone had a little battery left, so I replied to Attikus—the one man I trusted to save me.

Vanessa: *Help me. In some warehouse with a canopy over the canal dock. Suite 207. Modern Research Group. They drugged us.*

A boom sounded next door, and I quickly tucked away my phone.

"Help!" a man shouted.

"Get him!" Tiffany shrieked.

Footsteps approached, and a scuffle occurred outside the door. I got up and peeked through the window, seeing two men trying to apprehend a man with a pale face.

"Get the fuck off me! What did you inject me with?" He kicked and punched the men with significant force.

They charged at him again, and he defended himself well.

"Did someone give him too much Serum99?" Tiffany cursed. "He's too strong."

"We gave him the new one, Serum100," said one man.

"Fuck!" Tiffany barked. "You weren't supposed to give him that until tomorrow, when Dr. Messina is here."

"What the hell is going on?" a familiar voice demanded.

Tiffany looked scared as Brody Harris stepped into view and shot the madman.

"Sorry." Tiffany jerked. "He didn't react well to the serum."

Brody glared at her. "Get rid of his body. Hurry and finish what you were hired to do, or you won't get paid." He turned and left.

I slowly made my way back to the mattress. The man whose sneaker had hit my ribs opened his eyes and looked right at me.

I put a finger to my lips.

He sat up, glanced around, and muttered a curse. "Come with me," he whispered. "Hurry." He had curly brown hair and a large build.

Could I trust him?

He crouched and moved to a cabinet filled with medical supplies, shifting it aside to reveal a vent. He removed the screen and gestured for me. "Go."

What if this was a trick? What if he was pretending to be a victim like me?

I didn't move. "Why should I trust you?"

"I discovered this evil research program a month ago. I had an interview scheduled with a news station but never got to it. Someone drugged me while I was at a restaurant." He glanced toward the door, then back at me. "Hurry. We need to get out to save the others." He looked at all the unconscious bodies.

Intuition told me to trust him. I crawled through the dark space, and he was behind me.

"Keep going," he urged.

"How do you know about this vent?"

"I helped renovate this building months ago. It'll take you to the garage near the street."

When I got closer, I heard a buzzing noise. A metal dragonfly with glowing eyes flew up to me. It moved past me to the man behind me.

"Shit," he said.

"What?" I asked, crawling toward the street noises. Hope sprang to life.

"I think they're spying on us. Move faster."

The dragonfly lit up the crawl space, allowing me to hurry. As soon as I got to the street, I was going to run like hell to get help.

Sirens echoed in the distance.

I came to a metal grid and pushed at it. "It won't budge." The dragonfly flew out of the tunnel through the small space between the bars, leaving us in the dark again.

The crawl space was too small for me to move aside for the man. He should've gone first. Something hit the metal bars, startling me. Then someone unscrewed the metal grid and tossed it aside.

A face popped into the opening. "Vanessa?"

My heart leaped to see Attikus. He helped me out while Orion assisted the other man.

Attikus wrapped his arms around me for a long moment. I fell into his embrace as tears streamed down my face. I'd been in survival mode, and the severity of the situation was only now settling over me.

"You must've been worried," I said into his wet shirt. "Sorry."

He veered back and brushed my tears away. "We'll discuss it later. The police will want your statement. Then we're heading to the hospital to have you checked out."

Attikus held up a hand as I opened my mouth to protest that I was fine. "Non-negotiable. You need to get checked. He does too."

I looked at the man. "He helped me escape."

With one arm around my shoulder, Attikus turned to the man. "What's your name?"

I'd been so focused on surviving that I hadn't asked his name.

"Jackson Hewitt."

Attikus reached out his hand for a shake. "Thank you for saving my wife."

More police officers arrived and spoke to Orion, and I recognized Detective Farmer.

Jackson shoved a hand through curly hair. "I hope the authorities get to all those people in there. This group is evil."

Attikus nodded. "If you don't mind, I'd like to ask you some questions about the group. I want to catch those responsible for it."

"Yeah, anytime."

The two men exchanged numbers.

"If there's anything you need, or if you need a lawyer to fight them for whatever reason, let me know," Attikus said.

"Thanks for the offer. But I think I'm okay."

Detective Farmer came to talk to Jackson while another officer spoke to me.

Throughout the entire conversation, Attikus stood beside me, listening. I had gone after Dr. Messina because of Attikus. I'd wanted to help him the way he'd helped me.

When I finished speaking to the detective, Attikus looked at me. "Just a quick visit to the hospital and I can take you home, okay?"

I nodded, but then my legs gave out, and I collapsed into his arms. He scooped me up and carried me to his car.

CHAPTER SIXTY-ONE

ATTIKUS

I WAITED outside the exam room while the nurse checked Vanessa.

The door opened, and Nurse Amy waved me inside. "She's fine, but she needs to rest and take it easy for the next few days. It was a traumatic experience. The doctor will be in shortly to examine her again before she's discharged."

"Thank you." I walked over and sat down on the edge of the bed, taking her hand in mine. "It's all good news."

She looked at my cane. "Did you use your cane to unlock the grid?"

I showed her the bottom portion that held lock-picking tools, screwdrivers, and other supplies.

"Wow. That's an innovative cane," she said. "I can't believe your curator is among the ten people the police saved. How's he doing?"

"I don't know. I had to make sure you were okay first."

She placed a hand over mine. "Go check on him. The doctor should be in soon."

"Okay. If you need anything, shout." I kissed her forehead.

"I'll be fine. Go." Laughing, she pointed to the door.

I walked down the hallway to Joseph's room and sat in the chair beside his hospital bed. "How are you doing, my friend?"

"Better now," he said. "Sorry, the workload must've piled up while I was gone."

"Stop being a workaholic." I shook my head, looking at his long gray hair that desperately needed a trim.

"Takes one to know one." He smirked.

"I see you didn't lose your sense of humor. Nothing to worry about. Agnes took care of everything."

His eyes brightened, revealing an affection I hadn't seen before. "She's amazing, isn't she?"

"Something going on with you and Agnes?" I asked.

"Not really. It's mostly me secretly loving her for years." He chuckled. "It all started when she fixed my chair and repaired the sink in the office bathroom."

"You know how to do that," I said, loving the spark in his eyes. He would recover from this horrific event.

"Yeah, but she's better at it. Especially in her maintenance overalls. So damn hot."

I laughed, my shoulders shaking. I let him talk about Agnes for a while.

"You know, after coming so close to death, I realize that life is too short." He sat up and shifted the IV tube aside. "I'm going to tell her how I feel."

"Go for it." There was nothing better than seeing my curator and maintenance manager together. They'd make a fabulous couple.

"Want to talk about how you got into this dangerous situation?"

"As your curator, I like to attend local art exhibits. There was an exhibit near the Canal Walk. Small event with fantastic art. I overheard two people talking about you and an event in Boston. I turned around and saw the First Lady and some guy. She didn't seem as friendly in person as she did on TV. I think she recognized me but said nothing."

"You jotted down an art auction event in Boston on your calendar."

"That's what the First Lady mentioned." He nodded. "I never got the chance to tell you. The next day, I took a stroll along the Canal Walk after dinner. A man walked past me and jabbed a needle into my arm."

"Was this the guy who was with the First Lady?" I asked, showing him a picture of Dr. Messina.

"Yes. He's also the doctor monitoring everything. He shoved me into a trunk or van—I wasn't sure. Then I heard him call the First Lady on speaker."

Anger surged through me. Why was the First Lady involved in kidnapping and injecting people with dangerous drugs?

"How long were you out? Did the First Lady talk to you when you came to?"

"She asked me about your life and your weaknesses. I told her I only worked at the museum and didn't know you well. That you weren't the best boss, so we didn't talk." He flicked a look at me. "She didn't believe my lie and injected more meds into me. It made me weak."

"She did it, or someone else?"

"She did it," he said. "There was evilness in her eyes. She said I'd be useful. I assumed she was going to use me to blackmail or hurt you."

"Well, she didn't get to. You're safe now."

Was the First Lady working for Ashton? Or maybe The Trogyn?

"I was in another building with other people. But then they

moved everyone. I pretended I was unconscious but saw the number 207 on the new building. So I changed the date on my watch and dropped it, hoping you or someone would find it."

"I did. But I didn't know what the numbers meant."

"Yeah, it was a long shot. But I tried."

A knock sounded at the door, and Agnes poked her head in.

"We were just talking about you." I waved her in.

She entered with a bag of food. "Oh, yeah?"

"I've got to go. Rest up." I winked at Joseph. "Do what you need to do. Life is too short."

"I just saw Vanessa," Agnes said. "She looks well."

"She is." I leaned in and whispered, "Make the workaholic eat and rest."

"Got it."

After a hot shower with Vanessa, I tucked her into bed and lay next to her.

She described her ordeal. "They're experimenting on people with dangerous drugs. I saw a man go crazy from Serum 100. Did they locate Dr. Messina and Brody C. Harris?"

"The authorities are on it. Their faces are everywhere in the media worldwide."

"Worldwide?" Her eyes widened.

"Musepaper and Orion's media companies have extensive reach. They'll be caught. Don't worry."

"Before I forget, you need to check this." She reached for her phone at the charging station. "Brody bought an artwork from me."

She told me how she'd inserted a tracking device Vivian

had given her into the painting. "I haven't looked at the tracker recently. Maybe that can help locate him or something."

"My Lily Pad has some spying skills. I'll look later. You need to rest."

Her eyes warmed. "I'm part of the Super Spy Girl group."

I laughed. "What's that?"

"A group of intelligent women with unique missions. Sort of like the Bond girls." Mischief gleamed in her eyes. "My mission, For Your Heart Only, is complete."

I smirked. "What exactly is that mission?"

"To see if your feelings for me are real. We've had several painting sessions where you confessed your love for me. So they're real."

"You could've just asked me, and I would've told you."

"But I wouldn't have believed you." She kissed my cheek and dropped her head on my shoulder. "Actions speak louder than words."

When she fell asleep, I kissed her forehead and thanked the heavens for keeping her safe for me. I tried to extract her hands from my arm, and she murmured, "I love you, Attikus." She breathed. "Even your cane."

I smiled and replied, "I love you more than you can imagine."

I could have lost her—the only woman who held my heart. The only woman who loved me and all my flaws.

My vendetta against Ashton blazed into my head. If vengeance consumed my heart, Vanessa was the lifeblood that eased it.

Was the First Lady responsible for everything? Did I have another enemy besides Ashton? Were they working together?

If something happened to Vanessa, I'd scorch the world for her.

I entered my office, logged into Vanessa's tracker, and noticed she had several recordings. When I listened to the first recording, fiery blood surged through my veins. I called for an urgent meeting with my friends.

CHAPTER SIXTY-TWO

ATTIKUS

THAT NIGHT, I informed the boys that Vanessa and Joseph were doing well.

"That's great to hear," Remi said.

I raked a hand through my hair, releasing a sigh. "Thanks for your help with the drones."

"Anytime, man," Grayson said.

"You look tired." Forrest sipped from his tumbler. I should've gotten one for myself prior to this meeting. "Do you want to postpone this meeting until tomorrow?"

"No. I need to give you information while it's still fresh in my head. Besides, I need to spend time with Vanessa tomorrow, so the schedule might be too chaotic."

"Okay. What do you have?" Remi inquired.

"The First Lady injected Joseph, asking him questions about me."

"As in the President's wife?" they all asked at once.

I nodded. "Seems like she's involved in these dangerous drug experiments."

"What did you do to her?" Royce asked.

I was about to tell him I wasn't sure yet when Orion popped onto the screen.

"Sorry, guys. My meeting ran late."

"No worries," I said and caught him up.

"I spoke to my contacts in the CIA," Orion said. "They confirmed there are military research programs that use torture techniques and powerful drugs for behavioral studies like mind control. There are research centers in Canada, Texas, and Wyoming. He said there could be smaller ones that aren't listed in the database."

"The one in Providence just got exposed," Arrow said.

"Why would there be one in Canada?" Grayson asked.

"Maybe the Canadian politicians are colluding with our government, who knows?" Royce drank from his water bottle. "Politicians are corrupt everywhere."

"I wish Paul Exinor could've given us more information before he died," Forrest said. "His brain was bleeding. I couldn't stop it."

"Not your fault," I told him. "He gave us some clues to work with. We know they're using agents who are against their horrendous experiments. Some even threatened to expose it, so the people running the program had to get rid of them. They injected the agents with the drug, manipulated their minds, turned them crazy, and forced them to commit the crimes. Then they killed the agents."

"The President has to know what his wife's been up to. Even if a CIA agent exposed the program, who has the power to stop the First Lady? The President. The couple has been lying to the country—to the world." Orion scratched his chin. "Who are they? What is their agenda?"

"That's what we have to find out," I said. "Listen to this. It's Brody C. Harris talking to the First Lady." I played the recording from Vanessa's files.

"This is for you from the Harris family," Brody said. *"We know how much you love art."*

"Really? It's very thoughtful of you. Thank you," Madeline replied. *"The Starry Truth is an exquisite painting."*

"More people are waiting to congratulate you, honey," said President Collins.

"Please put this with my belongings to take home," Madeline told someone.

"Yes, ma'am."

Shuffling noises and a door closed.

"That recording was days ago," I said. "There are others, but the conversations aren't as clear. The painting must be hanging in an open room with many people."

"This proves that the Harris family is working with the President and his wife," Arrow said.

It was time I offered my suspicion. "She's not his wife. She's his husband."

Grayson snorted. "What are you talking about?"

"Look at this." I showed them a picture of Ashton when he was in high school and a picture of Madeline side-by-side. She'd had multiple plastic surgeries to enhance her cheekbones, soften her jawline, and make her nose smaller. All her procedures were done at Brigham and Women's Hospital in Boston. Despite the surgeries, certain features remained the same. "Ashton C. Lindor is Madeline Claude-Collins."

"What the fuck?" Remi moved closer to the screen.

"I see the resemblance." Orion sat back in his chair. "Holy Shit. We have a transgender First Lady."

"I know Madeline is Ashton because of how she speaks. Her voice is softer now, but she has certain unique traits she can't get rid of. The way she emphasizes the word 'really' stands out. It always annoyed me in high school."

"This presidency is a sham," Royce said. "Why does he have a British accent?"

"He's acting the role," I said. "He was in the high school drama club. So he's used to pretending."

"Was he gay in high school?" Remi asked.

"He had a girlfriend, but not for long," I said. "Then again, he could've been acting to hide his true sexual preference. I don't know."

"So the President's gay . . . I'm just thinking out loud." Grayson crossed his arms. "He marries a man who got a sex change to be a woman. Why?"

"There's more to this story. We just have to unravel it." I rubbed the tension building at the back of my neck. "There's nothing wrong with being gay. He could've said my wife is transgender. So why lie to the entire country?"

"Because he wouldn't have won the presidency," Royce said. "The country would have been divided."

I nodded in agreement. "His transition ensured nothing changes within the presidency. The country has a President and a First Lady."

Grayson scratched his head. "I still can't believe this. It's so . . . out there."

"Madeline Claude-Collins." Orion pursed his lips, thinking. "Claude—the name rings a bell. Hold on one second." He went off the screen. I heard him typing in the background. Then he blurted, "Fuck. I think I found something. Check it out."

A list of names flashed onto the screen:

Ashton C. Lindor: enemy #1.

Bobby C. Cooney: enemy #2.

Harry C. Sullivan: enemy #3.

Stephen C. Perry: high school principal.

David C. Johnson: judge overseeing Attikus's case.

Mike C. Matthews: police officer #1 who covered up the attack.

Benjamin C. Jones: police officer #2 who covered up the attack.

Anthony C. Young: fire investigator who gave false report.

Dillon C. Harris: heir #1 to Harris Pharmaceuticals.

Brody C. Harris: heir #2 to Harris Pharmaceuticals (cousin to Dillon).

Richard C. Muller: artist specializing in male genitalia at Boston Auction.

Jim C. Caruso: police officer who didn't help Vanessa's case.

"What do you guys see?" Orion asked.

"I see a C repetition." Grayson formed a C with his fingers. "Pun intended."

Orion came back onto the screen. "I just searched what their initial C stands for, and it's Claude."

"What?" Royce shook his head. "They're related?"

This mystery around Ashton just took a darker path. "Milton told me the Claude family is one of the wealthiest in Europe with ties to old money."

"They are," Orion grunted. "We don't like them. The Reimann family and the Claude family don't do business together."

"Why?" Remi asked.

"Their banking family is a lot older than my family," Orion said. "Napoleon Claude started the business, and his empire expanded to England, Germany, Sweden, Russia, and other countries. Despite their expansion, they wanted to keep their massive wealth within the family. Like the Rothschilds."

Forrest made a face. "Incest?"

"One of their daughters admitted it during an interview," Orion replied.

"No wonder they're all messed up," Royce added.

"But some of them broke free and married outside of the family." Orion turned from side to side, stretching his neck. "That's why we see the likes of Ashton, Brody, and others. These people are proud of their lineage, hence the initial C."

"Ashton is part of a powerful family." I yawned. "Why did he change his gender? It's not to hide from me. What's his agenda?"

"I think we've got enough to go by," Remi said. "We'll all look at the President and his wife. Go to sleep, Attikus."

"Thanks, guys."

I shut off the computer, returned to the bedroom, and washed up. Then I slipped in next to Vanessa, hugging her close. This entire investigation had morphed into a complex mystery. My friends and I didn't have time to discuss how The Trogyn fell into the mix. That could wait for another day.

Madeline Claude-Collins had some balls, but they won't save her from me.

CHAPTER SIXTY-THREE

ATTIKUS

A FEW DAYS LATER, the news broke that Brody C. Harris's body was found in the street with a gunshot wound. Either his own family or The Trogyn got to him.

My men found Dr. Messina disguised as a woman hiding not too far from the Canal Walk, where the illegal drug experiment took place. The doctor probably assumed people would look for him elsewhere, but I had a team focusing on the area. My drones and the camera footage around Providence caught him exiting a grocery store in a dress.

What was the deal with these men dressing as women? Dr. Messina was being held at Calvin's farm.

With my cane, I walked into Calvin's warehouse and entered a room where Dr. Nico Messina sat in a chair with his hands tied behind his back.

"All yours." Calvin got up from his chair and left with his three men dressed in black.

I didn't want to waste time, so I asked, "Why did you kill Dr. Noah Marks?"

Dr. Messina knew exactly who I was. "Because they told me to."

"The Trogyn or the Claude family?"

"They're the same thing."

He confirmed my suspicion.

"Dr. Marks didn't want to kill you for us, so he had to go. He knew too much." His thighs quivered. "When I looked for you the next day, you'd already been discharged from the hospital."

"Did you have anything to do with my family's murder?"

He shifted uncomfortably in the chair. "We sent toxic fumes into the house vents to knock them out before starting the fire. If I hadn't done it, they would've killed me." His lips trembled. "Your family was dead before the fire. So there wasn't any pain."

Did the fucker think that made it any better?

I lifted my cane and pressed a tiny button on the top. A blade flipped out. I jabbed it into his chest, and blood stained his white shirt.

He screamed. "Fuck!"

I twisted the blade, and he screamed louder. I wanted to pierce his neck, but I didn't want him to die so soon. So I jabbed his abdomen instead. Another painful cry erupted.

"What is Madeline Claude-Collins' agenda?" I asked, yanking the blade out.

His body quivered. "Serum100. It's a radical serum that targets certain areas in the brain quickly—from newborns to older adults."

What the hell?

Anger surged through me. "This is for the vulnerable people you want to hurt." I thrust the blade, puncturing his thigh. His scream filled the room as I asked, "Why?"

"Mind control," he whimpered. "They want to control everyone. It's social engineering!"

"Tell me more about Ashton Lindor." I yanked out the blade.

Ashton was groomed at a young age. His family ranked high within The Trogyn empire. All The Trogyn leaders were linked to the Claude family. Back then, President Charles Collins was a school police officer. His connection to the school systems allowed him to watch over Ashton and the other members' children. He later became a congressman and rose in the political arena to assist the crime organization.

"Did he volunteer at the Sandal Crest Elementary School?" I asked about my mother's employer.

Dr. Messina nodded. My mother had trusted the wrong police officer. Instead of helping her, Charles Collins reported her to The Trogyn.

"So Ashton is the current leader of The Trogyn?"

"Yes. But he has a large family support system that's all over the world." Dr. Messina winced.

"Who's the next leader if something happens to him?" I had to eliminate every one of them.

Dr. Messina gave me the order of the succession. "Victor C. Steinberg, Francis Claude, Jason Bankers Claude, and Emilio C. Rothschild. That's all I know."

"Now I need a list of all the members. Who has this information?"

"Two accountants." He hissed in pain.

"I'll need the accountants' names, all the members' businesses, hideaways, properties, bank accounts—everything."

"I can't," he said as fear overwhelmed his face.

"You *can*. Think of this as your redemption." I stared into his eyes. "For every delay, this will happen." I used my blade and pierced his thigh again.

Twenty minutes later, Dr. Messina gave me what I needed. I walked out of the room and told Calvin that the doctor was ready for the farm animals.

CHAPTER SIXTY-FOUR

ATTIKUS

THREE DAYS after Dr. Messina's death, the media storm began. My friends and I had released some information to the hungry media to nibble on. The news outlets couldn't stop talking about the Claude family, the CIA, Harris Pharmaceuticals, or The Trogyn. Different news stations created their own theories of what had happened and the crimes that involved powerful people across the globe.

Although we also leaked information about the First Lady resembling Ashton Lindor, no other media outlet mentioned it, except for Musepaper. I was certain the President and his people had ordered the media to leave him and his wife out of the drama.

I knew those involved were busy trying to patch up all the holes in their massive organizations, but there were too many. People had already peeked in and seen things. This was only phase one of my plan.

I wanted them on edge.

Vengeance had propelled me until Vanessa entered my life and took over the steering wheel. My heart was hers. Everything I did—and would do—was for her. Today, I needed to focus on my love.

I glanced at my watch and smiled, imagining her leaping with joy. Turning off my computer, I walked into the kitchen and found Vanessa stirring a pot.

"I have to run out. Do you need me to pick up anything?" I asked.

I loved seeing her in my kitchen. Her presence warmed the house better than any fireplace.

She didn't know it yet, but I had bought her apartment building. When I reached out to the landlord to pay the rest of her lease, he told me he was selling it and moving to Florida. I took the opportunity and bought the building for a fair price. It was prime real estate, with a ground-level studio space. She could always go back there to paint whatever she wanted. When I bought it, I didn't realize how handy that space would come to be.

"Can you get some scallions? I forgot to buy some. I'm making you the chicken porridge you love so much."

"Thank you for loving me." I wrapped my arms around my beautiful girlfriend and kissed her. "You should grow scallions in the greenhouse. Everything is growing like crazy."

"It's fabulous, isn't it?" Her eyes brightened. "You checked it out? I can start cutting lettuce and cucumbers to make a salad soon. I plan on planting scallions and ginger too." She placed a lid on the pot. "I have a proposal. Can you please start another greenhouse so I can grow everything I need for my terrarium? I can buy local, but I also want to grow my own plants."

"It'll be here next week." I kissed her.

"Thank you! How did you know?"

"I can read you, Lily Pad." I smiled. "It's obvious. You successfully used the greenhouse to grow food for us to eat, so why not grow plants for your terrarium? That way, you can control what you're getting."

"You're the best." She threw her arms around me. "This is why I can't stop cooking for you. One way to show you love someone is by cooking for them." She turned back to check on the porridge.

"You're going to make me fat."

She rubbed my stomach. "Your abs are made of stone. Nothing can make them fat."

"It must be those edible painting sessions that burn a lot of calories." I grinned. "We should do it multiple times a week. We'll have our own collection of abstract art."

"You still want to display those paintings in your museum?"

"Of course." I shrugged a shoulder. "It'll be called *Paintings of Passion.*"

Her eyes gleamed with amusement. "Your friends will see parts of your ass. Are you okay with that?"

"I've got a nice ass. Nothing to be ashamed of." I touched her chin. "If you're okay with your friends seeing your boobs and other parts of your body, why should I be shy?"

She sighed in defeat. "You're a strange man, but I love you."

"I love you too. See you soon."

When I was with Vanessa, my world had so much color—so much love. It practically oozed out of me. That sounded cheesy, but it was the truth. I didn't know how else to describe it. When a man admitted that love oozed out of him, he was hopelessly in love. There was no going back.

I smiled like a fool as I got to my car and drove off. I couldn't imagine my life without her. The journey to this moment had been difficult, but it was worth it because of Vanessa. She was the blessing I came home to every day. Because of this, I'd do anything to protect her.

I'd give my life to ensure the woman I loved was safe.

I stopped at the grocery store to pick up scallions and four bouquets of flowers. Then I drove to Vanessa's apartment building, entered the hallway, and took the elevator up to her apartment. As I walked through, I made a mental checklist of all the things that needed an update. The walls needed a fresh coat of paint; the lighting was outdated, and the rug needed to be replaced.

I arrived at her apartment and knocked, even though I had a key.

When the door opened, Mom Gigi and Ellen greeted me with hugs and gestured for me to enter. Hannah Lam sat on the couch drinking something.

She placed her cup down, rushed over, and embraced me. "Thank you for helping me escape."

"You're welcome." I offered each woman a bouquet, saving one for Vanessa.

"Thank you. You're so thoughtful." Hannah took the flowers and brought them to the kitchen sink while Mom Gig and Ellen placed their bouquets on the coffee table.

My team had extracted Hannah when a van took her and other inmates out to the highway for a cleanup. Though Vanessa had told Leo she no longer wanted him to extract her mom, they had refused. So I changed tactics and killed them before they could get to her. The inmate, Hannah Lam, was now considered dead. A dead body was dressed up as her to make it look like an inmate from The Women's Facility had died in a van during her community work.

She returned with a vase of flowers and placed it on the coffee table.

I reached into my pocket and pulled out her new social security card, driver's license, and passport. "For you to start over."

"Heidi Lam," she muttered, looking down at the cards. Her

hands trembled and tears streamed down her face. "I don't know what to say. A simple thank you isn't enough."

"I love your daughter, and I want her to be happy. Getting you out of prison has been her priority all these years."

The rescue occurred two days ago. But I wanted things to die down a bit before I informed Vanessa.

"Can I see her now?"

"That's why I'm here. Vanessa is making chicken porridge. I think your presence is going to make her day. "

I looked at Mom Gigi and Ellen. "You're invited to dinner too."

"Even if you hadn't invited us, we would've barged in," Ellen said. "I'm proud of you, little brother."

"A compliment from you usually means you want something. So what is it?

She punched me in the biceps. "Can't a sister compliment her brother?"

As they piled into my SUV, Heidi asked, "Can you please stop by the Saigon Bistro? I would like to get some *bánh mì*. Haven't had them in a long time."

"Excellent idea. They're one of my favorites too."

"Since we're there, we might as well go in and say hello to Hope," Mom Gigi said.

"Who's that?" I asked, pulling into a parking spot.

"You'll see."

I couldn't believe that my mother and sister knew Vanessa's mom. I'd only discovered this revelation when Heidi had asked to use my phone to call her friends. When she'd typed in Mom Gigi's number, we'd stared at each other for a moment.

Life was filled with unpredictable moments, and this was one of them.

We entered the restaurant, and like before, it was crowded. But Mom Gigi walked straight through the kitchen to the back and toward the office. The chef, cooks, and servers nodded at her as though she were a VIP member.

What was going on?

She knocked on the office door three times.

The door opened, and an older woman with gray hair stepped out. I'd seen her work at the front desk a few times.

"Hope, look who we have." Mom Gigi placed a hand on Heidi's shoulders.

Emotions overwhelmed Heidi as she embraced Hope. The women cried happy tears.

"I'm so happy you're safe," Hope said. "I heard on the news about the chaos near the highway."

"I'm safe, thanks to Attikus."

Hope smiled at me. "Mom Gigi has told me a lot about you."

"We're heading to see Vanessa," Heidi explained. "We should set up a time to catch up. I have an apartment now."

"I can't wait." Hope patted Heidi's cheek. "It's been a long time, but you look as beautiful as always."

"I'd like to order like six *bánh mì*, if that's okay?"

"Of course. It's on the house. Do you want anything else? Fried rice, noodles, a mango shake, some fresh spring rolls?"

"Sure. I haven't had them in a while."

An hour later, we all returned to the car and headed home.

I turned to Mom Gigi, sitting in the front seat. "How do you know Hope?"

"We're friends from a long time ago. I'll tell you when we get to your house. Vanessa would want to know too."

I couldn't wait to see Vanessa's surprise.

CHAPTER SIXTY-FIVE

VANESSA

AFTER ANOTHER SPRINKLE OF SALT, I scooped up a small spoonful of porridge to taste. Satisfied with the flavor, I prepared a bowl for Attikus and one for me, leaving them out to cool.

"All you need is a sprinkle of scallions and black pepper," I told each bowl.

Recently, I'd been talking to myself or humming when I painted, cooked, or did the chores Attikus didn't want me to do. He had a cleaning service that came once a week. Still, there was something satisfying about removing your own mess.

The self-talk and humming were probably my version of Attikus's whistling. It was joy coming through us.

I didn't know why, but I felt a lightness around me. Just pure happiness. Perhaps that was love. I'd never considered myself a wonderful cook, and I'd never enjoyed being in the kitchen. But seeing Attikus's face when he gobbled up my food warmed my heart.

I heard the garage door open and placed the lid on the pot.

Removing my apron, I hung it up. Footsteps sounded behind the door that led to the garage. *Lots of footsteps.*

When I opened the door, my heart erupted with shock and sheer happiness.

I screamed with delight. "*Mẹ!*" Fearing this was a dream, I veered back and looked at her. "Is it really you?" Tears flooded my eyes and spilled over.

She cupped my face and cried, "It's me, baby."

"Hi, Vanessa." Gigi poked her head out from behind my mom.

"Oh, my gosh. Let me get out of the way." *Mẹ* scooted to the side to let Gigi, Ellen, and Attikus through.

I met his smiling eyes. Though I didn't know the entire story, I knew my mom was here because of him. How much more could I love him?

"How did you get here? The news said there was a casualty during the highway cleanup, but they didn't give details."

"Hannah Lam no longer exists. Your mom is now Heidi Lam." She looked over at Attikus and offered an appreciative nod.

I'd been devastated worrying about my mother's safety, but Attikus told me not to worry. My love had been orchestrating things behind the scenes. I assumed the rescue wouldn't happen for another month. Now I understood why he'd been working late.

"Thank you," I told him and looked back at my mom. "I'm so happy you're out of that horrible place."

Attikus led Gigi and Ellen to the kitchen table, where he placed a tray of food from Saigon Bistro.

I embraced *Mẹ* for a long moment. We sobbed with happiness, relief, and gratitude. I couldn't believe I was hugging her. It was surreal. Only days ago, she was still in prison, and now she was in my home.

"Let's eat, and we can catch up." *Mẹ* grabbed my hand. "We have all the time in the world now. I bought some *bánh mì* for us."

As I walked to the table, Attikus placed flowers in a vase and smiled at me. Then he took out the scallions, preparing to chop them.

"I can do it," I said.

"No, you catch up with your mom. I've got this."

"Let me." Gigi yanked the scallions from him. "Don't want my son losing a finger."

After Gigi chopped up the scallions, we moved to the spacious dining table instead of the kitchen table. We'd never had this many people in the house eating. The joy on Attikus's face showed he didn't mind it at all. This was his found family —my found family too.

We chatted, ate, laughed, and cried. My heart filled with joy as I looked at Attikus, sending him invisible kisses, hugs, and all the gratitude he deserved.

The doorbell rang, and Attikus furrowed his brow, heading out of the kitchen. "I'm not expecting anyone."

"I am." Gigi lifted her hand.

Attikus and I exchanged puzzled glances. I hadn't even had time to inquire how Gigi knew my mom, and now someone else was at the door.

When Attikus returned, he brought Agnes with him.

Attikus looked at Gigi and Agnes. "Do you have something to share?"

Mẹ got out of her seat and threw her arms around Agnes. "So good to see you!"

Attikus moved to stand beside me. "Is it me, or did this day just get even stranger?"

"It's like a movie that makes no sense, but somehow, it does." I looked at Ellen, who didn't seem bothered by any of this. She scooped up a spoonful of porridge and shoved it into her mouth.

When she saw me looking at her, she offered me a thumbs-up.

"I think we're the only clueless ones." I gripped his arm.

Agnes looked over at us. "Come on. Sit down, and we'll explain everything."

CHAPTER SIXTY-SIX

ATTIKUS

VANESSA SAT down at the table, flanked by me on one side and her mom on the other. She looked anxious about what Agnes wanted to share. My curiosity was piqued too.

How had I not known about Agnes, Mom Gigi, and Ellen? I flicked Ellen a look, and she just smiled.

"Don't worry, it's not bad news," Agnes said from across the dining table.

"What have you been hiding from me?" I asked.

Mom Gigi wrapped her fingers around her cup of tea. "Agnes, Heidi, and I have known each other for a long time."

"You have?" Vanessa blurted. "From where?"

"We're part of the Lunch Lady Club." Mẹ placed a hand over mine.

"I thought that was just a small meeting with your friends after work," Vanessa said.

"It was a small meeting that grew over time," Agnes said. "A lot of the lunch ladies are moms who worked those hours so they could be home with their kids after school. Their pay sucked, so we often had other jobs on the side."

"Then we met someone who changed our lives," Gigi said, looking at me. "Your mom, Susan, discovered Harris Foods LLC—the company supplying food to the schools—also owned a pharmaceutical company."

"Harris Pharmaceuticals?" I asked.

"Yes," said Mom Gigi. "Susan started looking into it and found evidence that children were eating food with ingredients that made them sick."

"Kids suddenly got rashes, developed respiratory issues, depression, anxiety, mood swings, and so on," Vanessa's mom said. "I noticed the mental changes, especially in kids I was familiar with."

Mind control and behavior patterns.

Milton's words echoed in my head. The Trogyn, the CIA, Harris Pharmaceuticals, and Harris Foods LLC were all linked.

Vanessa gripped my thigh under the table, revealing how much she wanted to hurt these people. I covered her hand with mine, trying to soothe her, even though I felt the same way.

"The principals of the schools and the superintendents were all in on it." Agnes sipped from her tea mug. "They chose what vendor to feed our kids. It was always Harris Foods LLC."

Agnes continued to tell us that my mom had started the Lunch Lady Club. I had assumed she was a regular lunch mom at the school. Pride, regret, and anger surged in me. She had died trying to do what was right.

Vanessa rubbed her hand on my thigh, and I looked at her. We didn't need to say anything to each other. Her eyes told me she understood my emotion.

The Lunch Lady Club started out small but grew to include other moms from different cities and states.

"When Susan gathered evidence that connected Harris

Pharmaceutical to Harris Foods LLC, she wanted to report it to the police department." Mom Gigi clasped her hands together on the table. "She spoke to a school police officer, who suggested she set up an appointment to talk to the police chief."

"But then your whole family was murdered the next day." Agnes pressed her lips into a tight line.

I swallowed, trying to calm the rage building inside me as I connected the dots. "Was his name Officer Collins?"

Agnes nodded.

"I would've died from my injuries if I hadn't been transferred to the hospital," I said.

This wasn't a question but a fact. These people had wanted to obliterate my entire family because my mother planned to expose their evil intentions.

"Fate led us to kill Dillon Harris that day in the alleyway." Heidi wrapped an arm around Vanessa. "I knew his family would blame us for everything. We didn't have a chance against them back then."

"These people need to pay," Vanessa seethed.

"They will," I said calmly. Everyone turned to look at me as though they heard more in my voice. They were right, but I didn't want them to worry. "But it's going to take time. Do you have any of the evidence my mom gathered?"

"Sadly, it burned with the house," replied Mom Gigi.

I looked over at Ellen, who had been sitting quietly, listening to our conversation. "Was Ellen a lunch lady too?"

"Hell, no." She made a face. "I don't have the patience for that. My mom was friends with Gigi." She held the fresh spring roll in her hand, preparing to dip it into the peanut sauce. "When she passed, Mom Gigi adopted and taught me everything about the Lunch Lady Club. I'm now their outstanding accountant." She smiled, dumped the spring roll into the dish of sauce, and bit into it.

I looked at Mom Gigi. "You have a knack for harboring orphans."

"Some kids deserve to live, and some don't," she said without blinking.

"I concur," Agnes, Heidi, and Ellen agreed.

They didn't know that two out of the three boys she referenced were already dead because of me. I'd spare Mom Gigi the heartache of knowing her son had blood on his hands.

We ate and chatted some more. Agnes told me the Lunch Lady Club was still active, but not in the same capacity. They feared Harris Pharmaceuticals would go after them. They weren't wrong. This was a multibillion-dollar company with dangerous people protecting their assets.

My hatred toward them was so powerful, I was afraid the throbbing vein in my neck would burst.

Around nine o'clock in the evening, Agnes saved me a trip by driving Vanessa's mom back to her apartment and Mom Gigi and Ellen home. Vanessa wanted her mom to stay the night, but she refused. She wanted to have her own space to appreciate her freedom first. Vanessa promised to visit her every day.

When the house was quiet again, we sat on the couch in the living room with our hands linked.

"Thanks for this extravagant plan. How did you get the key to my apartment?"

"I own the building now."

"I can't keep up with you." She kissed my cheek. "It's like you have three brains all functioning at the same time."

I gathered her into my arms. "I'm still trying to absorb what I've learned today about my mom knowing your mom."

"It's surreal and incredible."

Mom Gigi said the lunch ladies only met to discuss issues and talk a little about their families, which was why she didn't know Vanessa when she first met her. She only found out from Agnes, who had visited Heidi in prison. She knew who Vanessa was when she married us in Maui.

"Do we need to inform your mom about our fake marriage?" I asked.

"Yes." Vanessa nodded. "She'll want to hear the truth from us."

"Okay."

"She's staying at my apartment now, so I can pay the lease."

"Don't insult me, Vanessa."

She stiffened, straightened up, and considered me. "I don't mean it in a bad way. It's your property, and she's living there. I can't have her stay for free."

"Who says she's staying for free?" I pulled her to me. "You're my girlfriend, and you're paying me with your cooking and painting sessions." I smiled, rubbing away the worry between her eyebrows. "I have a lot of properties, and I'm not losing any money by letting her stay there."

"Are you sure?"

"Absolutely, Lily Pad."

She poked me in the chest. "Now I want to know how you extracted her safely. I thought you were just going to have your lawyer ask for a new trial."

"That was the original thought, but I got some more information that made me revise the plan. Leo was going through with the rescue, even though you told him not to."

"What?" She bolted up. "Why? They already got the money, which I took as a loss."

I told her how Leo was using the extraction to create chaos for the city and the prison. That her mom was going to die—to create disorder—so they could launder illegal drugs for The Trogyn.

"I can't believe there's a drug lab in the prison's basement."

I described how my team pretended to be correctional offi-cers driving the prisoners to pick up trash. They also got a woman's body from the morgue the night before and dressed her in the same prison outfit. When the three attackers came, my men assisted the women to safety and killed the attackers. My men torched the van with the corpse inside. The city assumed Hannah Lam was dead.

When I finished the story, Vanessa gawked at me. "That sounded very calculated and complex."

"It was."

She hugged me. "If I'm ever falsely incarcerated and put in prison, I want you"—she pinched my cheek—"to be the maverick who masterminds my escape, okay?"

I chuckled. "Okay. But no one will dare touch you."

She rested her head on my shoulder for a moment. I looked down when I heard a little snore.

I didn't tell Vanessa that my lawyer would sue the city on her behalf so she could recuperate the money and time she'd lost. The City of Providence and its officials owed the Lam family much more than money could ever offer.

My Lily Pad had an emotional day. I could share this news with her later.

CHAPTER SIXTY-SEVEN

ATTIKUS

A FEW WEEKS of stability and no chaos gave Vanessa time to focus on her mom and her art gallery. Vanessa's mom and Mom Gigi had been hanging out at my house often. Ellen joined whenever she could. Agnes and Joseph even stopped by a few times.

My house had never been this full of life. But I loved it and decided to host more gatherings.

The more my circle of people grew, the more I feared retaliation from Ashton. I didn't give a damn that his new name was Madeline. He would always be the vile Ashton Lindor to me.

Vanessa and I had a lunch gathering at the Krazee Tavern today at one in the afternoon. The boys and their significant others, along with Mom Gigi, Ellen, Heidi, Agnes, and Joseph, would be attending. Remi had reserved the banquet room at his restaurant for us.

I walked into Vanessa's studio and saw her standing with hands on her hips, staring at the painting of Madeline Claude-Collins. "It looks eerily like her."

Vanessa crossed her arms. "I can't believe she didn't cancel the order. Instead, she wants it for an event at the Silver Cloud Hotel in three days."

"That's probably because you told her you were finished with the painting."

"I guess so. Madeline must know I'm your wife by now. She didn't when she first placed the order, but surely she does now."

"I'm sure she knows," I said. "She's a narcissist. Since she ordered a large painting of herself and already paid you half, she's going to want it, regardless."

"You're right." She sighed. "I don't have any more custom art lined up. Thank goodness."

"How are you delivering this painting to her?"

"A delivery service will ship it to the Silver Cloud Hotel."

"That's a good idea. I don't want you anywhere near that hotel."

She took my hand in hers. "Ready for lunch?"

"You go ahead. The boys and I have to stop by Remi's place to sign early copies of WaterFyre Rising."

"You have early copies already?" Her eyes filled with excitement.

"We selected a group of gamers from around the world to download the early copies to play and promote them. But these physical copies are collectible items that we'll give out as prizes for those who get us the most pre-orders."

"That's amazing." She embraced me. "I'm so proud of you and the boys!"

"You inspired a large portion of Level Seven, so thank *you*."

After Vanessa left, I headed over to Remi's house to sign the physical copies.

Remington, Grayson, Royce, Forrest, Arrow, Orion, and I stood around the dining table and lifted our whiskey tumblers, celebrating our success.

We'd have a large celebration with everyone later, but right now, we needed this comradery.

"The game has grown over the years. Each of us created a world that symbolizes our fears and dreams," Remi said. "Thank you for being part of this incredible journey with me."

"Thank you for starting it all those years ago," Grayson said.

"To WaterFyre Rising—may it take over in a positive way." Orion clinked glasses with us.

We chatted for a few more minutes, discussing The Trogyn, the President, and his wife.

"Everything has come down to them. We've got this." Forrest slapped me on the shoulder. "We'll get Ashton and eliminate The Trogyn forever."

Phase two of my plan began today.

"We should get going before the girls look for us." Arrow gestured to the door.

Grayson and I rode with Remington while the other boys hopped into Orion's SUV.

We stopped at a red light, and I turned to my right to see a large eight-wheeler truck heading toward us.

"Fuck."

But another vehicle smashed into our car and flipped us over.

CHAPTER SIXTY-EIGHT

VANESSA

INSIDE THE KRAZEE TAVERN, we sat around chatting with my mom, Gigi, Ellen, Agnes, and Joseph. The appetizers and drinks were delicious. Watching Agnes and Joseph together made me so happy. I understood why Attikus had been so worried about Joseph—he was a father figure to him.

Nerves churned in my stomach, and I placed a hand over it. My left eyelid kept twitching. I didn't want to think about it, but usually, those things signified a bad omen.

"What's taking them so long?" I asked the girls.

They checked their phones, but no messages appeared.

Michelle's phone rang, and she picked it up. "Where are you?" She listened intently. "What? Oh, my god." Her face transformed into dread. "Okay. I'll let them know. We'll be there."

My heart hammered. "What happened?"

The chatter in the room stopped, waiting for Michelle's response.

With trembling hands, she lowered her phone and said,

"There was an accident. An explosion. Remi, Grayson, and Attikus are dead."

My heart froze as shock overcame my body. I couldn't believe it. It had to be false. I just saw him this morning. I forced myself into survival mode. "What hospital?"

Michelle was about to tell me when Audri fainted. Vivian caught her just in time. Gigi called an ambulance and rode with Audri to the hospital.

Natalie and I clung to each other as Vivian drove us. Ellen took my mom in her car. Agnes and Joseph told us they'd meet us there. I was in no condition to drive. I'd probably run everyone over.

I was functioning in a daze of shock. My body felt detached from my head, and my soul was nowhere to be found. Somehow, I gathered my strength to step one foot in front of another. I supposed that was better than shattering into tiny pieces.

Attikus. I needed to see him. What happened to him?

When we arrived, I got out of the car and lost my balance. I braced a hand on the car, inhaling and exhaling to gain fresh oxygen.

Dear God, please give me the strength to survive this awful day.

When we entered the hospital waiting room, Forrest, Royce, Arrow, and Orion all rose from their seats.

I felt like I was floating, but I managed to look at Forrest because he was standing closest to me. "What happened?"

"An SUV hit Remi's car and flipped it over," he said. "The SUV burst into flames, and Remi's car caught on fire. It happened so quickly."

"We were a few cars back and rushed out as soon as it happened." Royce embraced a teary Michelle. "But the explosion was too big. They didn't stand a chance."

Somehow, I found myself sitting while my mom rubbed

circles on my back. Elena and Vivian consoled Natalie. I wished I could ease Natalie's pain, but I was paralyzed by my own. Audri was in an exam room, and Gigi was with her.

How could this be happening? I only saw him a few hours ago.

I gathered my strength so I could walk into the room without falling.

"Do you need me to go with you?" *Mẹ* asked.

"No. I'll be okay."

I pushed the door open, entered the room, and saw him on the stretcher. I didn't recognize his face. It was severely burned. The only thing I recognized were the clothes he wore that morning. My fingers trembled as I touched a section of the torched clothing.

Anger and pain knifed me over and over. I didn't want to remember him this way. Emotion surged in me, hot and angry. The dam broke, and I sobbed, dropping to the floor.

Attikus had such a bright future ahead of him. A video game to celebrate with his friends. I never got a chance to tell him I wanted to stay married to him and start a family.

Anger, grief, pain, and vengeance pumped through me.

Was this what he experienced all those years ago as a teen?

I knew who was responsible for this tragic accident today. Anger surged like hot lava, overflowing inside me. Anger numbed the other emotions, so I clung to it. Wiping the hot tears from my eyes, I vowed to make Madeline Claude-Collins pay tenfold.

CHAPTER SIXTY-NINE

VANESSA

AGNES, Joseph, and my mom told me they'd help with the funeral arrangements while I revised the painting for Madeline. I couldn't get myself to call the morgue to talk about his burial. I just couldn't do it.

My only saving grace was ensuring that Madeline paid for Attikus's, Remington's, and Grayson's deaths. Audri lost her lover and brother in one day. I didn't know how she was holding up.

Tell her your plan.

My girls needed to be part of this as much as I did. I wasn't alone. I picked up my phone and sent a text to the group chat.

Vanessa: *Got a plan. Can we meet?*

Audri: *Where?*

Natalie: *When?*

Vanessa: *In an hour? At my place—Attikus's place.*

Kiera: *Be there soon.*

Michelle: *Not gonna miss it for anything.*

Vivian: *Should I bring anything?*

Vanessa: *No, thanks.*

When the girls settled in my living room, the doorbell rang. I walked over and opened the door.

"*Mẹ*, what are you doing here?"

"I know what you're up to." She cupped the side of my face. "I want to help." She stepped inside.

I didn't want to involve my mother in this mess. What if things went wrong? She could be sent back to jail.

"I don't know what you're talking about." I closed the door.

She leveled a stare at me. "You're my daughter. I *know* you. You want vengeance. I want it too."

Tears filled my eyes. "I don't want you involved."

"I'm already involved. He was my son-in-law. He got me out of prison, gave me a new life, and asked me for permission to marry you." She flared her nostrils. "I want these people to pay."

"He asked you for permission?" I asked. "When?"

"When he told me about the fake marriage." *Mẹ* embraced me. "You did so much for me, Vanessa. My heart hurts for you. We do this together. We eliminate Madeline and President Collins, and The Trogyn will crumble."

I couldn't convince my mom to go home. She was stubborn like me, but having her perspective would help me avoid unseen obstacles. She took my hand, and I led her into the living room. All the girls had made themselves coffee or tea. I embraced Audri and Natalie for a long moment. We cried together, and that relieved some of the massive pressure in my chest.

When the tears dried up, Audri, Natalie, and I sat together on the long couch.

I blew out a breath. "The plan involves me and my painting."

I told them my plan and what they could assist with, and they gaped at me.

"That's dangerous." Elena rubbed her growing stomach. "But my reporters will be ready to bombard the couple with questions. I'll call in other media outlets that I trust."

"Good idea because Madeline will only invite those who will do as she demands," Michelle said. "I'll write about the President and his wife's corruption on my blog."

"Great idea," I said and looked at Vivian. "I need your high-tech devices."

"Whatever you need."

"I prefer you not put yourself in that situation," said Kiera. "But I understand why you need to do this." Her outgoing character had dimmed from all the grief in the air.

I didn't have the energy to ask how the other boys were doing. We were all dealing with grief in our way.

The girls told me they had gathered a list of companies associated with Harris Pharmaceuticals and Harris Foods, LLC.

"Give it to the boys," my mom said. "They'll know what to do."

Hurting these people was my way of getting justice. As for recovering, that would take years—probably a lifetime.

I turned to my mom. "I need you to get me some blueberries."

"Blueberries?" Natalie asked.

"It's Madeline's favorite."

"The Lunch Lady Club will take care of that," *Mẹ* said.

Who knew the Lunch Lady Club would have a hand in taking down members of The Trogyn?

"Can I see the painting?" Audri asked. She looked like a walking zombie. I didn't dare look at myself in the mirror.

I took everyone to my studio.

"That's a huge painting," said Michelle.

"We'll be there with you to help with all the details." Vivian touched my arm.

"The First Lady is hosting an event to raise money for Brigham and Women's Hospital."

"That's where she got her plastic surgeries done," *Mẹ* said.

"How do you know?" I asked.

She smirked. "I know a few things."

When everyone left, my mom stayed behind. "Do you need anything else besides blueberries?"

"No, thanks."

"How about *Atropa belladonna*, the berry from the nightshade family?"

How could she know what I was thinking? I was going to find them in the woods later.

"You have some?"

"No, but I know who grows them."

"I'll take some then. Thank you." That would save me time.

She patted my hand. "I'm glad you're using your botany knowledge for this."

CHAPTER SEVENTY

VANESSA

VIVIAN HAD BOOKED a suite in the Silver Cloud Hotel using a false alias. All the girls accompanied me except our pregnant friends. They would arrive when the event started, even though I'd told them to sit this one out. I didn't want anything to happen to them in case my plan didn't work, but I had stubborn friends who didn't listen to me.

Audri, Natalie, Vivian, Michelle, and I woke up at six in the morning to get ready. The event was scheduled to start at noon, but we wanted extra time in case we had to adjust.

The painting was in storage beside the banquet hall. I had alerted the hotel staff that I didn't want to risk the First Lady seeing her portrait. I wanted her to be surprised. The manager understood and told me to ask the front desk for a key when I was ready to transport the painting to the banquet hall.

After my friends and I freshened up, they dressed in jeans and T-shirts that read We Love the First Lady. I wore a skin-colored leotard and tossed on a First-Lady T-shirt over it with knit pants. I'd seen videos of Madeline's supporters wearing these shirts to her events, and they made it easier for us to maneuver around the hotel.

Natalie carried my makeup bag, and Audri held my garment bag. I carried two plastic containers. One had strawberries and raspberries. The other contained *Atropa belladonna*—a poisonous berry that looked exactly like blueberries. To a person who wasn't familiar with this deadly nightshade, it looked safe to eat. But the *Atropa belladonna* contained tropane alkaloids, which increased the heart rate and caused delirium, vomiting, hallucinations, and respiratory failure.

I didn't want the President and his wife in prison. That was too easy. What if they paid someone off? Or what if they escaped? I couldn't risk that. They deserved all the pain before death came for them. I'd always been a kind person, but I'd learned that some people didn't deserve kindness.

Audri got the key and told the staff we were moving the painting to the banquet hall, prepping for the event. It took two of us to transport the giant painting safely. Natalie locked the door as soon as we entered. A wide-screen TV was mounted on the wall at the front. Two more TVs were secured to the side walls. The hall didn't have any windows. Musical instruments were already set up in a corner for a local band. About twenty tables with white linen tablecloths and chairs were scattered around the room. A flower centerpiece and reserved name tags sat on each table. A few tall tables stood beside the refreshment area. We carried the painting to the front of the room near the TV and leaned it against the wall beside a table reserved for the First Couple.

I took off the T-shirt and draped it over a chair, revealing my nude leotard. I opened the makeup bag and painted my face to match how Madeline looked in the painting. It disgusted me, but I was doing this for Attikus, me, my mom, the boys, my girls, and all the people who had been hurt by Madeline or The Trogyn.

Natalie helped me dress in the poufy gown made of canvas fabric. I'd painted the gown to match the floral background. All I had to do was position myself how I'd painted the figure of the First Lady. I would be a three-dimensional figure with a floral dress popping off the surface. On any other day and for any other reason, this would be an innovative art piece for a museum. But today, I was using this method to capture my enemies.

I positioned myself. "What do you guys think?"

Standing farther away, Natalie squinted. "Move one inch to the right and tilt your head a little."

I did as she directed.

"Perfect." Natalie walked up to me, adjusting the gown.

"I don't know how you do it. You, the dress, and the painting are aligned perfectly," said Michelle. "It's impeccable."

"Thanks." I smiled warmly.

Michelle and Natalie attached sections of the dress to the Velcro pieces that were hot glued to the painting. This helped keep the dress in place.

The long hem hid my feet, which were in flats in case I needed to dart to safety.

Audri placed the pretty bowl of *Atropa belladonna* berries at the front table, where a sign read Reserved for the First Lady. She also added bowls of strawberries and raspberries.

Vivian inserted two tiny recorders into the painting and a mini camera. Madeline wouldn't have allowed me to attend knowing who I was. So this was my way of infiltrating her event.

Time flew by, and I ate some snacks the girls had brought with them.

I couldn't have done all of this without my friends' help. Elena's Musepaper would blast details about today's event to her wide audience. Natalie designed the dress with the hidden pockets so I could hide a knife in case I needed it. I painted over the canvas dress, blending it into the background of the painting. Kiera would take photos of the event to give to Elena and Michelle. Michelle's blog would release pictures and info to her international audience. Vivian's cutting-edge devices provided video and audio to support Elena and Michelle's media coverage. Audri's jewelry company was holding a fundraiser to support all the victims of The Trogyn. Anyone who donated would get a free bracelet from her new collection.

I could've disguised myself as a patron in the audience and watch the event unfold, but I needed to be up-close to Madeline. She had killed my love and my friends. I needed to see her *eat* the poisonous berries. I was a breath from danger, but I didn't care.

"We're heading back to the suite to prepare for the event." They had purchased tickets under false names in case Madeline had their real names banned.

The girls all stood in front of me, looking worried. "Are you okay?"

"I'll be fine. Thank you for all your help."

"Thanks for giving us an actual Super Spy Girl mission," Michelle teased.

Audri and Natalie held hands.

"Our boys would appreciate this," Audri said, sorrow filling her eyes.

"I needed this too." Natalie forced a smile.

"The boys only know part of the plan. We'll share the rest of the details when we return to our rooms." Vivian wrapped an arm around Michelle. "They'll get mad. But, hey, we can't just sit around and do nothing when they place themselves in danger for us all the time."

The girls and I had gone through several plans to help our boys at our Chill and Chat, but nothing was finalized. We thought we had more time.

This idea had formed in my mind like a deadly disease that developed inside a body filled with sorrow, hatred, and anger. Attikus's death triggered my vendetta. I didn't tell the girls or my mom that I would die with Madeline today if the situation called for it.

When the girls left, I stood in silence. One dim light glowed in the far corner. In the quiet, I heard Attikus's voice in my head. My heart was in pain from missing him so much. The pain throbbed all over my body. I felt it in my veins, in my lungs, in the air that I breathed. It hurt to live. I imagined my bodily cells trying their best to heal me. But my suffering wasn't a cut that could be bandaged or fixed with a pill. I didn't know if I could ever heal from this deep wound. I would do anything to see him again. Tears approached, but I shoved them down. The wetness would ruin the paint camouflage. As I waited for time to tick by, I replayed the day I last saw Attikus. My chest constricted.

I love you so much.

A noise sounded at the two doors, and the hotel staff wearing all black entered, flicking on the lights.

"Wow, look at that exceptional painting of the First Lady," said the bald man as he prepared the appetizer and refreshment tables near the entrance, which was on the opposite side of where I was.

Don't come over. Don't come over.

It was so hard not to blink. I prayed no one stared at the painting long enough to notice my eyes.

The staff brought in seven paintings on easels with

numbers on them. Minutes later, two employees gestured for three men wearing colorful suits to enter. They walked over to the band area, grabbed their instruments, and practiced a tune. Thirty minutes later, people arrived, browsed the paintings, and stopped by the appetizer table. Some attendees wore classy gowns and suits, while others wore unique outfits that told me they were artists. The crowd seemed to be a blend of the wealthy, creative types, and doctors who wanted to support Brigham and Women's Hospital. One doctor still had on his white lab coat.

"Look at that painting." A woman in a black dress yanked at her spouse's arm and pointed at me. "It's gorgeous."

Nerves twisted my stomach.

"That's a cool piece," said the man in the navy suit. He walked up to the painting with the woman. "I don't think it's for sale though."

I held my breath, praying they'd take a seat at their table below the platform.

"It's not for sale," said a man with the wild purple hair. "There's no number on it. That masterpiece would be awesome in my new movie, though."

"Maybe you can ask the First Lady to borrow it." The lady smiled.

"Please take your seats, everyone," said the staff member wearing a little black dress. "The First Couple would be arriving soon."

I breathed out a sigh of relief as people walked to their assigned seats.

Minutes later, President Collins and Madeline Claude-Collins walked through the door. She wore a red gown with thin straps and a full skirt. Her blonde hair had wavy layers that looked stiff. The President wore a tuxedo, looking powerful and proud.

"Hi, Mr. President and First Lady!" exclaimed the woman who had come up to the panting earlier. She gestured to Madeline's gown. "I *love* your red dress."

More people agreed and tossed out compliments at the First Lady. Beaming, she loved the attention.

"Thank you. The House of Dior creates exceptional artwork, don't they?" Madeline smiled.

"You look like a fabulous artwork!" said someone.

I wanted to roll my eyes at these people who were probably at this charity to gain favors from the First Couple.

Madeline's face brightened. "You're too kind." Then she turned to everyone in the room. "Thank you for coming." She placed her hands on her chest. "Thank you for supporting Brigham and Women's Hospital. Look at this incredible art and place your bids before it's gone."

The band lowered their tune as the President and Madeline took turns with their speeches about how the charity would benefit the innovative medical research conducted at the hospital. When the speeches finished and answered some questions, everyone took a break for refreshments, and music boomed. Chatter grew in the room as more people entered the room and walked around looking at the paintings. There were no more seats available for the late arrivals. I spotted my friends in the back corner. The girls were chatting amongst themselves while keeping an eye on me. The boys spoke to a group of men dressed in dark suits. The girls must have told them everything already. Conversations about art and medical research surrounded me.

After talking to a group of people, Madeline excused herself. She grabbed her husband's hand and walked straight to the painting of herself. They stood studying the painting, looking up and down. No one was on the platform with them.

"Darling, look at this portrait," Madeline said. "Isn't it gorgeous?"

The President whispered in her ear. "You're so hot."

"You too." Madeline beamed. "Life is good, baby. Those fuckers are dead. I'm sure the other guys won't be bothering us anymore. God is on our side." Since her face was turned toward the painting—toward me and away from the crowd—the evilness in her eyes blazed to life. I wanted to sink my nails into those devilish eyes and rip the sly smirk from her face. She ran a hand down the skirt of the canvas dress, admiring it.

"Three guys are dead." President Collins smirked. "The Claude family sent CIA agents and European assassins to ensure they died. Too bad someone killed them before we could. But I supposed that conclusion worked out in our favor."

"I wonder who killed them?" she asked.

"Probably another enemy."

"True. I hope it was a slow and painful death." She flicked him an amused look. "To get the job done appropriately, my family sent the top officials in the CIA. Whoever it was saved them time and trouble." She rattled off their names as though she were proud.

His smile widened. "I know. I put them in the CIA for you. Just wanted to make sure you remember."

"I do." She patted his cheek. "The Trogyn owns the CIA."

"We'll own the world soon enough." President Collins wrapped an arm around his wife.

"We're untouchable." She smirked. "If only the American people knew our family caused the last two presidents' assassinations. America has been compromised for a long time. People are so fucking stupid. They don't even know we're brainwashing them." She laughed. "We can sell them shit, and they'll buy it."

"You die if you don't comply." The President grinned.

Madeline kissed his cheek. "But you're different." She palmed him. "You know *exactly* how to comply." She took his hand and shoved two of his fingers into her mouth, sucking them. "I loved how you sucked my dick before I became a woman to be your First Lady. I miss it so much."

"I'm excellent at it, aren't I?" He looked at her with darkened eyes. "But so are you—Ashton Claude Lindor—the best cock sucker even at sixteen." He growled quietly. "If only the country knew how amazing you were."

"Really?" she emphasized. "You want to share me with the country?"

"Never."

What the hell? I wanted to puke. I couldn't believe what they were talking about in public. The crowd had increased along with the buzz of conversation, drowning out their chatter. Still, they should have kept their sexual innuendo at home.

But I was glad their arrogance allowed the recorder and the camera to capture everything.

What did they mean by someone else getting to Attikus, Remi, and Grayson before their assassins could? If they hadn't killed Attikus and his friends, who had?

"President Collins!" someone shouted across the room. "Do you have time for some questions?"

The couple turned, and I recognized a reporter from Musepaper. Elena and Orion were standing with my friends in the corner. Elena and Orion probably placed several of their people around the room to ask questions and help control the narrative. More men stood in the back row, probably Orion's security team. People dispersed to the side of the room because there wasn't enough seating.

"Of course, but after the video about the wonderful studies at Brigham and Women's Hospital," President Collins said, glancing around. "Wow. Look at this. We have more than a full house today. So glad you could join us to help raise money for this amazing hospital. Enjoy the food and drinks."

Madeline sat down and glanced at the bowls of fruits and trays of cookies reserved just for her. She touched the reserved sign as though she was stroking her own ego. She took a small plate, grabbed a sugar cookie, bit into it, and scooped up some blueberries. My gaze stayed on her as she placed a berry into her mouth. She chewed and swallowed it. Then she arched an eyebrow, probably wondering why the sweet berry's taste turned bitter. Those were the properties of the *Atropa belladonna*—initially sweet with a bitter and acrid aftertaste.

When the President sat down, she rose to speak about the artwork and the cause. President Collins scooped berries onto his plate and ate. Happiness spread throughout my body.

The couple relaxed in their chairs, eating casually as the patrons enjoyed their snacks in their seats or at the high tables. Chatter and music continued to boom.

Suddenly, the three wide-screen TVs turned on with a question flashing against a black screen: *Do you know who is the real Madeline Claude-Collins?*

CHAPTER SEVENTY-ONE

VANESSA

THE ROOM WENT QUIET, and the band stopped playing.

The President and his wife exchanged perplexed glances.

"What does that mean?" asked a woman with the short brown hair. "Does the First Lady have a different identity?"

"Is there something you'd like us to know, First Lady?" asked a man in a corduroy jacket. "We're here to support your charity, so we'd like to know the truth."

Conversations erupted amongst the tables as they waited for a response from the First Couple.

I smirked knowing the woman and man who asked the questions probably worked for Musepaper.

A second later, videos of Ashton Lindor as a high school teen splashed onto the screen. It was a clip from a performance of *Macbeth*. The cast got to introduce themselves.

"That looks like you, First Lady," said the short-haired woman.

"It does," said another reporter. "Do you have a brother?"

"Where's my assistant?" Madeline searched the room.

"Jack!" The President called out to the secret service agent whom I had met before. He was nowhere in sight.

The President and his wife both placed a hand on their chests, signifying their increased heart rate and difficulty breathing.

"Is that the First Lady in the video?" someone asked.

"That's not me!" Madeline shouted, losing her British accent.

"But it looks so much like you." A woman reporter snapped a photo of her.

"All of you—get out!" she shouted, blocking her face with her forearm.

"But we paid for the event," said a man sitting with his wife.

Looking pale, the President glanced around, probably looking for his people. Where were they?

A side-by-side image of Ashton and Madeline popped onto the TV screen.

A computer voice said, "President Charles Collins and his wife have lied to you. Madeline Claude-Collins is a transgender woman from the wealthy Claude family. They're running a powerful crime organization called The Trogyn, and they own Harris Foods, LLC and Harris Pharmaceuticals. They are feeding your children poisoned food, making them sick. They're forcing you to buy medicine from their company. These are the evil people around you." Images of the members flashed onto the screen. "The CIA is compromised by The Trogyn. They're killing Americans everywhere. This is how Madeline reacts when she doesn't get what she wants. She was only sixteen."

The video played the recording of Ashton beating Attikus. It stopped when Ashton's face was clearly visible.

"Stop it! Jack! Where the fuck are you?" She shouted for the secret service. "They're lying. They're trying to smear me."

"What happened to your British accent?" asked someone in the crowd.

Conversations erupted, and people left with fear, anger, and confusion on their faces.

"Look!" someone exclaimed. "There are more TVs out here with different videos."

"Check your phones!" said another person. "It's on social media everywhere."

"Wait, that's the President and his wife talking just now. Same event. They're wearing the same clothes."

I smiled, knowing Vivian and Elena were blasting the new video recordings caught by devices embedded in the paintings. Tears ran down my cheeks. I could hear and smell justice approaching. Karma's presence rang like a bell. My friends deactivated the recordings and the camera. There was no need for the public to see how the President and his wife would die.

After everyone had left, Orion closed the doors to the banquet hall. The only people in the room were my friends and Orion's security team in the back.

Madeline bolted from her chair, knocking it down. The chair hit the display cart filled with berries and dessert. The cart flew toward my legs, but I shifted, letting it slam into the painting. Madeline whipped her eyes to me. There was no need to hide anymore. I detached myself from the painting, wearing a one-of-a kind gown.

Madeline glared at me, and then she smirked. "Too bad Attikus isn't here to see me kill you."

My friends stepped forward, preparing to help me. But I held out a hand. "You're in no condition to kill anyone, Madeline. Or should I say, Ashton?"

She charged at me but stopped as pain strained her face.

She gripped her chest, and I smiled, loving that poison was flowing through her systems. Her left shoulder dipped more, probably because pain overpowered her effort to straighten herself.

"It's a marvel that my husband destroyed your shoulder back then when *three* of you beat him."

I remembered watching the video and seeing Ashton wince from Attikus's punch.

"Doesn't matter now, does it?" A sly smile slid onto Madeline's face. "He's *dead*."

President Collins gasped, hunched over, and collapsed onto the chair, looking worse than Madeline.

"My chest," he groaned. "Something's not right."

"Something is *extremely* right." I described his symptoms. "The *Atropa belladonna* is slowly tearing down your respiratory system." I tapped my head. "You'll start hallucinating as your brain deteriorates."

"Bitch!" Madeline lunged at me, gripping my throat with her manly hand.

I clawed at her with my sharp nails and pulled her hair. The blonde wig shifted, clinging to the side. I reached into my dress pocket, grabbed the knife, and stabbed her in the stomach.

"That's for Attikus!" I pushed her away, creating distance.

Madeline growled in pain, stumbled, and yanked out the knife. Her blonde wig fell to the ground, revealing a shaved head.

"Vanessa!" the girls shrieked with worry as the boys stepped closer to the platform.

"I'm okay." I gestured for them to stay where they were.

I wanted to see life end in Madeline's eyes. I wanted to see her suffer for all the lives she'd hurt. Most of all, I wanted her to pay for taking Attikus away from me and for killing

Grayson and Remi. Her death would help me grieve for Attikus.

The *Atropa belladonna* didn't affect Madeline as quickly as her older husband, who was barely alive in the chair.

"I'm going to kill you!" Hatred blazed in Madeline's eyes as she gripped the knife and rushed toward me again.

"Touch her again, and you'll be begging me to end you."

The voice was like an electric shock through my system. It jolted my heart, giving it new life. Everything in the room faded to the background as I turned toward his voice. When Attikus's face emerged from the group of security guards standing behind Orion, I released a sob of joy, shock, sadness, and anger. All these emotions battled in me, pushing tears to the surface and down my face.

Am I imagining this? Is it really him?

Attikus stepped up to the platform and brushed my tears away with his fingers. "It's me, Lily Pad." He kissed my forehead.

I sucked in a breath at his touch—his presence. He was real in the flesh. But the joy I felt was mixed with anger. Why had he kept me in the dark? I pushed the anger aside to deal with it later.

"No." Madeline glowered at him. "It can't be." She held a hand to her bleeding wound. "You should be dead."

Attikus stepped in front of me, creating a protective barrier between me and Madeline. "Things aren't always what they seem. You, of all people, should know this."

Blood continued to leak from the wound, but Madeline didn't seem to be affected by it like I had hoped. Perhaps her multiple surgeries and access to illegal drugs had messed up her body.

"Ashton, I can't breathe . . ." President Collins looked at his wife for help.

"You fucker!" She gathered her strength and lunged after me, but Attikus kicked her. She fell against the table but regained her composure.

"The berries are delicious, aren't they?" I smirked. "The deadly nightshade is toxic—just like you."

"You fucking bitch!" she exclaimed, her fists clenched.

A loud boom sounded from the door. I glanced toward it, looking worried.

"That's The Trogyn empire collapsing." Attikus said. "You should watch the videos of your family's businesses being destroyed. The high definition and audio effects are fantastic."

Happy tears streamed down my face as I stared at my love. God had heard my prayer. But now I had to deal with how Attikus had kept me in the dark about his plan.

I glanced at my friends, who looked equally shocked.

Attikus met my eyes. Love and so much more swam in them.

Oh, I have questions for you, Whistler.

"You good?" Remi asked Attikus, holding Audri's hand.

Attikus nodded. "Thank you."

My friends exited through a hidden door that blended in with the wall.

The only people left were Attikus, Madeline, her husband, and me. Drool slid down the side of the President's mouth.

Attikus walked up to me with his cane. "I missed you."

I'd missed him too, but I couldn't say it right now. The past three days had been hell, thinking he was dead.

"I'm going to kill you both!" Madeline charged at us.

Attikus stepped in front of me, drew a sword from his cane, and slashed off Madeline's right arm. It thudded to the floor.

"That's for charging at my wife." He seethed. "This is for my father." Attikus stabbed Madeline in the gut, and she wailed. "This is for my mother." He pierced one thigh, and blood gushed out. "And this is for my sister." He plunged the sword into the other thigh and yanked it out.

My body jerked as I watched Attikus unleash his rage. Cries of pain filled the room. I should feel bad for Madeline, but then I thought about all those lives she had ruined.

"This is for me." Attikus stabbed Madeline's wrist, knee, and ankle. Blood splattered all over the floor.

When he lowered his sword, I saw the names of his mother, father, and sister engraved on the blade. Now I understood why he always carried that cane.

"How does it feel to live with an injury that I caused?" Attikus tapped Madeline's left shoulder with his sword.

Madeline flared her nostrils, wanting to hurt Attikus, but was in no condition to do so.

"I read your medical files from Brigham and Women's Hospital." He smiled. "Your injured shoulder can't be repaired. You *can't* escape me." He glared at her. "Why did you become a woman?"

Heaving, Madeline glowered. "So you wouldn't find me . . . fucker."

A smirk slid onto Attikus's face. "You were that scared of me?"

"Jack." Her eyes glazed as she looked at Attikus. The hallucination had begun. "Take us home. Don't let Attikus find us."

"Why are you afraid of him?" Attikus asked.

"Not afraid, Jack." She moaned. "Always be cautious of a man with nothing to lose. He'll turn the world upside-down to find you." She started mumbling to herself.

Attikus walked over to the President, whose face was twisted with fear and pain. The President gasped for breath as he tried to escape Attikus, but he couldn't move.

"My mother came to you for help, but you betrayed her trust. You betrayed your country—your people. You're a pathetic man. This is for my mother, your country, and all the lives you've ruined." He stabbed the sword into the President's gut twice. The President called his wife's name as blood poured out of him.

Madeline was delirious and hallucinating. She looked at Attikus. "Jack, take us out of here. Now!"

I saw the closure on Attikus's face as he turned his gaze away from the President and Madeline. He wiped his sword on a napkin from the table and returned the sword to the cane scabbard. Taking my hand, he led me out the side door, leaving the President and his wife to bleed to death.

"We can't leave them there," I said. "The hotel staff will find them."

"No, they won't." He lifted my painted hand for a kiss. "I own this hotel. Someone will clean up the mess. Let's go home."

CHAPTER SEVENTY-TWO

ATTIKUS

A MONTH LATER, Vanessa was still mad at me and living with her mother in her old apartment. I only had so much patience. She'd told me she needed time to think things through. A month was long enough. I walked into the studio at her apartment, carrying a gift bag, and knocked on the door.

She opened it. "Yes?" Her dark hair was in a messy bun. She looked beautiful in her stained T-shirt and ripped jeans.

"May I come in?"

She shrugged. "Go ahead. You own this building."

Vanessa walked back to her fantastical painting of a lotus reaching for a floating island with a waterfall dripping with gold water. An intricate world lay beneath the lily pad and the surface of the water. I recognized the buildings around the City of Providence. Her color preferences had evolved to pastels instead of the bold, dark shades she'd favored before.

My love was transforming before my eyes. The darkness no longer existed in her.

"That's a gorgeous painting," I said.

"Thanks." She continued working, ignoring me.

"I love you," I said, standing beside her.

She stopped, turned, and met my eyes. Love radiated from her face.

"Can we please talk?" My heart quickened, fearing she'd say no.

She closed her eyes and released a sigh. When she opened them, she nodded. "Let's sit over here."

We walked to the old couch, and I sat beside her, leaving the gift bag on the floor. "Are you okay?"

She looked pale and exhausted. I blamed myself for her condition.

"I'm okay. Nothing sleep won't cure."

"I know I said this already, but I'm truly sorry for not telling you about my plan. I wanted to keep you safe. If I'd told you, I feared The Trogyn members would spy on you for your reaction." I took her hand in mine. "Your emotional state drove Charles Collins and Madeline Claude-Collins to believe my friends and I were dead. This led The Trogyn to loosen their security and become more careless."

She swallowed. "Go on."

"The boys used this carelessness to attack their multiple headquarters and hideaways. They had several in all the fifty states and many around the world. We destroyed all of them."

Her mouth dropped open. "How did you know their locations?"

"Dr. Messina had a list since he was one of their top elites. He gave me a clear picture of the intricate web within The Trogyn. Once I eliminated Ashton and the line of succession, they wouldn't have any more legs to stand on. There would be no leaders. No more hideaways, no more money, no more resources. They'd have nothing. The Trogyn would crumble."

She leaned against the couch. "So there's no more crime organization?"

"The Trogyn is gone, and the Claude family and their associates are scrambling from all the scrutiny, lawsuits, and people backing out of their businesses. The government is cleaning house at the CIA. It's going to be hard for the American people to trust their government again."

"What about Harris Foods LLC and Pharmaceuticals?"

"Thanks to you and the girls, we shut down over two hundred businesses associated with the Harris companies, and the owners are cooperating with the officials. Not only that, but Detective Farmer has also been appointed the lead investigator. He's put together a great team. We can trust he'll deliver the justice everyone deserves."

Vaness swallowed. "What happened to the bodies?"

"Farm animals got them," I said, not wanting her to know the details of Calvin's farm.

"What kind?"

"Alligators, tigers, wolves."

"Those aren't farm animals!" she exclaimed. "Are you referring to a different farm?"

"*Very* different."

She looked at me for a moment. "We need honorable men and women to hold office. The country needs change. The world needs change."

"Maybe this will inspire people to step up. But who knows? Politics is its own monster. The Trogyn was one of many." I sighed. "I'm tired of fighting, of planning—of watching my back."

"You've avenged all the victims of The Trogyn." She turned and cupped the side of my face. "You and your friends saved a lot of people."

"You had a huge role in it too." I gripped her hand. "If you're not safe or happy, there's no point in saving the world, Vanessa." I looked her in the eye. "You reached into my heart and repainted it a beautiful color." Her eyes softened on me. "You're the varnish that prevented my tattered soul from fraying."

"Attikus." Tears welled in her eyes.

"Our home is cold and lonely without you. I've been replaying our time together." My heart quickened with emotion. "In the quiet, I can hear myself. Most of all, I can hear your heart beating for me. You've been through a lot because of me. I'm sorry I hurt you."

"I was ready to die with Madeline that day," she confessed. "I didn't know how to make the pain stop. I thought if I watched her die, it would make me feel better."

"I faked my death to protect you, but I didn't realize my plan pushed you front and center of danger." Guilt multiplied in my stomach. "I watched your every move, so I know the pain I've bestowed on you. My cameras were placed all over the hotel, which I owned under an alias. I had to ensure you and the girls were safe."

I kissed her hand. She didn't yank it back, which was a good sign.

"You know, the boys and I would've gotten the President and Madeline from the confessions of the people they worked with or blackmailed. But when I saw your plan, I revised ours. Yours was better."

She smirked. "That just means you should never keep your plans from your wife."

"Never again. I learned my lesson."

"We've weathered a major storm." She stared at our joined hands.

"Your mom knew the truth, but I asked her not to tell you."

"That's why she agreed to stay home that day. Did she tell you about my plan?"

I nodded. "She had to. She didn't want to risk you getting hurt. I gave her my word I'd keep you safe."

"I love you." She looked at me. "But I need you to do something for me to earn the ultimate forgiveness."

A tremendous burden slid off my chest. I'd do anything for her. But the amusement in her eyes made me cautious about declaring that.

"Audri and Natalie already forgave their significant other," I said.

She leveled a stare at me. "They've been together a lot longer than we have." Her eyes narrowed with a hint of wickedness. "Plus, I'm not as forgiving as they are. I need my man to put in the work."

"Okay. What do you need me to do?"

"Chores and art. I need you to mop the kitchen floor, vacuum all the rugs, and do the dishes—the old-school way. No dishwasher allowed. Do this for a month."

I stared at her as the wild demand sparked a flurry of crazy images in my head. I hadn't done these chores in a long time. "We have a cleaning service to do all that."

"But I want *you* to do it. There's joy in cleaning up your own mess. Plus, positive energy loves it when you—the home-owner—put in the work." She smirked. "How much do you love me? Let me count the ways."

"Tomorrow can be day one," I said, taking on the challenge.

She smiled. "Are you sure about this?"

"Do you need me to draft up a contract?"

She smirked. "No."

"So that means you're moving back with me today?"

"How else will I monitor these chores?" She smiled and rested her head on my shoulder. "I'll get you a pretty apron to wear while you clean, Whistler."

"I'll wear whatever you want. I'll even clean in the nude for you."

She laughed, and I had my Lily Pad back. "About the contract—"

"It never really existed. I never gave it to my lawyer." I kissed her lips gently. "It was just a piece of paper to help you believe I would help you."

"You're such a cunning man." She shifted to straddle me and cupped my face, squishing my cheeks together. "You asked my mom for her permission to marry me?"

"I did, and she said yes."

"When did you plan on telling me this?"

"I wanted to right away, but you didn't want to talk to me."

She sighed. "I'm confused—"

I gently extricated myself from her, dropped to my knees, and pulled out a gold box. "I never got the chance to ask you like this. So I want to fill in all the blank spaces now." My heart thundered with anticipation. "Will you marry me, Vanessa?"

More tears overflowed her eyes. "Yes, you silly man."

Rising, I slid the brilliant-cut diamond ring on a petrified wooden band that matched her other ring onto her finger.

"It's gorgeous and so unique." She stared at the ring, moving her hand so it caught the sunlight. "I love it."

"I'm happy to hear that."

Vanessa embraced me, pushed me back down on the couch, and straddled my hips again. It seemed like this was her preferred position. "But you still need to do the chores."

I laughed. "Okay."

With sparkling eyes, she squished my face. "There's one more part to the groveling."

"What is it?" I asked through puckered lips.

"I want you to sketch a hundred images. It can be of anything. This will inspire you to create art again."

"Done."

"That was easy." She gave me a loud, sloppy kiss.

I reached for the gift bag on the floor and gave it to her. "For you, my demanding, perfect wife."

Beaming, she opened the gift bag and pulled out the sketchbook. Flipping to the first page, she saw herself and sucked in a breath. She flipped through all the pages, studying each illustration and its date.

"There are over a hundred illustrations of you. So that task is done."

Tears slid down her face. "You're a fabulous illustrator, Attikus."

"You've reignited the artist in me. Thank you." I got up from the couch and pulled her with me. "Do you want another wedding ceremony?"

"No need for that. A reception with family and friends would be nice. Nothing big."

"Anything you want."

"Was the marriage certificate also false?" she asked. "Is Agnes a fake justice of the peace?"

"The certificate is real. We're married, love. And Agnes is the real deal."

She looped her arms around my neck. "That saves us time. But I want another honeymoon. Same place."

I smiled. "We can do that after I finish my chores in the nude for you."

She gripped my hand. "Let's go home now. I want you to demonstrate that for me."

"It'll *sweep* you off your feet, baby." I scooped her up and headed home to show my wife all the ways I loved her.

VANESSA AND ATTIKUS
EPILOGUE

Another month later

Vanessa

We'd returned from our honeymoon in Maui last week, but no one attacked us this time. We'd spent most of our time on the private beach and flying to nearby islands.

Today, I was supposed to be resting, but I was too excited. Attikus was out celebrating with his friends and gamers they had flown into town. These gamers had a huge role in promoting WaterFyre Rising, especially the day President Collins and Madeline Claude-Collins died.

The gamers saw and heard everything that was recorded. They also saw the faces and names of The Trogyn members, information about the Claude family, and all those who had worked for them, including royalty, supreme court judges, governors, senators, police chiefs, CIA agents, FBI agents, doctors, celebrities, athletes, Nobel Peace prize winners, lawyers, priests, and so on.

My husband and his friends wanted the world to know The Trogyn weren't made of thugs but of respected people whom society revered and trusted. The shame game was played that day. The WaterFyre Rising reached an audience beyond the boys' expectations. Its excitement was unstoppable. People were already asking if there would be more games in that world.

These billionaires had sprinkled details about the crime organization into the game, leaving breadcrumbs for them to find the treasure. For those who found the treasure, they could enter portals that enabled them to play other games.

I glanced at the time on my phone. Attikus would be home in an hour, and I had something to show him. Smiling, I wrapped two abstract paintings I'd finished last night without him knowing. I never imagined I could love a man this much and have it returned the same.

Attikus didn't use a cane anymore. He'd retired it to the safe room, where his precious family items were stored. He'd also bought a property adjacent to the museum. Grayson was designing a few options for Attikus to review.

I blushed thinking about the exhibit room where he planned to host the *Paintings of Passion.* Nobody would know that abstract art was created by two lovers having fun. We'd added more to the paintings after the fact, but the first layer had started with passion, love, and laughter. The artist for the collection was Whistler L. Pad—a wonderful blend of Whistler and Lily Pad.

Attikus saved one abstract passion painting for his office. That artwork portrayed him posing for me on the chaise. I made it so we could hang it in our home and not have to answer questions from friends or family.

Once the gifts were wrapped, I set them aside and misted the three terrariums I created two days ago. One was for Attikus to take to work, one for Joseph's office, and another for Agnes. They were now living together.

Attikus had a lot of plants in his office, and he'd already set up the third greenhouse for me. My plant business was growing. I'd taken up the retail space next to the gallery for my plant collection and hired five new people. Two of them were my mom's friends from prison—Sheila Brown and Josephine Smith. They were released with Attikus's help and also received monetary compensation from the city.

I set the terrariums aside, sat down, and gulped a glass of cold water. I would've made some fresh spring rolls and Vietnamese crêpes for him, but I was exhausted, so I'd ordered from Saigon Bistro, and my mom delivered my order to me. She worked part-time at the restaurant to help her friend Hope.

Mẹ didn't need to work, but she wanted to. The city had awarded me ten million dollars for wrongfully imprisoning my mother and getting her killed during the rescue. Even though it was another body impersonating my mom's, the city didn't know that. But my mom donated a portion to a women's shelter and children's charity. *Mẹ*, Mom Gigi, Ellen, and Agnes started the Lunch Lady Club Program, which helped fund healthy foods for children across the country. The programs worked with farms willing to provide children with fresh fruits and vegetables. I was so proud of her.

My mom, Mom Gigi, Ellen, and Agnes held their Lunch Lady Club meetings at Saigon Bistro, like how the Smart A.S.S. had our Chill and Chat gatherings at my art gallery. The power of friendship and women working together was something we wanted to continue for generations to come.

The garage door opened, and nerves stirred inside me. My husband was home. I would've gone to the door to greet him like I usually did, but I was too tired.

Attikus entered the kitchen, whistling a lovely tune as he kicked off his shoes on the mat and looked at me.

"Where is my Lily Pad?"

"Right here waiting for you." I smiled.

He approached, gave me a kiss, and studied me. "You look exhausted. What did you do today?"

I told him what I'd done today.

"No wonder you're tired." He glanced at the terrariums. "These are gorgeous. Joseph and Agnes will be thrilled." He looked into his terrarium. "You know my office now looks like a rainforest, right?"

"Yup, and so does mine." I beamed with pride. "All the wonderful plants and flowers are promoting positive energy and producing healthy air for us."

"Do you want three more greenhouses to play with?"

I knew he was putting together the third one for me, but I figured I'd need more soon. I wanted to grow fruit trees all year round.

"Thank you!" I gripped his face. "How did you know I wanted that?"

"Because I'm the best husband out there."

My heart was so full. "You are an amazing man." I kissed him. "And I'm so lucky to be your wife."

"I'm the luckiest man because I have a creative *and* naughty wife."

Laughing, tears formed in my eyes. "Love is like a plant that can tolerate all kinds of weather—sun, rain, wind—to grow into something more. Our love is that versatile plant."

He folded himself on the stool beside me and took my hands in his. "I'm like your bamboo or willow tree—extremely versatile. We can deal with anything that comes our way."

"In a world of storms, I'm reminded that a blade of grass survives while a big tree collapses easily." I breathed. "The little things matter. Reading with you, sketching with you, cooking with you, walking in our yard, and listening to your silly plant jokes—all those things make my life worthwhile. So thank you for being the magical blessing in my life."

His eyes warmed. "I love you more than you could ever know." He reached for a tissue on the table and dabbed my eyes. "You're crying a lot these days."

I gestured to the two wrapped paintings on the table. "Those are for you. I made them."

"You were supposed to rest today."

"I was too excited. I'll rest tomorrow."

"That's what you said yesterday."

I rolled my eyes. "Just open the gift."

He opened the gifts and stared at the baby pink and baby blue abstract paintings. I studied his face as a series of emotions washed over him. Appreciation, gratitude, wonder, and revelation.

He whipped his gaze at me. "You're pregnant with twins?"

I nodded. "We're gonna be parents!"

Attikus

I thought I was already a blessed man with Vanessa in my life, but this news made my life even more precious.

"Life is a painting, and I'm living a masterpiece now because of you." I wrapped my arms around my wife, loving her and our babies. Joy radiated from me. I kissed the top of her head. "Is this why you've been tired?"

She nodded. "I didn't want to tell you until I finished these paintings. They can go above the cribs."

"How far along are you?"

"Just two months. The doctor did a blood test and confirmed the sex."

I frowned. "I want to be at all the appointments with you from now on."

"Yes, please!" She fell into my embrace.

"Let's go to the living room." I scooped her into my arms and lowered her to the couch. She was carrying two babies inside her. I could only imagine the energy that took. That explained her moodiness the past few weeks. I assumed it was her menstrual cycle or working too much. I hadn't expected this, but I was grateful.

Smiling, she patted the seat beside her. "Do you want to have the baby shower at our place or somewhere else?"

"We can have it here. It'll be more comfortable for you. We

have plenty of room to host." I placed a hand on her belly. "Hello, there, little ones. I'm your daddy."

She laughed. "Anything interesting happen today besides playing video games?"

I sat back, pulling her close. "Detective Farmer called me."

She stiffened, looking up at me. "What happened?"

"Nothing to worry about. He's helping his detective friend in Boston investigate a murder. They found the suspect's apartment, but he escaped. He had one of your paintings on his wall."

Vanessa sat up. "What painting? Can you describe it?"

I pulled my phone from my pocket and showed her the picture of a rose with petals and thorns.

"That's *A Petal for Your Thoughts*," she said. "He came into the shop a few times, asking if I had any bleeding hearts flower paintings. Seemed like a friendly man. He wore a red cap and dressed casually. We might still have some old recordings of him on video."

"You'd make a brilliant detective. I'll check out the recordings and give the detective what we have. If the Boston detective wants to speak to you, we can stop by when we visit my friend, Kain Kessler. He's right outside of Boston."

"Who is he?" she asked.

"A friend I met when I was undergoing physical therapy many years ago. He recently expanded his workout studio and invited me to visit. We haven't had time to catch up for a while, but he purchased a copy of WaterFyre Rising and reached out."

"I'd love to meet all your friends," she said, snuggling into me.

I told her the boys and I wouldn't retire the V.A.T.V. mission. If that mission needed us again, we'd be there. For now, the Vigilantes Against the Villains was a hobby. I continued telling her about my day when an adorable snore escaped her.

I glanced down and smiled at the beautiful woman in my arms. A surge of protectiveness and love overwhelmed me. I loved my little family so much. I watched Vanessa for a long moment, imagining my life with her and our children. She was everything my heart and soul needed, and I couldn't wait to meet our babies.

AUDRI AND REMI
EPILOGUE

Months later

Remington

I woke up early to the warm Hawaiian weather. My wife was curled beside me, wearing nothing. I had on boxers. Surprisingly, she was also awake and looked at me with adorable brown eyes.

"Morning, Sexy Dot," I said, brushing my finger over the beauty mark on her lip.

"Morning, DLS. You're up early." She traced my lips with her finger.

I couldn't believe she still called me DLS—Dangerous Line Segment—after so many years. But I loved it. It reminded me of our beginning. She was my best friend's sister—someone I never thought could be mine.

We'd married a week ago in Providence and landed in Honolulu yesterday. Audri and I took our time getting married. We loved each other but didn't want to rush. But it was time for us to make it official and perhaps start a family soon.

Her name was now Audri Wu-Starke. Everything I owned was hers.

"I want to watch the sunrise with you," I said.

She sat up and glanced out the wide sliding doors, which offered a gorgeous view of the ocean. Her gorgeous breasts bounced temptingly. "Excellent idea. Let me get ready."

"Not yet." I grabbed her hand, keeping her in bed. I captured a nipple, loving it.

"Baby," she moaned. "We did this all night."

"I could do this all day and all night. You can look at the sunrise while I suck on these gorgeous breasts."

"There's plenty of time for that." She laughed. "I want to document our honeymoon first."

"What do you mean?"

Audri

I hopped out of bed, flicked my long hair back, and posed for my handsome husband. He whistled, making me laugh. Life with this man was a dream come true.

"You'll love the memory book when I finish it."

Desire darkened his eyes as his boxers tented.

Shaking my head, I slipped on my pink silk robe, tied the belt at the front, walked over to the desk, and grabbed my DSLR camera. I brought it back to the bed and snapped pictures of his gorgeous face. Then I took pictures of our messy bed, the candles, the flowers on the nightstand, the rugs, and the little details of this gorgeous vacation home he owned. His staff had decorated it for our honeymoon, adding a lot of adorable details.

"Give me." He wiggled his fingers and got out of bed. "I want pictures of you too."

Smiling, I offered it to him. After taking a few images of me, he gave me back the camera.

"Put on a shirt and shorts." I gestured to his body. "If you behave, you can have your gift early."

"A gift?"

"Yes." I wiggled my eyebrows, placed the camera on the table, and washed up with him in the double sink in the bathroom.

Love and joy burst in me. This man loved me so much, and I didn't have words to describe it.

When we finished, we walked out to the beach, and the pink horizon greeted us. A sliver of the sun brightened in the distance. I looped the camera around my neck and carried the gift bag in my hand. Remi snapped pictures of the landscape with his phone. He aimed his camera at me, and I made several silly faces at him.

"Those are going in the book."

"No, they're not."

"Yes, they are."

I walked a few steps behind him so I could capture my man walking. When he peered over his shoulder, looking for me. I got about fifteen pictures of his stunning face.

"Are you the crazy paparazzo that's going to sell my photos for an obscene amount of money?" He wrapped an arm around me and kissed the side of my head.

"How did you know?" I grinned.

When we got to the table and chairs facing the horizon, I nudged him down and placed the gift bag in his lap.

"For you, the love of my life." I stood and watched him holding the bag. "Open it."

He pulled out the metallic gift box, removed the lid, and grinned at the leather bracelet I'd made for him.

"Is this from your new men's jewelry collection, Love is What You Wear?"

"Yes." I nodded. "The collection launches next month. This is the first one I made. The others are done by employees." I helped him put it on.

It looked fantastic next to the friendship bracelet I'd made him years ago, which was also leather.

He glanced at the two bracelets. "Perfect."

"You inspired this aged-leather twist design." I grinned, pride soaring through me. "We already have ten thousand preorders."

His eyes widened. "That's fantastic!"

I picked up the camera and snapped some pictures of him and me.

"I love you, Audri." He stood and took me into his arms.

"I love you too." I fell into his embrace, loving him more than he could ever know.

We took a bunch of pictures of the sunrise.

"We should do this every day to see how the color changes," I suggested.

"Let's do the same for the sunsets."

An hour later, he grabbed my hand. "I have something to give you too."

"What?"

"A marathon."

I made a face. "What do you mean?"

"A sperm marathon."

I burst into laughter.

"Let's see which of my sperm can get you pregnant." A wicked smirk flashed onto his face, and he yanked me to him. "Let's start a family. I want mini Audris or mini Remis running around the house."

Warmth bloomed in my chest. That was my dream too.

He scooped me into his arms so fast I almost dropped my camera. "The first race starts now!"

With laughter and love, we started our baby-making marathon.

MICHELLE AND ROYCE
EPILOGUE

Months later

Royce

Lightning flashed and thunder boomed, the sound resonating throughout the house.

"What a wild storm. I hope the rain will stop soon," Michelle said, snuggling closer to me on the couch where we were watching a nature documentary on TV. She had a bag of sour cream potato chips in her hand. She reached into it, grabbed a chip, and offered it to me.

"No, thanks, Angel," I said, admiring her tray of snacks on the coffee table. An assortment of nuts, gummy bears, chocolate, cookies, and a bowl of fruits. "Didn't you have dinner an hour ago?"

She slid me a glance. "Do you have a problem with that, Viking?"

We'd been together long enough for me to know that she usually ate when she was stressed or on her menstrual cycle. Experience had taught me to tread carefully. Though there was a storm outside, there could be an even bigger storm inside.

"No problem at all, my love." I kissed her head. "Just thinking we'll have to refill your snack pantry soon."

"Yes. We'll head out when the storm breaks. I'm craving beef jerky and pizza."

I laughed. "Pizza isn't a snack. "

She leveled a stare at me with her big brown eyes. "Anything can be a snack if you cut it into small pieces."

Like I said, I had to be careful.

"Okay, whatever you want. As soon as the rain stops, we'll go out."

Michelle and I had married six months ago in Iceland. It

was a quaint wedding at one of my excursion sites. Family and friends enjoyed their time at the hot springs and mud baths that Iceland offered.

I loved Michelle so much. She was the blessing that made my world worthwhile. When life was dark, she was the Northern Lights that gave me hope and happiness.

"Oh, my God." Michelle opened her mouth as a lion captured a deer, dragging it away. The lion cubs rushed off somewhere. Tears streamed down her lovely face. "That's so mean."

I wanted to remind her it was a survival of the fittest. The lion needed to eat too. But I feared if I said anything right now, she might kick me off the couch. She'd been overly sensitive lately.

I rose from the couch.

"Where are you going?" she asked, tearing her gaze from the TV screen.

"To get a drink. Want anything?"

"No, thanks." A pause. "Actually, maybe a bowl of ice cream, please?"

"Okay." I looked at all the snacks on the coffee table. The only thing missing was ice cream.

Thunder boomed again. Michelle leaped off the couch, rushed up to me, and grabbed my hand. What was going on with her today?

"Are you okay?" I asked.

"What do you think, Viking?"

I scooped some Cookies and Cream into a bowl and handed it to her. "I think you're acting strange."

She scooped up the ice cream with her spoon. "Open up."

When I did, she fed me ice cream and smiled. "What makes you think I'm acting strange?" She dragged me back to the couch, placed the bowl of ice cream on the tray, and looked at me. "Tell me. How am I different?"

Her face had a lovely pink hue. Her curious eyes bored into mine.

"You're snacking like crazy. And you're overly sensitive and clingy."

"Do those traits annoy you?" she asked as a curly strand of hair fell across her face.

I tucked it behind her ear. "Is that a trick question?"

"No." She grinned. "Do you want to know the real reason I can't stop snacking?"

"Is work stressing you out? Do you have your period?"

"It's neither, Viking." She touched my cheek tenderly. "You've got mail. It's been sitting at your desk for a few days."

"Huh?" I hadn't been in my office in three days. I'd been busy promoting the WaterFyre Rising game with my friends. The game was a worldwide hit, and the sales had surpassed our expectations. My friends and I had a meeting with a Hollywood producer who wanted to adapt it into a movie.

"Let me go check now."

"Okay. I'll wait here." She popped a grape into her mouth.

I walked into my office and saw a white rectangular box beside my keyboard. Did she get me a new pen? I opened the box and saw the positive pregnancy test. Joy burst inside me as I threw the tester up into the air, caught it with my hand, and rushed back to my wife.

Michelle

I heard him rushing out of the office and smiled to myself.

"Angel!" He picked me up and kissed me.

"Viking, you're squeezing too hard."

He released me, kissed me again, and drew back. "I'm sorry I didn't know."

"Men." I rolled my eyes, then smiled. "It's okay. Now you do."

"How far along are you?" Royce asked.

"Eight weeks. Still early days. I haven't told my mom or anyone yet."

"We're having a baby." His eyes gleamed. "We're going to be parents." Shock and love covered his face, making him look adorable.

We'd talked about starting a family a while ago. But I didn't want to start until we got married. When I missed my period and the sudden fatigue hit, I knew something was different. Then I couldn't stop eating, so I bought a test, and it confirmed everything.

"Get used to me eating all the time."

His smile stretched. "I'll make sure you have an unlimited supply of food."

Prior to meeting Royce, I struggled with an eating disorder. But my Viking had developed an app that helped me fight my monsters.

I feared this new craving for food would trigger the illness again. But this situation was different. I wasn't eating from stress or trying to look pretty for a competition—I was eating to feed another human growing inside me.

"I'm so happy." I embraced him.

"Me too."

"Do you want to know the gender or keep it a surprise?"

"I want to know."

"Great! Come with me to next month's doctor's appointment. They can tell from the bloodwork."

"I'll accompany you to all the appointments."

With joy bursting in my heart, I grabbed his hand and dragged him back into his office. "Let's browse ideas for the baby room. Boy and girl."

"Anything you want, my love."

NATALIE AND GRAYSON

EPILOGUE

Months later

Grayson

I'd been traveling for the last two weeks to complete a building project with a Californian company. I was supposed to be home on Friday but finished everything two days early. So now, I was in the driveway of my home, preparing to surprise my wife. I'd missed her so much. Two weeks without her was horrendous, even though we'd spoken on the phone every day. It wasn't the same as having her beside me.

She'd been working on her Fall Collection and couldn't accompany me like she usually did.

With a bouquet of flowers in hand, I entered the house. It was unusually quiet. I knew she was home because her car was in the garage. I would have pulled my car into the garage, but she would have heard me opening it.

She wasn't in the living room or the kitchen, so I made my way to her design studio. Warmth burst in my heart as I found my wife standing with her back to me, working on something on the table.

I leaned against the door frame, watching her work.

Love spread through my chest. I remembered a time when I came home from work, and the only thing waiting for me was the cold, empty house.

Natalie had changed everything for me. She had brought warmth and color into my life. I was about to enter when she lifted her arms, holding up a T-shirt with bold letters that read, *You're gonna be a Dad!*

What?

My mouth opened as I stared at the T-shirt. Joy and shock overwhelmed me.

Was she trying to surprise me? I wasn't scheduled to be home for another two days.

Quietly, I backed away from the door. I left the house, climbed into my car, and reversed to the far end of the street. I took a moment to let everything settle. We'd been trying for a baby for six months. Sadness had overcome her every time she got her period.

I'd seen the disappointment and anxiety on her face. But things had shifted.

This incredible news was what we'd been waiting for. My life was about to change for the better. Sheer joy erupted inside me. I wanted to rush to my wife, gather her into my arms, and hold her close.

But I had to wait. She wanted to surprise me, and I'd give her that.

After a few more minutes, I called her.

"Hey, Buttercup. What are you doing??"

"Oh, you know, just working on the next collection. How's my McDimple? Your meetings went well?"

"Yes. Guess what?"

"What?"

"I miss you."

She laughed. "Miss you too, silly."

"Guess what else?" I asked.

"What?"

"I just landed. Finished early, so I flew home. But I'll be at the office for a bit. Want me to pick up dinner on the way home?"

Natalie

Oh, my gosh! Excitement surged and rolled through me.

"Okay," I said as I tried to calm my nerves. "I want a little of everything. Some pizza, chicken wings, lo mein, and sushi."

He laughed. "Have you been starving yourself the last few days?"

"Nope. I'm just craving a lot of things."

"Okay. I'll be home around six thirty."

"Sounds good."

My heart raced as I clicked off the phone. Grayson would be home in three hours. That gave me enough time to set everything up to surprise him. It was a good thing I'd started on the T-shirt design earlier this week.

We'd wanted to start a family for a while, but things hadn't been aligned until now.

I placed a hand over my belly. "I can't wait to meet you, little one. We're going to love you so much."

I couldn't begin to explain the feeling of being pregnant, of knowing that a baby was growing inside me. Would he or she look like Grayson or me?

Smiling, I looked at the T-shirt I'd screen-printed. It came out perfect. I folded the shirt and placed it inside a box with pink and blue tissue paper.

I hadn't told my mom or my friends yet. I wanted to share this incredible news with my husband first.

After putting the baby books and magazines away and making sure no clue was left anywhere in the house, I dropped into a chair to rest. Exhaustion tugged at me.

After resting for a while, I strode into the kitchen, poured myself a glass of cold water, and downed it. I heard the garage door open, and excitement thrummed through me.

Three hours had flown by. My heart raced as I poured another glass of water.

Grayson entered through the kitchen door with two bags of

takeout. He placed the bags on the kitchen island, walked over, and embraced me. "I missed you so much."

"Missed you too." I tightened my grip around his sturdy body.

He drew back and kissed me gently. "I'll be right back. Need to get the rest of my stuff."

"Okay. I'll prep the food. Smells delicious."

Grayson returned with an enormous bouquet and a box of pastries. "For my beautiful wife."

I smiled as I got out a tall vase and added water. "What's the occasion?"

"Just because I love you. Let me." He placed the flowers into the vase, adjusting them as best he could. Then he embraced me. We stood in the kitchen, hugging each other for a long moment.

"Are you okay?" I asked. "How was the business trip?"

"Everything went well. I'm just glad to be home."

I led him to the living room couch and ushered him to sit down. Sitting next to him, I picked up the silver box and gave it to him. "I have a gift for you."

Smiling, he took the box, opened the lid, and removed the tissue paper.

He took out the T-shirt, and tears filled his eyes. "This is the best gift I've ever received. Thank you."

Love overflowed inside me. I threw my arms around him. "We're having a baby!"

His arms rubbed my back. "Yes, we are, and you've made me the happiest and luckiest man on the planet."

KIERA AND FORREST

EPILOGUE

Months later

Forrest

One more week, and Kiera and I would meet our little boy. I stood in the baby room with its light green walls and accents in baby blue and taupe. A white crib sat against the wall with an adorable Need Name sign at the top. We hadn't settled on a name yet. I'd made a dresser and a bookcase that matched the crib.

We'd received many gifts already for our little guy. He didn't have a name yet. Kiera and I had three names we were toying with, but we wanted to wait until we met him before deciding.

"Hey, BaMBu Beast." She waddled up to me in her maternity dress. "What are you doing?"

I grinned at the nickname she'd given me. I had a new respect for pregnant women after seeing what Kiera went through. The sleepless nights, the cramps, and the physical changes of carrying all that weight around. As a doctor, I knew the changes, but seeing my wife experience it firsthand helped me understand the miracle of nurturing a baby from conception to birth.

"Just admiring the baby's room." I welcomed her into my arms, kissing the top of her head. "How was the nap, Kitty K?"

"It was okay." With a hand on her lower back, she sat in the comfy rocking chair.

"Do you need a massage?" I asked, knowing she'd been experiencing back pain.

She shook her head. "I can't wait to get him out of me." She flicked me a regretful look. "No offense to you or our little man, but I'm tired and extremely uncomfortable. I can't see my feet, and I have to pee every twenty minutes."

Laughing, I sat on the ottoman in front of her. "I know, love." I took her hand in mine. "You look beautiful."

She snorted and rolled her eyes. "You're just saying that to be nice. I don't feel beautiful. I feel like an agitated fat whale."

I stifled a laugh. "You're gorgeous to me. You have a lovely glow about you. You're carrying our bundle of joy, and that's a lot of work. So thank you."

"I know I've been cranky." Her face softened. "But you'd be too if you couldn't sleep and your back hurt." The baby kicked, and she gasped. "I think he's practicing martial arts so he can compete with you when he comes out." She licked her lips. "I'm thirsty."

"Water or juice?" I rose from the ottoman.

"Water. I'll come too. I need to move." She reached for my hand, and I assisted her up.

Then she gasped. "Oh, no."

"What happened? Are you hurt?"

She looked at the puddle of water on the floor.

Forrest

Excitement and fear set in. I dealt with urgent situations all the time at my health clinic. But my wife's water breaking froze me for a moment.

Get yourself together!

"BaMBu Beast, it's time." Kiera's calm voice snapped me out of the shock.

I had expected excitement, but her calmness surprised me. It was the complete opposite of her energetic self.

"Are you okay?" I asked.

"Been waiting for this day. Can you clean up the mess while I get dressed?"

"Do you need me to help you?"

"I'm good." She waddled off as I got a towel to clean the floor.

When I finished, I went to our bedroom, but Kiera wasn't there. I found her sitting on the bench by the garage door.

She held the hospital bag on her lap and smiled at me. "Let's go."

I sat beside her and wrapped an arm around my lovely wife. "Are you nervous?"

She nodded. "Are you?"

"Yes. But I'm also very excited. Let's take this moment to appreciate the quiet one more time." I grinned at her. "Because when we return, it won't be quiet anymore."

Tears gleamed in her eyes. "Okay." She rested her head on my shoulder. "I can't wait to meet him.

I placed a hand on her belly. "Be good to your mom and come out quick, okay?"

A kick shifted my hand. Kiera and I looked at each other with wide eyes. Then we laughed.

"I think he wants us to go now," Kiera said.

"I agree." I took my wife's hand, led her out to the SUV, and situated her in her seat comfortably. "Let's go meet our little boy."

VIVIAN AND ARROW
EPILOGUE

Months later

Vivian

A dragonfly landed on my arm as I sat on the dock behind my summer home and waited for a fish to nibble the bait. Life had been chaotic, but things had finally died down. My dental office had expanded to include several dentists. I'd cut back my time there to concentrate on creating more gadgets for the government.

But this week was reserved for my love.

"Any bite yet?" Arrow asked.

I turned and watched my handsome husband walk toward me. He wore a pale yellow T-shirt that hugged his muscular body and cargo shorts. He smiled, and my heart raced like it did when we first started dating.

"Not yet," I said.

He placed down a tray of lemonade and a bowl of diced watermelon. With a fork, he poked a piece of watermelon and held it to my lips. "Open up."

"It's juicy and sweet, thank you." I placed the rod into his holder, shifted in my chair, and stared at him.

He arched an eyebrow. "Something on my face?"

"No. Can I ask you something?"

He snorted. "Since when do you need my permission to ask anything?"

"Never." I laughed. "Are you bored?"

He placed down the watermelon and looked at me. "No, why?"

I shrugged, wanting to ask a question that had been bothering me. I played with my pink flip-flops, wondering how I should bring up the topic.

He reached over and tipped up my chin. "What's wrong, Tulip?"

"Nothing's wrong." Nerves stirred inside me. "I was just wondering if you feel left behind."

"Left behind? What do you mean?"

"You know. All your friends are pregnant and getting ready for a new chapter in their lives. But you're—

He got out of his chair, grabbed my hand, and led me to the edge of the dock. He took off his sandals and removed my flip-flops. "Sit with me."

Our feet kicked the surface of the water like little kids.

"I want you to understand something, okay?" He lifted my hand to his lips. "I'm happy for my friends with their expanding families. But I'm in love with my family as is. We'll have kids when the time is right for us. I don't need to be a father now. Besides, having Kaylee is like having a kid. So parenting isn't new to us."

A burden lifted from my chest. "Right now, I'm happy the way things are. I want to travel and see the world with you first." I squeezed his hand. "In two years, I want to have kids with you."

Arrow

"Whenever you're ready, I'm ready." I kissed her. "So, this has been bothering you?"

She bumped shoulders with me. "Well, yeah."

"You should have said something to me."

"It's a sensitive topic, Bullseye. What if you wanted kids, but you were afraid I wasn't ready? But if you ask, the other might feel obligated to start. I don't know. Maybe I'm over-thinking things."

"You're definitely overanalyzing again." I wrapped an arm around her. "You can ask and tell me anything. I love you and this amazing life we have together. I would love to have mini versions of you and me running the house, but that's the future. Right now is what I want to focus on." I leaned into her ear. "I want to concentrate on you and the many ways I can pleasure you."

"Great minds think alike." Mischief gleamed in her eyes. "Do you know what I'm thinking now?"

"That you want to duel with me. Winner gets to pick a role-playing game." I ran my fingers along her lips.

"What kind of role-playing game do you have in mind?"

"Where you're the hot princess trying to save your land, and I'm the powerful warlord you must defeat."

"What's the princess wearing?" she asked.

"A beautiful dress that offers him glimpses of her smooth skin."

"She has daggers hidden in that dangerous dress," she added.

"Doesn't matter. Those daggers will be his when he claims her."

Vivian's lips curved into a wicked smile as she placed a hand on my thigh, moving slowly toward my bulge. "That sounds very exciting. I can't wait to battle with him." Then she shoved me away, got up, ran off, and offered a challenging laugh. "Catch me if you can, Warlord Bullseye."

ELENA AND ORION

EPILOGUE

Months later

Orion

We had a C-section scheduled for next month. Though the doctor informed us both babies were healthy, I was nervous for them and Elena. I supposed that was a natural concern for new parents. Excitement and fear stirred inside me, but I didn't let her know. I couldn't wait to meet my son and daughter.

Holding Elena's hand, I guided her to the chair in our backyard that was lit with string lights and lamp posts. The sky had darkened to navy dotted with stars.

"Where are you taking me?" she asked.

"You'll see soon." I checked to ensure her blindfold was secure.

While she met with her friends last week, I had my new Reimann Telescope V4 delivered. This was the upgraded version my company had created.

"You're coming to the chair, and I'm going to help you sit down."

Once she was seated, she asked, "Can I look now?"

I removed the blindfold.

She blinked, looked at the telescope in front of her, and squealed. "This is the new one?"

"Yes. We got it early. No one in the world has it yet.

Her face beamed. "That means we'll get to discover new constellations in other galaxies.

I laughed. "We've done that many times already."

"But not for our babies." Her eyes gleamed. "Let's look for a constellation and dedicate it to them." She reached for my hand. "You knew that, didn't you? You knew what I was thinking."

"I did."

"I love you, Orion." She pulled me down for a kiss.

"I love you, Elena."

I pressed a button on the side of the chair. It elevated her seat so she could access the telescope easily.

"Fancy chair," she said. "What galaxy should I look toward today?"

"How about we try to discover one?"

"Really?" Her eyes widened. "Can we do that?"

"We sure can. This telescope can see farther than any other telescope out there."

"Hear that, my sweet babies?" She glanced down at her belly and rubbed it. "We're going to discover a new galaxy together."

Elena

I couldn't describe how happy I was to look into the universe with my husband and unborn babies. Magic stirred in the air, and my heart thumped with joy.

I swiveled the telescope and zoomed. "Look at that beautiful nebula. It looks like a pregnant woman, doesn't it?"

Orion laughed as he looked at the screen on the side, reflecting on what I saw. "It does. But you're more beautiful."

"Look at those stars and planets! That blue planet has three rings and five moons. Am I seeing this right?"

"Yes," Orion confirmed.

"Am I still looking at the Andromeda galaxy?" I asked. Orion knew more about astronomy than I did. The vastness of space and possibilities continued to astound me. When I felt overwhelmed, I looked up at the sky, and my issues became minute. There was an infinite field of magic out there that hadn't been discovered.

"You're way past Andromeda, Sunshine."

"Really?" I shifted in my excitement. "So, this is a new galaxy?"

Orion pressed some buttons on the keyboard. "It's five hundred million light-years away. It's a spiral-shaped galaxy, similar to the Milky Way."

"Gosh, there are so many stars." A thrill rushed through me. "Am I seeing this right? I see two suns.

"There are two suns."

"Wow." Hope surged in me. "Has this been discovered?"

"Yes." He leaned over and kissed me. "You just did."

"Oh, my god!" I gripped his forearm, squeezing hard. "I don't know what to name it yet. But I don't want anyone else to discover and name it before I do." Concern etched my voice.

He smiled. "Don't worry. No one will name it before you. Like I said, this is an advanced telescope. You're able to see things no other scientists can see. This telescope isn't available for another six months." He pressed some more buttons on the screen. "I just took a snapshot of what you saw and recorded. I'll submit it to the International Astronomical Union in France. It'll be under my company name as a place holder. Once we think of a name, we'll update the data. How's that?"

I threw my arms around him. "You are the best!" I gripped his face and kissed him. "Our kids are so blessed. They'll get to discover incredible things before anyone else."

"We'll make sure they're loved and make this world a better place for everyone."

With that, my husband linked my hand with his as I browsed the universe in awe and appreciation.

Thank you so much for reading the WaterFyre Rising Series! If you enjoyed this series, you'll love the new Etched Series. You can preorder **Etched in Ink** now!

Check out The Maverick Bonus Scene: The Billionaire's Chores.

ABOUT THE AUTHOR
NADIA HAN

Nadia Han is a contemporary romance author. She's a dreamer, a visionary, and a believer in karma and kindness. She lives in Massachusetts with her husband, two children, and a cat, and enjoys the unpredictable New England weather.

Nadia started out writing and illustrating children's books when her kids were small. But she decided to write romantic suspense stories featuring diverse characters for herself. She loves escaping into different worlds and for that reason, she also writes otherworldly romance under a different pen name.

When she's not writing, she practices yoga, reads, explores nature, watches K-dramas, and eats all kinds of foods. Nadia is also an artist. She loves spending time playing with paint and other artistic mediums. She believes creativity is important for the mind and the soul. It helps her become a better writer because she can guide the reader to see things from a different perspective.

facebook.com/authornadiahan

instagram.com/authornadiahan

bookbub.com/authors/nadia-han

amazon.com/author/nadiahan